UNCLE OTIS

Shawn A. Lawson

authorHOUSE®

AuthorHouse™
1663 Liberty Drive
Bloomington, IN 47403
www.authorhouse.com
Phone: 1 (800) 839-8640

Published by AuthorHouse 01/22/2020

ISBN: 978-1-7283-4436-2 (sc)
ISBN: 978-1-7283-4434-8 (hc)
ISBN: 978-1-7283-4435-5 (e)

I

GETTIN' HEAVY

Pascagoula, Mississippi

The gulf breeze blew through Inez Taylor's thin, grey hair. She rolled slowly across the short bridge, just down the street from her house. The placid sound of the tires along pavement – barely audible over the gentle rustling of the leaves along the creek. She closed her eyes - recollecting a time when the bridge was wooden, and the road was dirt. Her daddy used to come down to this creek – cast his lines, on cool summer afternoons. Things had changed so much – transformed in what seemed to her, like the blink of an eye. She remembered herself so long ago, as the little girl, in the summer dress, carrying her daddy's minnow bucket down this road. The waft of air was hitting the sweat on the back of her neck - cooling her from the summer heat. The humidity - unequivocally brutal this summer, had her constantly doing the laundry, to keep her clothes from smelling sour. Luckily, there were only a few weeks of summer left and God willing – they would be cool. Come September, the weather would break - it always did.

Inez was pretty good at predicting the weather around these parts. She'd lived in Pascagoula her entire life. A fifth generation native, she claimed. She hadn't ever even traveled further than Mobile in all her life, which was not too far across the Georgia border. She'd never felt the need to - she was as fine as wine, right here at home – always had been. Inez had come from a tough line of Mississippi cotton people, who had always taken care of their own. After emancipation, they never relied on anyone for support, but themselves. They weren't in need of a single thing that they couldn't provide on their own. Her family had always lived off of the land, *their land*, and roughed it out through the worst of times. That's the only way that she knew. It was how her parents were raised by their parents, and how she was taught.

She was tough and she was a survivor. She'd once heard that one of her distant relatives was brought to the docks of Pascagoula, aboard a slaver straight from Africa. The land where she and her husband now lived, was the same land that her family had occupied ever since they won their freedom - and when she said won, she meant won! The war wasn't only won by the white folk. Many black folk laid down their lives in the struggle, too. Don't tell that to any white man around these parts though. They were likely to get upset, and even though she wasn't afraid of any white man - she didn't need any trouble. White folk have been known to get a little crazy in Mississippi, from time to time. She didn't have any intention to go aggravating them. No sir, she had made it seventy two years, without any trouble and she didn't need any now.

On the other hand Jasper, her husband, had never known when to keep quiet. When he was a bit younger, it seemed like he went a looking for trouble on the regular, from the whites. He was never the kind of man to take the verbal abuse from the crackers, without having a few words to say of his own. He had quite the temper back then, and it'd caused quite a bit of grief over the years - for them both! They'd been married for forty seven years now, and it was only in the last ten or so, that he'd stopped getting in so much trouble. Shoot, Jasper had his own bed down at the jail house for a while, and nary was a police man that didn't call him by his first name, when they saw him in the street.

He was a good man though - had always come home when he wasn't locked up and had never raised a hand to her. He was a good father, too. Lionel was the apple of his daddy's eye when he was a young boy. Even though the boy was grown now, Jasper still let Lionel get away with too much. Sometimes, a man needs to hear the truth from his father, instead of what he wants to hear. Lionel had let his wife throw him out of his own house, and he just went without a fuss. He came to his daddy, and instead of Jasper telling Lionel to man up and to go on back to his own house, he let the boy move back in. Living with his parents wasn't no place for a forty-two year old man to be. Inez meant to say something to the both of them about the situation, and soon. They were all going to sit down and have a come-to-Jesus meeting, if he was gonna' stay for any length of time, cause she sure wasn't going to be doing a grown man's laundry, unless it was her husband's.

She vowed that she would work that out with the two of them later. It had gone on for long enough! But for now, she was going to enjoy her afternoon walk - or ride, was more like it. She had been a riding in this here wheelchair for the last five years - ever since the stroke had disabled the left side of her body. Woke up one morning and couldn't move a muscle. Difficult and scary as it was - she pulled through. She was a fighter - a survivor!

"How much further you want to go?" Jasper asked. He was her legs now, pushing her up Orange Grove Road - the narrow, paved way that ran past their home and on up to the old oak tree. The one that she used to play in as a young girl. A crow cawed from a tree branch overhanging the road.

She looked up at the bird, just as it was chased from its branch by a smaller and much quicker bird, protecting its nest. As the crow flew away, it cawed again, as if to warn them all that he'd be back. "Just a bit further." Inez said, "Just up to the oak tree today."

Jasper knew exactly what tree she meant. The old, live oak that stood along the edge of the road, just around the next bend. It was the only destination that she ever wanted to visit, when she was out for her evening walks.

"You ain't tired, is ya'?" Inez teased.

"Naw, Naw I ain't tired...you just gettin' heavy, is all."

Inez reached around to smack his arm, bringing a chuckle from Jasper. "You better watch yo' tongue, old man...or I'm gonna cut it out yo' mouth when you sleepin'."

"You better watch you'rn, or I'll leave you down here by this oak tree."

"You better not..."

"I will," Jasper picked.

"Just hush, and let me enjoy my ride!"

He did.

2

After sitting under the oak tree long enough for Jasper to smoke a cigarette, the two returned to their home. The baby blue paint that jasper had put on the wood board a few years back, was fading to the point that it almost looked white. The summer sun had been hot this season. Maybe, she thought, she could get Lionel and Jasper to paint it before winter set in. As the two came around the bend and their driveway came into view, they noticed an unfamiliar car parked behind Jasper's Buick. "Who could that be?" Inez wondered aloud. Jasper pushed her up the driveway slowly and took a good look into the empty car, as they passed by. There was nobody inside of it, and nothing that Jasper could see gave him any indication as to whom it might belong. There was an empty 7-11 hotdog box, with mustard smeared along the edges and a couple of beer cans on the seat inside. Jasper looked around the yard, then up and down the street, to see if there was anybody around, but he couldn't see anyone.

"You suppose it's Lionel?" Inez asked. Her voice was a little shaky, at the peculiarity of finding the strange car parked in their driveway.

"Must be," Jasper said, a little uneasy himself. "Why ain't he at work though?" He pushed Inez's wheelchair up the wooden handicap ramp - the same ramp that he and Lionel had built for her right after she'd had her stroke. They approached the front door. The screen was closed, but the main door was ajar. "Did we leave the door open?" Jasper asked, as Inez was wondering the same thing. He pulled the screen door open and wrestled the wheel chair into the living room. At first glance, nothing looked out of sorts - the room was in the same order as he remembered leaving it. The TV remote was still on the arm of the easy chair - the quilted throw blanket over the backrest. A pile of Inez's Better Homes and Garden magazines were stacked on the coffee table and no lights were turned on. Everything seemed just fine with the place, until a long haired white man came from out of the darkness of the hallway, holding a gun.

Jasper felt his heart drop out of his chest and hit the floor. For a second, he couldn't catch his breath to speak.

Inez was the first to say something, "Who the fuck is you?"

The long haired man didn't answer her. Though he was dressed in nice clothes, his skin looked like he was in desperate need of a bath. Like he'd worked hard all day, down at the shipyard, and just put on his clean clothes, without showering. Only he was dirtier than that – he looked rotten - his eyes, his skin, his hair, his teeth – everything. He asked his own question, like he didn't even hear hers, "Where's Lionel?"

Jasper finally caught his breath and started pulling Inez's wheelchair back out of the front door. "He ain't here, now you need to go on and get." Just as his back reached the screen door, it suddenly opened from the outside and another man stepped inside, this one wearing panty hose over his head, and he pushed Jasper back into the room. They wore similar clothes - the kind that you might have found at a thrift store, maybe back in the eighties. Both had on long leather jackets, despite the heat. The second man stayed behind Jasper and Inez, between them and the door.

"I ain't gonna ask you again, old man…Where's Lionel?" the dirty man barked.

Inez, realizing that there wasn't any way for them to escape, did the only thing that she could think to do. She began yelling at the top of her seventy two year old lungs, "HELP!" The man at the front door simply closed it.

"Shut up, old woman…we ain't gonna' hurt ya,'" He said, rather unconvincingly.

"Fuck y'all, and get the hell out of my house," Inez said.

The man with the gun laughed. "You're pretty feisty…for an old cripple."

"Don't you talk to my wife like that, Boy," Jasper said. Just then, he was hit in the back of his head with something. He didn't know what it was, but it felt a lot like a Greyhound bus. He went sprawling across the room – crashing down on top of the coffee table - breaking the legs off and leaving him in a pile of broken wood, and Better Homes and Garden magazines. He felt the back of his head with his hand, and it was immediately covered in blood. Through his ringing ears, he heard Inez crying, "Oh Lord, Oh my Lord!" She tried to wheel herself over to her husband, but only made it halfway, before she was spun around by the man with the gun. "Now, look here, Bitch! We ain't leaving till you tell us where Lionel is staying."

"What y'all want with Lionel?" Inez asked, through her tears.

"That ain't any of your business," the man at the door said. His voice sounded older – more gravelly.

"Let's just say…he owes me some money," the man with the gun said. He knelt directly in front of her wheelchair. His breath smelled of beer, mustard, and decay. He smiled with a set of rotten teeth. "Now look, this has gotten a little out of hand." He motioned at Jasper on the broken table, "We didn't come here to beat up on a couple of geriatrics. We came here to talk to Lionel and get my money back. All you have to do is tell us where he is, and we will leave you and your husband alone to go on watching Sanford and Son and eating your watermelon, or doing whatever your kind does on these beautiful, lazy afternoons."

She knew where he was supposed to be. Lionel was supposed to be at work at the shipyard, at least that's where he told her he was going, when he left early this morning. "I don't know where he is," Inez said, through her tears. "Now get the hell out of my house 'fore I call the law on you sons-of-bitches."

The man by the door stepped forward and punched Inez in the back of the head with the brass knuckles – the same ones he'd laid the old man out with. She tipped forward out of her wheelchair - falling face down, onto the rug that her mother had given to her and Jasper, the day that they were married, back in 1967. She never even tried to catch herself as she fell, taking all of the impact with the floor, directly on her nose. Inez Taylor died within sixty seconds of landing on the carpet. Upon seeing his wife struck in the head, Jasper picked up a broken table leg and scrambled to his feet. He managed to take a single wobbly step towards the man that had hit his wife, with every intent of smashing his brains out through one of his ears, when a bullet hit his chest, knocking him back onto the broken table. Jasper watched the two men scramble out of the front door, knocking over Inez's wheelchair as they went. The car engine started up, and he heard it back out of the dirt drive. He ignored the pain in his chest and his shortness of breath, long enough to pull himself over to his wife. She had not moved a muscle, since she was hit in the head. He rubbed her back until he died beside her, on their living room floor.

3

Hampton, Virginia

S parks flew as Allen Blackwood made his way down the dimly lit corridor - flashlight in hand. The temporary lighting, run along the ceiling, was not sufficient enough to see into the darker recesses of the building. The blackness ahead was momentarily interrupted, as another series of sparks flew - someone was welding overhead. All that Allen could see of the worker creating the fire shower, was the bottom half of his legs, on top of the ladder – the rest of the man was hidden among the pipes in the ceiling. Allen stepped into an open door to avoid being struck by the flaming hot debris. His plastic hardhat was no match for the superhot metal. Luckily, this room was on the exterior of the building and was lighted naturally by large windows. Allen tried the light switch to see if it worked, while he was waiting for the welding job to finish. The switch did nothing. These rooms were supposed to be complete, according to the update that Allen received from his coworkers earlier this morning.

Allen sighed, pulled the handheld radio from his belt. Keying the microphone he said, "Come in, Randall."

Randall's voice scratched back over the radio, "Go ahead."

"Who wired the lights in room four-o-seven?" Allen asked.

"They ain't working, are they?"

"How'd you guess?"

After a brief pause, Randall crackled. "Carl's on his way…"

It was going to take Carl a few minutes to reach the fourth floor of the Chamberlain Hotel. There were only a couple of passage ways that could be used, since the entire building was under construction. The old hotel had been built in 1928 and was long overdue for a remodel.

A private group, along with the City of Hampton, acquired the property, formerly owned by the government, and planned to use it as their centerpiece in a massive project designed to revitalize the area. *Fat chance of that*, Allen thought. This city has been flat-lined for longer than Allen had been alive. He lit a cigarette, standing beside an open window overlooking Ft Monroe and the Chesapeake Bay beyond. The poison burned his lungs. He exhaled and stood watching the smoke as it left his mouth and passed out of the open window, dispersing into the early summer air.

A soft breeze carried the scent of his clothes up to his nose. He smelled of cigarettes, whiskey, and the woman that he'd met last night. What was her name? Did she even say? Surely she had, but it would have been one of the few things that was spoken after they left the bar last night. He'd met her before – Tina? Tanya? He knew it, he was sure of it, but his mind was still foggy from the amount of alcohol that he'd consumed. She'd still been there in his apartment sleeping, when he'd left for work this morning. He successfully crept out of the door at 6:00 am, so as not to wake her. Talking sometimes just made things difficult, especially when sober. What would he say anyway? *Hi, how are you doing? Thanks for last night. By the way; what did you say your name was?*

He hoped that she'd be gone by the time that he returned home. He didn't intend to be rude, but wasn't looking forward to seeing her again, anytime soon. Besides, he'd noticed the slightly discolored area around her ring finger. She'd never mentioned it, and he never asked, but it didn't take a scholar to figure out that she was probably married – most likely, a military wife with her husband deployed away. Poor guy was overseas fighting a war, while his wife was lying in Allen's bed. Allen felt a twinge of remorse, but quickly dispelled it. From what little he could remember, he hadn't picked her up. It was the other way around, and for all he knew, the recently removed ring was the result of a divorce. He hoped that it was the divorce thing, but he really didn't care one way or the other. He had no intention of ever seeing her again - or so he told himself now. One thing was for sure – he would have no company tonight - he needed to get some sleep tonight.

He looked around the city from the window. Fort Wool, with its stone walls and towers, was just across the water, on a small man-made island. The island and the fort were both the brainchild of Robert E. Lee, when he was an Engineer for the U.S. Army. Allen had always been appreciative of the historical significance of the Hampton area. Unfortunately, the city had done a very poor job of keeping that history alive and there wasn't much left to spark the interest of the tourist. Nothing like the larger neighboring cities, such as Williamsburg, Norfolk, and Virginia Beach. Vacationers passed right through Hampton every day, without second thought, on their way to the more popular spots.

Allen had grown up just a few miles away from where he was standing right now - over in Buckroe Beach. Back in the 1920s, the Chicago gangsters used to vacation at Buckroe and the neighboring town of Phoebus. It was so well traveled by the mobsters, that Phoebus even received the nickname of "Little Chicago" by the gangsters. The notorious Al Capone built a house between Phoebus and Buckroe, which still stands today. The 1920s was the era that the locals liked to glamorize, but Hampton's tough reputation goes back even further than that. Allen had read somewhere that after the pirate Blackbeard was killed, back in the 1700s, his head was brought to Hampton Harbor, and hung from the old wooden Hampton River Bridge, as a warning to others who might get the bright idea to become pirates. Allen's family even claimed to be distantly related to a pirate that once sailed with Blackbeard. He had no idea how they would know such a thing, but it was a cool story to tell his friends, none-the-less. One thing was for sure, even though the pirate and gangster days were long gone, Hampton still carried the reputation of being a tough town.

Allen watched a tug boat trudge slowly through the Bay, towards the Hampton River and wished that he was on *it,* instead of here. The low steady drone of the diesel engines, plowing across the waves, could clearly be heard, as black smoke pumped out of the smoke stack.

The cigarette left a bad taste in his mouth, and he wished that he had something to drink. He looked at his watch - it was only 11:15 am. He was going to have to make it all the way until noon before he could get to his car and finish off his flask of whiskey. It would help him make it through the remainder of the day. He considered bringing the flask inside the building, so that he could nip it from time to time, but decided against the idea for fear of being caught drinking on the job. He found that lately he needed something to help him get through the day. He despised the people that he worked with, and he hated construction work in general, but it was all that he knew. There weren't a whole lot of options for uneducated people these days. Not when college grads were flooding the workforce and taking all of the jobs that didn't require so much manual labor.

Allen promised himself that he was going to go back to school someday, but that had never happened. He was thirty one now and couldn't imagine himself ever having to study for another exam. Things could be worse, he guessed. He was a site foreman for the company he was working for, and although he was in no danger of getting rich, he was paying his rent - usually. Allen felt like he fit in with the people of this profession. It was tough work physically. That, and the lack of any education at all necessary to perform it - it was where all of the rejects of the fucked up American society wound up. Respectable companies won't hire people with serious criminal records, but a construction company was happy to have the body on the jobsite. It was a rough trade to be in, and an even rougher one to be in charge of. It was a little sketchy when you had to convince a man who'd just been released from prison, to do something he didn't really want to do, just because you asked him to. Allen had been in a number of scraps with people on the job in the past - mostly because his tolerance of people was very low – made especially so when he'd been drinking.

Carl walked into the room, breaking Allen from his thoughts. He tossed the cigarette out of the window, but didn't turn around - Carl didn't immediately say anything either. The man was about the same age as Allen, but looked a few years older due to premature greying hair. It was Allen's opinion that Carl only had a job with the company because he was dating the boss's sister, Patricia. That said, Allen needed to be guarded around him, because word always got back to the boss, via Carl.

"Randall said for me to come up here," Carl finally explained. Allen faced him, and noticed immediately that Carl had made his fifteen minute trip to the fourth floor, without any tools or a ladder, and therefore he couldn't do any work without wasting another fifteen minutes retrieving them.

"I thought we were finished wiring the lights in this room." Allen said.

"Me and Jonas did," Carl said. Jonas was another shining star in Allen's opinion, and happened to be Carl's best buddy.

"Well then…" Allen tried to control his frustration, "…you and Jonas need to get some tools, grab a ladder, and do it again…because you and your pal evidently didn't do it correctly the first time."

"Well… it was Jonas who wired *this* room…" Carl began to put the blame on his buddy. It was one of the things that Allen disliked the most about the man. He never took responsibility for his own actions.

"Just go get your gear and fix it!" Allen didn't have the patience to listen to any of Carl's excuses right now.

Carl left the room, just as Randall came in carrying a ladder. "He came all the way up without his tools, didn't he?" Randall asked. He was smiling, because of a running joke that he and Allen had about Carl being an idiot.

Allen just shook his head, "He's consistent…I have to give him that much!"

"Consistently bad!" Randall joked. "You ready for lunch?"

Randall Jefferson was a black man - standing five feet, eleven inches tall, and was about three hundred pounds. He looked like a human bowling ball, but despite being more than a little on the fat side, he was as strong as a Brahma Bull. Randall had also grown up in Buckroe. He and Allen were friends since middle school, and he was also one of the most sincere people that Allen had ever met. "What are we eating today?" Randall asked, after setting down the ladder.

"I'm going to skip lunch," Allen said, without looking his friend in the eyes. He could feel Randall's eyes scrutinizing him.

"You gonna be eating with your other best friend, Elijah Craig, again today?" Randall asked, with a twinge of sarcasm in his voice. Elijah Craig was Allen's whiskey of choice, and Randall knew it.

Allen glanced up at Randall's face. He was trying to get a read on if his friend was kidding around, or not. Based on the disappointed way that Randall was looking back at him - he guessed the answer was - *not*.

Randall exhaled, "Look, I ain't one to be all up in someone else's business, but it seems to me like you've been letting that shit rule you for quite a while now." Randall shook his head the way a disappointed father might shake his head at a son – one who was making the wrong choices in life. "I'm all about the partying and having fun, but you need to separate that shit from your work life. It's going to get you in trouble."

The things that his friend was saying made sense. Allen knew that he'd let the drink sink its hooks in him. Hell, he was more aware of it than anybody else, but he also knew that Randall didn't realize that the two of them were at different points in their life right now. Randall had a wife and a young child. He had people around him all the time – people that cared about him - Allen didn't. There were women that came around once in a while, but only for a drink, or whatever the high Allen could provide them at the time. Other than that, he was alone. It was depressing to go to work every day, only to go home every night to an empty apartment. His routine was a miserable existence. After work some nights, all he'd do was nurse a bottle – watching TV until he fell asleep, only to get up the next morning and do it all over again. When it was warm outside, he spent the evenings, sitting on the steel balcony that adjoined his front door, with a steel staircase that ran down the back of the building. If it was especially hot it was his best option, since the apartment he rented didn't have any central heat or air, and it could get quite muggy in the summertime.

Other nights he went down to the local watering hole, the Big Horn, and drank there, but that could get expensive. He could buy a whole bottle of whiskey for what he spent on a few drinks down there. The sad truth was that his life, as a whole, revolved around spending his time alone while trying to decide on where he was going to pop the top on the next bottle. It had become his only pleasure, and no matter how hard Randall tried, he just didn't understand how miserable it was for Allen to be sober. Randall could stand there and talk to him all day, and it wasn't going to change the fact that he was going for a drink, just as soon as the lunch bell rang.

Allen knew that he was probably to the point where he needed professional help if he was going to quit, but that was only *if* he wanted to quit. Right now, he had no intention of doing any such thing. "Yeah, thanks for the concern," Allen said. "I'll keep that in mind."

Randall shrugged his shoulders. His disappointment was apparent, "Whatever man! Just know that if you need someone, Shannon and I are here." Randall turned and walked out of the room, at the same time Carl and Jonas back came in.

"Where do you want us to start?" Carl asked.

Allen looked at Carl - lit another cigarette and without saying another word - left the room.

4

It was a quarter past five when Allen walked into the company office. The reception area was small. There was barely enough room for the two chairs placed on either side of a large potted plant that had grown nearly tall enough to reach the ceiling tile.

Allen popped a hand full of Tic-Tacs into his mouth, to freshen up his breath. He preferred chewing gum, it masked the alcohol better, but the mints were all that he could find on short notice, in the truck glove box. He'd taken a couple of swigs from his flask while he was out in the parking lot, and he didn't want Chip, *his boss*, to smell it on him. Now he was standing in the small lobby. There was an open receptionist window to his left, and to his right, a white door with dirty finger marks all around the handle. A cheap picture of a sailboat adorned the only open wall. It was the kind of picture that Allen imagined someone could pick up at a yard sale for a couple of bucks. Allen poked his head in the window and saw that there was nobody at the desk. He tried the door, knowing full well that it would be locked, they were in Hampton after all. Of course it was locked, so he leaned his head through the receptionist window again and yelled, "Chip?" There was no answer at first. He called again, and as he did, Chip Avette's sister, Patricia came waddling around the corner from somewhere in the back. She didn't say hello, she ignored that Allen was even standing there, and simply pushed a button under the receptionist desk. The door behind Allen made a buzzing noise.

"He's in his office," Patricia finally said. Allen pulled open the door and went in.

Chip Avette was indeed in his office and was on the telephone as Allen entered. Chip was a big man, standing nearly six feet four and moderately overweight. He had once been in pretty good shape, but years away from

13

field work and even longer away from his youth had packed on the extra pounds. He wore a crisp white shirt and tie, with business slacks - he always did. Allen felt a little under-dressed in the dingy jeans and the t-shirt that he'd worn all day on the jobsite. Without breaking from his conversation on the phone, Chip motioned for Allen to sit in the chair across from his desk. Allen ignored the gesture and used the time to look around Chip's office. The whiskey was beginning to take an effect and he was afraid that if he were to sit down, the room would start spinning faster than it already was.

Hanging on the wall were numerous plaques for donations made by the company to little league baseball teams, and a couple of blown up pictures of Chip and his late father, fishing from the back of a very substantial boat. There was also a picture of Chip's very plump wife, Shelly. Allen always had to fight back the urge to call her Lulu, since she reminded him of the fat lady from the Dukes of Hazzard TV show – right down to the hairdo. He knew them well – they'd grown up in the same neighborhood. As he looked at the picture, Allen felt himself sway a little, deciding that it was time to sit down. He took the chair Chip had offered him. Sitting now, he looked out of the office door and across the hall to find Patricia at the receptionist desk, staring directly back at him. Allen despised the girl and was pretty sure that she felt the same about him. It didn't help the situation that she was Carl's girlfriend - he and Carl loathed each other.

She was chewing on a piece of gum that made Allen think of a grazing cow. He couldn't help but chuckle and waved goodbye, as he gently pushed the door closed, so that he didn't have to look at her anymore. Chip finished with his phone call. "Sorry about that," He hung up the receiver, "Freaking supply companies!" He pulled his desk drawer open and removed an envelope, then tossed it onto his desk in front of Allen. "Look…I know that it's late and you've worked hard all day, so I will make this as quick and painless as I can." He motioned for Allen to pick up the envelope.

Allen opened it. Inside, he found a check for five hundred dollars made out in his name, "What's this?"

"It's some extra money, to hold you over for a couple of weeks."

"What do you mean?" Allen asked, confused.

"Look…" Chip said, "…I'm not one for beating around the bush…

you know that…so I'm going to give it to you straight. I'm laying you off for a couple of weeks, to give you some time."

"Give me time…for what?" Allen could feel his blood pressure rising, causing the room to spin a little faster.

"Look, I don't know how to put this gently, so I'm just going to lay it out there," Chip explained.

"You keep saying that…so please, do."

Chip took a deep breath, he was clearly uncomfortable, "You are a hard worker…maybe the best I have, and I hate to lose you right now, but you are also the biggest liability in the company. I've heard from multiple people on the job, that you've been drinking on the clock. That is a serious safety violation and could bite us all in the ass, if something were to happen to you or someone else, because you were drunk."

Allen's mind was racing, "Who said that?"

"I ain't saying who…" Chip explained.

Allen cut him off and stood, "I'm gonna' put my foot in Carl's ass… and then I'm gonna…" he felt dizzy and sat back down – leaning his head against the back of the chair.

"You don't need to be in here talking like that…wait…" Chip said, noticing Allen's mannerisms, "Are you drunk right now?"

"What…no…what the fuck, Chip?" Allen argued. In fact, he was more than a little drunk. Maybe, he should have eaten lunch. The nip that he took in his truck, shouldn't have had this kind of effect on him.

Chip rubbed his forehead. "Look…you need to take some time to get yourself together. I'll call you when work picks up and see if you're ready to come back. In the meantime, you need to get some help."

"Oh, screw you man…who in the fuck do you think you are?"

"I'm trying to be your friend, but you are making it real hard for me." Chip kept an even voice, even though he was losing his patience.

"You aren't my friend." Allen's words were slurring now, "You're just an asshole who used me to make a few bucks for his company, and by the looks of your charity donations and your fucking fishing trips, you've made a pretty penny off of me."

"I didn't use you Allen," Chip said, "You were paid for your work."

"Call it what you want, motherfucker, but I don't see nobody else around here going on fishing trips."

15

"What in the hell is your fixation with fishing trips right now," Chip laughed. "You're not making any sense."

"Don't laugh," Allen felt his blood beginning to boil, "I'm serious!"

Chip shook his head in disappointment. "Allen, you used to be a cool guy. What happened to you?"

For some reason, this question infuriated Allen - maybe because it was true, or maybe just because he was intoxicated and wanted a reason to be angry - but he was filled with rage. "You know what Chipper…" Chip hated to be called Chipper, and Allen knew it, "…you used to be a guy that would never have let his hoe-bag sister, date such a piece of shit such as Carl Raymond."

Chip sprang from his desk chair, with the intention of smashing his fist through Allen's face, but he caught himself, before he went too far. "Get your drunk ass out of my building," Chip said, pointing at the door. His voice quivered, he was so angry.

"With pleasure…" Allen stood and swung open Chip's office door so hard that it bounced off of the wall. He stormed past Patricia who was standing beside the phone, at the reception desk - more than likely getting ready to dial 911, if things got out of hand. She refused to make eye contact as Allen passed her, but said "Asshole," as he went.

"Fuck you, and your boyfriend," Allen mumbled, slamming the exterior door.

5

His cellphone started to ring at the exact moment he placed his key into the lock of his apartment door. He was feeling a little bit embarrassed by his behavior at work earlier in the afternoon. Somewhere deep down inside, he hoped that it was Chip calling, so that they could talk a little more civilly, but he knew that Chip Avette was not the kind of man to reach out after what happened.

He was tired, more than a little hung over, and the sound of the phone was ringing was no different to his aching head than nails on a chalkboard. Allen pushed the door open with his foot, as he pulled the phone from his pocket - checking to see who the caller was. He took a deep breath when he saw that the caller ID read, *Mother.* He closed the apartment door and hit the decline button. The last thing that he needed right now was more drama. He could already guess what it was that she wanted this time. *Stan was kicking her out…again, or Stan was going on vacation without her.* Though he tried to be there for her when she needed him, right now he just couldn't deal with it.

He walked into the bedroom hoping that his friend from last night was gone. She was, but he found a note lying on the floor. It was scribbled on a pad next to his mattress - which was also on the floor, since he didn't have a bed frame.

Thanks, See you around.
Tina

He tossed the notepad back to the floor and went to the refrigerator to grab a beer. Then, he fell onto the couch - just a single step from his refrigerator in this small two room apartment. Technically, it was three rooms if you counted the bathroom - or three and a half if you threw in the tiny clothes closet with the folding doors. The apartment was the opposite of lavish, but it kept the rain off of his head and with the plug-in space heater that he'd bought at Wal-Mart, it stayed cozy enough through the winter months. The accommodations were also about all that Allen could afford and now that he was jobless, he wondered how much longer he'd be able to pay the landlord.

He popped the top on his beer and exhaled deeply. Finishing his first cold one with only a couple long gulps, the cell phone began to ring for the second time. Not bothering to turn on the lamp - *the 7- Eleven across the street kept his place pretty well-lit with its parking lot lights* - he grabbed the phone off of the counter and answered it this time, after glancing at the ID, "Hey mom, what's up?"

"Hey Alley...I didn't think that I was gonna get you." His mom had called him Alley since he was a kid, when her third husband coined the nickname. The guy was an asshole who always came up with stupid names for people. Somehow, the nickname stuck around - the husband had been replaced - a couple of times over.

"What's up?" Allen didn't bother with the small talk.

"Is there something wrong with your phone?" She asked. "I've been calling all day."

It had actually only been one other time, "About what?"

"I have some bad news. I thought that I should pass it on to you."

"What's the bad news?" Allen regretted asking, as soon as he did. He imagined that he'd opened the door for another one of her boyfriend complaints. She'd been living with a man for years, and complained about him incessantly. Sometimes, Allen just wanted to scream – fucking leave! If you are that unhappy – LEAVE! But he knew that it would do no good, she wouldn't leave until she found someone new to partner with, at least for a little while. The only one she hadn't been able to latch onto for any length of time, was his real father. Allen had never met the man, and didn't even have his last name. That was why Allen's last name was the same as his mother's – Blackwood. Apparently, his father wasn't around at the time that Allen was born. She'd always been guarded with any information about him. Even after Allen was old enough for the truth, she'd continued to lie and protect his identity. From what Allen could tell, she'd become pregnant when she lived in Mississippi, and moved to Virginia shortly after. That was about all that he knew. That and the man's first name was Stephen.

He sipped his beer and was prepared for the sob story that preceded most of their conversations. Instead, she skipped to the point. "It's Uncle Kirk…he's sick," she said. Kirk was one of her five brothers, and by far Allen's favorite uncle. Never knowing his own father – Uncle Kirk had always been a positive male figure in Allen's life. Kirk and Aunt Elizabeth lived in Mississippi, but used to visit the family in Hampton on a regular basis. He was really the only one of her brothers to ever come around much. Allen could remember his mother and stepfather sitting in the smoky kitchen around the dinette table, playing cards with Kirk and Elizabeth. That had to be back in the early eighties, when Allen was maybe ten years old. He wasn't sure why he remembered the card games. Maybe, it was because it was some of the very few good times that he remembered anyone ever having in that house.

On one of those visits, it just so happened that Allen had gotten a bad report card, or hit one of the neighborhood kids, or had been caught telling a lie - *it was hard to keep up with his infractions, real or imagined -* and was being punished. Only thing was, his punishment back then wasn't the way that punishment went by today's parenting standards. Even the smallest transgressions usually resulted in belt spankings with the pants down, so that the belt could make better contact with the skin – followed by being put in the garage, or confined to a certain corner of the house for ridiculous amounts of time, sometimes as long as a week, sometimes longer. The only reprieve was to go to school, or the bathroom, and then it was back to the corner.

Uncle Kirk had come to visit during one of these punishments, and must have felt sorry for Allen, because when he left to head back home to Mississippi, he took Allen with him. It turned out to be one of the most memorable summers of Allen's childhood. He'd held an affection for Kirk and Elizabeth ever since.

Regretfully, Elizabeth died of cancer a few years back and Allen hadn't made it to her funeral. From what he'd been told, she was buried in a family cemetery somewhere in Mississippi. Kirk must be pretty old himself by now. "What's wrong with him?" Allen asked.

"It's his lungs…one of them quit working altogether, and the other one is only half working."

"That doesn't sound good," Allen said.

"It isn't," his mother agreed. "Jennifer said that he can't walk more than a couple of feet, without having to stop for a breath." Jennifer was one of Allen's cousins, by his Uncle Elmer. She lived in Mississippi too and was evidentially still pretty close to Kirk.

"How old is he now?" Allen asked.

"Let's see…" his mother started doing the math in her head. Allen could picture the dusty wheels turning in her feeble mind, "Elmer and I are sixty-two, and so that would have made Conrad sixty-five. Kirk has got to be sixty-seven by now."

"Wow," Allen said. "Time flies, don't it? It seems like yesterday when I spent that summer down there."

"That's been about twenty-five years ago," she trailed off for a minute. Allen assumed that she was recollecting. He hoped that her memories of the past were fonder than his were. "Time sure does move quickly." She said, "You know, there ain't very many of them left."

"Who are you referring to?" Allen asked, before finishing his second beer and tossing the bottle in the trash.

"I'm talking about our family…especially the old timers. All of momma's brothers and sisters are dead. Daddy's are all gone too…except for Otis."

Allen's grandma and grandpa had been dead for about five years now. They passed within six months of each other, the way that old people often do, when they've been married for so long.

"Otis?" Allen asked. He remembered some of the family down in Mississippi, but he didn't recall an Otis. "Have I ever met Otis?"

"I think that I took you to Uncle Otis's house once, but you were small…maybe two, or three. You probably saw him when you were down there with Kirk and Elizabeth that summer, but maybe you didn't realize who he was." She paused and as an afterthought she said, "He's rich."

"Wait a minute…" Allen said, remembering that summer, so long ago "…I do remember the rich guy." Allen looked out of his window at the cars passing by on the street. The day was all but gone over the horizon, but the orange hue of the setting sun still hung just over the treetops. He was thinking back to that summer. "I remember him showing up to Kirk's house, for a cookout or something…driving a really nice car. The cousins all talked about how much money he had, but I didn't realize that he was family. That was Otis…huh?"

"That was most likely him."

"How did he manage to get wealthy, while our side of the family stayed so poor?" Allen asked. He thought of the small house, on the deprived side of town, that his grandparents had rented for the last twenty years of their life. It was hard to imagine why they had lived in such squalor, while somebody related to them was filthy rich.

His mother paused a moment before she answered. "I'm not sure how he made his money, but he and Daddy didn't get along." Allen noticed that the pause before her sentence was usually the same one that preceded her lies. He'd heard it a thousand times, but didn't say anything. He just couldn't quite figure why she would lie about Otis's wealth. Then she said, "You should call down there sometime…talk to them."

"I don't know about that," Allen said. "It's been a long time. They probably don't even remember me."

"Yes they do!" She said, "Every time I talk to them, they ask about you."

"No kidding?"

"They do. You should take a trip down there some time. They would love to see you."

Allen rubbed his forehead with his fingers, "maybe I can find him while I'm down there."

"Who?"

"Stephen," Allen knew that she wouldn't discuss it, but thought he'd mention it to see if today would be the day that she'd crack. Someday, she'd have to tell him more, but it wouldn't be today.

She took a noticeable breath and then said, "yeah, maybe so. But you should really go see your uncle…and it might be the last time that you get to see Otis too! He's getting old."

"Yeah, maybe sometime I will. Right now though…I'm gonna' need to be looking for a job."

"What happened to your job, Allen?" She asked, with a bit of sarcasm. She may as well have said, "*What did you do now, Allen?*"

"I got fired…" Allen said, "…it's probably for the best. The company I was working for was a bunch of jerks anyhow?"

"What are you going to do?" She asked.

Allen thought about the question for a minute, before saying. "I really don't know, but look…I just got in. I'm beat, and need a shower."

"Alright, I'll talk to you soon…Love you," She said.

Allen hung up the phone.

After finishing with his mother, Allen polished off the twelve pack and fell asleep still wearing his jeans and t-shirt.

He woke up the next morning with the sun shining through the window. It must have been eighty degrees inside the small room. There wasn't any air conditioning to stave off the summertime heat. The problem was that if he installed a window unit, it tripped the breaker. The house was old, and not equipped to support the modern luxuries.

The house had been built around 1911. In recent years it had been sectioned off into five different apartments. Allen's was the smallest of the five and only accessible by a narrow set of steel stairs, which went up the back of the house from the driveway. He opened the door to the landing at the top of the stairs and stepped outside into the late morning air. It was already humid and the sun made Allen's eyes hurt. He closed them and rubbed the sleep away. When he reopened his eyes, Mr. Gulledge was standing at the bottom of the staircase. The old man was looking up at him with what Allen felt was more than a little disdain. Maybe it was all in Allen's mind, but he never felt like the property owner liked him very much. Rufus Gulledge was a somewhat short, but stout man - about sixty years old. He was a Vietnam War veteran - a Huey helicopter pilot from what Allen had gathered. He now owned a small carpentry business. He had gray thin hair and a matching grey mustache. He was wearing his trademark jeans with a red pocket tea-shirt. A pack of Marlboro cigarettes, sticking out of the pocket. In his hand he held a can of white paint and a paint brush. Allen had learned through his time as a tenant that Rufus didn't beat around any bushes with unnecessary conversation.

"I thought you'd be working…" Rufus said, "…you have the day off?"

"Yeah, I'm taking a little break." Allen didn't feel like he needed to explain his personal situation with the landlord.

The old man nodded his head. Allen could tell that the Rufus wanted to ask more questions, but he didn't, instead he said, "You just make sure that you don't take any breaks from paying your rent on time."

"I've got you!" Allen said, "What are you doing…with the paint?"

"This place looks like shit…" Rufus waved the brush around in a circular motion, to encompass the whole house, "…I'm gonna have the outside painted next week. I was going to put a coat on the railing of this staircase, hoping that it dried before you got home. Apparently, *that* plan is blown to shit." Rufus set the paint and brush down on one of the stairs and pulled a cigarette from his pocket. "If you have some time off, maybe I can give you a break on your rent. I was thinking that you could paint your apartment yourself."

Allen knew immediately that he didn't want any part of that deal. Rufus Gulledge had a way of working agreements in his own favor, screwing you in the process. "Hey you know, I wouldn't mind taking you up on that offer, but I'm heading out of town for a few days." This was a total lie, but as it came out of his mouth, it didn't seem like such a bad idea. He had a couple hundred dollars in the jar in the kitchen. That could provide him gas to get him to Mississippi and back, if he was frugal. Hopefully, he could hook up with some of his family and not even have to worry about meals while he was down there.

"Oh yeah?" Rufus said, "Where are you headed?"

"Pascagoula Mississippi, to see some family."

II

PAINFUL AWARENESS

Pascagoula, Mississippi

A dirty, red sedan drove slowly past, in front of the house - breaks squeaking – rods tapping, like the driver would be lucky to make it to the end of the street before the engine quit altogether. It crept along the narrow road, past the police scene – the lights from the patrol cars infringing on the otherwise quaint neighborhood. Neighbors, who would usually be eating dinner by now and watching The Family Feud, instead standing in their lawns, trying to catch a glimpse of whatever was going on at the Taylor house.

The driver of the red sedan stopped completely, when Officer Jenkins, who was directing traffic on the small thoroughfare, held up his hand. The officer then waved for a police van with STATE FORENSIC UNIT painted along the side in big black letters, to back out of the driveway. Once the van was clear, Officer Jenkins motioned for the red sedan to carry on.

Instead, the driver - an oversized white woman, *whose cleanliness matched that of her busted car*, rolled down her window and asked the Officer what was happening. Jenkins didn't answer, but directed the lady to keep moving.

Standing in the yard, Mississippi State Police Detective, Lashauna Trudeau watched as the woman drove unhurriedly down the street, taking in as much of the police activity as absolutely possible, before disappearing behind the tree line on the far end of the property. Lashauna thought, *If only people were that fucking nosey when the actual crime was taking place, it would sure make her job a lot easier.*

Detective Trudeau turned around to face the old, blue house again.

27

She stood alone. She liked to have a few moments to herself at the crime scene, to get her thoughts in order. She didn't want to hear anybody else's opinion of what may have happened here. Everyone would have a theory, from the uniforms to her superiors. She traditionally ignored them all. She didn't want anyone else's thoughts and ideas corrupting her own. It was her way of doing things, and had been for years.

Her partner, Detective Leonard Menard stood on the small porch, at the top of a handicap ramp, interviewing the officer that was first on the scene. She and Leo were thorough, and knew the importance of getting all of the statements done at the scene while it was still fresh in the mind of the interviewee. Leo knew what questions to ask – the ones that she, as lead detective, would want to know the answers to. They'd worked together for three years and had cultivated a successful process. She watched Leo, with a bit of admiration, as he talked to the patrolman. Leo was a transfer to the Mississippi State Police, from the New Orleans PD, five years ago. He was short, but stocky and good looking, for a Creole that had grown up poor. He'd learned the value of hard work at an early age. His father demanded that Leo and his siblings carry their own weight when they were young. At forty-six, he was an exercise fanatic, and he drove Lashauna crazy with his constant nagging about her bad eating habits. He brought with him the experience of working in a big city like New Orleans, yet he lacked the instinct that should have propelled him to the highest ranks of the department by now. Nonetheless, Leo was a by-the-book policeman. The two of them made a good team. Lashauna liked to act on instinct, which was a gift that some people naturally possessed. Leo was excellent at filling out paperwork and following policy - which Lashauna detested. In her opinion, they were a match made in policeman heaven. She heard the footsteps approaching from behind her, but didn't turn around. She knew immediately who they belonged to - the only person who had the balls to disturb her while she was having her alone time.

"What's the story Trudeau?" Captain Harrelson asked.

"Two dead inside," She answered, "Husband and wife. The estimated T.O.D. is approximately twenty-four hours ago. The lady was in a wheelchair and died of unknown causes…most likely the blow to the back of her head. She was found face down in the living room, and out of her chair. There is some dried blood on the back of her head, but not a lot of bruising which leads me to believe that she wasn't alive for long, after the blow. The husband more than likely died from the gunshot wound to his chest, but of course, we will wait for the coroner's report on both before we make any further assumptions."

"Murder weapon?" The Captain asked.

"There wasn't so much as a BB gun found inside the house, so we assume that it left with the killer. It doesn't appear to be a burglary since it doesn't look like anything was taken." She sighed, "We don't have very much at all right now, Captain."

"Skip the bullshit, Lashauna," Harrelson said, "What do you *think* went down?"

Lashauna faced him. She had a savage look in her eyes. The same look that he would have expected to see on a hungry lion, as it caught the first scent of potential prey. He found her fiercely attractive, but it was more than her beauty that attracted him, it was her aura. She was the kind of woman that could lure you in with her beauty, and then tear you to shreds for nothing more than the sport of it. Standing at a tall for a woman six foot, Detective Trudeau was the daughter of a white father, a French fisherman who had died several years ago. Lung cancer, Harrelson thought he'd overheard once. Her mother was a black Creole lady, who was rumored to be a voodoo priestess, in her younger years. The combination of her parents gave Lashauna a caramel completion and blue eyes, that were almost as clear as crystal. Harrelson found it hard to stare into them for too long at one time, afraid that he would be drawn in with their magnetism - and lose his mind forever. He was convinced that her mother had in fact been a voodoo witch. Lashauna had evidently inherited quite a bit of her mother's craft, and perhaps she wasn't even aware of it.

"I don't know why, *yet...*" She was saying when Harrelson regained his composure, "...but it looks like someone went into the house while the two were out. I'm working on where they might have gone...maybe for a walk?"

"How do you know they were out?" Harrelson asked.

"There was mud on the wheelchair wheel and a slight track of it coming in from the front door. If it were old, it would have dried and been scattered in other areas of the house. I'm not one hundred percent sure, but that's my first intuition. When they returned, someone was waiting on them. The attacker hit the old lady...it may be what killed her, and then shot the husband. Not sure in which order it happened," Lashauna explained.

"What else have you got?"

"That's it right now. We're getting some statements together." She gestured towards Leo, who was finishing up with the patrolman on the porch and walking towards Lashauna and Harrelson.

"Let me know what turns up," Harrelson said, as he walked toward the house. He patted Leo on the shoulder as the two passed in the yard.

"Sure thing, Captain." Lashauna said. She watched Leo as he reviewed his note pad. "What do we have so far?" She asked her partner, when he approached.

Leo flipped back a couple of pages, "The uniform said that he responded to a call from the neighbor. She evidentially stops by occasionally, to chat with the old lady. When she came by today, she found the door ajar, and when she pushed it open, she saw the deceased in the living room floor."

"Did she go inside?" Lashauna asked, wanting to make sure that the crime scene had remained preserved.

"She said no. The uniform ..." He flipped the page "...Officer Markelson, was the first inside. Once he confirmed the deceased, and cleared the house of further threat, he came outside and waited by his patrol car."

"Do we have an ID on the deceased?"

"Yes, Mr. Jasper Taylor, and his wife Mrs. Inez Taylor, both of them were in their seventies. "Here is an interesting find...they have a son who, according to the neighbor, is recently estranged from his wife, and is now living here...in this house...with his parents."

Lashauna looked at her watch. It was nearly seven o'clock in the evening. "Do we have a name for the son?"

"Lionel Taylor," Leo read from the pad.

Lashauna looked up at the horizon. It was a beautiful pink and orange sky, mixed with various shades of blue. She loved the gulf coast. She loved the way the air smelled, as it picked up the fragrance of the swamp lily and mixed with the clean gulf breeze, coming up off the beach. Her eyes dropped from the sky to the driveway, where Officer Markelson's patrol car was backing out to the main road, to make room for the coroner's van. As the patrol car moved, she caught a glimpse of something on the ground.

As she walked over to the object, she had a thought. She'd been in this area her whole life and went to school not far from where she was standing. It was her school days that came to mind, as she remembered a somewhat troubled boy that was a year or so ahead of her in class. It was a much smaller community back then. So when someone got a reputation for being a bad kid back then, everyone knew it. The name Lionel Taylor was one that she remembered quite vividly. "Figure out which room the son is sleeping in. We need to search his belongings." she said, as she stopped the coroner's van from pulling all the way up, so that the object wouldn't be covered again.

"I'm on it," Leo said. He followed her to the driveway. She was standing over what appeared to be an empty 7-Eleven hotdog box, which had been run over by a car tire. There was dried mustard along the edge of the box. She looked from the box, all around the yard and back to the box. "What are you on to?" Leo asked.

She pointed at the box with her pen. "Get this entered into evidence."

Leo would never question Lashauna's direction - it was more out of respect of what he'd seen her accomplish over the years, than fear of angering a superior. So, when he asked, it was only out of curiosity. "What are you thinking?"

She stood up and motioned with her hand around the yard. She said in a manner that was like a teacher trying to evoke the thought of her students, "It may be nothing...but, look around the property and tell me what you notice."

Leo stood speechless, trying to pick up on what she was alluding to. He looked around the yard for a few seconds before he said, "Ok, tell me... what I should be noticing?"

"The old man was tidy...inside of the house, and out. He just came home from a walk pushing his wife's wheelchair up the driveway."

Leo noticed the wheelchair tracks through the soft ground along the edge of the driveway when Lashauna pointed to them as she spoke. "He wouldn't have let trash just sit in his driveway without picking it up," She continued, "There's not another piece of trash anywhere on the property that isn't in a trashcan."

Leo couldn't help but smile. The intuition that this woman possessed was mind blowing. "I'll get it bagged up."

"Oh, and one more thing...ask Officer Markelson if he had a 7-Eleven hotdog on his way here," Lashauna said. "I'm going to talk to the neighbor, to see if we can get an idea of where to find Lionel."

2

At the Taylor residence, they'd found nothing more than some dirty laundry and a box of unopened mail in the son's bedroom. The detectives used the address on the mail, to match a low rent apartment complex downtown. She and Leo had gone to the address. It turned out to be a run down, four story complex - dirty and unkempt. Shutters were broken, screens were torn, or missing from the windows altogether. Other windows were covered by plywood, having never been repaired after Hurricane Katrina. Trash was scattered everywhere, pieces of it blowing in the Gulf breeze, as Lashauna and Leo stepped out of their police car.

"Nice place," Leo said, with a facetious tone.

"Yeah," Lashauna agreed, "People don't understand that just because they're poor, doesn't mean that they can't be clean."

Lashauna knocked on the unit door with the address 2B on the frame above. Knocking caused a couple of the neighbors to open their doors, to see what the commotion was. They stood inside of their apartments - their doors cracked just enough to see Lashauna and Leo standing in the hall. The onlookers appeared scared – helpless, behind the safety chains and the wooden doors that separated them and the dangers of the outside world. The look in their eyes made Lashauna feel that if she were to take a single step in their direction, they would scurry away like feral cats. One of them, deciding that there was nothing interesting happening, closed their door, securing it with the loud click of the dead bolt. The other onlooker gave Lashauna and Leo dirty looks as she continued to watch. Lashauna flashed her State Police badge, and tried to engage the lady in conversation, to learn about the residents of 2B, but the lady was not willing to tell Lashauna anything and kept repeating, "I don't know!" To every question that she was asked. A man came walking down the hall with an armload of groceries and headed for the apartment next door. When the detectives approached him, he claimed that he could not speak any English, even though he was clearly an African American. "No abla English," the man said, as he hurriedly put his key into the lock, to which Lashauna remarked that he was the blackest Mexican that she'd ever seen.

Leo got on his cell phone and contacted the landlord, hoping to have the door opened. Luckily, he was able to reach the man, and the whole time they waited for the small, greasy landlord to arrive - Lashauna had a terrible feeling that they were going to find more dead Taylor family members inside the apartment. Much to her surprise, they found no such thing.

Once Mustafa, the Landlord, arrived and figured out how his key went into the lock (*it took him three attempts*), he opened the door into an empty apartment. Mrs. Taylor and the children if she and Lionel had any together, were gone - along with everything else in the apartment. It was completely vacant. Lashauna had hoped to get a recent picture of Lionel Taylor from his estranged wife, but there was nothing left of the pictures that used to decorate the apartment, except for the slightly discolored outline, where they had once hung on the dirty walls. Leo called the local police department, to report the missing wife - now known as Denise, thanks to the clerk at the police station. She was able to pull the name from previous records. Leo learned during his phone call that Lionel had been arrested on drunk and disorderly charges about a month ago and was photographed at that time, during booking.

Gaining this information prompted a trip to the City of Pascagoula, Police Department. The main precinct was located just off of Highway 90, on Live Oak Avenue, not far from the apartment. With a mug-shot photo now in hand, and a copy of Lionel's rap sheet to go with it -the two detectives were headed to Reggie's Sport Bar - a location notorious to the local PD, as a hangout for the rejects of the local society. It was mentioned in the arrest report as a place frequented by Lionel Taylor. Lashauna could tell that Lionel liked to party, and if he were still in town – it might be a good place to start looking. According to the old folk's neighbor - Inez used to complain about Lionel's drinking. The neighbor lady was very clear that Lionel didn't stick solely to the liquid spirits either. She said that Inez had a concern about Lionel bringing illegal drugs into her house. Lashauna doubted that the illegal drugs in question could be as simple as marijuana.

No, she was sure that the drugs, or *drug* if you will, was heroin. It had become an epidemic in this part of the country over the last several years.

Drugs or not, she couldn't figure out why Lionel would kill his parents. What would be his motivation? The prying neighbor said that she hadn't seen his car in the driveway since last night. It just didn't make any sense, and far as Lashauna could tell - there wasn't anything to be gained by killing the parents – no money, no inheritance - nothing. The old people were broke. With exception to their social security checks - they didn't appear to have any money coming in at all. Plus, all of the so-called valuables were left in the house. The TV, a small amount of nearly worthless jewelry, and Jasper's tools. Even the old man's car was still in the drive way. Lashauna had seen many crimes of passion over the course of her career, and very few of them resembled the level of absolute spineless, uncalled for violence that she witnessed in the Taylor house. Who would beat the crippled old lady in the back of the head? If Lionel had wanted to kill her, there were certainly more humane ways to go about it. Things just weren't adding up. She turned the cruiser onto the final stretch of highway before they reached the bar.

"So, do they even let white guys into Reggie's Sports Bar?" Leo joked.

Lashauna smiled, "Only if he has some soul."

"I guess you are going in alone partner…the "has soul" box was not checked on my paperwork."

"Oh come on, everyone has a little."

"Well," Leo smiled, "I did watch the Jeffersons when I was a kid."

"I'm not sure that show had a lot of soul." Lashauna smiled.

"Bullshit, have you ever seen George Jefferson dance? That's the moves that I took to the prom, baby girl!"

"No kidding," Lashauna laughed at the thought of Leo doing the George Jefferson dance in his high school gym, "How'd that go?"

"Not great," Leo teased, "I had a hard time keeping the girls off of me, and it upset my prom date."

"Well," Lashauna consoled, "I'm sure that he got over it, in time."

"Yeah…wait…what?"

Lashauna laughed again, and then her mood turned more serious when she said, "I don't think that Lionel is our guy."

"What makes you say that?" Leo asked.

"It just doesn't fit," she explained, "I'm not saying that he isn't somehow indirectly responsible, but I think when we find him, we are going to have to inform him that both of his folks are dead."

Leo thought about it. The case had the potential to be so easily open and shut. In a way, he had hoped that it would be, but she was right as usual, it just didn't have the feel of other cases. "So what are you thinking?"

"Right now, I'm grasping at strings, but I *do* think that they were killed *because* of Lionel. Somehow…drugs…the wife…the separation… somehow…I don't know. It's the only thing that makes sense. Other than him and his lifestyle, his parents appeared to have lived in a pretty secluded world."

"All right, all right," Leo nodded his head. "We can work that angle for now. I can see where you are coming from." She smiled again and Leo considered opening the door and jumping out of the moving car to avoid the thoughts of infidelity that went racing through his mind. Her sexual magnetism was off of the charts. The scary thing was, Leo was pretty sure that she had no intention at all of displaying it. It happened naturally. She was undeniably, a very dangerous woman. She had the ability to lure you in with a single helpless, sensual look and then before you knew what was happening, she could rip your limbs from your torso and feed them to you through you own ass. Quite a woman - yes indeed!

Lashauna pulled the car into the busy parking lot of Reggie's Sports Bar – parking around the back of the building, near the dumpster. She turned on the overhead light, to review the file that they'd obtained at the station. She studied Lionel's photo for memorization. It would be easier than carrying the photo around the bar and holding it up next to people, to see if it matched. She closed the file and shut off the overhead light. "You ready?"

"Let's get this over with!" Leo said, "Me and momma are supposed to be watching some TV tonight."

"Oh, really? What are y'all watching?" Lashauna asked, in a vain attempt to sound interested in the fact that Leo had a life outside of his work.

"The Walking Dead," Leo said.

"You may be in luck! You may see some zombies in here" She said, as they reached the double wooden doors to the establishment. They were

35

painted bright red, against a dark brown exterior. A dim light was shining down directly overhead. Leo couldn't see any windows on the exterior wall, a fact which he noticed walking up, but had assumed that it was just the side of the building that they came down. "Odd design," He said, as she pulled open the front door. Even before she had the door fully open, they could hear the music blaring. It was a *Boys to Men* song, from way back. Leo followed Lashauna down a dark hallway, which opened up into a single large room. In it was a dance floor, surrounded by tables and chairs. Smoke filled the top half of the room, so it was hard to see faces, given the fact that the dim lighting didn't improve in the main room. It wasn't a weekend, so the place wasn't as packed as Leo figured that it could get. Even so, there were quite a few people in the main area, and all eye's fell on the white guy in the business suit, who had just entered where he didn't belong. It didn't help matters that the honky was entering with a beautiful black woman, and from Leo's quick observation - the best looking one in the establishment. These people looked rough - ridden hard! Lashauna - feeling the tension - took him by the arm, like they were together, and walked to the bar, where two open stools were waiting. Leo sat with his back to the counter top, looking out at all of the resentful eyes staring back at him.

Lashauna motioned for the bartender - a large black man, dressed in a tattered New Orleans Saint jersey and a black bandana, tied around his head. The man acknowledged her with a nod of his head and then took his time coming down, even though he didn't appear to be very busy. While they waited, she looked around the room, starting with the wall behind the bar. There was a partition of liquor bottles stacked all the way to the ceiling. Lashauna saw all of the major labels. She didn't have to perform a taste test to determine that they had been refilled with the cheap, bottom shelf variety alcohol and was now being sold as top-shelf liquor. It was an illegal practice, but hard to prove. Besides, a drunk didn't know the difference. Behind the bottles, there was a dirty full sized mirror stretching about midway down the bar. Other than the bottles and the mirror, there was nothing else to speak of hanging on the walls. In fact, there were no decorative pictures, or none of those neon advertisement signs hung anywhere in the room. The lighting was dim and there was smoke hanging at ceiling level, due to the lack of proper ventilation and nearly every table had a cigarette smoker. It hung like a cloud over the bar inhabitants.

After running out of seemingly mundane things to do, the bartender walked over and leaned on the bar in front of Lashauna. His face was inches from hers when he said, "What'll it be?" His eyes were shifting from between Lashauna and Leo, waiting to see if the white guy would react to the disrespect shown to what was assumed his woman.

"A couple of cokes." Lashauna said, never moving her head, to get the bartender out of her personal space.

"I don't sell cokes."

"Pepsi will do," Lashauna said.

"I don't sell no Pepsi, either." The bartender looked directly at Leo, as he said it.

Lashauna sighed and pulled her badge from the pocket of her suit jacket. She laid it on the bar between her and the bartender. He stood up straight when he saw it, totally retreating from her space, by taking a couple of steps away. "What?" she asked, "No more intimate conversation?"

The bartender grabbed a towel from the bar and began to clean some glasses, which were stacked in a rack, near where he was standing. "What do y'all want?" The bartender gave Leo a look as if to say, *I should have known that there wasn't any way a guy like you, could be with a woman like her.*

Lashauna picked her badge up off of the bar. "I want you to come back over here, so that we can talk."

"What? Am I under arrest? I ain't done nothing wrong." The man was obviously going to be tough to get answers from. Like many inner city people, he showed a blatant disrespect for authority. Lashauna and Leo were used to it; they dealt with his kind on a daily basis.

"We didn't come in here to arrest *you*, but the way things are going… I'm not convinced that I won't leave here without taking you with me," Lashauna said.

The bartender shrugged his shoulders, "You ain't got nothing on me! I'm just minding my bar."

"This is *your* place?" she asked, "Are you Reggie?"

"Yep…" He said, "…and if y'all ain't got no business wit me, I would appreciate it if y'all would vacate my premises. I'm trying to run a business here."

Lashauna nodded her head empathetically, and then said, "Reggie, to be honest with you, I would personally find great pleasure in leaving this shithole right at this very moment, but I'm here for a reason, and until I'm satisfied with the service that I receive from you, I'm afraid that I won't be going anywhere." Lashauna's voice never showed any emotion. Leo stood and walked over to the entrance door, to prevent anyone from making a quick escape. He didn't want Lionel rushing out of here, before they could identify him and the smoke was so thick, it was hard to see faces.

"Here's the problem, Reggie," she explained, "We are here looking for a man named Lionel Taylor, and I plan on hanging out in here until I find him. So, do you know where I can start looking?"

Reggie walked a little closer to Lashauna and said, "Look around you lady. You're outside your comfort zone! You're in my world in here. I ain't gonna tell you shit! You think that just because you come in here, with your little Cracker Jack puppet over there, and flash yo' badge around, it's supposed to scare people into turning snitch? That shit don't happen here." Reggie's voice grew louder and louder. A couple sitting near the door got up to leave, but Leo showed his badge, and ordered them to sit back down at their table. Reggie watched and then said." Y'all motherfuckers better have a warrant, or I'm gonna have yo' asses!"

"I don't need a warrant, Reggie. This is a business that is open to the public, and I don't need special permission to come in during business hours, but since you are in the mood to speak of legal documents, then I should bring up the fact that you don't have your state liquor license displayed." She motioned to the bare walls all around them. "Now...I'm not accusing you of not having a current license," She smiled at him, "I'm sure if I were to ask, you could provide me with a copy of it right away, but you should know that it *is* a violation to not have it displayed behind the bar. You'd probably only be fined a small amount and put on some kind of probation, and of course, be required to display it in the future." Her eyes never left his, as she explained, "But, by chance, if you *didn't* have a current license to sell liquor...Well then, we have a more serious problem, don't we? Seeing as how almost everyone in here is drinking *something*...and we are both painfully aware of the fact that you don't sell any fucking soda."

Reggie's shoulders slumped and his eyes went to the floor.

"Where is he?" She asked, like it was a matter of fact that Reggie had the answer

"He's asleep in my office."

"And your office is…"

"Past the restrooms…second door on the right."

3

The dark hallway stunk of spilled beer and vomit. The soles of their shoes stuck to the floor with every step. Lashauna imagined that this place hadn't seen a mop in years – maybe ever! The music started up from the jukebox again, as the detectives came to a door labeled with a sign that said, simply – KEEP OUT! Other than the restrooms on the other side of the hall, this was the only door. Leo slowly turned the knob and pushed it open. His hand was on the butt of his pistol, as he did so. He insisted on going through a door before his partner, if there was potential for danger on the other side. Chivalrous for sure, but it drove Lashauna crazy. She hated to be treated like a lady on the job. Women had fought long and hard to get equal rights in the workplace, and the fight was not over. There was still a certain degree of sexism that existed. She was as tough, maybe tougher than most of the men that she worked with, and with no disrespect to Leo, who was a fine officer – she stood a better chance of making the correct, split second decision, if things went sour on the other side.

She knew that Leo's heart was in the right place, and she was convinced that it wouldn't make a difference to Leo, if his partner were a woman or a man. He would still insist on going first. It's just who he was. Lashauna waited patiently - keeping an eye on the hallway leading back into the main area of the bar. She didn't want anybody sneaking up on them while they were in this confined space. From what she could see, there wasn't a rear exit from this hall. Most likely, it would be found in the office that they were about to enter. They were trapped in a bad spot if anything were to go wrong. Leo poked his head into the room and then swung the door fully open, so that Lashauna could see.

Lionel Taylor was fast asleep on a deeply stained, green couch, which looked like it had been salvaged from the curbside of a road. Lashauna debated if she would even run the risk of sitting on the thing - much less laying her head on it to sleep. Lionel hadn't stirred with the intrusion - his peaceful slumber explained as they walked into the room. There were empty syringes and rubber surgical tubing on the floor, beside the couch. There were also a few small squares of aluminum foil, not far from one of the syringes, and a glass pipe. The kind used for smoking crack - or more likely Lashauna thought, heroin.

"It looks like our boy here is off in wonderland at the moment," Leo said. He picked up a small wooden box from the floor and looked inside.

"What do you have?" Lashauna asked. Leo held up a small bag of marijuana.

"That's it?"

"I'm afraid so…whatever else was in here, has apparently been smoked by sleeping beauty over there," Leo gestured to Lionel. "What do you want to do?"

Lashauna sighed, "Let's take him in on the weed possession, and let him sober up in the drunk tank. We can have the EMT's take a look at him, to make sure that he's alright. They can also do a toxicology on him. Tomorrow, we can sit him down and find out what he knows about his parents."

Leo stayed in the office with Lionel, while Lashauna went out to the car to call for a black and white to take Lionel to the station. She didn't want to transport him in her car, which turned out to be a very wise decision. Lionel puked twice in the back of the patrol car, on the way to the station.

Greenville, South Carolina

The red check engine light lit up on the dash board, just seconds before all hell broke loose under the hood. Smoke began to pour from both of the front fenders of the nearly used up Land Rover. Allen bought the truck used for what he thought was a reasonable price, considering it was a high mileage vehicle, but it had been nothing but problems, since he first drove it off of the used car lot. He'd replaced the hoses, the radiator, the belts, the alternator, and some kind of air compressor for the shocks, which evidently, only the Europeans are using in their vehicles and charged a king's ransom for. By the way the smoke was billowing from the front end of the truck, it looked like the radiator had gone again.

"Son of a bitch," Allen slammed the gear shifter into park, and instinctively grabbed his empty flask off of the passenger seat. It'd been empty since he took the last swig a few hours back, as he passed through Charlotte. He unscrewed the lid and tilted it to his mouth, hoping to get even a single drop on his tongue for the taste – alas nothing, the container was bone dry. He screwed the top back on – tossing it back onto the seat next to him. It was close to dusk, and the traffic was dying down. Allen had been on the road for about ten hours and was looking forward to getting some sleep - *so much for that now*. He climbed out, pulled the hood up and was engulfed in the sweet, acrid smoke cloud that was caused by the antifreeze hitting the hot engine. Once the smoke cleared, he was able to check and didn't see any leaks in the radiator. *Maybe*, he thought, *it was a hose*. He followed the small hose from the radiator, to where the overflow tank should have been, only to realize that the overflow tank was completely missing. The only remnants of the tank were the two little plastic tabs, which used to attach it to the inside of the fender. *Just great,* Allen thought, *where in the hell am I going to find a replacement overflow tank for an old Land Rover?*

He remembered seeing a sign about five minutes before the engine trouble started that had said, *Greenville, Next Four Exits.* He hadn't been paying very close attention at the time, but he was sure that he hadn't passed more than one of the said exits to Greenville. He walked to the back of the truck and opened the door. He wanted to hang a rag out of the window, so that his truck didn't get towed while he took what could be a long walk back to town. As he was searching one of his bags for a sock or something suitable, he heard a vehicle pull in behind him.

He turned around to find that an older model, dark brown Chevrolet pickup truck had pulled over to help. An old man - Allen estimated him to be in his mid-to-late sixties - was climbing out of the driver side door. Allen couldn't help but to notice that the old man was big. Not fat, but built large. He had likely lost some of his muscle mass in his twilight years, but he was still NFL linebacker material. The old man was wearing jeans and a faded Fleetwood Mac t-shirt that said 1977 World Tour. It even had the dates and locations printed on the back. To top off the vintage redneck apparel, he was wearing a brown, trucker style baseball cap.

"Havin' a little trouble are ye?" He asked, as he walked past Allen on his way to the front of the Rover. By the way the old man walked past without introducing himself, Allen couldn't help but wonder if he was talking to Allen, or the broken down truck.

"Yeah," Allen gestured to the front of the Land Rover, "I seem to have lost my antifreeze reservoir."

"Well let's take a look at it…see if we can patch it." The old man walked to the open hood. Allen followed. When he got to the engine compartment, he stood quietly and rubbed his chin for a full minute before he said, "Correct me if I'm wrong here, fella', but it appears that we are going to have to figure out where the dang thing went…before we can even *think* about patching it."

Allen couldn't help but laugh. The old man chuckled too.

"Come on," the old man said, "I'll give you a ride into town."

Allen accepted.

Once they were inside the old man's vintage pick-up, he introduced himself as MJ MacAulay, with a firm handshake. He then proceeded to slide an Elvis Presley tape into the first working eight track player that Allen had seen since he was a kid. As *Big Boss Man* startled to rattle from a couple of jerry rigged speakers, thrown haphazardly in the back of the cab, MacAulay explained that he was a mechanic, and had his own shop, over in the town of Mauldin. He explained how it would be no problem for him to get the Land Rover back in running order, once they found the replacement parts. Allen had a little bit of knowledge regarding automobile repairs, and knew that it wasn't a very big deal to replace the plastic reservoir tank. He was just happy to have a ride - especially once he realized just how far he actually was from the nearest auto part store. It took a good fifteen minutes worth of interstate speed to reach the exit. It would have taken Allen hours, maybe into tomorrow, to walk the same distance.

They arrived at an Acme Auto Parts Super Store, which was situated in a strip-mall, next to an Italian restaurant that had no shortage of dead flies, turned belly up on the plate glass window sill. Allen walked to the driver side of the pick-up, and thanked the old man for his trouble. He told MJ that he would catch a cab back out to his truck, but the old man insisted on waiting and giving him a ride back out to the truck. "No need to waste your money on a cab," MJ said. When Allen gave him a look that asked, 'are you sure?' MJ shrugged his shoulders and said, "Southern hospitality, at its finest. What can I say?"

Allen went in – standing at the counter for about ten minutes, as the man behind it searched the, evidently endless, inventory of the store, on his grease stained computer. Allen was beginning to wonder if the man actually knew what he was doing on that machine, or if he was writing a short story, while Allen stood there and waited - growing impatient and craving a drink. Finally, the auto part salesman, who comically matched his computer's filth said, "Naw," and shook his head. Allen waited for the rest of the sentence to come, but it never did.

"Naw? Allen repeated, "naw what?"

The salesman turned away from his dirty computer. "Can't get it! It's a dealer only part."

"Dealer only? Where is the closest Land Rover dealer?"

The counter salesman, *Hank, by his name tag*, pulled a giant phone book from under the counter. It was the second time today that Allen had seen relics from the past, put to use. He wasn't even sure where to get a phone book these days. Everyone used their cell phones to find numbers in these modern times – times that had evidentially not made it all the way down to Acme Auto Parts, in beautiful downtown Bumfucked, Hickville.

The salesman wrote down an address and a phone number on a yellow sticky pad and handed it to Allen. "It's up on Laurens Road. They're probably closed by now. They might have it in stock...or they may have to order it."

Allen considered thanking the man for the obvious possibilities, but instead he thanked him for the address and walked back out to the parking lot. It was fully dark now and MJ was sitting in his pickup truck, under one of the parking lot light poles. He was listening to an early version of *I'll Never Let You Go Little Darling*, on his Elvis eight track. He turned down the volume on the King of Rock and Roll who, *in Allen's opinion*, was whining like a miserable school girl, through the static filled speakers. Allen silently said a little prayer to the gods of music, thanking them for not forcing him to be in the truck while that song played in its entirety. "What's the word?" MJ asked.

Allen shook his head in defeat. "No luck! I need to wait until tomorrow and check with the Land Rover dealership."

"Well..." MJ looked at his watch, "...what do you want to do?"

Allen considered his options. None of them were good, since he barely had enough money left in his pocket for gas to get all the way down to Mississippi. There was no telling how much the part for the truck was going to be. "I hate to ask, but could you give me a ride back to my truck?"

"Sure...what are you going to do once you get there?"

"I suppose that I'll get some sleep, and figure out how to get to the dealership tomorrow," Allen said.

"Oh, horseshit!" MJ said, as if the mere mention of that plan disgusted him, "Get in and we'll go pick up my flatbed. Let's get that broke down piece of British shit, off of the interstate and pull it back to my garage. I've got a little living space in the back of the shop. You can sleep in there tonight...and tomorrow, we'll go get the part."

Allen was stunned by the generosity and stood beside the pickup's window for a few seconds, before he said. "I really appreciate your offer, but you've done enough already, and I don't have any money to speak of. I couldn't possibly pay you for all of…"

"Look here kiddo…" MJ cut him off, "…I'm hungry, and I don't want to sit here bickering back and forth. I ain't expecting anything from you, and I wouldn't have offered, if it was going to be a problem." He looked at Allen. He had a very captivating aura about him. Allen had only known the man for a couple of hours and already, he respected MJ. He was the kind of man that Allen wished he could spend more time with and get to know. The man had integrity, and displayed authority without losing his humor.

"You married?" Allen asked.

MJ gave him a strange look. "Yeah, I am…why?"

"I'm just making sure that you aren't some weirdo, gay, serial killer or something."

"Let me assure you, if I were…I wouldn't be wasting my time on some small dicked, butt ugly, broke assed child, such as yourself," MJ laughed. "Now get in the damn truck, before I leave you here."

Allen got in.

5

It was midnight before they got back to the shop - Allen's Land Rover in tow. Over the course of the evening, the two had plenty of time to talk. There wasn't a radio in the tow truck and, *thank goodness*, no eight track blaring the King of Rock and Roll, through shitty speakers. So there was little else to do, but get to know each other a little better. MJ talked about his wife for a while and then his daughter. By the sound of things, they were a close knit family. He asked Allen some carefully selected questions - mindful not to pry too deeply. MJ was therapeutic in the way he communicated. Like a trained professional - his office, the greasy cab of a tow truck – his patient's couch – the worn bench seat. Allen found it easy to talk to him. He told MJ about getting laid off from work, and about his sabbatical to Mississippi - to try and discover his family roots. He left the drinking problem out of the discussion, because the word *problem* wasn't a good way to describe it – it was more like a hobby! But either way, it was not something that Allen wanted to discuss.

MJ didn't pass judgment, or even comment when Allen spoke of his estranged relationship with his mother. He simply said, "Everyone has got their own demons to exercise. She is most likely the way she is, because of something in her past. If you get to know her better…rather than keep pushing her away…you may get a better understanding of why she does the things that she does." It was wise words. Not necessarily words that Allen really wanted to hear, although he nodded his head and didn't say anything to the contrary, to keep from disagreeing with a man that had gone so far out of his way helping him. Allen changed the subject to sports and politics as they finished what seemed like their journey across the entire state of South Carolina.

Finally, they pulled into the parking lot. The building was white cinderblock and had two large garage doors in the front - MacAulay's Auto Repair professionally painted in red and black letters across the wall over top of them. The sign matched the one on the door of the tow truck. The small parking lot was full of vehicles that Allen assumed were waiting on repair. "Looks like business is good," he remarked.

"I can hardly keep up," MJ said. "You should see the lot in the back."

"How many people do you have working for you?" Allen asked.

"Just me and my son in law," MJ said. He pulled the tow truck on the side of the building and put it in park. "Just lock it up! We'll get your truck down in the morning."

They walked to the building and opened a side door. MJ stepped into the darkness and then turned on the overhead lights. The work area was surprisingly tidy for an auto repair shop. The floor was painted a spotless grey and was polished to a shine. The vehicle lifts were clean and there was a line of tall red toolboxes along the back wall.

"Wow," Allen took it all in, "Nice shop!"

MJ nodded his head, as he walked to a door in the rear of the shop. Allen noticed that the later into the evening that it had gotten - the less talkative MJ had become. "There is a cot back here, and a shower in the way back." He turned the lights in the back room on for Allen to see his way. It wasn't much bigger than a closet, but along the wall there was a small military style cot. Other than the cot, there was half of an old high school locker, positioned in one corner and a tattered poster of Farrah Fawcett, the one in the red bathing suit, hanging on the wall opposite the door – there was nothing else in the room.

"I need to be getting home," MJ explained. "I'm sure that Trudy is still up and she'll worry herself until I get in,"

"Alright," Allen said. "Thank you, again...for everything!"

MJ waved his hand between them, like he was swatting at a gnat. "Don't mention it. I'll be here in the morning around eight. Tony, my son-in-law, opens up around seven. Don't be alarmed when you hear him come in."

"No problem," Allen said, as MJ headed out.

Allen lay down on the small cot and stared up at Farrah. He felt his eyes getting heavy. The beautiful face of Farrah began to blur and he was sound asleep, even before the sound of MJ's pickup could no longer be heard in the distance.

6

Allen woke just before 4:00am. His mouth was dry – craving something, but not water. His head hurt and when he sat up his hands were shaking. He got up and searched the garage – hoping that MJ didn't have some sort of security system that would go off and bring the cops. The last thing that he needed was to explain his current situation to some local backwoods sheriff's deputy. He was hoping to find a hidden bottle of booze, that MJ or his son-in-law might have stashed away – no luck. He'd never really expected to find any in the first place, but what self-respecting alcoholic wouldn't try. Looking around the shop did give him a new appreciation for the level of professionalism that MJ had in his work. The place was organized and tidy. Nothing out of place – right down to the red oil rags, all folded and placed neatly on a shelf. Satisfied with his snooping, and knowing that he couldn't get back to sleep without a drink, Allen decided to get some fresh air. Despite the cleanliness of the garage, there was still a lingering smell of antifreeze and motor oil, and it was making his headache worse. When he got outside he noticed that MJ wasn't kidding about the rear parking lot. It was full with cars, from one end to the next, waiting to be worked on. Some of them might be junkers, but others had the license plates, indicating that they were still registered to someone, while others were down right nice cars. At least one was a classic muscle car that someone had obviously sunk some serious money into. For something to do, he walked the lot looking at the cars. He couldn't bring himself to go back inside the empty garage and wait for seven am to roll around.

As he walked, he noticed a creek behind the fence, running into the woods and decided to follow it for a while. A hike through the wilderness may do him some good. Allen loved being outdoors – always had. He and his brother used to spend all summer building forts and playing war with their friends, back when they were young boys. Walking along the creek bank reminded him of those times – a simpler life. It had all seemed to change so quickly. Sometimes, he wished that he could go back.

The exercise and the fresh air helped him to temporarily forget that he desperately wanted a taste of whiskey. After about an hour, he decided that it was time to head back and get cleaned up, so that he could be ready when MJ showed up. His new friend was going to take him to get the parts for his truck. He was pouring sweat by the time that he returned – letting himself in through the back door that he'd left unlocked. He was really looking forward to a warm shower, but due to the fact that there was no water heater in the building – he took a cold shower instead.

Tony, the son-in-law, was actually thirty minutes early that morning – meeting Allen as he was coming out of the shower. The encounter was especially awkward since Allen didn't have a towel wrapped around him as he walked around the back room of the shop. He thought that he was going to be alone for another thirty minutes and was in no hurry to put his clothes on, which were on the cot across the room.

"Whoa…sorry," Tony said. He was glancing comically back and forth from Allen, standing in the nude, and the Farrah Fawcett poster on the wall in front of him. He quickly backed out of the doorway.

"I's not what you think," Allen said, hurriedly putting on his clothes. "You're early…I thought you were going to be here at seven." Once dressed, he went out to the garage, to properly introduce himself.

Tony Moretti was not a small man, but he was shorter and thinner than Allen. He was forty something, olive skinned and had thinning black hair. Tony was wearing, Allen assumed, his regular work attire - a pair of tan coveralls and a faded blue cap that had the MacAulay's Garage logo on the front. Topped off with a red shop rag hanging from his back pocket. He was pulling the chain to open one of the garage doors, as Allen came from the back room.

"I guess it's too late for a normal introduction," Allen offered his hand. Tony shook it, then wiped his hand on his rag. "Anything I can help you with, to open up the shop?"

"Yeah sure," Tony secured the chain for the first door and moved to the second. In a thick northern accent - not a dialect that Allen would have expected down here this deep in the south, he said, "You mind catching the light switches over there." He pointed to the far wall. Allen turned all of the switches to the on position and heard the hum of the ballast for the overhead lights, as they flickered on. The sound was much like a mosquito caught in a bug zapper.

He followed Tony out of the side door and helped him move a tire rack to the edge of the parking lot. After a couple more tasks, with Allen helping out where he could, Tony grabbed the keys for the tow truck off of the front counter. With the Land Rover still attached, he expertly backed both trucks into the garage. Then, he disconnected Allen's truck, and pulled the tow truck back outside. By the time he returned, Allen had the hood popped and was searching the back of his truck for his set of tools. Tony took a look at the engine and said, "Looks like you lost a small hose also."

"A hose...how can you tell?" Allen joined Tony under the hood, to see what he was talking about.

"Right here..." Tony pointed to a small nipple protruding off of the radiator. "This is an O-two ain't it?"

"Yeah"

"Then there's a hose that attaches here and hooks to the reservoir bottle."

Allen looked at Tony, "How do you know that?"

"I've worked on one or two of these before...they're notorious pieces of shit."

MJ called the shop phone not long after they'd opened and said that he was going to be a little late. When Tony relayed the news to Allen, he assumed that MJ was trying to catch up on some sleep, since the two had stayed out so late the night before.

His assumption was wrong, MJ showed up at 9:30, with all of the parts needed to fix the Land Rover. Tony was inside the shop at the counter assisting a customer who was picking up their vehicle, while Allen was finishing up pulling a tire rod off of an Oldsmobile Cutlass. He wanted to help out, to stay busy, and Tony had agreed to let him work.

"Well...well, look at you," MJ said, as he came through the garage door carrying a box with the parts. He set them down on the work table, "We're gonna make a mechanic out of you yet."

Allen smiled, and said, "I know just enough to be dangerous."

M.J. walked over and inspected the tire rod. Then he looked under the fender of the Cutlass. "Don't forget to pull off those rubber bushings when you replace the tire rod. It's best to replace those while you have the whole thing apart."

"Sure thing...do you have any in stock, or do we need to order them?" Allen asked.

"We order them," MJ said. "There are so many different sizes that we can't stock them all."

Allen wiped his hands while MJ was under the fender of the car.

"Hand me the flat head screw driver," M.J. said. Once the bushing was free, M.J. came from under the car and stood beside Allen at the work bench, "So you met Tony...what do you think?"

Allen was a little bit surprised by the question. "What do you mean?"

"I'm curious, what is your opinion of the man? He's married to my daughter, and I am just trying to get some outside feedback." Then he added, "Sometimes you can't see the forest for the trees. You know what I'm saying?"

Allen smiled, "Well M.J., to be honest with you, he seems like a good guy. I mean, he's hard working...from what I can tell, but I really haven't had a whole lot of time to get to know him. We have been pretty busy this morning."

"What about the Italian thing?" The old man asked, with a straight face.

"I don't see where that would matter," Allen said.

"Grand baby's..." M.J. said.

Allen laughed. "I wouldn't be too worried about that. There are some really good looking Italian people."

"Yeah, but did you get a look at that little pug faced son-of-a-gun in there? He ain't one of the good lookin' ones."

This made Allen laugh even harder. He looked at the old man with the white hair and the greasy fingers, holding the rubber bushing from the Cutlass and thought of how lucky Tony was to be able to call this man family. Allen shrugged his shoulders and said, "At least the Italians make great cars."

"You got that right." M.J. tossed the worn out bushing into the trash can. "Too bad the British don't. Speaking of which...let's get yours fixed."

"About that…" Allen said. "…I really don't have much money on me right now, and I don't even know what kind of price you could put on the level of help that you've already given me, but I want you to know that I intend to make good on it. I could call my brother…see if maybe he could wire me some money…just let me know the price."

M.J. pulled the parts out of the box. "How much money have ya' got in your pocket right now?"

Allen did the math in his head, deducting the gas and food expenses from yesterday on the road. "Without looking…I'd say, I probably have about four fifty, maybe four seventy five."

"To your name?" M.J. paused what he was doing.

Allen nodded, "…that and the value of the Land Rover."

"That ain't much, is it?"

"No…it isn't."

M.J. put his hand on Allen's shoulder, "Boy, I ain't one to judge, but you need to get yourself together." He looked Allen directly in the eyes as he spoke, "I don't know you very well, but I'm a pretty good judge of character, and you've got a whole lot more to offer this world, than the little bit you have contributed so far. Don't think that I haven't noticed the whisky flask on your front seat and the way your breath smells." He patted Allen's shoulder and then went back to separating the parts from their boxes, getting them ready to install on Allen's truck. "You don't owe me nothing today…but after you take some time with your family, I want you to get serious about being somebody. Do some good for *yourself,* because if you don't, nobody else is really going to give a shit about you, son. Nobody is going to be looking out for you…other than you."

Allen heard M.J.'s words, and for the first time in a long time, he felt like he wanted to do right by himself. Not only to show the old man that he could, and not only because he wanted to, but because M.J. wanted him to. "Why?" Allen asked.

"Why…what?'

"Why are you being so kind to me?" Allen asked. "You don't know me from the next guy. Why are you helping me?"

M.J. faced Allen, "To be totally honest with you boy, I asked myself that same question while I was on my way to pick up these parts for your truck this morning…" He held out his arms "…and the answer is…I really don't know. I've seen many a person pass through here, and I ain't ever lost a moment of sleep for not helping any of 'em, but I see something in you, Allen. Beyond the feller who can't hold a job and drinks a little too much." M.J. shrugged, "I see myself in you. I see the son me and Trudy lost when he was a baby. I see a damn fine man who just needs a little help to get going." He held up the replacement reservoir for Allen's Land Rover. "This here cost me one hundred and sixty four dollars...you can owe me that. The rest I do because I want to...because I feel like you just need a little help getting going again."

Allen felt like hugging the old man, but somehow he knew that M.J. wasn't the hugging type. "I'll repay you...for all of it."

"Well, why don't we just worry about that later? Right now, let's focus on getting this piece of shit put back together. I'm sure that you're ready to get back on the road."

Surprisingly, Allen wasn't in a hurry at all.

Pascagoula, Mississippi

The interrogation room was small - roughly six feet, by six feet. The walls - painted white with grey tile on the floor, and a two way mirror along one whole wall. Still somewhat intoxicated, Lionel Taylor sat in a wooden chair, facing a small stainless steel table that was situated in the center of the room. He was a thin, lanky man – and not only thin because of the drug use, he would never have to worry about carrying extra weight – it wasn't in his body chemistry. The clothes that he wore were stained and smelled of animal urine. Despite the hangover and the dirty clothes, Lionel wasn't a bad looking man. He had kind eyes, and a decent smile – marred by bloodshot and lack of a toothbrush. He didn't come across as dangerous, in the opinion of the police officers – just another mild mannered junkie. The table had a large steel ring, anchored directly in front of where Lionel was sitting. He'd seen it before – been handcuffed to it before too. He found some comfort that he wasn't wearing handcuffs this go around and he didn't intend to have any put on him, so he kept his hands in his pockets while he waited. The Detective that had introduced himself as Menard when he was brought in, stood behind Lionel, with his hands in the pockets also.

Detective Leonard Menard was dressed in brown pants and white dress shirt, with his leather holster draped over his shoulders, minus his gun. As a rule, it had to be checked in with the duty officer before they could enter a room with a prisoner. Not that Lionel Taylor was necessarily a prisoner at this point. Though he'd been arrested and charged with public intoxication last night, he was released by the magistrate this morning, with a citation to appear in court in three weeks.

Lionel sat quietly and began folding his newly acquired legal paperwork into a paper airplane. When he was finished, he sailed his creation at the door, just as Lashauna came walking in. Whether it was intentional or not, it mattered little to Lashauna. She had a surprisingly high tolerance to the antics of lowlife criminals. It wasn't the first time someone tried to get under her skin, and it certainly wouldn't be the last attempt. She'd seen much worse than some loser throwing paper airplanes. She stepped inside the door and closed it behind her. She was holding a file folder in her hand and opened it. "You might need that paperwork later," she gestured to the paper airplane on the floor.

"I ain't worried 'bout no paperwork," Lionel said, with a dismissive wave of his hand. "Why am I still here? The man said I was free to go an hour ago."

"That was on your public intoxication charge, you are here for something else," Lashauna explained.

Lionel leaned back in his chair and crossed his arms. She knew that this was Lionel's glorious moment to try and represent himself as a badass, the way that all criminals try to do when they are talking with the police. They act like they have a law degree from Harvard, but usually wind up either saying something incriminating, or just sounding like a complete dumbass. It was very rare that she encountered someone that actually *was* educated in the law. She appreciated those rare encounters because it tested her own knowledge, and measured how far she'd come in her profession.

Unfortunately - this was not the exception. When she sized up her competition – the skinny, ashy-lipped tweaker sitting across the table from her – she realized that it was going to be a lot like Michael Jordan, playing one-on-one against a third grader.

The idiot rambled on, "…and secondly of all, sleeping in the back room of a bar, ain't public intoxication and number two…I ain't done nothing else!" The detective let his words hang in the air between them for a few seconds. Lionel sat uncomfortably in his chair waiting on a response, while the lady detective's crystal blue eyes burned right into his own - his body shivered.

"Don't we know each other?" Lashauna finally asked. "Didn't you go to Gautier High School? Class of ninety-three?"

Lionel appeared thrown off. He scrutinized the ID badge that Lashauna had hanging around her neck. By the way that he was squinting, it was obvious that he couldn't read the name written on it. "Lionel Taylor," she said his name, as she read it from the file in her hands. "Your folks lived out on Orange Grove Road." She smiled at him, which caused him to smile in turn. "Didn't you play football in high school?"

"Baseball too!" Lionel boasted. "Have we met before?" He was still smiling at Lashauna, like he was working his pickup game in a local bar, and not in the interrogation room of the local police department.

Leo - watching from the corner - shook his head and rubbed his brow. He couldn't help but feel sorry for the poor guy. He'd seen it happen on many occasions. She reels them in, they tell her what she needs to know and then she tears them into pieces. As beautiful as she was, there was a sadistic side to her that showed up occasionally when she was on the hunt.

"Yeah, we have actually," She said. "We went to school together…for a year or two. I was a couple of years behind you. I think you were a senior when I was a sophomore." Lionel's smile grew larger.

Wait for it, Leo thought, as he stood behind the poor bastard, listening to the exchange.

"I was also the one who arrested you last night, while you were… *sleeping,*" Lashauna made the quotation gesture with her fingers. "Resting like a little baby at your buddy's bar. Nestled snugly into a substantial pile of used drug paraphernalia!"

Lionel's smile faded. He looked over at Leo. The cop just shrugged his shoulders as if to say, *you had to know it was coming.*

"Where did you get the drugs?" Lashauna asked. Her voice was flat like she was simply asking what he wanted for dinner.

"Wha…I didn't have any drugs on me," Lionel's smile quickly turned back into a scowl of anger, mixed with defiance.

Lashauna nodded her head in agreement, "Your right! They weren't on you…they were *in* you." She tossed the file folder onto the table in front of Lionel. "That's a toxicology report from the blood that you donated for testing last night. It shows very high levels of methamphetamines in your system."

"Blood test…I didn't agree to no blood test," Lionel shouted, and started to stand up until Leo put his hand on Lionel's shoulder – pushing him back into the chair.

"Oh, well that's the neat thing about our medical laws, Lionel." Lashauna explained, "When someone is found in such a state of unconsciousness, and appears to be having a medical emergency, it is well within the rights of the first responders to draw blood and have it tested. Just in case they need to administer medication, to counteract whatever is wrong."

"It don't matter what you got from that report. You can't use that shit in court." Ironically, Lionel did seem to get smart at this point - because he was right. Lashauna wasn't sure if he was only getting lucky, or if he had experience from previous run-ins with the law. It didn't matter, either way.

"Agreed," She said. "If I were here trying to bust you on being a worthless junkie, then you would win the prize," a small victorious grin crept back onto Lionel's face, "but I'm not worried about your pitiful drug habits!" She continued, "Except for maybe who supplied them to you, if you are willing to offer up that information...out of the goodness of your heart, of course. No Lionel, I wish it were so, but it's not! My business here today is trying to find out who killed your mother and father."

Leo buried his face into his hands. *Sadistic and heartless*, he thought, *Sadistic and heartless.*

"Wha..." Lionel said. He began to tear up - his voice cracked as he spoke. "What did you say?"

Without a trace of emotion in her voice, Lashauna explained, "Your mother and father were killed the night before last. Someone came into their house and murdered them both."

Lionel was crying full-on now. "How?" He asked. He didn't know it, but that was the right question to ask. By inquiring how it was done, Lashauna knew that he didn't do it – not directly at least.

"At this point, and according to the coroner's report, your father died of a gunshot wound to his chest, and your mother was bludgeoned to death."

"Bludgeoned? What's bludgeoned?" Tears were streaming down his face.

"She was hit in the head with something," Lashauna explained, with the same even voice that she had spoken in the entire time. "I am pretty sure that you didn't hold the gun Lionel, but I need to know who you have been messing with, because I find it ironic that not long after their drug using, tramp of a son moves back in their house...they get killed."

"Go fuck yourself," Lionel spit on the folder that was lying on the table in front of him. "This ain't on me. I didn't cause this to happen."

"Say what you will," Lashauna picked the file folder up and wiped the spit off with her hand, "Give me some names, and let me do my job, because I *will* find who did this to your parents." She then wiped her hand off on the sleeve of Lionel's t-shirt.

Lionel pulled his shoulder away from her hand. "Oh, so you want to help me, huh? Is that it?"

"No Lionel!" Her voice was still calm and even, "I don't give a shit about you. I am only in it for your parents. They didn't deserve what they got…." She walked to the door - opened it and stopped, "…you on the other hand, *will*!"

Leo grabbed Lionel's elbow, to help him to his feet. "You're free to go," he said.

"Let me know when you want to talk." She left the room.

8

Pascagoula, Mississippi

Allen missed his turn the first time and after realizing that he must have gone too far – he made a U-turn and came back. It was pitch dark and he couldn't see anything beyond his headlights. There was not-so-much as a porch light anywhere in the distance. He was getting a little bit concerned, since the only civilization that he'd seen for the last twenty minutes was a dilapidated shack along the river, *long since abandoned*, a few miles back. Until the sun went down, all that he'd seen had been forest and swamp. He was in the middle of nowhere and if this old piece of crap truck broke down on him again, he might never be found. The alligators and the bugs would surely pick his bones clean before daylight. The thought made him nervous and more than a little vulnerable. He was a city boy – and though he hadn't stepped out of the truck in hours, the amount of bugs hitting his windshield, as he drove down the long road to nowhere, told him that that there was very little in the way of civilization this deep into the swamp land. Out here, nature ruled. He passed another Alligator Crossing sign before he came to the one that he was looking for. He turned his Land Rover between two brick pillars, with gaudy concrete lion statues sitting atop them. It was after 11:00 pm, so he eased slowly along the long driveway.

The trip from South Carolina had taken a little longer than expected, since Allen didn't want to push the Land Rover too hard. He kept it at about five miles-an-hour over the speed limit, the whole way. The night was eerily silent, aside from the hum of his engine. It was difficult to be sure if he was in the right place or not, since he still didn't see any houses. Along the way, there had been nothing but woods for what seemed like miles, broken only by the occasional bridge that spanned creeks and marshes, with signs and names like Kings Bayou, and Crooked Bayou, and the Pascagoula River. The I-10 Bridge coming into town had been one of the longest that Allen could ever remember crossing. He'd never given it much thought before, but as a child, he heard his relatives talk about their homes in the Bayou. He got the feeling that Pascagoula was a town that was literally floating atop a swamp.

He was driving down a private drive, which was immaculately manicured and evidently very long. To him, this looked like the entrance to a museum, or maybe a college campus. He rounded a bend and came to a clearing in the trees, passing beside a large lake situated on the left. He starting to doubt his course, and was considering turning around, when a building appeared from behind the trees. It was an enormous log home, with two river stone chimneys and a large wrap around porch. The whole thing was lit. The lights shining up from the ground, revealing the massive structure, making it resemble a small version of a hotel that Allen had visited once, called the Great Wolf Lodge. He slowed the truck, not sure if this was the right place. Then, he noticed that the doors were open to a large detached garage, and there appeared to be someone standing in the doorway, waving at him. It was probably just southern hospitality, or the beginning of a scene straight out of a scary movie. In reality, it was just someone wondering why some idiot was driving down their driveway, in the middle of the night. To avoid looking suspicious, Allen drove forward to the parking circle, in front of the garage. He rolled down the driver side window as the person, *it turned out to be a woman*, approached his truck. As soon as she was in the beam of the headlights, Allen recognized her as his cousin, Jennifer. She was older and heavier than he remembered. It had been going on twenty years since he'd last seen her.

"Hey there!" She was smiling big, "running a little late, ain't ya'?"

"I got a little side tracked along the way," Allen turned off the engine and opened the door. They hugged. "How are you? It's been a long time."

"I'm doing great," she said.

Allen remembered that it had never been Jennifer's style to complain even if she wasn't doing alright. She was always a positive person when they were younger.

"That's great." Allen said, he felt like he should ask the humdrum required questions, per the rules of social etiquette, but he didn't really have any interest in getting into a long conversation after driving the better part of two days. What he really wanted was a shot of whiskey and some sleep. She did him a favor and didn't waste time with anymore useless chatter. He'd love to hear all about what she had going on - tomorrow.

"Move your truck into the garage, then we'll go inside and get you settled." She pointed at an open area, just inside the massive garage.

"It's fine out here," Allen said. "It's not exactly garage kept, if you couldn't already tell."

Jennifer looked at the truck and smiled. Allen remembered her good sense of humor. They used to entertain each other pretty easily. "It's not that," she said. "My mother's car was stolen just the other night."

Allen looked around the property. He couldn't see any signs of civilization, anywhere. "Out here?" he asked. "Who would come all the way out here to steal a car?"

"Don't know, but Uncle Otis said we should all park in the garage, until he gets some cameras installed. Luckily, whoever it was, only got Mom's Lincoln and not one of Uncle Otis's from the garage. It would be hard to replace one of those."

Allen saw what she was talking about, as he pulled his beat up Land Rover into a garage that was nothing short of a classic car museum. Allen - always a huge fan of classic automobiles - was in awe. There were cars everywhere. In the far corner, he could see a 1968 Mustang, 427 Cobra Jet. There was also a 1967 Olds Hurst, an early 70's Ford Torino, convertible and his own personal dream car, a Lime Green, 1969 Dodge Charger. There were probably fifteen cars altogether, some of which were under car covers, along with five vintage motorcycles on the far end of the building. Hell, Allen had watched enough American Pickers, to know that the old gas station signs decorating the place were worth a small fortune. There were three common vehicles, parked in the area where Allen was now pulling his truck. He assumed that they belonged to Jennifer and whoever else was in the house. One thing was for certain, these people weren't hurting for money.

"Who all lives here?" Allen asked, grabbing his duffel bag from the truck.

"This is Otis's house," she explained, "but Uncle Kirk, along with me,

Ronnie and my Mom and Dad. We have been staying here helping to take care of him. It's been more Mom doing the taking care of, since Dad is trying to run the dealership."

"The dealership?" Allen asked.

"Yeah," she said, "Otis owns a Ford dealership in town. My dad has been running it for him for a couple of years now."

"Is Otis in bad shape?"

"He has his good days, and bad ones. Kirk and Elizabeth were here helping out first. Then, after she died and Kirk fell ill, Mom and Dad came to help both Otis and Kirk."

Jennifer's dad was Allen's uncle, Elmer. He was also the twin brother of Allen's mom. Allen was always told that he looked just like Elmer. Allen didn't know if he did or not, since he hadn't seen Elmer in twenty years.

According to Allen's mother, Uncle Otis was more than ninety years old - which explained his health problems, but Kirk's health was a mystery. "What is wrong with Kirk?"

"His lungs have pretty much stopped working. He has a hard time breathing. Walking even short distances, gets him winded." She led him into the main house through a side door and into a massive kitchen. When they were inside, her voice dropped to a near whisper, "He waited up for you as long as he could. He told me to tell you that he would see you in the morning."

"What caused his lung problems?" Allen asked.

"Not sure, he never smoked. They just went bad. I guess it happens to some people, right?"

"I guess so." Allen was in awe of the size of the kitchen that they had just entered. He grew up in entire houses that were smaller than this room. "Where did Otis get all of this money?"

She held her finger to her lips, as they walked up a wooden grand staircase that reminded Allen of the one from the Titanic movie. "He made it back in the old days…different businesses. Running moonshine is the rumor," she smiled like she'd told a joke and shrugged her shoulders. "Never Know!"

"Moonshine?" Allen repeated, "No shit?"

"No shit," She agreed. "He still tinkers with the old family recipe, from time to time" Finally, after walking down a long hall, they came to a bedroom. "This is where you can sleep. The bathroom is two doors down, if you need it."

Allen entered what he presumed was the guest bedroom and found that it had nicer furnishings than any hotel room that he had ever stayed the night in. The bed was a king size sleigh that must have cost a fortune. He was pretty sure that everything in the room was an antique. Not the kind of stuff that you typically find in a guest bedroom. He tossed his duffel bag on the bed. Compared to the fine linen, it looked as out of place as he felt, in the grand bedroom.

"Need anything else?" Jennifer was still standing at the door.

"A stiff drink," Allen said.

"I'll bring up a bottle and a glass. What do you like to drink?" She asked.

"How about some of that old family recipe?"

9

A lawn mower woke Allen from the best night of sleep that he could recall in recent memory. The mattress that he was laying on was so soft, that he felt like he was floating in the air. He sat up, wiped his eyes with the palms of his hands, and looked around the unfamiliar room to find a clock - no luck. He kicked his legs over the edge of the bed, and noticed the Mason jar sitting on the nightstand - still a quarter full of moonshine. He couldn't say for sure, but he guessed the jar was only about half full when Jennifer brought it up to him, just before bed. An empty glass sat beside the Mason jar, so Allen did what any self-loathing alcoholic would do - he poured the remainder of the brew into the glass.

The family recipe was some of the best moonshine that Allen had ever tasted, and it packed quite a punch. Allen had slept like a baby, all night long. That may have something to do with the long drive, but he was sure that it had more to do with the bottle. After finishing his liquid breakfast, he dressed and embarked on the huge undertaking of finding a bathroom in this gargantuan house. He needed to get washed up and get ready to meet the rest of his family - some of them for the first time. The home was extraordinary. The walls were real wood panels, with intricate wood trim - not the cheap, trailer park wood panels, common in the homes that Allen frequented. It was Buckingham Palace variety. The floors were carpeted so thick and soft, that it rivaled the mattress that Allen slept on. There were paintings hanging on the wall which, *based on the quality of the rest of the décor,* had to be originals and likely worth a fortune. Allen was sure that one was an original Gabe Leonard, one of his favorite artists. A Georges Seurat was hanging beside it, on the other side of the hall, a Steven Hannah – a little known, but highly sought after artist that Allen had learned about in an advanced art class, back in community college.

Allen found the restroom and after a couple of minutes of trying to adjust the fancy shower nozzle, he cleaned himself up. After his shower, he made his way downstairs. Jennifer was in the kitchen, mixing a salad in a very large bowl. "Hey there...sleep in much?" she teased.

Allen looked at the clock hanging on the wall. It read 10:45am. "Sorry..." He said, "I guess I needed it."

Jennifer smiled and said, "That, or Uncle Otis's shine was a little too much for you to handle." She reminded him of a younger version of his mother.

"Yeah...maybe it *was* the shine. That stuff was pretty good."

"*Pretty* good," Jennifer repeated, "Some would argue different. Most people say it's extraordinary. At one time, people paid a pretty penny for that stuff. Quite a few pennies actually; that shine is what built this house."

"No way," Allen said.

Jennifer grabbed a fresh tomato and began chopping it. "Uncle Otis has made quite a fortune in these here parts, and rumor is that it all started with that recipe."

Bootlegging, Allen thought to himself, *Must have been quite the operation to afford the luxuries that he'd seen around this house.* "What's the big salad for?" Allen asked, as he grabbed a piece of tomato from the cutting board.

"It's for our family get-together this afternoon."

"Get-together, what's the occasion?

She finished the tomatoes and moved to the cucumbers. "We don't ever really need an occasion. We all try to have supper here at least once a month. Otis and Kirk have always insisted on keeping the family close.... although, today I guess you could say we are having it for you."

"For me? Wow, now I'm feeling the pressure. Let's hope that I can live up to the expectations."

She smiled again. It was an innocent smile and it made her look young again – like she'd looked the last time that Allen had seen her. Somewhere over the last twenty years, Jennifer lost her little girl figure and had put on a few pounds. She wasn't necessarily overweight, but she was starting to show the body of a middle-aged woman. There were traces of grey in her hair, at the roots and Allen wondered if she would already be completely grey if she didn't dye her hair regularly. Seeing her, made Allen feel a little old himself. She was only four or five years older than he was, which put her in her mid to late-thirties. Allen looked around at the empty kitchen. "Where is everyone?"

"Well, Mom took Otis and Kirk down to the lake in the golf cart. Dad's at the dealership, taking care of some urgent business and the rest of the gang won't be here until around two this afternoon."

"Who's coming?" Allen was feeling a little uneasy about seeing everyone after so long. He'd heard stories from his mother that his cousins could be a little less than welcoming at times. Backwoods rednecks was a term that was thrown around from time to time. Allen didn't remember very much about them, other than they were all older than he was and judging by the stories that he'd heard, they all had trouble with the law at one time or another. He didn't know how he was going to be received, as the outsider. He didn't have anything in common with them that he knew of. One thing was for sure, Allen was no redneck. He embraced his culture and all, but the whole redneck thing with the camouflage outfits, orange hats, and big trucks, was ridiculous. Hunting gear had a purpose, but it was certainly not meant to be the attire that someone should wear to church. He wasn't for sure, but based on the part of the country that he was in – he expected that more than a couple of his relatives were going to show up for the cook-out wearing something neon orange. Allen, being from the city, was usually happy with blue jeans and a t-shirt.

"I think that most everyone will be here," Jennifer said.

"Wow, that's quite a list." Allen said sarcastically, he stole a cucumber and popped it into his mouth.

Jennifer shrugged her shoulders, "It's hard to say for sure who will come, but the whole family was invited."

Just then, they heard the whine of the golf cart approaching the back door. "There're back," Jennifer led Allen out of the kitchen door and onto the back patio. Riding past the pool was the trendiest looking golf cart that Allen had ever seen. It was painted orange and black and had a lift kit that set it a good two feet off of the ground. The knobby tires were attached to large chrome mag wheels. It had a roof hanging over six white leather seats, and the whole thing appeared to be straight off of some kind of "pimp my golf cart," competition show.

At the wheel was a middle aged woman, that looked so much like Jennifer, Allen had to make sure that the younger version was still standing beside him. She wore tan shorts and a white blouse, and her hair was completely grey. Beside her in the front passenger seat was Allen's Uncle Kirk, he was dressed in blue jeans and a tan short sleeve cowboy shirt. He was in his late sixty's now, but still had enough hair on his head to wear his famous pompadour hair style. The same one Elvis made famous in the fifty's. On the next row of seats sat an old man that looked a lot like Colonel Sanders from the Kentucky Fried Chicken box. He was sitting with an air tank propped between his legs and had a plastic mask attached to his face, with a thick rubber band. Even with his oxygen mask in place, there was never quite a man that carried the elegance of his generation, any more so than this one. He was dressed in navy blue slacks and a crisp white shirt, trimmed with a black bowtie. Allen could see the smile on the old man's face even from under the mask. Patsy Blackwood brought the golf cart to a stop, just feet from where Jennifer and Allen were standing.

"Well I'll be…" Kirk said, with what Allen thought was a troubling amount of wheezing in his voice, "…If you don't look just like Clara!" Kirk stood up with effort and walked a few steps over to greet Allen. Patsy got out and steadied him by his arm. Allen and Kirk hugged. "Been a long time boy," after he and Allen finished their embrace, Kirk said, "You remember Uncle Otis, don't you?"

Otis was still sitting in the cart, but held his arms out for Allen to take his hands. "Welcome home Allen," Uncle Otis said, with a gravelly voice. Allen assumed that he meant to say welcome to *my* home, but didn't correct his elder.

"How was your trip out here?" Patsy inquired.

Allen shrugged, "Eventful, but I'm here now, and that's all that matters."

"You got that right," Kirk smacked him in the shoulder, with quite a bit of force for an old man with lung issues, "and we're proud to have you. Get in," Kirk suggested, as he sat back down in the golf cart, "Patsy can drive us around, so you can see the property."

Patsy held her hands up in protest, "I told you I can't be a driving y'all around all morning. I need to help Jennifer get something cooked if y'all want to eat supper in a little while." Kirk and Otis looked at each other and then at Allen, as if it were on queue.

"I can drive," Allen suggested, taking the hint.

"All right then," Kirk said. "We didn't like the way she drove anyhow."

Allen got behind the wheel and Uncle Otis leaned forward into earshot of Allen. "Women drivers and all…" He whispered.

"I heard that Otis," Patsy said. "I'll remember that when you two want me to drive y'all around tomorrow." Otis and Kirk snickered.

Allen drove along the trails on the property for about an hour, without seeing the same area twice. The estate was enormous. Otis said that he owned three hundred and sixty four acres on this bit of land, which implied to Allen that there was more property elsewhere. The cart trails meandered through the forest, which would occasionally open up to large grassy areas that were shaded by Weeping Willow trees, covered in Spanish moss. At times, the path took them near the swamp, which seemed to be on all sides of the property. Kirk pointed to a section of high ground that was largely open land. It was undoubtedly the highest piece of land that Allen had seen on Otis's property. There was the roof of a building jutting up on the other side of the hill. Kirk directed Allen to it. The building turned out to be another house, situated along the river. It had a main building that Allen assumed was a guest house and attached to it, was a boat shed. Kirk told Allen to pull up alongside a flat bottomed boat that was sitting on a trailer, beside the shed. From that spot, Allen could see what looked like swamp for miles and miles. "That there is King's Bayou…" Kirk said, and pointed off to his right. The swamp had a river running through the middle of it, "And out there is Whiskey Bayou."

Allen liked the sound of that. "I'm assuming that's where people used to make moonshine," he said.

"Not just anybody," Otis said. "Our family has been on this land since the Revolutionary War. We have made this bayou home for over three hundred years. This here hill, we are standing on, was documented on property deeds going back to the founding of the State of Mississippi. It has always been named Violent Hill."

"Violent Hill?" Allen wasn't sure if he'd heard Otis correctly.

Otis nodded and continued, "It was named so by the Indians, after two tribes met here in a bloody battle over control of the swamp. That was long before any white man ever set foot on it, or on the continent for that matter. It is also where my daddy brought me, and his daddy brought him, when there was important family business to discuss." A cool wind blew the decayed scent of the swamp past the three men. Allen looked at Kirk, who was skinning a small stick with his pocket knife. Kirk caught Allen's stare and smiled, "She called us and filled us in on what's been going on with you."

"What...the hell does that mean?" Allen asked, confused.

"Your momma! She called a couple of days ago," Otis said. "She told us that you have been fired and that you were drinking too much."

"She also said you were living in a shithole." Kirk added.

Allen could feel his blood pressure rising. All that he had wanted from this trip was to come and visit his family, maybe to locate his father. He wanted to get to know them and not have any of the usual dark clouds of life hanging over his head. Leave it to his meddling mother to screw that up for him. "I'm doing all right." Allen downplayed his situation, out of embarrassment. "The job sucked to begin with, the place I'm staying ain't so bad, and I may drink a little more than I should, but it ain't out of control."

Kirk threw the stick that he'd been working on to the ground. "Well, we ain't tryin' to get into your business, other than to just let you know that we're here for you. I know that we ain't never been too close, you being raised in Virginia and all, but you are family, and we would never turn you out." He faced Otis; to Allen it seemed like he was getting permission from the old man. Otis nodded. "How long you staying?" Kirk asked.

"I hadn't really thought about it, to tell you the truth." Allen said. Initially, he had been so focused on getting here, he hadn't thought about going back. "I guess I'll stay a week, if that will be alright?" Allen glanced from Kirk to Otis.

"That will be fine," Kirk said, "and if you decide to stay longer...your welcome to do that too." He brushed the wood shavings from his jeans. "Uncle Otis may even have some work for you to do while you're here, so that you can earn some money. How's that sound?"

"That sounds good...real good." Allen didn't tell them, but he was down to his last few bills and until now, wasn't sure just how he would have gotten the gas to get back to Virginia.

"Drive us down to the pier and let's see if we can spot us a gator." Kirk pointed straight ahead, towards the bayou.

"A *real* gator?" Allen didn't hide the excitement in his voice.

Otis patted his shoulder "Don't worry boy. The gator won't get you... besides there's creatures out here, a lot more dangerous than a gator."

10

Allen reclined in the Adirondack chair and let the cool, freshly cut grass massage the bottoms of his feet. He closed his eyes for a moment, feeling like he could go back to sleep, but decided that napping at a cookout, where he was the guest of honor, would be in poor taste. Instead, he forced his eyes open and stretched his arms above his head. The setting of Otis's property reminded Allen of a park. The lawn from the back of the house all the way to the tree line, hundreds of yards away, was immaculately manicured, broken only by the stone paths. Fruit trees were strategically placed all over the property.

He stretched his legs out and felt small in the openness of the back yard. He watched from his chair, as a couple of his cousins, Tommy and Dewayne, were busy on the other side of the pool, cooking up another round of barbeque ribs on the smoker. A warm breeze was carrying the sweet smell of the barbecue smoke across the yard and past Allen, making his mouth water. Another of Allen's cousins was sitting beside him.

Robert Blackwood, was Uncle Kirk's only son and as much as Allen admired Kirk – he could never seem to get very close to Robert. On several occasions, Allen had tried to strike up a conversation, but nothing he said seemed to take hold. Robert would give a one or two word answer, and that was it - sometimes only nodding his head, without commenting at all. Allen had given up trying to break through about twenty minutes ago when Robert had gone to sleep. In his mid-forties - Robert was apparently on the low end of the brainpower spectrum. That could possibly explain the lack of conversation.

Allen had grown up listening to his mother tell stories of Robert's many failures, more so than any of his other cousins. Robert had been arrested for a few ignorant things over the years. Once, he changed the price stickers on a toolbox that he wanted to buy. He took a lower price tag from a different one and got caught. That was back in the days when things were less electronic than they are today and crimes were easier to get away with – unless you were Robert.

Robert had a wife and two young girls that were in their early teens. Somehow, he'd managed to stay married for most of his adult life. Nancy, Robert's wife, was on the other side of the yard sitting by the pool and stuffing her face with Chips Ahoy cookies like Nabisco wanted their bags back. Sweet lady, but not much to look at. Nancy, like her husband, wasn't going to win any scientific awards. She talked slow and deliberate, like someone trying real hard to form complete sentences. There were gaps and random, unexplained pauses, leaving the listener confused. Allen imagined that stimulating conversation was something that was entirely absent in the Robert Blackwood household. He could only hope that the teenage daughters didn't suffer the lack of intelligence like their parents, but based on the way that the two of them came today dressed like a couple of twelve year old East End hookers, it didn't leave Allen with much hope. The girls were now in the pool with Jennifer, who had her baby boy, Ronnie in the shallow end floating around in circles.

Allen looked at Robert, still asleep in the chair beside him and wasn't sure if it was due to the isolation, way back here in the Mississippi Bayou, but Robert, who was just a few years older than Allen, wore his hair in the same nineteen fifties pompadour style, like the older generation and Allen was also pretty sure he shared a clothing closet with them too.

Robert had on tight jeans, which had to be as uncomfortable as they were ridiculous and the same style of cowboy shirt that Kirk seemed to prefer. The style was more befitting the older man, who at least had been alive when the look was popular. On Robert - it just looked like a Toy Story costume!

From behind, Allen heard voices that he wasn't familiar with and turned around to find two men, who weren't at the party earlier. One of them had long brown hair, pulled back in a ponytail. He was wearing jeans like everyone else, and instead of cowboy attire, he was wearing a black t-shirt, with a Pink Floyd logo on the front. He looked rough around the edges and Allen got the impression that he wasn't the kind of person you'd want to have around for too long. The man could have passed for a vagrant. He looked dirty, wild - unkempt.

The man that arrived with ponytail was shorter and scrawnier, but looked similar. The two could be brothers – probably were! The smaller one lacked the insane killer eyes that ponytail had, but looked dangerous just the same. He had a Jim Carey haircut, from the movie Dumb and Dumber, and he *was* wearing one of the cowboy shirts, which evidently - made *him* family! "Who's that?" Allen roused Robert from his nap.

Robert groaned, as he turned in his chair to take a look. "That's Johnny and Chris."

"Where do we know them from?"

"They're our cousins!" He looked at Allen, who must have been wearing the question mark on his forehead. "Uncle Conrad's boys."

"Oh, ok..." Allen said, still not sure if he'd ever met either one of them before. If he had, it must have been when he was a child. Being that his mother was one of the youngest of his grandparent's children made most of Allen's cousins quite a bit older than he was. If Johnny and Chris were Uncle Conrad's children, then they were probably two of the oldest cousins that he had. Uncle Conrad was the first born of Clara's siblings and was almost twenty years older than Allen's mom. Conrad Blackwood died of lung cancer several years back.

Allen watched as Johnny and Chris walked over to the grill, where Tommy was rolling hotdogs over the flame. Dewayne was standing nearby, with a cigarette in one hand and a can of Coors in the other. Tommy and Dewayne were the only children of Bernard Blackwood, the second oldest of Allen's mother's siblings. Bernard was still living in Virginia. Allen had seen Tommy and Dewayne a few times over the years, since they visited their father regularly, and he lived only minutes from where Allen had grown up. Truth was, Allen didn't really know them any better than he did the rest. He couldn't hear what was said, but Chris said something that made Dewayne break out laughing. Johnny pulled a hotdog off of the burner with his fingers and ate it. They looked like a close knit family.

Behind them, Jennifer, Aunt Patsy and Nancy were in the shallow end of the pool, playing ball with Jennifer's two year old son, Ronnie. Allen watched Jennifer as she mothered the toddler. The baby giggled, making Jennifer laugh and hold Ronnie above her head, which made him giggle again. Jennifer had been married just long enough to get pregnant. Her husband Scott, left before the baby was born, claiming that he wasn't ready for a family, and that he felt trapped by their relationship. Jennifer had kind of been feeling the same way. The only difference was that the jerk-off Scott wasn't the one carrying the baby – she was, and she couldn't just walk away from that. She'd done pretty well given the situation; as far as Allen could tell she looked to be a good mother. Allen noticed that she tended to the baby all the time while she was at home. He'd learned that she also worked as a receptionist at the car dealership that her father, Elmer, ran for Uncle Otis.

Elmer was the youngest of his mother's brothers. He and Clara were fraternal twins. Elmer had spent most of his adult life in the Army, serving in two wars and retiring a Command Sergeant Major. Now, as far as Allen could gather, Elmer spent his days running the family owned car dealership.

Allen watched little Ronnie, splashing around in the pool with his water wings keeping him afloat. He was laughing, while chasing a floating ball around. His happiness reminded Allen of a time when things were simpler. A smile crept across his face, as he envied little Ronnie's innocence.

From the corner of his eye, Allen caught a glimpse of someone coming around the corner of the garage and toward the group in the backyard. It was a skinny black man, who looked like he was in desperate need of a shave. At first glance, Allen mistook him for a gardener, or some other type of hired help.

Then, Johnny spotted the man coming at about the same time that Allen did, and said, "What the fuck?" He started walking over to meet the man half way across the yard with Chris, Tommy and Dewayne right behind him.

"What's all of this," Allen asked Robert, who opened his eyes lazily and then, seeing what was transpiring, jumped to his feet fully awake. He jogged to catch up to the others, who were almost to the stranger. Allen, not knowing what was going on, but being smart enough to recognize when things was getting ready to go south, started over to the crowd, now gathering in the middle of the yard.

Kirk was walking slowly in front of Allen as he got closer to the group. "What's going on Kirk?" Allen asked.

"Nothing that your cousins can't handle…" Kirk said, calmly, "…and nothing you need to be involved in." Allen watched as the scene unfolded on the other side of the lawn.

11

Ten minutes before the confrontation began to play out in Otis's yard, Lashauna and Leo watched Lionel Taylor from the edge of a tree line. They were in their unmarked patrol car, as he parked along the shoulder of the road, and got out. Leo was relaying everything that he saw in detail to Lashauna, looking through his binoculars. Lashauna had pulled the car to the edge of a clearing, just far enough to where they could see Lionel, but he couldn't see them - unless maybe, if he was looking for them. In this case, he wasn't. They'd been following him for better than an hour now and Lionel hadn't given them any indication that he was aware of their presence.

It had been a slow, time consuming endeavor tailing him. After releasing him from custody, he caught a city bus, just a block from the police station. Then, after getting off the bus, Lionel walked the half mile back to Reggie's bar, to pick up his car. Leo questioned Lashauna's decision to tail the guy. Especially, if she was leaning toward the fact that he wasn't the one who killed his parents.

"Two things..." she said, "...first, I want to get a location on his vehicle and get a mold of the tire treads, to compare to the ones that we found in the parent's driveway!"

"Don't we know for certain that his car was there on a regular basis?" Leo asked, and immediately he regretted asking the question, based on the look that she was giving him. It was a look that said - *Really? Is this your first day on the job?* She didn't actually say it, but she didn't have to. She explained her assessment, as an educator would to a pupil. She had a way of letting you know that she was miles above you intellectually, without making you feel inferior - unless of course you were a bad guy, and then she made it obvious - ruthlessly and painfully.

"We need a baseline..." she explained, "...we know the car that the old couple drove and we can eliminate their tire tread marks. We need to get Lionel's to eliminate his marks, and whatever tire marks are left, will hopefully match the person responsible, when we find him."

Leo understood. *Simple*, he thought, *yet miles above.* "What was the second thing?" he asked.

"We just told him that his parents were murdered." She pulled a piece of gum from her pocket and placed it into her mouth. "He is very emotional right now. If he knows anything...or even has an inkling of who might be responsible...I am banking on the fact that he is on his way to see that person right now."

They had the conversation as they followed Lionel's sedan through town and then out to the edges of the King's Bayou. Now, they were sitting in the car, on the dusty back road, watching Lionel rummage through his trunk.

"What in the hell do you think he's looking for?" Lashauna asked.

"No telling..." Leo said, "...maybe he has a flat. Or maybe, he's looking for a map. What if we're just following around a junkie, who doesn't know where in the hell he's going?"

"Based on where we are, I would have to disagree."

"What do you mean by that?" He lowered the binoculars.

"Come on, you telling me that you haven't ever heard of the Blackwood family?" she asked.

"Can't say that I have..." Leo leaned back in the passenger seat and propped his knee up on the dashboard, the way someone who was taking a rest during a long road trip would. "...should I?"

"I wasn't sure just how far their notoriety had traveled over the years. I guess the legend never made it down to New Orleans."

"Well, New Orleans is where I moved when I was in high school," Leo explained. "My folks had a place just outside of St Louis before that." He peered through the binoculars again. Lionel finished rummaging through his trunk and was now sitting on the hood of his car. "What do you suppose he is up to?"

Lashauna shrugged her shoulders and rolled down her window. The car was getting stuffy with the engine turned off and the AC wasn't running. "I don't know. Maybe, he's waiting on someone."

"Well sis, looks like we've got some time." He tossed the binoculars onto the dashboard. "Why don't you tell me about these Blackwoods?"

"Where do I begin?" She said. "Most of what I've heard is urban legend. Tales told by high school kids. I didn't really believe most of what I heard at first, but as a senior in high school, I did a paper on local legends. I was a good student of course, so I did a thorough job with my research. I pulled local records from the library...newspapers, census reports, everything that I could get my hands on and the more that I read, the more I began to believe the urban legends."

"So, get on with it already," Leo said.

She flipped him the bird - he smiled - she continued, "The facts are, that back in the twenties, Clyde Blackwood was a tenant farmer, who worked for some of the local land owners in exchange for a place to live and enough food to feed his family. He had a wife named Ellie, whom he'd married back in Scotland. The two of them sailed to America right after the First World War.

Once they were in America, they had three children; a little girl named Betsy and two boys Artie and Otis. The family was very poor when they arrived and lived in one dilapidated shack after another, sometimes in barns, elbow to hoof with the farm animals. They were constantly moving from one town to the next, to keep up with the work. It bothered Clyde that he had to raise his family in such substandard conditions. He worked hard to try to get ahead of the bill collectors, and when his children were still young, he put them to work, helping out where they could. The Blackwood family had a longstanding reputation of being hard workers, going all the way back to Scotland, where the family was responsible for tending to Church property. Rumor was that somewhere down the line... they were related to a pirate that had sailed with Blackbeard."

"No shit?"

"As far as I know, some dude named Murphy Blackwood."

"That's cool!"

"Yeah, well it might explain what happened next!"

"What's that?" Leo asked.

"I'm getting there," Lashauna said, "Meanwhile, Clyde taught his children the value of hard work. On the side, to earn a few extra bucks here and there, Clyde dabbled in making his own whiskey. It didn't take him long to make a name for himself locally, as the preeminent bootlegger. His whiskey was highly sought after, all over Mississippi and beyond. Just about the time that he'd made a name for himself, prohibition took effect."

"Lucky for him!" Leo added.

"Right?" Lashauna agreed. "Once prohibition was in full swing...he started making money hand over fist. It wasn't long before he gave up his share cropping gig altogether and ran his whiskey still full time. Within a couple of years, he was able to buy a piece of property and build a house out along the swamp. The property was named Violent Hill, I think after some old Indian legend and he called his estate by that name from then on. As his boys grew, he taught them the family business. Betsy, the daughter, helped Ellie with household chores for a while, but she was supposedly quite the tomboy and quickly gravitated to the bootlegging operation with her father and her little brothers. Clyde was happy to have her around, since the boys could be pretty mischievous at times, and she helped keep them in line. Having her around helped Clyde concentrate on his business. Rumor has it, the kids were moving the whiskey over to the other counties, by the time that they were ten or eleven years old. Clyde raised them to be tough. He knew that they had to be, if they were going to be useful to the operation. There are stories of young Betsy and the two boys delivering the shipments to the far reaches of Mississippi...all alone... just the three of them."

"Wait a minute..." Leo said, "These kids were driving cars across the state, at eleven years old?"

"Not by road..." Lashauna said, "...by boat...out on the swamp."

Leo sat up straight in the passenger seat. "No shit?" He faced her, "The kids were out in the swamp by themselves, making moonshine runs, before they had even hit puberty? Those kids were bad asses!"

Lashauna agreed, nodding her head. "So, it turns out that Clyde made some enemies in some of the other counties, by taking away pieces of their bootlegging business. His recipe had become renowned. One bootlegger in particular, who lost some of his business to Clyde, was Alter McLaughlin.

McLaughlin was an Irish immigrant, who'd set up just about every illegal operation that you could think of in Biloxi. He supposedly had quite a few cops and judges on his payroll, and was said to be connected to some big time gangsters up in Detroit. When Alter McLaughlin wanted something done in southern Mississippi, he wasn't accustomed to being told no. Anyhow, one day Clyde was approached by some men out on the swamp, while he was on his way back home from making a run. It turned out that Alter McLaughlin wanted Clyde to go into business with him. It is said that McLaughlin asked Clyde to quit distributing as an independent, and cook for the McLaughlin organization. Clyde refused on the spot. He already had a pretty good thing going, working for himself. He didn't want to be tied to someone else. Much less with someone with McLaughlin's reputation. When Clyde refused, the men quickly turned from recruiting Clyde, to warning him to stop selling in their territory, *which in McLaughlin's opinion was all of Mississippi.* Clyde was not easily intimidated and ignored the threats. All went well for another month or so, that is until one night when the children were making a routine run, from Violent Hill out to the Whiskey Bayou, for a drop off.

Even under the full moon, it can be hard to see the faces of the people around you in the bayou, so the children had no idea that the people waiting at the old hunter's shack, out in the middle of the bog, was not their usual customers. It turned out that it was five of McLaughlin's men. McLaughlin had gotten wind of the whiskey drop, by beating it out of one of Clyde's regular customers."

"Whaaat?" Leo said, "This is like, some serious prime time movie stuff."

"No kidding...right?" Lashauna said, "But, I'm pretty sure that it's all true."

"So what happened to the kids?" Leo checked Lionel with the binoculars again, to make sure that he hadn't moved.

"Well...the story goes that the men beat all three of the kid's up pretty bad...broken ribs, broken noses, that kind of thing. When they were finished beating on them, McLaughlin's men lined the three kids up along the water's edge, telling them that they were going to be executed. One of McLaughlin's men held his gun to Betsy's head. Artie and Otis could do nothing but watch and plead for their sister's life. Before the man pulled the trigger, he was distracted by the sound of a boat motor, off in the distance and hesitated. Artie and Otis used this opportunity to dive into the swamp and swim away into the darkness. For whatever reason... Betsy didn't jump in."

"She was probably frozen with fear...the poor kid," Leo said.

"Yeah, more than likely, but none the less, she didn't get away when her brothers did." Lashauna popped another piece of gum into her mouth. "A couple of hours after the children were supposed to be home, Clyde grew worried and went looking for them at the shack. He found Betsy. She was beaten nearly to death and had been raped. Apparently, after the boy's fled, McLaughlin's men had grown angrier and had their way with her. It later came out that they claimed to have never intended to kill the kids in the first place, they were just trying to scare them and to send a message to Clyde. Betsy was unconscious and needed medical attention. Clyde searched for his sons for as long as he could, but could delay no longer in getting his daughter to the hospital. He saw to it that Betsy was safe and being taken care of by the doctors, and left her at the hospital with Ellie. By the time that he returned to his boat, to go and look for Artie and Otis, it was nearly morning. He found them both climbing out of the swamp and walking down the dock. They were wet and cold and they were badly injured from the beating that they took. On top of the injuries that they had received from McLaughlin's men, the boys were covered in mud, and had been nearly eaten up by the bugs."

"It was a miracle that they weren't alligator dinner," Leo added.

"You've got that right..." She said, "...those were some tough kids."

"So, what happened?"

Lashauna picked the binoculars up off of the dashboard and took a look at Lionel for herself. He was laying on the hood of his car. "Do you think he went to sleep?"

"No telling," Leo said, "Finish the story. Did Clyde take care of business, or what?""

Lashauna smiled at him, "Alright, Alright...Jeez, I feel like a school teacher at story time here. So, the boys were treated for their injuries, and were able to tell Clyde who was responsible. It seems that the assholes that did this, were calling each other by their first names while they were around the kids. Clyde wrote down all of the names that the boys could remember on a piece of paper and kept it in his pocket from that day forward.

The boys bounced back pretty quickly and Betsy recovered in time. Clyde, who by this time had made more money than he could spend in the next couple of years, laid low for a few months. He continued to brew his whiskey, but he stockpiled it and stopped selling it altogether. It wasn't more than a month later that Clyde and the boys were out working on the property, when they saw a boat coming down the river. Betsy was not with them this time, since she had become a bit of a recluse after what happened. When Clyde met the boat at his dock, it turned out that it was four of McLaughlin's men, coming to broker a deal for some of Clyde's whiskey. All of the customers that were formally Clyde's, were complaining about the quality of the whisky that they were getting from McLaughlin's people.

Here's the thing,' Lashauna said, "up until now, Clyde had a pretty good idea about who it was that was behind the attack on his family, but he could never be sure that it was McLaughlin. All that he had to go on was the list of names that he carried in his pocket, and whether it was an act of ignorance, or just the fact that these men were so brazen that they didn't care, he didn't know, but when everyone introduced themselves, Clyde recognized two of the four men's names from his list. Artie and Otis also identified the men from the sound of their voices. It's amazing how certain things get etched into your mind, when you think that your life is about to end. In this case, it was the voices of the men, since the boys could see little else in the swamp that night a couple of months ago."

"What did he do…kill them on the spot?" Leo asked. "I can't blame him."

"No…" Lashauna said, "…he played it cool. He wasn't only interested in getting the men who had *done* this to his children. He wanted the man who'd ordered it."

"No shit?"

"No shit!"

Leo looked through the binoculars again. "What the hell?"

What?" Lashauna asked.

"Our boy Lionel is headed off into the woods." Leo watched him jump a fallen tree and disappear into the brush. "Let's get the plaster kit from the trunk mixed and get that mold of his tire real quick. What do you say?"

"I like that idea," Lashauna pulled the keys out of the ignition switch, got out of the car and popped the trunk. She pulled a plastic bag of the powdered plaster from a tackle box, and a bottle of water from her lunch cooler. She got back in and slowly eased the car up to Lionel's bumper, while Leo mixed the plaster in a coffee mug. They both got out this time and Lashauna watched for Lionel to return, as Leo took off his suit jacket and got down in the road to apply the plaster to Lionel's back tire. He held it in place as it dried. "So go on…finish the story," He said.

"The short version is, Clyde agreed to deal with McLaughlin. He began selling his whiskey to McLaughlin's men, who took distribution to every corner of Mississippi. Within a year nearly every speakeasy on the Gulf Coast was selling Clyde Blackwood's brand. Clyde meanwhile, was biding his time. Working his way deeper and deeper into McLaughlin's operation. He earned their trust, and he even befriended several key members of the operation. He eventually identified, or had a pretty good idea, of every individual that was directly involved in the beating and rape of his children.

Then one night, as a business gesture to McLaughlin and his men, Clyde invited them to a celebration that was held on his property, on Violent Hill. It's been estimated that as many as fifty people showed up for the party. Nearly everyone from McLaughlin's business was there, most with their wives, or girlfriends. The drink of the night was some of Clyde's special batch. Little did anyone know that he had made a barrel of his whiskey mixed with arsenic and he, his wife and his two sons, served it to everyone who was drinking, everyone except for Alter McLaughlin, and the five suspected rapists. Within fifteen minutes, just about everyone at the party was dropping like flies out on the Hill, where the party was being held. By the time McLaughlin and his men realized what was happening and tried to flee back to their boat, Clyde, Artie, and Otis met them at the dock with guns drawn. The other survivors, *just a couple of the wives that fortunately didn't drink,* were allowed to leave, but McLaughlin and his five men, with their hands bound behind their backs, were marched back up the Hill among McLaughlin's dead and dying associates. There they were made to kneel under the moonlight. It has been said that all of the men pleaded for their lives. With Ellie, Betsy, Artie and Otis looking on, Clyde never said a word to them, as he cut the throats of four of the men who had attacked his children. One of the men tried to get away, but he was quickly gunned down by Ellie as he ran. Alter McLaughlin supposedly offered everything that he had, in order for Clyde to spare his life. Clyde slapped McLaughlin's face openhanded and called Betsy forward. He handed her the knife and she stared the Irish man in the face, the face of the man responsible for what happened to her, as she pushed the blade into his throat. Rumor is that Clyde and the boys took all of the dead bodies and threw them into the swamp, for the gators to dispose of."

"The gators were eating well that night," Leo said, from under the fender of Lionel's car.

"Fifty plus people disappeared that night and the only survivors...the women that were allowed to leave...never would say what they had seen, or where their husbands had disappeared to. It has been said that they were visited by Clyde and warned that the rest of their lives were going to be cut very short, unless they forgot everything that they had witnessed on Violent Hill. None of them ever spoke.

Clyde ultimately took over the entire state with his bootlegging operation. It seemed that with McLaughlin's disappearance, there was quite a void left in the illegal whiskey operation. Clyde made a fortune filling that void."

"Jesus Christ..." Leo pulled the plaster mold off of the tire and got up. He looked it over to make sure that he had gotten a good sample. He held it out for Lashauna to inspect. "What do you think?'

"Look's good to me." She answered, still staring through the woods. "You know...ironically, I think that Violent Hill is not far through those woods."

Leo wrapped a plastic bag around the mold and put it into the trunk of the car to dry. "You think he is heading out to the Violent Hill property?"

"Maybe..." She said, "I think that the Blackwood family still lives out there."

"What kind of business do you think Lionel would have with them?"

"I'm not sure..." She returned to the car, "...but whatever it is, it can't be totally above board...or he would have skipped his hike through the woods, and used the driveway."

Leo got in. "You want to check it out?"

"Oh, hell yeah..." She started the car and drove.

12

llen watched from across the yard, as Johnny and the black man exchanged unpleasant words. Tommy, Dwayne, Chris, and Robert were all assembled behind Johnny. To Allen, it looked like some kind of ridiculous cafeteria high school fight. The spectacle of all of these grownups acting like a bunch of children did not make Allen proud to be a part of the group. Johnny was pointing into the visitors face, as he raised his voice louder and louder, to yell over what the other man was saying. Robert and Chris were pointing over Johnny's shoulder and shouting their own comments at the man. Allen couldn't really understand anything that the black guy was saying, since it was drowned out by all of the others. He could however understand some of what Johnny was shouting, *"You had better get your fucking story straight, boy,"* and somehow it was the *"boy"* part that Allen knew was going to ignite the chaos. For a second, Allen had a feeling that he was watching something straight out of the sixties civil rights movement. Allen was beginning to feel sorry for the guy, *who from Allen's experience growing up in a rough neighborhood*, was very close to being mobbed. Then, on the other hand, nobody asked the guy to crash the party, so maybe he was about to get what he deserved. Either way, Allen wasn't about to let it go without at least trying to defuse the situation.

Allen glanced over at his family and was surprised to see that none of the old guys appeared to be the least bit worried about what was going on. Almost like it was commonplace to have altercations with strangers in the back yard around here. Not even the ninety-plus year old Otis appeared even slightly worked up over what was happening. The only people who had any concern at all were Jennifer and the other women, as they ushered the children out of the pool and inside the house.

Spit was flying out of Johnny's mouth as he screamed in rage, *"You come onto my family's property and accuse me of something like this? You've got a lot of nerve, asshole! I'll bust your teeth out of your..."* his intensity was growing, until something in the driveway caused him to stop mid-sentence. Allen looked and saw a large sedan coming toward the house. The group in the yard noticed the car also, and they all seemed to settle down a little bit. The sedan came to a stop at the edge of the driveway, not far from where the group stood. A man and a woman got out of the car. Allen could tell right away, without ever seeing a badge - they were cops!

The man was short, stout, and was dressed in a grey suit. Allen also noticed that he had dirt stains on the knees of his pants. His brown hair was combed neatly in a business style, but he also seemed a bit rough around the edges. To Allen, he looked more like someone who would be a construction worker, rather than a policeman.

The woman on the other hand was put together very well and very attractive. She didn't belong in a squad car, any more than the Taliban belonged at a peace rally. She had light brown skin that matched her business suit, and while her partner looked as if he had purchased his suit from Wall-Mart - the suit she wore, looked like it was custom made for her in Italy. She had very little in the way of makeup and in Allen's opinion, it would have been a crime to cover her natural beauty. The two cops walked over to the assembly, who were all standing quietly as the detectives approached. Elmer walked forward to greet them. Otis, Kirk, and Allen walked slowly behind him.

"What can we do for ya?" Elmer asked, as he stepped between the cops and the rest of group.

The woman cop said, "I'm Detective Trudeau..." She flashed her badge, "...this is Detective Menard. We are with the Mississippi State Police Department."

Elmer said defiantly, "Ok...now that we know who you are...why are you here?"

Lashauna took her time answering the question. She made eye contact with every single one of them before she spoke. Like she was taking note of who was present. Allen got the impression that she was incredibly confident and brave. He could tell that she was used to controlling situations, and not the other way around - no matter how hard Elmer was going to try.

"We found a disabled car out on the road," she finally said, "wasn't sure if it belonged to any of you."

"A disabled car?" Elmer said, and looked at Lionel. "What kind of a car?"

"A Ford Taurus…maroon…mid-nineties," Leo answered.

"Well, it must belong to him…" Elmer said, and gestured towards Lionel, who was now staring at the ground, but also clearly still seething with anger. "I had one stolen not long ago. I'd thought that y'all would be out looking for that one. Maybe this fella' knows a little something about that!"

"Did you report it," Leo asked Elmer.

"Damn right I did…and I ain't heard a word about it since."

"Whom did you report it to Sir?" Leo asked."

"To the goddamn police…" Elmer spat, "…who else?" This gave everyone a chuckle, except for the cops and Lionel, who continued to stare blankly at the ground.

"I think he means the local police department," Lashauna said, to her partner.

"Right!" Leo was trying to contain his temper.

Otis stepped forward, using his cane to steady himself. "If you don't mind me asking…what are a couple of big shot, state police detectives like yourselves doing chasing down a disabled car?"

Lashauna smiled at Uncle Otis, like he'd won a prize for being the only one in the group smart enough to ask the obvious question. "It just so happens, that it was the exact car that I was looking for…and I know that it belongs to my friend there…" She nodded at Lionel, "…everything alright here, Lionel?"

Lionel answered, without looking up at the detective, "Yeah."

"Come on…" she said, "…I'll give you a ride back to your car." Lionel hesitated for a few seconds and then he stepped out of the crowd and walked to the detective's car. "You gentlemen have a good day," she said, as she started to leave. Then she stopped and faced Uncle Otis, "Do you mind if I ask you your name, sir?"

"Am I in some sort of trouble?" Otis teased. He had a smirk on his face that reminded Lashauna of the one that George W. Bush used to wear, when he made his feeble attempts at being witty.

"No not at all," Lashauna said, "I'm just curious."

"Otis Blackwood." He held out his frail hand to her. She took it in her own and said, "Mr. Blackwood, I have heard quite a bit about you. It is a pleasure to finally meet you."

"The pleasure is all mine young lady." Otis said, and then he added, "I hope!"

She smiled at him, turned to face Elmer and said, "I will look into the investigation regarding your missing vehicle. You gentlemen have a good day." She joined Leo and Lionel at the car.

The Blackwood family watched, as the detectives pulled slowly out of the driveway.

13

"**W**hat in the hell was that all about?" Leo asked Lionel, "Why'd you go hiking through the woods and sneak up on that family picnic?"

Lionel didn't reply. He wasn't going to tell the cops a damn thing. He was going to handle this for himself, but first things first. He needed to be smart about it and not go getting hemmed up by the police beforehand. He had realized as soon as he approached Johnny that he'd made a mistake. Charging in head-on was a slip-up, especially when there were so many of them. Not to mention the fact that the cops had been tailing him. He needed to find Johnny alone somewhere, and then he was gonna make that son-of-a-bitch pay. *All this for what? Over some smack - smack that Lionel had every intention to pay Johnny for.* The thought of his mom and dad being dead caused Lionel's eyes to well up with tears again. He should have been there to help them. He swore to himself that he would make the bastard pay! Maybe, even make the bastard's family pay too. He pressed his palms to his forehead and leaned his head back against the headrest. *Jesus,* he thought, *I need something to even me out a little bit, so I can think.* Meanwhile, the honkey cop was in the front seat, running his mouth and Lionel hadn't heard a single word that he was saying. The lady cop pulled up to Lionel's car slowly and before she was even stopped completely - he opened the door, and got out.

"You're welcome…" Lashauna said, from her window, as Lionel climbed into his own car.

He ignored her at first, but then rolled down his own window. "Can I go to my parent's house?"

Lashauna looked over at Leo, who shrugged his shoulders. "It may still be a mess!" She said, "Do you have anywhere else that you can stay?"

"Yeah…but I need to grab a few of my things."

"Do you want us to follow you over there?"

"Y'all been following me everywhere else, so why even ask," Lionel said, and then, "No…I don't need no babysitters."

"Alright," Lashauna said, "I'll call over to the forensics people and let them know that you are coming. They should be out of there by now, but just to be sure."

Lionel rolled his window back and pulled away from the detectives. Lashauna rolled her window up also, to avoid being covered in the dust that was kicked up by Lionel's tires spinning on the dirt. She and Leo sat in silence for a few seconds before Leo said, "What in the hell was that about?"

Lashauna shook her head, "I don't know, but I would be willing to bet a dollar against a doughnut that Lionel thinks that someone in that group back there, had something to do with his parents' death."

"I think you may be right!" Leo agreed, "It looked like things were getting heated, right before we pulled up."

"That was Otis Blackwood." Lashauna said, out of the blue.

"The old man was the Otis…No shit?"

"No shit…" She said. "He's still looking good, for someone who must be pushing near one hundred years old."

"You ain't kidding. Who were the other people?" Leo asked.

"I don't know yet, but I think that we should look in to the missing car thing…and start finding out who all of them are. It would be safe to assume that by the way that most of them were dressed, in their John Wayne attire…they were probably all related."

14

The excitement from the episode in the yard had died down and most everyone had gone home for the evening. Allen helped Jennifer and Patsy clean up the paper plates and other trash around the pool. Once they were finished, he made himself a whiskey on the rocks and tried sitting by the pool in the peace and quiet. He wanted to relax, but it wasn't working. It was only mid-afternoon and Allen was feeling restless. He was still excited from the ruckus earlier. He went inside and tried watching TV with Patsy and Jennifer, but he couldn't get into the TV show that the women were watching. It was some fake TV judge, reading paternity tests to the dredges of society. After five minutes of the baby's momma and the accused father screaming back and forth, Allen got up and walked away. The TV exchange reminded him of the scene in the yard, between Johnny and the black guy, and he'd had enough of hearing people scream, so he decided to explore the house. Otis's home was a lot bigger than it looked from the outside. There were spacious rooms, beyond even more spacious rooms, and at one point Allen wasn't sure exactly where he was. He wandered, finding that all of them were decorated with fine furniture and decor. He took his time to investigate the small photos and decorations like he was in a museum. In a way, that's how the place felt. Eventually, he found himself in what he could only describe as the library, with tall wooden bookshelves along one wall, which was completely filled with books. Nearly every inch of the other three walls were covered with photos, and paintings of people. Allen found a collection of antique photos on one of the walls. He examined each of the black and white prints, looking for someone that he recognized. Most of the people in the old photos looked similar. Quite a few of them shared the deep set eyes that were a Blackwood family trademark, but he didn't know who any of them were. Eventually, he found a series of newer photos – maybe from the late sixties – early seventies. There were a few of his mother, taken at various stages in her life. In some, she was with Elmer, when the twins were elementary school age. Allen laughed when he realized all of these years later - his uncle still wore the same style clothes that he had back then, and with the exception of having less of it – Elmer's hair was pretty much in the same style also. Next to a photo of Elmer doing a youthful impersonation of Elvis Presley, there was one of his mother and another man in their early twenties. The photo had obviously been taken in the early seventies, based on his mother's miniskirt, beehive hairdo, and the plaid bellbottom pants that the young man was wearing. At first, Allen didn't think anything of the print, and almost passed right over it, but just as soon as he was about to dismiss the old photo, he lost his breath. He looked closer and realized that for the first time in his life, he was staring at an image of his father. The young couple was happy. The young man had his arms around Clara, as they posed in front of a car. Allen couldn't ever remember seeing his mother look so vibrant. This had to be taken right before she'd become pregnant with him. Before the weight of the world had pressed her into an almost unrecognizable shell of the beautiful young girl in the picture. Allen lingered a little longer on his parents, trying to ignore the empty feeling in his gut – the sensation that he'd lost something. Something that he'd never possessed – he moved on.

Down the picture wall a little ways, he found some images of his grandfather, from what looked to be the nineteen twenties or thirties, when Artie was a young boy. In one, Grandpa Artie, Uncle Otis, *who were both very young and dressed alike, in straw hats and dark overalls*, were standing beside a young girl wearing a black dress. Behind the children stood Allen's great grandparents, Clyde and Ellie. His mother had an old blurry photo of them in an album, back home. This photo was much better quality, Allen could see the features of his long dead relatives. Clyde Blackwood was tall and thin and had a head full of dark hair. He was handsome, rugged and had a scowl on his face that indicated that he was not entirely comfortable with having his picture taken. Ellie was thin and pretty, but she looked sad, the way that most people from that time period did in photos. Behind Clyde, Ellie and the children, was a sizeable wood framed house, with a large wrap-around porch. It was certainly not the palatial home that Allen was standing in now, but for the time period – it was probably quite a place. Artie and Otis were handsome, and even at that young age, they looked like a hand full of trouble. Allen's eyes returned to the young girl in the black dress. She was pretty and shared the good facial qualities of Ellie, but Allen didn't realize that his grandfather had a sister.

Allen was startled when someone from behind him said, "That's Clyde Blackwood in that there photo…your Great Grandfather." Allen turned around to find Otis standing in the doorway. "You remind me a lot of him, you know." Otis walked laboriously into the room. "The way you appear when I see you at certain angles…you have his eyes." Otis smiled, "He was also quiet, like you are. Some say that's the sign of an intelligent man."

Allen smiled, and said, "I was believing you, until the intelligent part."

"I'm serious," Otis said. "Maybe you don't give yourself enough credit."

"Thanks, Otis!" Allen decided to change the subject. "Who's the little girl?" He pointed at the photo.

Otis took the picture off of the wall and ran his thumb across the face of the girl in the photo. "That is my big sister…Betsy! Your great aunt."

"Is she still alive?" Allen asked.

"Not anymore," Otis said.

Allen wondered how he could have lived his whole life and never heard of her. He was close to his grandpa and couldn't remember ever hearing her name mentioned. "Where did she live?"

Otis hung the picture back up on the wall. "Right here, on the other side of this property at the old house. All the way up until she died." Allen could hear the pain in Otis's voice as he spoke. "She passed on when she was young…much, much too young!" Otis walked over to the bookshelf and scanned the titles, until he found the book that he was looking for. He thumbed through it, before he turned to Allen and said, "I need something to read on the crapper. I just finished a good one by that guy who writes all of those detective stories. What's his name? Lehay…or something like that… anyhow…he's a good writer."

Allen laughed. He'd read a couple of stories by Dennis Lehane, and agreed that the guy was one of the best in the business right now, but he didn't correct Otis. Allen noticed that the old man was breathing heavily and wheezing a little bit. "Where is your oxygen tank?"

"I left it in my office…I hate the damn thing…dragging it all around the house, like a fool."

"Let me help you back to your office then," Allen offered.

"I have a better idea! Why don't you go out that door there…" He motioned with his cane to a set of French doors, behind a heavy curtain, "…the garage is right around the corner. Get the golf cart and come back around here and pick me up."

Allen opened the door to the outside, "Be right back."

He returned within just a couple of minutes with the cart and helped Otis into the seat. The old man asked Allen to first swing around to his office to pick up the oxygen tank, and then over to the garage. He said that there was something there that he wanted Allen to see.

When they arrived at the garage, there was still a little bit of sunlight left in the sky. The horizon was painted shades of orange, pink and purple. Otis led Allen into the garage through a side door, past an array of classic vehicles and into the very back of the building. He walked up to an automobile that was under a heavy blue car cover. Allen could tell right away that it was an antique of some kind, based on the shape. Large fenders and running boards - he was drooling even before Otis gestured for him to pull the cover off and when he did, Allen was amazed to find that it was a pristine, black 1926 Model T. "That was my daddy's car," Otis said, and as they walked around it, Otis gestured to the lack of a back seat, "He modified it to carry his whiskey. Lightened it up where he could. There wasn't another car in the state of Mississippi that could run with it back then."

"It's amazing," Allen ran his hand gently along the roof edge.

"Then in 1941, he bought that one over there." He pointed at a dull grey, 1940 Ford Coupe sitting along the far wall, "He drove that one until the day he died."

Allen walked over and touched the fender of the 40 Coupe rubbing the V8 emblem. The car was pristine in every way, except for a few holes punched in the fender and a couple on the passenger door. There was no mistaking the holes as anything other than bullet holes. "How did he die?" Allen asked.

Otis smiled and his eyes watered from the corners. "Not by any of those," he said, "all of them there bullets missed everything but his leg.

He limped for a while afterward, but that was nothing more than a close call." Otis attempted to pull the cover back over the Model T, but with his cane and oxygen bottle in his hand, he was having a hard time. Allen hurried over to help.

When they were finished covering the car, Allen looked around the room in awe of the automotive history that was represented within the walls of this garage. "These cars are remarkable…" Allen walked over to a vintage Harley Davidson motorcycle. It was a black and beige two tone Pan Head, Hydra Glide that he estimated to be early nineteen fifties, "Do they run?"

"Like brand new," Otis bragged. "You want to take one of them for a ride?"

Allen couldn't hide the excitement in his voice. "What's that sixty nine Charger got in it?"

"A four-twenty-six, Hemi…."

"Where would we find the keys for that one?" Allen asked.

"Should be in it…." Otis said, with a smile.

"You up for a ride?"

Allen surprised himself with the level of restraint that he was able to display. He was careful not to drive so fast to scare the old man, but it was surely a lesson in patience. The car had enormous power, and Otis was correct in saying that it was in pristine condition. Inside and out, it looked like it had just come off of the showroom floor. Once out on the main road, the engine purred like it was brand new. They drove for a few miles, before Allen decided to turn around at a gas station. He passed a group of gawking onlookers – standing at the pumps - busy filling their modern day pieces-of-shit with fuel. Allen slowly pulled the vintage machine back onto the main road, wanting to savor the experience for as long as possible. It was then that Otis said, "Quit driving like a pussy and get on the gas a little bit." Allen smiled, and did as he was instructed, leaving a little rubber and a whole lot of smoke on the asphalt, as they pulled away. Otis laughed out loud and Allen realized that the old man was enjoying himself as much as Allen was. The ride home took considerably less time. When they reached the driveway, Allen slowed and crept along the dusty road, trying not get too much dirt on the car. "What is this thing worth?" Allen asked.

"Last I checked, it was in the neighborhood of about one hundred thousand…give or take. It's all original you know…never been restored. I bought this one myself in sixty nine. Paid about fifty five hundred for it back then."

"Not a bad investment," Allen said. When they got to the curve in the road that led back to the garage, Otis directed Allen to go straight and into the grass. At first Allen was a little reluctant to drive the classic car off of the drive and through the yard, but when he looked closer, he saw faint tire tracks - grown over due to lack of use. He followed the path unnervingly into a thicket of woods that were dangerously close to scratching the fenders of the car. When he came to an area of brush and undergrowth, he wasn't sure if he could squeeze the car into it, so he stopped.

"What are you stopping for?" Otis asked.

"I don't want to scratch the car," Allen explained.

"Damn the car! It'll be fine. Just drive, we're almost there."

Allen slowly pulled the car through the undergrowth, cringing as the small branches scraped against the sides of the hot rod. He looked at Otis, who was watching forward out of the window and either didn't hear the scratching, or really didn't give a damn about it, like he said. Once they were through the thick brush, the woods opened up to a clearing with an old house and barn occupying the highest point. One could have never seen either of the structures through the thick woods. Allen recognized the house from the photo of Otis as a child. This was Great Grandpa Clyde's house.

Allen parked the Charger. The house had probably once been painted white, but was now just bare wood with traces of white in the cracks. It had a large wrap-around porch, like Otis's current house, but this building was much smaller in size. "This is where you grew up," Allen said.

They got out and Otis stood beside the car, while Allen checked the fenders for scratch marks. When he was finished verifying that he wasn't responsible for damage to a car that was worth five times the amount he'd ever earned in a year - he stood and watched. Otis was standing silently, appearing to be lost deep in thought. Allen imagined how difficult it must be for him to have a monument to his youth, hiding out here in the woods, within walking distance to where he lived. Allen had moved around so much when he was young, that he had never really felt a bond to a childhood home, but all of Otis's life could be chronicled on this property. As he watched the old man, he felt sorry for him. He wasn't sure why exactly, but he did. Maybe it was because Otis had been left behind by everyone else. All of the ones in the old photo. All of them that had once occupied this secluded place in the world. He put his hand on Otis's shoulder, "You ok?"

Otis patted Allen's hand with his own and said, "No matter how many time I've come to this place over the years – I still get choked up, when I think about all of the happy memories that we had here as a family. I can remember me, my brother and my sister playing on that there porch like it was yesterday." Otis took a deep breath, "Time sure does fly."

"That it does!" Allen agreed. He could also remember being a child, but his recollections weren't always so happy. He remembered times like when he was hauled off by Social Services during his fifth birthday party, in front of all of the neighborhood kids, leaving them at the party with the birthday cake and all of his gifts. His mother was dealing with some substance abuse issues back then, and one of her bitter ex-boyfriends had notified the state, saying that she was a danger to the children. Apparently, all of a sudden the piece of shit took an interest in the well-being of Allen, after barely acknowledging that he existed over the year or so that he'd dated Clara. That day, Allen had carried only one of his presents to his new foster home with him – a rocket ship. He didn't know why he'd chosen to pick up the rocket – but he did. It was laying among the torn wrapping paper and boxes, as he was being led away by the social worker. Over the course of the next year, it became his only connection to his home – to his mother. When his foster parents would fall into one of their weekly trailer park boxing matches, five year old Allen would retreat into the dark bedroom - his sanctuary, and cry himself to sleep, while holding onto his rocket ship. No, there was no happy, playing on the porch moments that he could recall. No fond memories of a home that meant anything to him at all. When he was finally reunited with him mother, after a long drawn out court battle with the State, Clara had moved to a new apartment – perhaps, out of embarrassment over her child being taken by social services, in front of everyone else's children.

Seeing how deeply Otis loved his family - the dead and gone and the living, made Allen wish, for the first time in his life, that he had known more of his family years ago. Before he'd lost hope in the Blackwood name.

His mother had always said, *Blood is thicker than water*, but her actions always proved otherwise. Here in the last two days, Allen's bond with his family had grown considerably deeper, and yet he hardly knew any of them. Just the fact that he shared the same ancestry was enough for them to welcome him in. He was a Blackwood, and they accepted him for that reason alone. Uncle Otis was living proof that his mother's words had been right, blood was in fact, thicker than water. "Can we go inside?" Allen asked, feeling himself getting a little bit choked up too.

"Let's go see…" Otis willed his frail legs to get moving again. "…the worst case is that the floor will fall through." Allen gave Otis a concerned look. The old man smiled and shrugged his shoulders. "No big deal, if it does…then I can show you the basement." This made Allen laugh all the way up the porch steps and to the front door. To Allen's amazement, when Otis opened the door, the inside of the house was still furnished with antique furniture. There were drop cloths over some of the pieces, but a large portion of the couches and tables were uncovered. "Do you still use this place?" Allen asked.

"No…not really. Not in the last ten years or so. I lived here until the big house was completed in eighty-eight. After that, we used it as a guest house from time to time." Otis pointed at the staircase that led upstairs. "Go on upstairs and look around, if you like. I'm afraid I can't really get up and down the stairs very good anymore. I'm gonna' sit down here and relax for a little bit." The old man found a spot on the couch and sat down. Allen watched as Otis made himself comfortable on the old sofa – not missing the irony of just how much this house suited the elderly man. Otis's polyester slacks and grey wool sweater fit the decor of the house perfectly. It was like looking at a living Norman Rockwell painting.

Allen left his great uncle there on the couch and took a quick look upstairs. It must have been quite the place, nearly a hundred years ago. It was still impressive by today's standards. The layout was spacious and the furnishings that were left behind looked expensive. There were probably thousands of dollars' worth of antiques still in here. The floor was creaking a little too much for Allen's comfort and he wondered when the last time someone with his weight was up here, on the second floor. He wasn't fat, but he was sure that he weighed more than everyone else in his family, other than perhaps Tommy. He didn't feel very comfortable going any further than the top of the landing, so he turned around and went back down stairs.

Otis was sitting on the couch - his eyes closed - taking a rest. Allen continued his self-guided tour, walking through the dining room and into the kitchen. He tried to imagine Otis as a child, running around this house. Allen's great grandmother, Ellie, hard at work on the supper dishes in the kitchen sink. The sink was now old, cracked and covered with dust, but Allen imagined it clean and tidy, the way that he was sure his great grandmother had kept it. Being in here was like stepping back in time. The wallpaper was original to the nineteen-twenties, as was the flooring. The cabinets and countertops looked turn of the century. For a construction worker – Allen had seen many new building projects, and none of them had the character and attention to detail that this place had been built with. It was a shame that it was in such a state of decay.

Allen came upon a door just past the kitchen and he opened it. To his surprise, there was a staircase leading down to a cellar. It surprised Allen that a house built this close to a wetland would have a cellar, but he knew that they were on the edges of Violent Hill – sort of a geographic anomaly out here in the swamp, and the elevation must have allowed it.

"There's nothing to see down there," Otis had sat upright, and was talking to Allen from his place on the couch. "It's probably flooded by now anyhow. Daddy always had a tough time keeping the swamp out. I had an electric pump installed back in the seventies, but it hasn't run in years. The snakes and the bugs have the run of the place now-a-days."

"Shame," Allen said. He closed the door and returned to the living room. The floor under his feet gave a little, as Allen stepped on it and the wood made an uncomfortable popping sound. For a split second, Allen thought that it was giving way underneath him. He quickly stepped to another board and looked at Otis.

Otis smiled and said, "The old floor is going to give out completely one of these days."

"What are we here for Uncle O?" Allen asked. He didn't feel quite as comfortable wandering around the abandoned house anymore, now that he realized the danger of falling through the rotten floor. The old man sighed and then spoke in a quiet voice. Allen pulled a chair from the wall over to the edge of the couch, sitting down next to Otis. "I brought you over here to show you the old house. It is timeworn…run down. It really ain't worth much! The land it sits on would be better suited for some other purpose. The bitter-sweet memories that I have of this place are…just vague memories now. All of the people that ever held this place dear, with the exception of me, are all dead. I have thought about having it torn down on a number of occasions, but each time I started to do it, I came to the same resolution. It is a part of our family's history…and being such…it is important that it is preserved…because nothing can replace that history. Nothing can ever change that history either. The good and the bad…it makes us who we are. It defines each generation, whether they embrace it, or not. Thing is…you don't have to acknowledge your history, in order to be affected by it."

"I agree! Why don't you have this place renovated?" Allen asked.

Otis looked directly into Allen's eyes. Allen could see a spark behind the watery exterior of the hazel eyes, staring directly into his own.

"You are more like my daddy than any of the rest of them…" Otis said, "…you have the same glimmer in your eyes that he did. It's not just the look, I see a lot of his personality in you too. It's strange really! How you can be so much like someone that you have never met, just because you carry the same blood in your veins."

"I would have liked to have known him," Allen said. "Tell me about him."

Otis patted Allen on his knee. "There is way too much to tell in one sitting. He was a good father. He loved all of us. His family was important to him. There were things that he let his wife and children get away with that he would have never tolerated from anybody else. He was an upright man in general, but he had a mean streak. He didn't trust outsiders…a lesson that I could have learned from at one time or another. But Clyde could be downright brutal to anyone outside the family, if he felt like they were a threat to the rest of us. He was also quite a business man, and he made a good enough living for all of us to be comfortable, for a long time."

"I can see that!" Allen said, referring to the estate and the obvious fortune that must go along with having all of the luxuries that the Blackwoods of Mississippi enjoyed. "I have a couple of questions though. Why did your brother, my grandpa Artie, leave here and go to Virginia? Why did he give up all that the family had to offer here, and raise his children in near poverty? Why did my mother never come back out here, after I was born?"

Otis seemed to consider the questions by taking nearly a full minute before he answered the first one. "Your mother was raised in Virginia, away from the family. She came up without ever getting very close to us and I blame that on my brother, Artie. She came out once, right after she'd graduated high school and spent some time with us. She met a boy while she was out here. He broke her heart, and afterward, she moved back to Virginia."

"My father?" Allen asked. "Stephen Gilmour?"

Otis nodded his head. "She was pregnant when she headed back to Virginia. It was just another reason for Artie to hate me. He allowed his daughter to come visit, hoping to get her life started off right, and she went home pregnant and broken hearted. He blamed me for what happened to Clara, just like he blamed our father, for what happened to Betsy. He has always been a bitter man. He left home when he was still very young, and wandered every corner of Mississippi to spite Clyde."

"I don't understand…what happened to Betsy?"

Otis took a deep breath – wheezing a little when he did so. Allen offered to go out to the car and get the oxygen tank, but Otis waved him off. "Betsy," he explained, "…was hurt by some bad men. Men that my daddy did business with from time to time. It happened when she was thirteen and she was never right after that. Now-a-days, a doctor would say that she suffered from depression, or some other gobble goop, and give her medication, to even her out. Back then though…it went untreated. Hell, none of us had even heard the word depression used in any other context than the national economy. Momma and Daddy, both said that she just needed to work through it. That she would be alright in time…but she wasn't. She committed suicide two weeks after her fourteenth birthday. Daddy found her one morning in the barn, with her wrist's cut. She'd gone out there after everyone had gone to bed, and done it." Tears rolled down his wrinkled cheeks. "She bled out overnight, while the rest of us slept comfortably in our beds."

"Jesus…that's terrible," Allen said, "Did Great Grandpa ever find the men who hurt her?"

Otis nodded and wiped his eyes with the sleeve of his sweater, "He took care of them before Betsy died. It didn't make any difference in the way that Daddy felt though…after she died…he never forgave himself."

Allen wanted to ask, *took care of them how,* but decided that now was not the right time.

Otis kept talking, "My brother never forgave Clyde either. He felt like what happened to her in the first place, was my daddy's fault. Artie moved away, as soon as he was old enough to go. First up to Meridian, where he met Gladys, and then out to Virginia. Daddy tried to help Artie over the years, in any way that he could, especially once he found out that Artie, Gladys and the kids were living in insufficient conditions. Artie refused all of daddy's hand-outs and it wasn't until much later, that we found out that Artie had developed a drinking problem. He chose to let his own family suffer, to spite our father. When your uncles, Elmer and Kirk, were old enough, they moved out here. Then, your mother showed up. She was loyal to her mother and father, but wanted to have opportunities that she otherwise wouldn't have been afforded back in Virginia. She met the wrong boy. It didn't work out and she went back home to be with her momma. We wanted her to stay. She would have had plenty of help raising you here, but she insisted on going home. I think that her decision was partially from a broken heart, and partially out of embarrassment. We would have never turned her away, she was family. The same as you are, and we won't turn you away either!"

"What ever happened to Stephen Gilmour?"

Otis shrugged his frail shoulders, "One day he was here and the next… gone!"

"Just like that, huh?" Allen asked. "Never heard from him again?"

"Nah! He knew better than to ever show his face around here again after what he did. Her brothers would have never let that slide." Then he repeated, "He broke your mother's heart."

Allen had just one more question, "What about this job that you said you had for me?"

Otis said, "Well, it ain't your typical job."

Allen was no rookie when it came to hard work. He couldn't imagine that anything Otis needed done around here would be listed as extreme on the labor intensity charts. "Whatever it is, I'm your man!" Allen said.

Otis patted Allen's hand again and smiled. For a fleeting moment,

Allen could see the mischievous boy from the old picture. That child still existed, underneath the wrinkled exterior of his Great Uncle. Otis whispered to Allen, as if they weren't the only ones in the abandoned house, in the middle of the Mississippi swamp, "You don't have any affliction to breaking the law just a little bit...do you?"

III

WHERE ALL
THE WILD
THINGS HIDE

1

Allen was laying on his bed. He'd been thumbing through a Mad Magazine that was so old, the focus of the jokes was Russia, and a very young Sylvester Stallone. He was bored and anxious and not really reading the words on the pages, just more or less letting his fingers flip the yellowed paper, for something to do. He was startled by a sudden pounding on his bedroom door. He tossed the magazine aside and got up to open the door. Robert Blackwood, was dressed in a black sweatshirt and black jeans, *Allen thought that it was a pleasant change from his cousin's usual Hee Haw attire.* Allen put his watch on, while Robert waited by the door and as he began to put his wallet in his pocket, Robert stopped him, "You might as well leave that here..." Allen nodded acknowledging that Robert had a point. Based on the little information that Uncle Otis had shared back at Clyde's house, he and his cousins were going to be up to a little mischief tonight, and there wouldn't be any need for a wallet. Plus, it was best not to have identification, in the instance the wallet gets dropped. He tossed it back onto the nightstand.

"Is that the darkest clothes that you have?" Robert asked.

Allen looked down at his yellow t-shirt and blue jeans, like he just realized what he was wearing. "I may have a darker shirt in my bag," Allen said.

"Something with sleeves..." Robert said, "...the bugs are gonna' eat you alive."

"Bugs?"

"Yeah! In the swamp...I hear that on certain days, they can be really bad!", Robert said, with a twinge of sarcasm in his tone. "Like Monday, through Sunday!"

"We're going into the swamp!" Allen asked, "At night?" He was vaguely aware of the panic in his voice. Robert noticed it too and smiled, revealing a mouth that was short more than a few teeth, including one in the front. Robert walked to the door and said, "Hurry up and change…they're waiting for us down at the dock."

Allen found a dark shirt with sleeves and put it on as he hurried down to the driveway, where Robert was waiting. The sun was setting and a cool breeze was blowing in off of the swamp. Without having much to say to each other, Allen and Robert drove the short distance to the boat dock, located on the far side of Violent Hill. When they arrived, the landing was already bustling with activity. A dark blue van was parked near the dock and Allen could see the rest of his cousins moving things from the van to a boat that was tied to the pier. They were all wearing dark clothes also and were hard to see against the shadowed forest behind them. By the time that Allen and Robert arrived, they had the van empty of the supplies, except for one last duffel bag. Johnny was standing at the front of the truck, reading something by flashlight and although he looked up as they approached - he didn't speak when they got out. Allen, not really knowing what was expected of him to do and feeling a little out of place, decided that sticking close to Tommy was a good idea. He'd always liked Tommy the best of all of his cousins, since Tommy was usually even-keeled and didn't seem to always be trying to prove his machoism, like the rest of them. Tommy was a little bit heavier than the rest of his cousins, and had a thick mustache that covered his entire upper lip. Of the Blackwood family, there were two distinct DNA strands. One, with the dark hair and olive skin, was the more attractive and more like Allen's grandmother's side of the family. The other side was the pale, red haired side which took more from Artie and Otis's side of the family. Tommy fit into this second bunch, but what he lacked in good looks, he made up for with a good personality. He was standing with his brother, Dewayne, when Allen found them. They were under the porch of the boathouse, near the back of the open van. Just as Allen approached, Dewayne lit what looked like a cigarette, but as soon as Allen caught a whiff of it – he realized that it was some pot. He took a healthy drag, and then passed it around. As it came to Allen, he thought of passing it along without partaking in it, but instead he puffed, thinking to himself that maybe this wouldn't be a bad job after all. He'd never been much of a pot head - *whiskey was always more his thing*, but there were certainly worse ways to start a new job.

After a few minutes, Johnny came over with Chris and Robert, and took the joint from Allen before saying, "We've already loaded everything…" Then he pointed at Robert and Allen with his pinky, while holding the rolled cigarette, "…you two can unload by yourselves when we get back." There was something about Johnny that Allen didn't like. Johnny gave him the feeling of being around an aggressive dog - likely to attack at any moment.

Johnny took a long pull off of the joint before saying, "Let's go," through clenched teeth as smoke escaped the corners of his mouth. Robert grabbed the duffel bag from the back of the van and followed the others to the waiting boat. Dewayne and Tommy got on first, and took the front seats. Allen had to do a double take, to make sure that his eyes weren't playing tricks, when they both picked up rifles off of the floor of the boat. Robert passed the last bag to Johnny, as he climbed aboard and took up his position, behind the steering console. Robert pushed a button and the motor rumbled to life. Allen climbed aboard the flat bottomed craft and Johnny motioned for him to take a seat in the rear. Allen sat down facing the motor, as Chris and Robert untied the lines that moored the boat to the pier. Robert pulled slowly away and then Chris handed Allen a rifle of his own, before taking a seat next to him. Johnny sat next to Robert at the console. The running lights from the dashboard only lit half of Johnny's face. He looked at Allen and mockingly said, "You know how to use that thing?" Allen had shot an assault rifle at targets before and was pretty sure that he could figure it out.

"Am I going to need it?" Allen asked.

Johnny laughed, and gave Allen chills when he said to Chris, "You just never know…do you?" They both laughed in a way that made Allen start to regret being on this little adventure with them. Chris showed Allen where the safety was, and told him that other than flipping the switch, the weapon was ready to go.

"What's in the bag?" Allen gestured to the duffel bag. Johnny and Chris either didn't hear the question, or they both just blatantly ignored it. Allen was pretty sure that it was the latter, because they were both looking directly at him when he asked. He considered pressing the matter, but decided against it for now. The boat entered an area thick with cypress trees and vines, forming a natural canopy over the small river. The vegetation completely blotted out the sun, leaving the occupants of the small boat cool, damp and in near darkness.

Chris patted Allen on the shoulder and giggled when he said, "Get ready man, this is where all the wild things hide." Chris's words worried Allen, the same way that not knowing what was in the black duffel bag worried him. Where were they going? The boat trudged on, through the thick underbrush of the Bayou. Allen wondered if maybe he'd made a big mistake, by signing up for *whatever* this was that they were getting ready to do.

The boat motor lumbered along with a steady hum that Allen supposed could be heard for miles away out here. Not that the noise mattered much; Allen assumed that you could light off a bomb out here and no one was going to pay any attention to it. They were miles from civilization. It had been at least twenty minutes since they left the dock of Violent Hill. In that time, Allen's eyes had adjusted some, but not much. He could see well enough to know that he was where very few men had probably ever been. The thought entered his mind that all of their lives were completely dependent now on the small twenty-five horse power motor, attached to the rear of the Carolina Skiff. If anything were to go wrong with it right now, even something as minor as a rubber hose busting loose, they would all be eaten by the creatures of the wild, before they could ever get help. The river was only about fifteen feet wide, and on either side – marsh, swamp and trees draped with Spanish moss, all seemed to absorb any light that the night had to offer. In a few places scattered here and there, was dry land, but the underbrush was so thick that there was no way that a man could walk through it without a machete. Allen imagined that it would be a miserable fate to have to get through here on foot. The bugs and the reptiles would have a meal for sure. He could feel the large insects' dive bombing his arms and head even as he rode in the boat. They seemed to be impervious to the bug spray that he'd applied back at the van. Things could be worse though, he intended to give Robert a big thank you, when they got to wherever they were going, for giving him the heads up on wearing the long sleeves. He only wished that he'd brought more of the bug spray for his neck and face. The way that the bugs were biting and leaving welts - he was pretty sure his face would resemble Sloth, from the Goonies, before he made it back to civilization. The drone of the boat motor died down a notch, and Allen could hear the water catching up with the back of the boat, meaning that they were slowing down. He turned to look out in front and initially he didn't see anything. Then the faint glow of a small fire appeared along the left shoreline, up in the distance. Johnny stood and said to Allen, "When we get up here, stay on the dock, beside the boat."

"Sure, no problem," Allen said. He was perfectly fine with not having to do anything more complicated than staying with the boat.

Johnny grabbed the duffel bag and walked to the front to stand with Dewayne and Tommy. Chris was behind them, with the rope in his hand, waiting to tie off to the pier. Robert expertly brought the boat along the pier, as if he had done this a thousand times, and gauging by the way that Allen was the only one who seemed nervous – he probably had!"

The pier was attached to an old, dilapidated shack by a wooden walkway, which it was nestled into. If it hadn't been for a line of Tiki-Torches – the variety found at the local Wal-Mart, stuck in the ground along the path, Allen probably wouldn't have noticed that the shack was there at all since it was mostly covered by the forest. The people that they were meeting were already at the shack, as the Blackwoods docked the boat. A couple of the men came to the pier and Chris tossed one of them the rope. The man, large and white, with a full beard and wearing shorts with a flannel shirt, gently pulled the boat against the wooden pylons and tied it off. A different man, one that looked eerily similar to the first, tied off the front line.

Chris was the first to jump up onto the pier. He was followed by Johnny, Dewayne and Tommy. Robert walked over and said to Allen, "It looks best if you stand on the pier, next to the boat." Allen nodded. When Allen climbed out of the boat, there was a stranger standing there – an enormous man that had to be six feet six and every bit of three hundred and fifty pounds. Allen noticed that the guy looked as nervous as he was himself, and the man had a hunting rifle strapped to his shoulder. They made eye contact and Allen nodded - a hello gesture. Fatso just stared at him with a blank face like he was a Beefeater, guarding the Queen of England. Allen nonchalantly flipped the safety switch on his rifle to the fire position.

Johnny and Chris were walking up the path to the shack to join a couple more of Fatso's friends. They all went inside the small building. Allen could see the glow of a lantern through the cracks in the crude wooden planks. Tommy, Dewayne and Robert stopped about halfway up the path and waited. After several minutes of being inside, Johnny and Chris emerged – again carrying the black duffel bag. They walked quickly back to the boat and tossed the bag onto the deck with a heavy thud. Tommy, Dewayne and Robert all climbed aboard. Allen winked at Fatso, who was still mean-mugging, and then he followed his cousins onto the boat. The whole scene lasted for what Allen estimated to be about ten minutes. Robert fired up the boat motor, as Chris and Allen pulled in the ropes from the pier. They were off again, heading back the way that they'd come. No one was in the mood for talking on the return trip. Tommy and Dewayne sat at their places in the front, smoking cigarettes. Chris, Allen and Johnny were in the back, while Robert navigated the dark river. Allen didn't know for sure what laws he'd just broken, but he was sure there were more than a few on the list. He tried to convince himself that the trip was all about selling some of the family recipe whiskey, but quickly surmised that men don't meet in the middle of the swamp to exchange something that could be bought at the local ABC store. He also wasn't sure how much he was getting paid for this excursion – he and Otis hadn't discussed a price. Hell, they had barely discussed the work at all, other than to be ready at seven o'clock, for Robert to pick him up. Nonetheless, he couldn't help but to think that he had made some very easy money tonight – even if it was probably only going to be enough to buy a bottle of whiskey.

2

It was after nine o'clock when they got the boat unloaded, onto the trailer and back in the boathouse. Johnny insisted that cleaning the boat be left to Robert and Allen, since they'd been late getting to the dock - or so Johnny had claimed. Allen got the impression that Johnny liked being in charge. He also thought that Johnny was an asshole. Maybe, he just couldn't help but to be one all the time; some people couldn't. Allen didn't remember Otis telling him exactly what time to be at the boat dock - only that he would be picked up at a certain time, by Robert. Nonetheless, Allen kept quiet, as he and Robert struggled to get the skiff up onto the trailer. The other four were watching from the back of the van. When Robert and Allen were finished with the boat, Dewayne and Chris jumped into the van and drove away. Allen got into the bed of Roberts pickup truck. Tommy was in back with Allen while Johnny rode in the cab with Robert and the black duffel bag. Allen leaned against the bed of the truck. He faced Tommy, who was looking at the moon. It was peaking nicely over the dark hill, as they made their way back to the house. "What's in the bag?" Allen asked.

"What do you think?" Tommy said, without looking in his direction. He'd closed his eyes and was resting his head against the truck cab.

Allen was pretty sure of what it was, but truthfully he had never seen enough of it in one place to fill a bag of that size. "Is it full of money?"

Tommy didn't reply this time. He never even opened his eyes. "It is... isn't it?" Allen pressed.

"Why don't you just wait and ask Uncle Elmer what's in the bag." Tommy said, in his deep southern drawl.

Allen laid his head back against the cab also. "Fair enough," he said. He thought that maybe it wasn't just Johnny - maybe they were all assholes.

Tommy spoke again. "What's your momma up to these days?"

"She's doing alright – she keeps to herself mostly," Allen explained. Clara and Tommy had always been pretty close.

Tommy lit a cigarette, as the truck bumped along to dirt road. "I heard that she was having some problems with her boyfriend."

Allen shrugged his shoulders, "Yeah I guess so...she's always having some sort of problems with men." Allen looked at Otis's house off in the distance, lit up against the night sky. "Some things never really change... do they?"

"Yeah," Tommy puffed his smoke, "Maybe not!"

"Time flies...just passes right by us. Don't it?"

Tommy took a deep drag from his cigarette. "Time is the great taker... leaves noting in return!"

Yeah! That summed things up. Didn't it? Time had flown – leaving Allen nothing. No money, no job, no real family to speak of. If tonight had taught him anything, it was that he really didn't know, or even really fit in with these relatives. A couple he didn't even really like; he didn't have anything in common with any of them.

"How about you...you got yourself a steady girlfriend?" Tommy asked.

"No...not at the moment I don't," Allen said.

Tommy gave him a funny looking, sideways glare, "You ain't gay are you?"

Allen laughed uncomfortably, "What? No...not at all! Wait a minute... that wasn't a proposition was it?"

Tommy smiled, and threw his cigarette butt over the side rail of the truck. "You don't have to worry about that shit from me! I just wanted to make sure that we were on the same page, before I go hanging out with you in public. I don't need any of the fellows down at the watering hole getting hit on by someone that I bring in."

"Homophobic much?" Allen asked.

Tommy raised his hands. "Hey, it's a strange new world. If it's acceptable for them circus clowns to marry each other, then it should be alright for me to qualify the people that I associate with, by asking direct questions. Don't I have the right to say that I don't agree?"

"Not according to the Liberals," Allen said.

"Fuck them!" Tommy spat.

For the sake of not getting Tommy too worked up, Allen chose to not comment. Although he understood where Tommy was coming from, he wasn't going to get himself all spun up over a subject that didn't pertain to him, one way or another. He didn't care what other people were doing, if it didn't cause him any grief! *To each, their own!*

When the truck pulled onto the paved driveway, Allen figured that they were close to the house; thank god for small miracles. Another few seconds of talking to Tommy, and Allen would have bet that the next subject was going to be how the Democrats have ruined the country. Robert pulled up to the garage door and shut the truck off. Elmer and Patsy were walking out to greet them, as the four men got out of the truck.

"Everything go alright?" Elmer asked.

"Like clockwork..." Johnny said, handing the duffel bag to Elmer.

"Where are Chris and Dewayne?" Elmer asked.

"They're dropping the van off at the barn..." Johnny said, "...they'll be here in a minute."

"You boys come on in and I'll warm y'all some supper," Patsy said.

Allen followed the others to the dining room. Johnny stayed behind with Elmer. Allen assumed that they were discussing what had transpired on the trip. Patsy brought a whole tray of fried chicken out to the table at about the same time that Johnny came into the dining room with Chris and Dewayne.

Jennifer and Kirk joined the dinner party. Jennifer set baby Ronnie on her knee, when she sat down at the table. She picked up a spoon and fed the toddler some mashed potatoes from a bowl. Besides the chicken and mashed potatoes, there was also gravy, biscuits, green beans and corn. The spread was better than Allen could ever remember having at his house growing up, and that included any Thanksgiving dinner. Everyone dug in like animals and Allen was reminded of an episode of Duck Dynasty that he had seen. The people sitting around the table right now, in this elegant room, with these expensive dishes, looked about as out of place as a polar bear did in Arizona. Allen couldn't help but chuckle a little, as he helped himself to a large spoonful of potatoes. Halfway through dinner, Elmer popped his head through the door of the dining room and motioned for Johnny to come with him.

"It's time to get paid, boys!" Johnny said, as he tossed his napkin into his chair on his way out. He returned a few minutes later and Chris went out. This rotation went on until all of them around the table had taken their turn, except for Allen. When Tommy returned, he nudged Allen with his elbow, as he sat back down, and said, "Your turn, chief!"

Allen got up and walked out of the dining room door and into the hallway. Elmer popped his head out of Otis's office a couple of doors down, and said, "What in the hell are you waiting for? Let's get this done, so Otis and me can get something to eat!"

Allen quickly walked down to Otis's office and found the old man sitting behind an enormous oak desk. He was impeccably dressed, in a light blue suit complete with the black ribbon tie. Again, he reminded Allen of the Kentucky Fried Chicken guy. Allen double checked his watch and found that it was near ten o'clock. He was surprised to find the old man dressed in a nice suit, so late in the evening. Elmer closed the door, as Allen entered. The black duffel bag was lying on the floor at the old man's feet, just beside his desk. Allen noticed that it was now empty and had collapsed upon itself. Otis held his oxygen mask to his face with one of his frail hands and motioned for Allen to sit with the other. Allen took a seat, and Elmer sat down beside him, in a matching red leather chair. It was the kind of furniture that Allen would have expected to find in a lawyer's office. Otis lowered his oxygen mask and leaned forward, resting his elbows on his mammoth desk. "So...how did your first trip go?"

Allen decided not to make it sound too easy - just in case he didn't fully understand his responsibilities yet. "It went alright...I guess."

"What do you mean, you guess?" Elmer asked.

Allen explained, "Well...if all that you are asking me to do, is ride through the swamp on a boat at night, and then stand on a dock for ten minutes! While the others did whatever in the hell they did, and not tell me shit! Then it went well!"

Otis nodded his head and smiled, "Is that all that you thought that you were doing?"

Allen looked from Elmer to Otis, and back, "That's pretty much what I did tonight."

"Were you nervous?" Otis asked, "With all of the guns and such?"

Allen considered the question. It was the first time that he'd thought about it since they'd returned. "You know, at first I was a little uneasy about being out in the swamp, at night, on a small boat, but after a little while that didn't bother me. The guns didn't really bother me either. What *is* bothering me is the fact that I still don't know what in the hell we were doing out there."

"What do you think that you did?" Elmer asked. He had his hands crossed in his lap. With his business man haircut and white button up shirt, he reminded Allen of some kind of therapist, talking with a patient.

"Alright!" Allen was getting tired of the twenty question game, "Is this some kind of head shrinking session or what? If you guys don't want to tell me what we delivered out to that shack, in the middle of the swamp…then so be it! I don't need to know, but I'm not comfortable with this question and answer bullshit." He looked at Elmer and waited for the backlash. He was sure that his outburst would bring forth Elmer's notorious temper. Instead, his uncle sat there just staring at Allen. It was Otis who spoke, and this time he was speaking to Elmer. "He certainly has the Blackwood temper, doesn't he?"

"Sorry!" Allen said, "I'm just tired and need a drink. I don't mean any disrespect, but I didn't like being the only one out there who didn't know what was going on."

Otis pulled an envelope from one of his desk drawers and tossed it into Allen's lap. It landed with considerable weight. "It's I that should apologize to you, Allen. My instruction was for you to be briefed on what we were delivering, prior to you going with them. Am I to assume *that* didn't happen?" He looked at Elmer, who gave the universal *I don't know* expression. "Meet me at the garage at eight o'clock tomorrow morning. I'll make sure that you are fully aware of what you are signing up for." Allen nodded in agreement. "In the meantime…" Otis continued, "I think that you will find your pay for tonight's work more than fair!"

Allen opened the envelope in his lap and saw a stack of hundred dollar bills. He wasn't sure if he actually made a noise out loud, but in his mind, he gasped. He didn't want to be rude and count it out right now, but just from the brief glance, he was willing to bet that there were at least fifty bills there, maybe more. "Wow! Uncle Otis…Thank you!" Allen was sure that right now, he was holding more than he'd made in several months of working his old job.

"Don't mention it Allen." Otis said, "I appreciate you being here to help out."

Elmer stood up and walked over to the door. Allen took the hint, and stood up also. He shook Otis' hand before he left. Otis smiled at his great nephew and said, "I'll see you in the morning."

As Allen was walking out, Elmer said, "Y'all try not to get into too much trouble tonight."

Allen didn't have any idea what he meant by that, until he found Robert and Tommy waiting in the dining room. They were at the table with Kirk who didn't look very healthy. He actually looked much worse than just two days ago, when Allen first arrived. "Heard you did a good job tonight, Allen." Kirk said, as Allen entered the room. His voice was weak and wheezy.

Allen smiled, and said, "I'm glad that the expectations are so low, otherwise I may be in trouble."

Tommy said, "Bullshit...you did just fine!" He and Robert stood up "You ready to go?"

"Go where?" Allen asked.

Tommy and Robert exchanged glances and then Tommy said, "Nobody told you how we celebrate after a successful job? Damn Robert! I thought you were supposed to fill him in on things." Robert looked dumfounded. It was not a difficult look for him to achieve, in Allen's opinion.

"We're going to meet up with everyone else, over at The Kingfish," Robert explained.

"The Kingfish?" It sounded like a bar and a pretty good idea to Allen, "Let's get to it!" He said.

The three of them piled into Allen's Land Rover, but not before Robert made a wardrobe change into one of his signature cowboy shirts, *this one - bright red, with white piping on the chest and pockets*, accented with a pair of tight jeans. His outfit wasn't complete without the overly gigantic, silver and gold belt buckle that resembled a gladiator shield more than something used to hold your pants up. Not that Robert even needed a belt. Allen was sure there was no way that the jeans Robert wore would ever fall down. Hell, he might even need some help getting them off when they got back. Allen just shook his head in disgrace when he saw his cousin, knowing that he was about to be seen in public with a rodeo clown. He kept telling himself, no matter how embarrassing, it was family and he was only a guest here. Tommy was more manly and casual in his attire - flannel shirt, blue jeans and work boots – a style that Allen could appreciate. Allen was still wearing the clothes that he'd worn into the swamp earlier.

"You gonna start this piece of shit, or what?" Tommy teased, catching Allen daydreaming.

"Yeah…sorry!" He turned the key and the V8 started right up. The engine had never run as good as it did ever since MJ tuned it back in Greenville. Allen threw it into gear and headed down the driveway.

Tommy directed Allen along the back roads with the ease only a lifetime local would have known. The trio went down neighborhood streets that could be mistaken as a post-apocalyptic backdrop, with the dilapidated houses and rusted out hulks of automobiles every so often. Hampton, Virginia was by no means a mecca for the wealthy, and it had its own share of low income areas, but the level of poverty that Allen was witnessing, as they drove the back roads of Pascagoula, was shocking. It was borderline third world. They passed a bedraggled black lady, sitting on the edge of the road among the litter and trash bags - torn open, spilling their foul contents onto the street. She stared hopelessly at the passing vehicle, seeming to plead for help. Tommy noticed Allen's shock, "It's crazy that some people live like this, ain't it?"

"Yeah," Allen agreed, "what's with the war zone?"

"Katrina," Tommy said, "…most of the area was never rebuilt. The federal government failed these people, for the most part. There was some relief money, but most of it went to New Orleans. That was the only area that the media was concerned about. Nobody gave a shit about these people here in Mississippi."

They drove past a group of teenagers, gathered at the end of a driveway. The driveway was attached to a house that had plywood covering the door and the windows. Allen wondered if any of the teens actually lived in the condemned house. The boys stopped what they were doing, faced the passing truck, and took a few steps out into the street, like they were expecting Allen to stop. He guided the truck around them, never letting off of the gas. The teens were yelling something and one of them tossed a bottle as they went by. Whether or not it actually hit the truck was irrelevant, he wasn't about to stop, even if it had. Allen had grown up around rough people. He knew the look in their eyes – the way that they carried themselves. He could separate the fakers from the real deal, and he didn't have to look very close to know that these kids were noone that you wanted to engage in casual conversation with. It was best to not even acknowledge them.

Tommy directed Allen back out to the main road and they were only a short distance from a parking lot - just on the other side of a large, green sign that read, THE KINGFISH LOUNGE, in bright white letters. The building was shaped and painted like a barn and looked like it was pretty well maintained. The shrubbery out front was trimmed and the parking lot was clean, paying no homage to the residential area just a couple of blocks back. Allen pulled the truck in and found a spot in the front, next to a group of motorcycles - all backed into a neat row. Robert was in the back seat, haphazardly singing along to a Johnny Cash tune. In Allen's opinion, it was the best song that had been played on the shitty country music radio station for the entire trip. Allen only liked the old country music – not the new stuff. He could tolerate some of the modern singers that had the old sound, like Chris Stapleton, but the for the most part, he thought most of the stuff played on the radio these days was on the verge of unbearable. If he had his pick, he was more of a rock and roll guy. Having grown up with the greats like the Eagles and Fleetwood Mac – it was hard to listen to any of the unimaginative music this modern generation liked. Nevertheless, he wanted to be a team player and when Robert and Tommy both insisted that they couldn't go out drinking without hearing some country music - Allen conceded.

When he turned the engine off, the radio died with it, yet Robert kept singing along. *"...for you I know I'd even try to turn the tide...because your mine...I walk the line!"* He finished singing the song, as the three of them walked through the doors and into the bar. The building was larger inside than it looked from the road. Keeping with the barn theme, it was wide open, with exposed rafters and a wood plank floor. The place looked like an actual farm building to Allen - complete with hay bales and seating booths that were made to resemble horse stalls. In the middle of the room was a dance floor and behind that, a stage - decorated with country western décor. It reminded Allen of something from the Hee-Haw variety show that he used to watch with his grandpa as a kid. A banner was draped across the front of the stage reading,

DOUBLEBARREL DARRELL and THE BEERBELLIES,
Featuring, Raggedy Ann.
THIS WEEK ONLY!

A towering bouncer, dressed in overalls and a red and white checkered shirt, with a piece of straw hanging from the corner of his mouth, stood beside a hostess, who was grabbing three menus from the hostess stand. Tommy gestured that they wouldn't be needed and passed right by her. She was cute, but obviously very young - maybe a little too young to be working in a bar this late at night.

Johnny, Chris, and Dewayne already had a table on the far side of the room, near the very large bar. There were only a few empty tables remaining. The place obviously did good business. The table that the cousins were at was round - carved to resemble a wagon wheel. The table beside them was occupied by the bikers. They were all dressed in leather vests with matching patches on their backs. Allen didn't even have to look closely to know that the patch was some representation of a skull. He also didn't have to look very close to see that most of the men in the group had expensive haircuts and had probably been dressed in collar shirts and ties earlier in the day - working their 9 to 5 office jobs, punching keys on their computers while dreaming of going out with their buddies tonight, to pretend that they were some kind of outlaw biker gang. A couple of them were watching Robert as he entered and they shared a laugh at his red cowboy outfit. Allen completely understood the humor, but thought that they were just being assholes by laughing. Chris, sitting at the table next to Johnny, was wearing something similar to Robert - only he was dressed as the blue ranger. The bikers must have previously been poking fun at Chris's attire and then when Robert showed up - it just added fuel to the fire.

Allen took a seat facing the bar and Dewayne slid a glass of recently poured beer to him. Doublebarrel Darrell and the Beerbellies started playing music again. He turned in his seat to watch, as a woman with a guitar, wearing a dress that looked like it was made from old curtains, started singing in a high pitched voice that was painful to Allen's ears. To her right - a man in blue overalls, *they must be popular around here*, and a crisp white shirt - picked a banjo and sang back-up vocals. They both wore straw hats that were big enough to be umbrellas. Allen looked over at Robert and Chris and thought that with the outfits that they were wearing, they would look good up on stage with the rest of the clowns. As soon as the music started up, people all across the bar stood and started clapping to the rhythm and stomping their feet. A large crowd made their way over to the dance floor and fell into a line. Chris stood up, chugged the remaining beer in his glass and joined the growing crowd in the dance line. Allen watched as Chris disappeared into a line of people. Robert calmly finished his beer and stood up also. "Come on Allen…" he urged, "…let's see what you've got."

"I'll pass!" Allen smiled.

Robert hooked his thumbs on his oversized belt buckle, "What's the matter…afraid you can't hang?"

It was the first time in Allen's life that he could remember being called out to a line dancing competition, and honestly he was completely unprepared to answer such a challenge. He laughed and said, "No Robert, I'm afraid that I would be depressed for the rest of my life, knowing that I'd peaked so young, after partaking in such excitement. I'm just not sure that I am ready for that just yet!"

Robert shot a puzzled look, and quickly glanced around the table, to see if anyone else was confused by what Allen had just said. Clearly not understanding that Allen was making a joke Robert said, "Suit yourself," as he produced a comb from his back pocket and ran it through his pompadour, "…but don't be crying, when I wind up with all of the ladies."

"Sounds like the only people crying here tonight will *be* the ladies," Johnny joked.

Robert shrugged off the comments and strutted over to the dance floor. As he went, the bikers were laughing and pointing. It was obvious that their remarks were about Robert, and this time – with a little more beer in their system – they were getting pretty loud about it. Allen saw Johnny's expression change after one of their comments. It was only a flash, but Allen was sure that he saw something dangerous in Johnny's eyes. For a brief second, he was looking into the eyes of a beast in the wild. Allen took a sip of his drink and savored the taste. He hadn't had a beer in days and he couldn't remember the last time that he'd had one from the tap.

Johnny poured the remainder of the pitcher into his own glass and slid the empty pitcher over to Allen. "Your round!" he said. Allen thought that the gesture was a bit rude, but ignored it and looked for the waitress. She was missing in action – probably out back smoking a cigarette and taking a break from this horrible music. Allen couldn't blame her – thought of joining her!

"So…" Dewayne said, over a loud banjo solo, "What was up with that cop lady the other day?" He was talking to Johnny, but nervously spinning his mug in front of him on the table.

"What do you mean?" Johnny asked.

Dewayne stopped with the mug, and fidgeted with a small napkin. "Kinda weird, how she just popped up at the same time as that jackass Lionel, ain't it?"

Johnny shrugged his shoulders and took a swig of his beer. He wiped his mouth with his sleeve, and said, "What the hell do I care if the heat is following around that crack head? I don't deal with him anymore. 'Sides… she ain't got nothing on us, she would have popped us by now."

"She wasn't narcotics Johnny! She was homicide," Tommy said. "I heard that Lionel's parents were killed the other night." Tommy stared directly at Johnny. "Why was he at Violent Hill, Johnny? What did he say to you?"

Johnny slammed his beer mug down on the table so hard, that foam and beer spilled around the edges. It made such a noise that the bikers looked over to see what the commotion was. "What the fuck do y'all want? You bunch of noisy motherfuckers!" Johnny spat in the direction of the bikers, "Mind your own fucking business!" He paused, waiting for one of them to say something else. They didn't, so he turned back to Dewayne and Tommy, "I told you, I don't know nothing about what those niggers wanted…so stop bugging the shit out of me while I'm trying to listen to the music." He looked at Allen and barked, "Are you going to get us some fucking beer or what?"

If there was one thing that Allen hated, it was to be talked down to. Tommy sensed that Allen was fuming and elbowed Allen in the arm and said, "Don't pay him any mind! He don't mean no harm. He just forgets how to talk to people when he's drinking."

"Well next time, he better try harder to remember..." Allen said, talking to Tommy, but looking directly at Johnny, "...or he might mouth off to the wrong person!"

Johnny didn't reply. He pretended to watch the band, and never said another word. He just waved his hand at Allen, like he was shooing a fly. Tommy pulled a twenty dollar bill out of his wallet and tossed it to Allen. "This round's on me," he said. "It looks like there's an opening at the bar... and the bartender's pretty cute. Why don't you go over there and cool off a minute?"

"Good idea," Allen said, and stood up, "...but Johnny can get his own fucking beer." He walked away, leaving Tommy's money on the table.

Allen located an empty stool at the end of the bar and took it. He was fuming mad and was trying to convince himself of all of the reasons why he shouldn't go over to the table and punch Johnny in his throat. Who the fuck did he think he was after all? For whatever reason, Johnny's been nothing but a prick ever since Allen got to Mississippi, and Allen had no idea why. Suddenly, all of the anger and frustration that Allen was feeling left his body, and Johnny became the furthest thing from his mind. He had only been sitting on the stool for maybe a full minute, before she approached from the other side of the bar. The woman was a stunner! She was wearing a waitress shirt with the bar logo printed on the chest. She was so gorgeous she made the bar uniform look like an evening gown. Allen recognized right away that this woman didn't belong behind a bar – in this place or any other. He was surprised to see what he felt like was a genuine smile on the lady's face, as she walked over to his end of the bar. "I'm glad you walked away and didn't punch him," she said, grabbing a towel and wiping the bar in front of where he was sitting.

"Excuse me?" Allen wasn't expecting any sort of conversation.

"The jerk," She gestured over her shoulder with her thumb, towards Johnny, "I'm glad that you showed restraint."

"Yeah, why is that?"

"Because you look like a nice guy," she explained. "One who doesn't need the drama...and he's just a jackass who comes in here starting trouble all of the time. Can I get you a drink?"

"Yeah…sure, whatever you have on tap," Allen said.

She pulled a mug from under the bar top and filled it up with something dark. Allen thanked her as she brought it over and handed her a ten dollar bill. She walked to the other end of the bar where the cash register was located. Allen couldn't help but to watch her go. He guessed that she was in her mid-thirties at least, but her body was that of a twenty year old. She was put together extremely well. After a couple of minutes, she returned with his change. Allen waved it off and told her to keep it. "The beer was only four dollars," she said, but Allen still insisted that she keep it. It was a gesture that he would have insisted on even if she'd looked like Hillary Clinton. He was always a good tipper when he had the means to be, but after thinking about it, he sort of regretted giving such a big tip in this case. She probably got big tips all night long, from every man that came through here. Allen continued watching her, as she chatted with another customer down the bar. She was graceful - didn't miss a beat, or a chance to smile and make eye contact as she poured drinks and took the money. Bartending was a craft, and it was one that she'd perfected. Allen could see the almost hypnotic effect that she had on the men, and even some of the women. Money was flying from their hands, left and right. There were two tip jars - strategically placed at either end of the bar and they were both nearly over-flowing with money. After a few minutes, a man in a blue button up shirt made his way behind the bar and emptied half of the tips from the jars into a bag. *Clever,* Allen thought, *Leave some of it in there, to encourage more!* The pretty bartender was noticeably uncomfortable, as the man in the blue shirt passed behind her and said something that Allen couldn't hear. She smiled anyway, as his hands lingered a little too long on her hips. Blue Shirt got a ledger of some kind from below the countertop and on his way out, touched her hip again. *There you have it,* Allen thought, *Mr. Pretty Bartender.* None of these guys throwing money at her ever really had a chance, did they? She was just working them, the way a stripper worked the idiot's that sat at the edge of the runway. Only this woman was pretty enough to do it with her clothes on. *Oh well,* Allen sipped his draft, *the dream was nice while it lasted!*

He spun in his stool, facing the line dancing crowd, to see if he could spot a girl more his caliber, perhaps a fat one – blind, or mildly retarded. He was admittedly getting a little desperate these days. He hadn't been with a woman in months other than that barfly, Tina, and he'd been so drunk with her, he couldn't even remember any of the details. It wasn't that he'd had any trouble picking women up – he was a decent, if not semi attractive man. He'd just been too busy with his own self-loathing over the last few months, that he hadn't made the effort to try and meet anyone. Come to think of it, he'd replaced having women in his life with a bottle. He'd been content with that for a time, but right now he was craving a woman's attention. He was distracted in his quest to find a member of the fairer sex to hang out with, when he spotted Robert, among the line dancers. His cousin was holding firmly to his oversized belt buckle and dancing in a very animated style; one that appeared more like a nitwit trying to look like a country western dancer than an actual country western dancer. Allen couldn't help but laugh, as he watched the show that Robert was putting on out on the floor. After a few minutes, and as the song wound down, a voice spoke from behind him.

"That guy was really getting into it, huh?"

Allen turned around to find the bartender leaning on the bar right behind him. She was laughing at Robert also.

"Yeah," Allen said, "what a clown. Poor fellow will probably be ashamed tomorrow, when he sobers up."

She laughed, "Can I get you another beer?"

Allen looked at his glass and was surprised at how quickly he'd emptied it. He nodded in agreement. When she returned with his change, this time Allen took four of the one dollar bills and slid her two of them. She smiled at him and said, "You know...that usually works the other way around!"

"What's that?" Allen asked.

"The tips usually increase as the night wears on!" She stuffed the two dollars into the nearby tip jar. "What did I do wrong?"

Allen smiled at her this time. "I was tipping you big the first time, with the hope of getting your name. It didn't work out, so I thought I would save my money this time around."

"Demri," she said, and held out her hand.

Allen laughed and placed another dollar in it. "Well Demri, it's very nice to meet you!"

"What's yours?" she asked.

"Allen," he answered, and took the dollar back out of her hand.

She laughed again, "So, that's how it's going to be?"

Allen shrugged his shoulders and sipped his beer, "It's only fair."

A guy in a brown sport coat, down on the other end of the bar, began to tap his knuckles on the bar top, indicating that he needed a refill. She went to attend him. Every man in this place was competing for her attention. Allen couldn't help but think of what an asset she must be to the owner of the place. He imagined the customers that she must bring in all by herself. Across the room, he saw Blue Shirt, sitting in a booth alone, watching as Demri interacted with the customers. Allen guessed that he must be the owner. He was a small, well-groomed man. The kind of guy that gauged his self-worth by the possessions that he could acquire. It was a list that probably included a nice house, a Porsche – maybe a garage full of other man toys. Allen was also willing to bet that there was something between him and Demri. If not right now, surely at some point or another. The man had a packed house on a Friday night and apparently all that he could find to do was to sit and watch his girlfriend. *What an insecure prick*, Allen took another swig.

Blue shirt caught Allen staring, making him immediately feel like a weirdo. He tried to play it off, with a cliché raise of the beer mug, but the man only stared at him with an expressionless gaze. *Rude Prick!* Allen shook his head and faced the bar again. To his delight, Demri was heading back down to his end. Allen watched her eyes, as she approached and realized that they were not focused on him, but on something else, directly over his shoulder. Just as he turned to see what had distracted her, he was patted on the shoulder. "What's up 'cuz," Robert nudged in between him and an irritated looking, husky girl. She was wearing a blond wig, and had on a pink cowgirl hat. Robert wedged in with sweat pouring down his face and the collar of his shirt soaked through. Allen felt like crawling under the barstool to escape the forthcoming humiliation of being associated with the village imbecile. He'd decided on getting up and leaving, but knew that the gig was up. Everyone in the place knew that he and Robert were together by now. Besides, Robert was the only cousin who had really made Allen feel welcome since he'd arrived. So what if the guy was a spectacle. Instead of walking away, Allen teased, "Hey Robert. That was some mighty fine dancing out there."

"Told ya!" Robert said, "You can't hang!" It was a statement to which

Allen had no comment. He was doing his best to ignore Robert at the moment anyhow. Allen wanted him to leave quickly and thought that if he didn't have much to say, Robert would go back over to the table with the rest of them. Demri had gone back to the other end of the bar and Allen was hoping to god that she didn't come to his end until after Robert was gone. No such luck! She caught Allen's eye, smiled, and walked toward them.

"Hey, Robert," she said, when she got close.

Robert replied, "Good evening Demri, can I get a beer, please." She popped the top on a Coors and set it in front of Robert.

"You two know each other?" Allen asked.

"Sure do," Robert said, "We went to school together since about third grade. Ain't that right Demri?" He leaned over and whispered into Allen's ear, even though Demri could hear everything that he said. "We used to date!"

Allen damn near dropped his beer.

She leaned on the bar in front of them, "I don't know if calling someone your girlfriend in the fourth grade, even when they didn't agree with you, constitutes as dating, but ok! Whatever you say, Robert."

"She's always been a bit of a snob," Robert whispered again, only this time trying to hide his lips behind his beer bottle.

"I can still hear you, Robert," She said. He flashed her a toothless grin. "How do you two know each other?" she asked.

Before Allen could answer, Robert said, "That's my dad's, sister's, boy!" It sounded like something someone would say in a spaghetti western movie.

"We're cousins," Allen said.

She nodded and said, "Yeah, I got that."

Allen finished his beer in one final gulp, set the empty bottle down on the bar with a twenty dollar bill and said, "Thanks for the drinks."

He left Robert and Demri and passed the rest of his family at the round table as he headed towards the exit door. He'd had enough of the dark cloud of embarrassment that seemed to hover over these back wood redneck cousins of his and he decided to get some fresh air. On his way to the door, he noticed the man in the blue shirt still watching him. Allen met the strangers gaze as he went past the table. He thought that he could see confusion and jealousy in the man's eyes. Jealousy of the attention that Allen had been receiving from Demri, and confusion as to why Allen would walk away from her when he was getting it. Allen was a little confused by his actions also, but he couldn't take any more of Robert ruining his chance to make a good first impression. Instead, he went out of the front door, stood under the Kingfish sign, and lit a cigarette. He didn't smoke much anymore, but he always kept a pack with him, especially when he was drinking. He stood in the warm Mississippi evening, watching the traffic pass out on the main road. A group of people came out of the bar behind him and he could hear that the Beerbellies had started their second set. All the more reason to be outside he thought.

He finished his cigarette and stomped it out on the ground, and as he was walking back to the door, it flew open. A large group of people poured out from entry way. Behind the first wave, Tommy was escorted out, with a bouncer under each arm. He was followed by Chris getting the same service. Allen ran over at just about the time that the bouncers turned Tommy and Chris loose. "What the fuck?" Allen said, as Tommy jumped back at one of the bouncers.

"Johnny's in there fighting with the Bikers," he motioned to the bar. Allen started to go back inside when Johnny, Robert, and Dewayne came from around the back of the building. "Screw this place man!" Johnny was screaming like an immature teenager. He had a red cheek that was starting to swell - Dewayne had a bloody nose and was trying to stop the blood with the sleeve of his shirt. "Why in the fuck are they allowed to stay?" Johnny asked one of the bouncers. "Bring their asses out here so we can finish this."

The only response that he got from the bouncer, who was comically dressed in a red and white plaid tablecloth shirt and overalls, was a firm, "Sir, you need to leave."

Johnny got chest to chest with the bouncer, a man that could fill in as a silver back gorilla in his spare time, and said, "Well, fuck you too," Johnny pointed in the bouncer's face.

Luckily for all of them, Tommy grabbed Johnny by the arm and pulled him to the truck. Allen started the engine as the rest climbed in. Allen was about to put the truck into reverse when Johnny jumped out of the truck and ran over to the line of motorcycles. He pushed every single one of them over before running back to the truck, yelling, "DRIVE...DRIVE!"

Allen quickly threw the truck into gear and reversed out of the spot. As he put the truck into drive and mashed the accelerator, the front doors of the Kingfish flew open and a horde of angry bikers came swarming out, swearing and throwing beer bottles at Allen's Land Rover, as is sped out of the lot.

3

When Lionel Taylor was eighteen years old, he broke into the neighbor's barn - stealing a circular saw, a level, and a tool box full of hand-tools; he was caught and convicted of burglary. In all, the goods could have been purchased new for a few hundred dollars, at most. In court he learned that the law valued the tools at more than fifteen hundred dollars. Of course, that was the price after the neighbor tacked on some extra "missing" items, in an attempt to raise his insurance claim. If Lionel remembered correctly, a generator and a roto-tiller were on the list by the time that he went before the judge. He didn't remember seeing those items in the barn in the first place – much less ever leave the barn carrying all of that shit.

He'd likely never have been caught if he'd done what he originally intended to do, which was give the tools to his father, but addiction can cloud and distort a mind, and good intentions never get realized and rarely even remembered.

Instead of giving the tool box to his father, he took the stolen goods to a local pawn shop, to trade for some cash. Little did he know, the rightful owner of the tools had visited the pawn shop before he arrived and was looking for his property. The neighbor left word with the owner of the store to give him a call if someone showed up with the goods. Lionel fell right into the trap and took twenty dollars for everything that he stole. The pawn shop owner did as he was asked and contacted the barn owner, letting him know that a young man by the name of Lionel Taylor had just been in and sold him the level, the wrenches and screwdrivers, and the toolbox for twenty bucks. He failed to mention that he also took in a circular saw in the deal, but probably figured that it was due payment for doing his good deed to the barn owner. Oh, and by the way, he wanted his twenty dollars back once they apprehended Lionel - the thief.

The police were waiting for Lionel by the time that he made it back home. Luckily, his dealer wasn't anywhere to be found on the way home, or else he would have been charged with the drug possession to boot. He was charged, however, with stealing the items that he was actually guilty of taking, along with the items that he didn't take - the roto-tiller and the generator. The circular saw, generator, and tiller were never recovered. The barn owner profited because he screwed the insurance company by lying about the tiller and generator. The pawn shop owner profited because he got all of his money back, plus the saw which he probably sold for at least one hundred dollars. In truth, there were multiple criminals involved, but Lionel was the only one convicted. The justice system, huh?

Overall, Lionel spent three weeks in jail over the ordeal. It was not his only time locked up, but it was the first and that made it special – lessons learned in the value of cigarettes and Vaseline. It was also upon his release that he was legally unable to own a handgun in the State of Mississippi from then on. This didn't deter Mr. Taylor from giving Lionel a revolver, right after Lionel and Denise got married and moved into the apartment building downtown. Criminal record or not, Jasper Taylor wasn't going to let his son and new daughter in-law live downtown without some protection in the house.

Lionel sat on the edge of the bed, holding the .38 caliber pistol. The memories of his father brought tears to his eyes. He laid the gun on the bed beside him and walked over to a small table. It was covered with cigarette burns and small aluminum foil wrappers. It was the nicest room in the Rolla Rancho Motel, a throwback establishment to days long past that was only holding on by allowing payment by the hour. Lionel's prepaid four hour stay was down to the last twenty minutes. His intention had been to catch some sleep, but he found that it was impossible with his parents constantly on his mind – he couldn't rest. He considered calling Denise - telling her the bad news – considered begging her to come take him away from here, but he doubted that she would even answer the phone. She was finished with him - he knew it! She blamed the drugs, but he knew that she was done with him long before smoking this shit had ever become a problem. They were never right for each other. Sometimes that was how it went. She just happened to realize it long before he did. Besides, she was probably halfway back to her sister's house in Indianapolis by now.

There wasn't any reason to bring her into this mess anyway. What he was about to do would only tangle her up in a bunch of ugliness. No - he would keep her out of it. He owed her that much. Besides, he didn't need anyone trying to talk him out of it. That piece-of-shit, cracker-assed Johnny Blackwood was going to pay for what he did, and Lionel wasn't going to trust the system to get it right for him. He'd learned that the system didn't get shit right! Especially not when it was poor black accusing rich white - not in Mississippi! Lionel was going to do it himself. Johnny was going to get what he had coming, along with anybody else that got in the way.

Lionel picked his glass pipe up off of the table and lit the end with his lighter. The sweet, acrid smoke filled the pipe first - then his lungs. He held the smoke in for as long as he could, before feeling like his lungs were going to explode. Then he exhaled slowly and laid the pipe back down on the table beside the empty foil wrapper that formerly held the crack now coursing through his body. He immediately started to sweat and felt powerful - like he could tear the room apart with his bare hands if he'd wanted to. He stuffed the pipe into his pocket and went to the dirty sink, ran cold water into his hands and splashed it onto his face and neck. Then he grabbed the gun off of the bed, tucked it into the waist band of his pants and left the room, slamming the door behind him as he went.

4

T he alarm clock was buzzing loudly and apparently had been doing so for some time. Aunt Patsy came into the room to wake Allen up. He'd set the clock before dozing off with a spinning head last night. Things had grown considerably less interesting once he returned to Otis's house and left the company of his cousins. He'd felt tired before they'd gone to the Kingfish Lounge, but once they returned and after the excitement with the bikers, he was wide awake. He laid down, but couldn't get himself to sleep. Eventually, he just sat up in his bed watching the news. After that, he watched some talk show on comedy central, hosted by some cynical asshole who made a point to be as gross and absurd as possible. It was a feeble appeal to the younger generation of what Allen liked to refer to as a culture in decline. Eventually, he switched the television off and lay in the dark. His mind kept returning to the bartender, Demri. He hadn't even caught her last name. His somewhat impaired and very exhausted consciousness was convinced that she'd shown him a little more attention than the other men at the bar. Then again, what in the hell did he know? Even if that had been the case, it was before Robert, the Rodeo Clown, came over and made an ass of them both. He wished that he hadn't gotten up and walked away, but stayed and talked to her while he had the chance. He could have asked her questions that were driving him nuts like, do you have a steady boyfriend? What is your last name? Or, could I please, please have your phone number?

He'd finally fallen asleep around 3:00 a.m. Patsy roused him as she shut off the alarm. "Get up young'un," she said, as she pulled the curtains in his room open.

"Oh, come on…" He protested, as the morning sun hit his eyes. He pulled a pillow over his face, "I just need another hour."

"No can do! Otis is waiting for you in the garage," she said.

Allen sat upright in the bed and looked at the clock. It read 8:06, in big red blinking letters. He'd forgotten all about meeting Otis at 8:00 this morning. "Shit," he grumbled, jerking the covers off of himself and springing from the bed. Patsy covered her face and left the room, closing the door as she went. Before Allen realized it, he was standing in the middle of the room in his underwear. "Sorry Patsy," Allen yelled through the closed door, "At least I had underwear on this morning."

As she headed down the hall she said, "Get yourself dressed, boy and don't make your Uncle wait for you any longer than he already has!"

Allen threw on jeans and a shirt and hurried down to the garage where Otis was waiting. He found the old man with his walking cane in his left hand and a polishing cloth in his right. Otis was gently rubbing the fender of a 1956 Bellaire convertible. "Sorry to keep you waiting," Allen said, coming in the side entrance of the garage. Otis just waved him off and finished polishing the fender. "You know…" he said, "I've always liked this one. Let's drive *it* today."

They took the car out to the old house in the woods – this time, Allen stopped where the overgrowth hung over the dirt road and broke some of the branches back, so that he didn't have to worry about scratching this car, like he'd done the Charger. On the way out Otis didn't say much, but once they parked in front of the old Blackwood family home, he leaned against the hood and said, "I'm sorry that you felt like you were left in the dark during the swamp run. You have every right, as an active member of this family business, to know what it is that you are getting involved with. That being said, once I have shared with you what it is that I am about to share, you can by no means ever tell another soul. I don't think that you would. But if you did, the consequences would by severe…for us *all*!" Allen wasn't sure, but if he didn't know any better Otis had just threatened him. He was beginning to get the feeling that whatever was going on was a lot bigger than homemade moonshine.

Otis continued… "My daddy started this business back in the twenties, with the help of me, my brother, and my sister. He believed that there was no greater bond than that of a family and therefore, felt like there wasn't anyone on the outside that could be trusted with the family secrets. Ultimately, the business cost my sister her life, and it cost me and my dad our relationship with my brother…your grandfather! Dad and I did what we could to keep on making our whiskey. Distributing it far and wide, just the two of us; we kept the business alive. He always laughed and said that once I had kids, we would have more help. At the time, I thought that he was kidding around, but I later found out that he was serious. I married your greataunt Victoria, may god rest her soul, in nineteen thirty-eight, and we tried and tried to have children, and believe me…trying was the fun part…" He gave Allen a little wink and a smile, "…but it turned out that Victoria was barren and unable to bare children." Otis's thoughts seemed to trail off slightly. Then he continued, "Mom died first, and after a while dad died too. Then it was all on my shoulders to keep this family business alive. For quite some time I debated on whether or not to just quit running the shine altogether…take a legitimate job, but to do so, I would have been walking away from everything that my dad had spent his life working to build, what he'd sacrificed so much for! I just couldn't give that up. Years went by and I made just enough money to cover the ingredients of each batch, but you see money wasn't the problem. No sir, money was never a problem! Daddy had left enough of the green stuff so I'd never have to work another day in my life. Hell, if invested the right way, maybe two or three lifetimes. The problem that eventually came up was that the customers began to dwindle and the demand dried up. Good whiskey became easier to get and through legal means. I just shut the still down… didn't do much in the line of making anything at all for about twelve years or so. Victoria and I lived quietly out here in this house for several of those years. Then I built her the main house. She'd always wanted a big house. She dreamed of having family around someday and wanted room enough for everyone. She was so excited when construction began. She worried the builders over everything to make sure that it turned out just right. She would have driven the damn nails into the wood herself, if I would have let her. She stayed on top of everything and when it was finished, it was marvelous. Unfortunately, she was only able to live in it for about a year, before she got the cancer, and had to go stay in the hospital. My sweet Victoria died less than two years after we finished the house."

"Otis, I'm sorry, I know that must have been hard," Allen said, feeling the old man's pain.

Otis just kept on talking, like he didn't even hear Allen. He was disconnected from the here and now, reliving the past in his mind. "Her passing threw me for a loop! I didn't know what to do with myself at that point. One day I found myself sitting in my empty living room and I realized that without her...I had no purpose. There was no one left for me to take care of. Victoria was dead, my Mom and my Dad were both dead, Betsy was dead, and Artie was out on the east coast, doing whatever it was that he was doing back then. I spent much of my time taste testing my family recipes. Trying to dull the pain of being alone. At times, I contemplated sticking the barrel of a shotgun into my mouth, to end the misery of loneliness. I couldn't bear the idea of being left behind by everyone that I'd loved.

Through an act of desperation, I sent a letter to the address that I had for Artie and Gladys. In it, I begged for my brother to forget his blood feud and put the past behind us. He never replied; guess he wasn't willing to move on and let the past go. Never heard from him! But reaching out to my brother wasn't totally in vain. About six months after I sent the letter, two of his children whom I had never met until that moment, showed up at my doorstep. I had never laid eyes on them before that day, but as they stood on my doorstep that fall afternoon, there was no mistaking that they were Blackwoods.

The oldest, Conrad looked just like my daddy, Clyde. The other, Kirk looked so much like my sister Betsy, that I cried right there on the porch. The two boys...or, I should say men at that point in their lives, had a note from their mother Gladys, addressed to me. It said that the family was having a difficult time in Virginia and were living in near destitution. This was due mostly to the fact that my brother had become an alcoholic and rather than taking care of his family, he spent his time running the roads with whores and passed out drunk in alleyways far from home. He wasted the little money that he earned through odd jobs on poker and booze, when he should have been working a steady job and at home, taking care of his own. The boys told me that their father would stay gone for weeks at a time, and when he did come home, it was long enough to take whatever money his wife had managed to earn, and to beat on her and the children, if they had the audacity to mention him being gone all of the time. Before long, he would be off again, gone for weeks straight sometimes.

I was disappointed to hear that this was happening, and there was no way that I could let Gladys and her children…the last of my living relatives, go on living like this. This was the only family that I had left and I immediately wanted to take care of them. So I offered to take everyone in and provide a better life for them. I sent a letter to Gladys, saying that she and the kids should come to Mississippi and live with me, and hopefully we could convince Artie to do the same once he resurfaced again. Unfortunately, my letter arrived to Gladys at one of the rare times that Artie was home and he was the one that read it. He accused her of having an affair with me and from what I hear, he almost killed her from the beating that he gave her that night. Elmer and your mother were there at the time, since they were both too young to have traveled with Conrad and Kirk. I heard that he beat those kids around pretty good also. Elmer, being the boy, got it the worst. They told me that Artie nearly killed the little boy, who was only trying to defend his mother and sister. It wasn't until months later, when Kirk traveled home to visit his mother that he found out what had happened."

Otis and Allen walked around the side of the old house along a dirt path as they talked. Up ahead was a small cemetery - surrounded by a black iron fence and grown over with ivy. Beside the gate, leading up to a group of headstones, was a stone bench. Otis slowly walked over to the cemetery and leaned on the fence in order to catch his breath. He took a seat on the bench, leaving enough room for Allen to sit beside him. Allen didn't want to sit and instead inspected the headstones. It was the who's who of Otis's life. One was marked for Victoria Blackwood, one for Bessie Blackwood, one for Ellie Blackwood, and one for Clyde.

"What did Kirk do when he found out that grandpa beat everyone over the letter?" Allen asked. Otis took a deep breath of the oxygen from the bottle that he had draped over his shoulder like a purse. The plastic mask hung around his neck much like the way that a world war two pilot would have worn it. To Allen, Otis didn't look very much like a world war two pilot. He looked like a depleted old man. His eyes were hollow and bloodshot, his skin - white and blotchy. The neck that was showing from the collar of his shirt was thin, lacking any muscle at all. It was a miracle that it could still support the weight of his head. As Otis spoke, Allen could almost see the words as they came up his narrow throat. "I believe that if Kirk could have gotten his hands on Artie at the time…he would have probably shot him through the heart. But as was the norm, Artie was off on one of his adventures and he never came back home the whole time that Kirk was there, though Kirk waited for weeks. Eventually, without knowing if his father would ever return, Kirk decided to head back to Mississippi. He intended to bring his mother and siblings, but Gladys would have no part of coming. She insisted that Elmer and Clara go with Kirk. She knew that they would be safer out here with me. Elmer was willing and came without a second thought – the beating that he'd received had made up his mind that he never wanted to see Artie again. Clara, always the good daughter, insisted on staying with her mother. I've always admired that about her. Knowing full well that there wouldn't be anyone else around to take the punishment when her father came home… she still insisted on staying there with her mother."

"So, she stayed?" Allen was confused.

"No," Otis continued, "She wanted to, but Gladys insisted that she come with her brothers…reluctantly, she did."

"Is that when she met my father?" Allen was starting to put the pieces together.

Otis nodded, "Stephen Gilmour!" He said it like the taste of the words were bitter in his mouth.

Allen knew that there had been some bad blood between his mother and his father, hence, the reason Stephen had abandoned his pregnant wife and unborn son. From what Allen's mother had told him, the guy was a deadbeat and when he left in the dead of night so long ago, he'd actually done them both a favor. "Did you know my father very well?"

Otis shrugged his frail shoulders, "Nobody knew him well…he was a bit of a mystery. He stuck around here for a little while…just long enough for him and your momma to get smitten, then he was gone!" Otis looked at the ground as he spoke, "That fella was no good…he really hurt your momma."

"Why'd he leave?"

Otis toyed with a brown leaf with the toe of his expensive leather shoes, "Can't say for certain! Why do people ever do the things that they do?" He looked at Allen in the eyes, "Either love, or greed! That's all that motivates any of us…I guess!"

"Yeah…I guess!" Allen agreed.

Otis smiled, "I understand that once Clara was back at home with her mother and father things got a little better. Artie settled down a little bit as he got older, but by then, most of his family was out here with me. The three of them continued to struggle financially, all the way up until his death. Even then, on his death bed, he refused to have any part of my help." Otis took another breath from his oxygen tank. "But I can sleep at night, knowing that I tried…" He patted Allen on the leg. "…and having you here gives me the opportunity to do more!" He stood up, "My chance to atone for my sin's, if you will!"

Allen put his arm around his Great Uncle, "I appreciate that, Uncle Otis."

"I know you do!" Otis said, and then he continued his story, "About thirty years ago, with the expanded family here, and no work to speak of for anyone to do, we had to come up with a business, to keep money in everybody's pocket without draining the family bank. Seeing as the only thing that I was able to do to make good money was illegal bootlegging, it only made sense that we start up the family business again. The problem was, I had been out of the business for quite a while and by now, people could go down to the local liquor store and buy their whiskey without the risk of having run-ins with the law. No one was going to pay top dollar for bootleg anymore. It was the early seventies, and the new craze at that time was this thing called LSD. When I looked closely at the possibility, it didn't appear to be all that much different than bootlegging whiskey had been back in the old days. So we learned how to make it, and we found a way to sell it in bulk, using the same business model that my daddy came up with back in the twenties. It took some time, but we were able to work our way into the local market. Then we branched out from there. Soon, we were across the whole state of Mississippi, and then the Gulf Coast region. Within about ten years, we were making twice as much money as we ever did selling moonshine. Then it was ten times."

"So what we took into the swamp last night was acid?" Allen was shocked.

"No," Otis waived him off like the notion was preposterous, "LSD was the drug of the seventies. It was cocaine in the eighties and crystal meth in the nineties. Today, it's heroin."

Hearing the old man explain the drug trends of each decade was a little bit comical and despite the smile that spread across his lips, Allen was not sure how he felt about it. Drugs were never really his thing. Aside from being on the purchasing end of a few bags of weed, he'd never tried much. He most certainly had never been a drug dealer and becoming one had never crossed his mind either. He wondered, *just how in the hell could his life get any more complicated?*

Otis took notice of Allen's facial expression. It must have been one of concern, because Otis asked, "Is there anything that you want to ask?"

As a matter of fact, Allen's mind was flooded with questions. The one that came out when he opened his mouth was, "Why sell drugs?"

"Pardon me?' Otis said, with the air of the dignified southern gentleman that he appeared to be on the surface.

Allen was slowly beginning to see that there was a less admirable side to his uncle. "I could be wrong, but it looks like you have more money than you could ever spend. You have obviously lived a long and prosperous life. Why continue to take the chances?"

Otis took a drag of oxygen and asked, "How much money is enough?"

"What?"

"How much is enough?" Otis repeated, "You tell me how much money that I need, to make sure that all of my family is taken care of forever, and I will stop."

"Uncle Otis, it's not your responsibility to take care of everybody…"

"What do you know of responsibility?" Otis's face reddened. It was the first time that Allen had seen the old man lose his composure. "You have never been concerned with anything but yourself. My father vowed to take care of his family, and he risked everything, every single day that he lived, to see that it was done. He created this business…this beast. It became a powerful thing - a living thing. It grew and grew and needed constant minding. Though it was dangerous, it provided for our family beyond our wildest imaginations. When he died, it became my responsibility. I can't possibly just stop giving my family the means to provide for their own. I would be turning my back on the most important lesson that my father ever taught me, and that is to take care of your kin." He looked away from Allen. Otis watched as a gentle breeze blew off of the bayou and rustled the tops of the cypress trees. "Artie didn't understand that. He never learned that lesson. He always did what he thought was best for himself only. Look at what happened to his side of the family. Our father would be ashamed...I am ashamed. I will not let myself, or my family down like that...EVER!"

Allen didn't know what to say. He could see that Otis was upset, and in no way did he want to be responsible for causing the old man any grief, but it was at that very moment that Allen realized that he couldn't stay here. He just didn't feel comfortable being a part of something like this. Otis was wise and he could tell what Allen was thinking, without Allen saying so. He nodded his head and placed his hand on Allen's shoulder. "On some matters, we see things differently. I understand your reservations, and I respect them..." He looked Allen directly in the eyes again, and Allen couldn't help but to admire the dignity and respect that those old eyes commanded. Allen thought that Otis must have been quite a man back in the old days. "...you are a part of this family, whether you are a part of the business or not, and you will want for nothing, for as long as you are here. That being said, I wouldn't go and tell your cousins that you know what it is that we do. They might feel a little bit nervous when they learn that you decided to back out, once you learned the truth."

"No problem..." Allen said, "...I won't say a word."

"That's good..." Otis said, he patted Allen's cheek with his hand. It felt cold and frail on his face. "...now let me spend a few quiet moments with my wife, before we head back." Allen helped his Great Uncle with the latch on the cemetery gate. It was rusted and difficult to open, but with a little effort Allen was able to let Otis in. The old man stood in front of the family gravestones with his head bowed, Allen stood by the car and waited. While Otis prayed, Allen debated whether or not he had made a mistake by coming to Mississippi in the first place. Thanks for the surprise, mom.

5

Lashauna was sitting at her desk, reviewing photos of the Taylor crime scene. The pictures that were taken inside the house of the bodies made her skin crawl. She tried to not get emotionally attached to her cases, but sometimes she just couldn't disconnect. What had happened to these people really pierced her deep. The couple reminded her of her own parents. They were all about the same age. It was scary that one senseless, random act could take them from her in an instant. She wanted to call her mother – just to hear her voice, but as she reached for the phone, Leo came in carrying a brown envelope with a big smile on his face. "What's made you so happy?" He forgot about the phone call for now. He sat down across from her and tossed the envelope on top of the photos. "What's this?" she asked.

"That, partner, is the report on the plaster tire molds that we took from the driveway and from Lionel's car."

She opened the package and skimmed over the information. Like most police reports, it was diluted with acronyms and confusing verbiage - included so that the lawyers and the doctors could talk a little bit above the average citizen, while they explained things to a jury in court. In her opinion, it was a feeble attempt to try and justify the price that they had paid to hold their title. It should be written the way people talk to eliminate confusion. Lashauna dismissed most of the filler as unnecessary bullshit, and would be happy if the page had only one or two sentences - the necessary facts. Attached to the back was a diagram, an overview of the Taylor property and a location of all of the tire tracks found at the scene. She tossed the paperwork onto her desk and said, "Ok, so what's it say?" She knew that Leo would have already deciphered the jargon and he could summarize it quicker than she could read it. "Well, in a nutshell…you were right!" He explained, "We matched Lionel's tire tread pattern and those of his parent's car to *some* of the tracks…but that was expected right?"

"Ok," She leaned back in her chair and crossed her arms. She knew that Leo liked to talk things out the long way when he explained them. It helped him to put the pieces together in his mind. She was beginning to wonder if it would have been quicker for her to just read the report.

"So, what they found was a good set that didn't match those of either of the Taylor cars," he said with a smile. "The mystery tires, if you will, are a Goodyear all season triple tread with a match size of 255-60-17."

Still, she reclined in her chair and waited for the hook. She knew him well enough to know that he was stringing her along now. It made him feel good to be explaining things to her for a change. He leaned back in his own chair to match her posture. She smiled and thought that the only thing that he was missing in his moment of triumph, was a cigar.

He continued, "So, what was the type of car that Elmer Blackwood reported stolen, according to the police report?"

"Bullshit," she opened her desk drawer and produced the stolen car report that she pulled not long after leaving the Blackwood's property the other day. She found the line that stated the vehicle type. "…a 2008 Lincoln Town Car."

"…and guess what size tires are standard on a 2008 Town Car," Leo smiled.

"How do you know that?" She asked.

"I asked Google."

Lashauna reviewed the report. This time a little more closely. She hadn't paid very much attention before - when it was just a random stolen car report, but now she looked at the date that the report was written. "Leo, what day did we get the call to go to the Taylor's house?"

Leo looked up at the ceiling, as if the answer were written on the tile above his head. "I think it was the twentieth. I could check the report…"

"No…your right…it was the twentieth. I just wanted to double check." She handed him the stolen vehicle report. "Look at the date of this report."

Leo did. At the top of the page in the date column, it read 7/20/15. Leo looked up at Lashauna, "Is it a coincidence that Lionel showed up at the Blackwood cookout the other day?"

"Nothing's ever a coincidence," she said. "Contact the local PD and tell them to copy us on anything that they find related to this stolen vehicle." She started clearing the photos off of her desk. "I think it's time that we interview Elmer Blackwood regarding his missing car."

6

The boat bumped against a large cypress branch, which was floating in the dark, murky water. Johnny eased back the throttle a little and brought the skiff to a slow crawl. The last thing that he needed was to punch a hole in the fiberglass hull, way out here in no-man's-land. He looked all around him – nothing but swamp and forest. Although he'd been out here a million times over the course of his life – it was rare that he ventured this far out during the daylight hours. Things looked different in the daytime – foreign. Nonetheless, he recognized exactly where he was. Nearly every inch of the swamp looked exactly the same to someone who wasn't as familiar, but Johnny spent much of his childhood out here in the Whiskey Bayou. When he and Chris were little, back before their father had died, Conrad would bring them out here and drop them off. He told them that their Great Uncle Otis had found his way home from out here when he was only a young boy. If Johnny and Chris were worth anything, they could do the same.

Johnny remembered how terrifying it was to be all alone out here in the wilderness. *Funny thing, thinking back on it, it always seemed that he was alone, but Chris had been with him - hadn't he?* It had always seemed that having Chris with him was usually no better than being alone. His little brother was barely more than a piece of baggage that Johnny had to carry through the swamp and everywhere else they'd gone. Johnny had always known that his brother was - different. Their daddy called him thick-headed, or slow. Conrad used to say that Chris's brain orphaned his body at birth. Conrad had called them both names when they were young though. Conrad even told his boys that the reason that their momma ran off when they were young was because she was ashamed of her children, because Chris was slow, he would say and Johnny was mean spirited. *Fuck them!* Johnny muttered aloud to no one. He hoped that his mother and father were both burning in hell, all alone - right now.

He looked out into the distance and saw a deer through the trees. He remembered how it felt the first time that he'd killed one. It was the first thing that he'd ever killed. Even though he was only twelve or thirteen at the time, he remembered being aroused by the feeling of taking the life. Hell, even just thinking about it right now was giving him an erection. The rush that he got from deciding the life or death of a living creature made him shiver. It made him feel alive, more powerful – god like. He considered stopping the boat and satisfying his need to kill, but decided to postpone it for later – he couldn't be late for his meeting. He was excited and could feel the tingling in his abdomen. He would take his time with the animal. It was an art form that a master couldn't rush. Art - oh yes - there was an art to it alright!

When he was young, Johnny liked to spend a lot of time out here, since there was an abundance of wildlife - he could fulfill his need. He cultivated the desires that he possessed out here in this swamp. He thanked his daddy for that. If Conrad hadn't dropped them off and made them fend for themselves, Johnny wasn't sure that he would have ever realized the gift that he had. He'd tried to show Chris the beauty of it, but Chris was too thick headed to appreciate it. Chris killed, but without experiencing the pleasure of it, and even pulling the trigger took some time. From as far back as he could remember, Johnny had to fend for both of them when they were alone. The burden infuriated Johnny and there were times that he considered placing his knife to Chris's throat and doing them both a favor. Chris wasn't like him – he didn't belong out here. No one would have ever known. Johnny could have just said that Chris disappeared, or was eaten by a gator, and nobody would have cared, especially not after their father died. No one paid either of them any mind. Nowadays, Johnny was glad that he hadn't killed Chris though. His little brother had become quite a useful tool for him. If Johnny was the artist, then Chris was his brush, and if things went well with this meeting that he was about to have, then the two of them were about to paint a masterpiece.

He pulled the boat up to the same pier that he'd visited just days before with his cousins. Even though he didn't see anyone else, he noticed a small john boat tied on the other end of the dock. He reached for the gun tucked into the waist line of his jeans and thumbed the safety off. Johnny tied the boat off and climbed out of the skiff, as two men emerged from the brush behind the cabin. One of them was tall and lanky and the other was a little shorter with a pear shape. Neither of them had a terribly intimidating look, in fact the shorter one reminded Johnny of an oversized toddler. Both of the men wore camouflage shirts and ball caps. Johnny would have mistaken them to be a couple of lost hunters, if he didn't recognize the tall man as Henry Stokes, the person that he was supposed to be meeting. Henry worked for a man named Fintan LaRue. LaRue was a distributor – one with connections deep enough to reach across the country. The other guy wasn't LaRue though - Johnny had no idea who he was.

"I thought I told you to come alone." Johnny said, as they approached him.

Henry replied, "Man, I wasn't coming all the way out here, to the middle of nowhere, by myself." He gestured to the baby faced, pear-shaped man. "This here's Sammy, my brother in law...he's down." Johnny quickly pulled his gun and pointed it at the shorter man, causing both men to raise their hands with their palms face out. "Whoa...hold on a minute there..." Henry said. The toddler faced man didn't say a word, but looked to Johnny like he had just shit his pants.

"I fucking told you to come alone," Johnny yelled.

"He's down man...he's down...". Henry pleaded.

"What the fuck does that mean...he's down?" Johnny held the gun in Sammy's face. "...and why are you talking to me like I'm some kind of a saggy pants gangster?"

"Man, I ain't talking to you no kind of way, Johnny...I'm just saying he's good...he's my family. Now Jesus Christ man...please, put the gun down so we can talk some business."

Johnny held the gun on Sammy for a few more seconds, and then he lowered it. "Get him away from me! He don't need to hear anything that I've got to say."

Both of the men simultaneously let out a sigh of relief. "Go sit in the boat, Sammy," Henry instructed his brother in law. Sammy didn't hesitate - he quickly scurried to the john-boat. Once he was gone, Henry looked at Johnny and said, "Now that was a little uncalled for...don't you think?

Johnny placed the pistol back into his waistband. "What I think is that if we are going to do business together, then you need to learn how to fucking follow directions."

Henry, not wanting to get into a pissing contest with Johnny over who should be calling the shots in their business endeavor, let the remark slide and went on to business. He had no intention of being out here in this god forsaken swamp any longer than absolutely necessary. "So look here," Henry said, "We have the local distribution set up to move as much product as you can deliver. Most of the pieces are in place...we are just missing one key part...the product. You said that you were good for some heavy volume and all that I've seen so far was enough for me and my neighbor to catch a quick buzz with. When can you deliver?"

"Soon," Johnny said.

"Soon ain't cutting it, Johnny. Mr. LaRue has a lot of time and money invested in this and he is ready to start seeing a return on his investment."

Johnny lit up a smoke and looked out at the muddy water slowly flowing past the pier. Uncle Otis was the main distributor of heroin in the region, but was unwilling to branch out further than the Bayou. Johnny knew that there was more money to be made out there - a lot more. Henry Stokes and Fintan LaRue were the conduits to nationwide distribution and more cash than any of them had ever seen. If Otis was unwilling to branch out, then Johnny was going to seize the opportunity for himself.

The problem was that this deal was taking a little longer to put together than he'd planned. That cocksucker, Lionel Taylor, had set him back some time by stealing his money. Money that he needed to invest in the chemicals to make the product. Johnny would set Lionel straight soon enough. In the meantime, he knew that he needed to get his plan in motion. He'd waited long enough. It was time for him to step out of the shadows and become the man that he was destined to be. He flicked his cigarette into the water and said to Henry, "You'll have all that you can handle by the end of the month."

IV

THE DYING OF
THE LIGHT

Allen raised the hood of his truck to check and see how the repairs were holding up. He pulled the oil dipstick and was not surprised to see that it was at least a full quart low. Next, he unscrewed the top to his radiator, to check the antifreeze. Luckily, that didn't look too bad. The reservoir was still full with the bright green antifreeze, just like it had been when MJ filled it up a couple of weeks back. Right beside Allen, little Ronnie scooted along Uncle Otis's driveway, in his plastic Fisher Price car. The toddler was wearing only a t-shirt and a diaper, which was enough for the hot and humid afternoon. Ronnie looked up at Allen and grinned from behind a pacifier that was stuck to his mouth. Ronnie's mother, Jennifer, sat in a lawn chair, making an effort to keep out of the sun. Allen thought that by the way that she was dressed, she belonged in an old time beach photo, where all of the women were covered with oversized hats and sunglasses that were so large they could easily be mistaken for car windshields. She sipped on a glass of ice tea and was thumbing her way through the latest issue of a Glamour magazine. Meanwhile, Ronnie was in the middle of the baby's first fender bender, when he plowed his toy car into the door of Allen's truck with such force that it shook the truck slightly.

"Ronnie," Jennifer said, from behind her magazine, "…you're gonna have to get out of that thing if you don't watch where you're going."

Allen smiled at Ronnie who smiled back at him and then reversed slightly, only to pull forward and do it again. Allen thought that the boy most likely did it on purpose the first time, just to get a little attention. "Aww…he ain't hurtin' nothing," Allen said, "Besides, I'm sure that he gets his bad driving honestly."

Jennifer lowered the magazine from in front of her, "What is that supposed to mean?"

"Nothing…just that I can already see that he takes after you when it comes to driving…that's all," Allen replaced the cap to his radiator. "Wasn't it you that drove through the front of a clothing store while you were trying to park?"

"That was a long time ago…" Jennifer smiled. "Maybe you're right…I do suck at driving."

Allen watched Ronnie head down the drive and away from where they were. "Do you need me to go and get him?"

"Naw…he'll be fine." Jennifer didn't seem concerned that the toddler was getting farther and farther away. "You really leaving?" Jennifer asked, like she was having a difficult time wrapping her mind around the fact that someone could actually walk away from this kind of luxurious living.

"Yeah," Allen said. He wanted to give her an explanation why, but he didn't know how much she knew about the family business, and didn't want to be the one to spill the beans, if she was oblivious. "I've got some things to take care of back home."

"When are you going?" she asked.

"Not sure…soon though! Hey…do you mind if I use your car for a little while?" Allen asked, looking at his oil dipstick again. "I need to go find an auto parts store and get some oil for my truck." He didn't want to risk driving it until he filled it up. He was sure that it wouldn't take long for the engine to overheat in this scorching heat.

"Sorry…but I can't," Jennifer explained. "I have to be up at the dealership in an hour. Me and Ronnie are getting ready to go." She stood up, set her magazine and her hat in the chair, and began to walk down the driveway. Ronnie was cruising and on his way to the main road. "Ask Uncle Otis! He'll let you use one of his cars."

Come to think of it, that sounded like an excellent idea to Allen. It was another opportunity for him to drive that Charger that he loved so much. "Good idea!" he yelled to his cousin, as she jogged to catch Ronnie, who was moving double time with his little legs to try and get away. Once she caught him, the toddler started to cry when she pulled him from the toy car. She carried the baby on her hip and attempted to pull the car back up the drive by herself, until Allen went out to lend a hand.

2

The engine rumbled as Allen slowly pulled away from the curb in front of Bell Auto Parts. The two clerks and a customer gathered at the building entrance to admire the rolling piece of classic art. Allen took his time getting down the road, so that everyone could get a good look. He felt a sense of pride to be driving a car like this one. It was certainly a rare pleasure that very few people got to experience these days. He stopped at a red light near the store and instead of turning right to head back to Violent Hill - he decided to prolong the motoring experience and turned left instead. Since he was planning on going back to Virginia, he might never get a chance to drive this car again. He wanted to prolong the experience for as long as he could. He drove for another ten miles, before deciding to head back. He'd pulled into a department store parking lot to get turned around. Once he spun the hot rod around, he caught the sight of a familiar sign across the street. He sat with the engine at idle and both hands on the wheel, as he stared out of the windshield. He tried to find a reason why he shouldn't go into the Kingfish Lounge and see if the bartender, Demri, was working today. It didn't take long to decide that seeing her one last time was worth the short trip across the street. Even if she wasn't working today, a stiff drink might do him some good.

He parked the Charger in the back of the building, where the parking lot was a little less crowded. He didn't want to take the car back to Otis with any new dings. As he approached the building in the daytime, it looked a lot less manicured than it had the other night. He walked in through the same doors that Johnny had been thrown out of on their last visit. The stage, like the rest of the bar, had an empty, hollow feel to it. Instead of the crowds and loud country music, there were only a few people inside – the lunch crowd. Most of the patrons were gathered around the bar - finishing up their liquid lunches as they glanced nervously over their shoulders, to make sure that it wasn't their boss that had just come through the front door. The stage was deserted except for the instruments, set in their stands, waiting in the darkness for Doublebarrel Darrell and the Beerbellies to show up on Friday and bring them back to life. Music played from the juke box and this time it was good old rock-and-roll - a Soundgarden tune that Allen kind of liked. His hopes of running into Demri were dispelled when he noticed that the person behind the bar was not the stunner that had him subconsciously drive across town to catch a glimpse of, but instead a chubby blonde. He took a seat on the same stool that he'd sat in the other night and motioned for the bartender. The blonde smiled and said, "One second, Hon." She rushed around the bar carrying a ketchup bottle - delivering it to a table that was occupied by four construction workers, currently giving their lunches such hell that they didn't even acknowledge she was there.

Allen was watching - trying to decide how the food looked and if he wanted to grab a bite or not, when the door to the kitchen swung open and Demri emerged carrying a box of beer. Allen watched as she opened the cooler doors and arranged the beer bottles inside. As impossible as it were, she looked better today than she had the other evening. Her hair was pulled back, and she wore tight fitting blue jeans that showed her figure.

On her second trip down to Allen's end of the bar, she noticed him. Demri smiled and stopped what she was doing, "Hey there...you're back!"

"That, I am," Allen agreed.

"Allen...wasn't it?" She asked.

"That's pretty good. I'm shocked...and frankly a little bit flattered that you remember," Allen smiled.

She smiled also and was so beautiful that Allen almost fell off of his stool. "If I remember correctly...that info cost me a couple of dollars," she teased.

Allen laughed, "Yeah...sorry about that."

"No problem," she was leaning on the bar in front of him now, "Allen Blackwood, I presume?"

"Yep," he said, "Is that good, or bad?"

"I don't know...most of those Blackwoods are pretty rowdy!"

154

Allen nodded his head. He couldn't disagree, "I'm not like the rest of them."

"Is that so?" She said, "You're special, huh?"

"Not special...but different."

"What makes you different, Allen Blackwood?"

"It's a long story," he said, "I'll fill you in some other time."

"You want a drink?" she asked.

"Do you have time to have one with me?"

"Not right now...sorry," she motioned to the open beer boxes and the mess on the bar.

"Later?" he asked.

She looked at the clock and caught herself doing it. Allen got the feeling that she was having some sort of inner conflict. He felt like she was close to a yes, but he was still expecting to get a no. If she said no, he'd resolved himself to having just one drink and leaving this place never to return. He could live with the fact that he'd given it a try - nothing ventured, nothing gained. After a full fifteen seconds she said, "Sure, I get off in thirty minutes. We can have one together."

Allen tried to hide his excitement, "I'll be waiting right here."

Demri finished stocking the beer coolers and wiped down the bar. Blondie was taking over the shift, so she and Demri counted the draw from the register and emptied the tip jars. When they were finished, Demri came around to the other side of the bar and sat on the stool right beside Allen. Blondie came over to take their order.

"What are you drinking?" Allen asked.

"I'll just have a Bud! Thanks, Krissy," Demri said to the blonde.

"I'll have a Black and Tan, please," Allen said, and Krissy went to retrieve the beers. Allen pulled twenty dollars out of his pocket and laid it on the bar for the drinks. Krissy returned with the bottles and took the twenty. Allen said, "Keep the change."

Once Krissy went back to her busy work, Demri took a sip of her beer and then got right to the point, "So, what's your story?"

"My story?" Allen asked. Demri sounded like a reporter trying to get information from an informant. He liked her direct approach though, "Well, let's see. Where to start...I was in the orphanage, with all of the

155

other little children, when the rich bald headed man came and adopted me. It was a hard knock life, ya know?"

Demri laughed, "I'll bet you were cute in the little red dress."

"Yeah, no one could wear it like me."

"You're funny!" She was studying him and he tried to act like he didn't notice. "Now, seriously!"

"What part do you want to hear?" He asked.

"I don't know," she said, "If your life was a book would it be a comedy or a drama? You know...give me the footnotes."

Allen nodded his head, "I understand...Let's see...I think mine would be more of an adventure."

"Oh?" She said, "lucky me. I've finally met Indiana Jones." She smiled again and looked directly into his eyes. For the first time, he noticed that given all of her extraordinary qualities - her eyes might be her best one. "Where are you from?"

"You first," Allen said.

"I grew up here, in Pascagoula."

"Funny thing!" Allen teased, "me too."

"Bullshit, I've known the Blackwoods my whole life and I've never even heard mention of you," she said.

"Well...until two weeks ago I lived in Virginia." Allen pulled at the paper beer label, "I never came out here much."

"What do you do for a living?" she asked.

"I'm an electrician. I've also worked on cars," Allen added.

"Are you just visiting...or what?"

Allen laughed, "Wow, you are full of questions aren't you?"

She shrugged her shoulders and sipped her beer, "I'm sorry, I am just not used to sitting around hanging out with strangers. I have no idea what we should be talking about. Might as well get to know you a little."

She was direct, Allen would give her that much. "No problem, I don't mind. I appreciate you taking the time to hang out a few minutes."

"Look," she said, "I'm sorry, but I don't usually sit around and bullshit with customers at the bar, and I'm not exactly sure why I'm doing it now. I am a single mom and my priorities are one hundred percent dedicated to taking care of my children." She shook her head and stared into her half empty beer bottle. "I need to get going. Thank you for the drink." She set her beer down and stood.

"How old are your children?" Allen asked. She didn't answer - she just stood beside her stool. "I plan on sticking around a while if I can find somewhere reasonable to live," he added. She still didn't walk away. *That's a good thing*, Allen thought, *there's hope*. "I don't know my family very well. As a matter of a fact, I met most of them for the first time when I got here two weeks ago." Demri was still there. "Please...sit down and finish your drink. If you decide to leave after we've finished this round, you can go and I'll never come in here and bother you again. I promise...please." Allen stood up and pulled her stool out for her.

She thought about it a few seconds longer and then she sat back down. They both drank from their bottles without saying anything else, until Allen asked, "What's your kids names?"

"Landon is my baby. He's four, and Lindsay is six, going on sixteen." She waited to see Allen's reaction to the news that she had small children. Some people were turned off by a woman with children. There was no reaction from him at all. "Do you have any children?" She asked.

"No," Allen smiled, "I've never met a woman that was willing to have them with me."

Demri laughed and Allen motioned to Krissy for another round. Demri and Allen had two more drinks apiece and talked about everything from sports to divorce. A subject that Allen knew well from witnessing his mother's three failed attempts at marriage and a subject that Demri knew from firsthand experience. She told Allen all about her unfaithful ex-husband and their nasty divorce. It was a story that Allen found hard to believe. Who in their right mind, lucky enough to have a woman like Demri to come home to every night, would look elsewhere for attention? He decided that the guy must have been a complete douchebag. Demri added that she'd dated a couple of men over the last two years, but that nothing serious ever came from any of them. "I just haven't met anyone who fits into me and the kid's lives the right way," she explained.

Allen tried to imagine a distant world, far from where they were right then, where he might fit into her life, but he couldn't. This was the kind of woman that belonged with movie stars and professional athletes, not jobless drifters such as himself. If normal men, with normal lives and careers didn't fit into her life, then he never stood a chance.

At some point the conversation turned to Allen telling her his sob story of a rough childhood filled with welfare and social services. Demri found it hard to believe, since the Blackwoods of Mississippi were notoriously wealthy. He didn't go into all of the details about how or why the family splintered. He just said that a family feud had kept them apart all these years.

"Fifteen years ago, did you ever think that you'd be where you are now?" she asked.

Allen thought about the question and tried to recall where he thought he was fifteen years ago, "No, I guess not," he said.

Despite Demri's beauty, she had a down to earth way about her that Allen found refreshing. She talked easy and when he spoke, she seemed genuinely interested in what he was saying.

She asked, "So, you're looking for a house, are you?"

"No...not a house," Allen explained, "I don't really need a house, or a yard, or any of that. I'll probably find an apartment, or a room for rent. Something that doesn't sink the anchor too deep, you know."

"When are you going to be looking?" she asked.

Allen thought about it. He didn't really need to hurry since he could stay at Uncle Otis's as long as he needed to, but he didn't want to be there for too much longer. He was beginning to feel like a bit of a mooch, "Soon, I guess. I haven't really set a date - why? Do you know someone who has a room for rent?"

Demri shrugged her shoulders, "Maybe...it needs a little work, but I've thought about running an ad in the paper and renting out the apartment above my garage. It has its own bathroom and a small kitchen area. It's probably not what you are looking for though."

Allen tried not to sound too excited when he said, "Sure, I wouldn't mind taking a look at it. When is it going to be available?"

She gave it some thought, "That depends on what you are willing to live with, until I can get it fixed up." She smiled again, "Now, you know that if I rent you a room, you and I can never go out on a date right?"

"It's mighty presumptuous of you to think that I would go on a date with you either way." Allen laughed and took a sip of his beer. Demri smacked him in the shoulder. Allen said, "That sucks, really! But after listening to you talk for the last hour, I am pretty sure that if we did go out…it wouldn't take you very long to figure out that I'm not right for you either. Besides, I need a place to live worse than I need a date!"

"Alright then," she said. She grabbed a drink napkin and a pen from the other side of the bar and scribbled an address on it. "Come by tomorrow evening if you want to take a look at the room. I should be home by six thirty, or so."

Allen took the napkin and put it into his pocket. "I'll try to be there by seven," he said.

"Ok," she said.

"Ok."

Demri looked at her watch and said, "Oh my god, I need to get going. My mother has my kids and I'm supposed to pick them up in twenty minutes."

Allen chugged the remainder of his bottle, "Let me walk you out."

Daytime had turned to dusk. Pink and orange clouds stretched across the horizon and a cool breeze blew in from the Gulf of Mexico. They walked slowly – both of them enjoying the evening air. She carried her purse in one hand and her keys in the other. When they got to her Toyota, she unlocked it and Allen held the door as she climbed in. She started the engine and rolled down the window. "Thank you for the drinks," she said.

"It was my pleasure," Allen said, "anytime!"

"I'll see you tomorrow?" She asked.

"You sure will," He said, as she backed her car out of the parking space and drove out of the parking lot. He watched until she was gone. At the instant she left his sight, he missed her. He missed her being next to him - for a moment in time, being with him. He'd just met her, but god, there was something about her that he couldn't get enough of. He walked back to Otis's Charger and after sitting with Demri for the last hour, the car didn't seem very exciting. He couldn't ever remember feeling this way about a woman. Especially one that he hardly knew. He figured that renting this room from her was a very bad idea. She made it abundantly clear that if they did business together, there would be nothing else. The way that he felt right now, he didn't know if he was capable of being around her and not wanting her. He opened the car door and sat in the seat holding the napkin that she'd written her address on. He thought about crumpling it up and tossing it into the parking lot. He knew that it would be the smartest thing for them both, but he just couldn't bring himself to do it. She didn't need his baggage. Hell, he didn't even have a job at the moment and other than the roughly five thousand dollars that he had from the Otis job – he was broke. He folded the napkin up and placed it back in his pocket. He couldn't toss it. He wasn't that strong. He knew he had to see where this road was going to lead him. The possibilities were too great.

3

The return trip to Violent Hill was a blur for Allen. His mind had been totally consumed with Demri and he'd paid little attention to anything else since leaving her. Once back, he pulled Otis's car into the garage and under the flood light attached to the garage, returned to his truck to finish the oil change that he'd started hours ago.

Robert's truck was in the driveway, parked beside his Land Rover. It was a fairly new Chevrolet pickup - lifted up a good foot higher than it was designed to be and had large mud tires mounted on shiny expensive looking rims. It was exactly the kind of truck that Allen imagined someone that had more money than brains would drive. He didn't know for sure, but he was willing to make the assumption that all of his cousins drove something similar. Allen popped the top off of his oil filler and dumped the quart of new oil into his engine. He did the best that he could to get it all into the filler hole in the dark – only spilling a small amount. When he was finished, he replaced his engine cap, and turned around to throw the empty oil bottle away when he bumped into Robert. It scared Allen so bad that he dropped the plastic bottle. "Goddamn, Robert!" Allen exclaimed, "What's with the sneaking up on people?"

Robert chuckled and said, "Scared you didn't I?" He was dressed in all black, just the same as he'd been the night that they went into the swamp. Allen was about to ask why he was dressed like that, when Robert said, "You want to go with me on a little errand?"

"An errand, huh? For Uncle Otis?" Allen asked.

Robert shot Allen a toothless smirk, "Naw, this one's a little payback on a fella that owes me something."

Allen had no intention whatsoever of going on Robert's personal errand. "Sorry, I can't. I've got something important to do tomorrow. I need to get some sleep tonight."

"Suit yourself," Robert said, in a way that implied that Allen was missing out on something big.

"Who's going with you?" Allen asked.

"Just me and a couple of other fellas. Noone you'd know."

"Sorry I'm gonna miss it," Allen said, even though he wasn't. Robert climbed up into his oversized truck and fired up the engine. It sounded like a racecar that was revving up for a big race. Allen could only imagine the money that Robert had put into that truck. The dimwit took off down the driveway so fast and loud that he was sure Robert would wake everyone in the house. Allen could hear the obnoxious sound from the exhaust pipes all the way out on the main road. Once Robert was good and gone, Allen closed his hood and went inside. Tomorrow evening couldn't get here quick enough.

4

The next morning, Elmer Blackwood wheeled his Mercedes sport car into the parking spot with the OWNER PARKING ONLY sign hung on a post. As he was pulling into the lot, he noticed an unfamiliar Ford Crown Victoria sitting underneath the large roadside business sign that read **Blackwood Auto Sales**. The car looked like the same Crown Vic that had been in Otis's driveway the other day when the police and that drifter showed up. He intended to ask Johnny just what that was all about, when they had some time alone. He would have already done so if he'd seen Johnny, but his nephew tended to stay hidden until there was work to be done. Johnny didn't come around to Otis's very much. Elmer figured that it had something to do with the fact that Johnny and Chris liked to stay high ninety percent of the time, and they knew that none of the elders would tolerate that. The family operation was too risky to have those idiots intoxicated while handling business, not to mention using up all of the product. It was best to only bring them around when there were drops to be made.

Elmer sat in his car with the engine running. He tried to imagine why the state police woman would be here at his place of business. He ran the possibilities through his mind - Patsy's stolen car? He wished now that he'd never filed a police report when the Lincoln was stolen. He certainly wasn't going to miss the few thousand dollars that it was worth, and now he had the cops snooping around. They were dangerous - always looking for someone to slip up and say something that they could turn around, trying to trip decent people up with their suspicions. Incompetent assholes! Instead of going out looking for the stolen car, they were going to take the easy way and harass him to the point that he would rather forget about the claim altogether. In the end, it would all just be a waste of time and he still wouldn't have his car back. The Lincoln was probably being traded to the scrap yard right now, at this very moment. Some crackhead was getting a couple hundred bucks for Elmer's car, while these pencil-dicks sat in his parking lot with their thumbs in each other's ass. All that they were good for was harassing good people. Cops sucked!

As he sat working himself up into a fit, a frightening thought occurred to him. What if it wasn't the stolen Lincoln? What if it was the family business that they were here for? He got nervous and began to sweat. A fleeting thought cross his mind – he should run. He considered going back home, packing a suitcase and heading somewhere else for a while, until he was sure that they weren't on to the family operation. He picked up his phone and called Otis's house. If they were on to the business, then they would have surely started by storming Otis's property and seizing everything that they could. They wouldn't start with the dealership – would they? The phone rang a few times with no answer, and it made Elmer even more nervous. He put his car into reverse and just as he was about to back out of the parking space – Kirk picked up on the other end.

"Hello," Elmer's older brother sounded weak. He was raspy and breathing heavily into the phone.

"Kirk? It's Elmer…is everything alright over there?" Elmer knew that there was panic in his voice and couldn't help it.

Kirk inhaled deeply, "Everything's just fine here. What do you mean?"

"Where's everyone?" Elmer asked.

Kirk took another deep breath, "Well, Jennifer and Ronnie were just down here having breakfast with me. They've gone up to get dressed. She's going to head up there to the car lot. I believe Patsy had an appointment of some sort in town this morning, and Otis and Allen are still upstairs sleeping…why?"

Elmer watched the Crown Vic and didn't see anyone inside of it. He scanned the lot and couldn't see anyone other than Freddy, a recently hired attendant, setting out some promotional signs near the road. The detective was nowhere to be found. Maybe it wasn't the same car, he thought. Maybe, he was just being paranoid. "No reason! I was just checking in," Elmer said. He turned his car off and hung up the phone without saying goodbye.

He got out and walked through the showroom where a couple of Otis's classic cars were on display, along with some modern models with hefty price tags. The hood was open on one of the units for sale – a brand new Mustang GT 500 and as Elmer walked past the open hood, two figures stepped out from behind the car.

"Mr. Blackwood...good morning," the man detective said.

Elmer stopped in his tracks, not sure if he should run away, or not. "'Morning," he said. "What can I help you with?"

"Nice car," Leo said, "what's it worth?"

"Stickers on the window," Elmer said. "I'll get one of the sales people to help you, if you like." He resumed his walk to his office.

"That's the problem!" Lashauna said, "You can't always take things for face value."

Elmer turned and said, "Excuse me?"

"I was just saying that things aren't always what they appear to be," Lashauna said.

Leo piped in, "Ya know, the value of things...like cars...or people... especially people!"

"I get the feeling that you ain't here to test drive one of my cars, are you?" Elmer asked.

"No sir...we're not," Lashauna said. "Is there somewhere else that you would like to talk?"

Elmer was shaking, but led them to his office. The large room had an absurdly oversized conference table in it. He closed the door behind them and set his briefcase on his desk. Lashauna and Leo sat together on one side of the conference table and Elmer sat on the other. His mind was racing and butterflies were fluttering like crazy in his stomach. Elmer still didn't know why they were here and it was driving him crazy with panic. He was ready to give them everything that they wanted - incriminate everyone but himself in order to buy time and get out of here. Aruba would be nice, or somewhere like that. All that he had to do was get out of this room without hand cuffs and he was gone.

"Why are you acting so nervous?" Lashauna asked, Elmer.

"I'm not nervous," Elmer fidgeted with his shirt cuff, "I would like to know why you are here though. I'm a very busy man."

Lashauna leaned forward on the table. She sensed that there was something amiss with the way that Elmer was acting, but she didn't know enough about him to put her finger on it. "I'm sure that you are," she said. "I'll cut to the chase, Mr. Blackwood. It's this matter of your missing car."

Once he heard that this meeting was about Patsy's car and not the family business, Elmer took a deep breath and gained some confidence. He immediately felt the weight of an elephant leave his shoulders. He wiped his forehead with the sleeve of his suit jacket. "My wife's car," Elmer corrected her, "Have you found it?"

"No, unfortunately not yet, but we do have a couple of questions to ask you regarding the matter," she said.

"I already told the other cops everything that I know. Y'all are gonna have to do the rest. I thought that's what you got paid for." Elmer was defiant, and Lashauna recognized the sudden change in his demeanor, but she let it ride.

"Who had access to the car, Elmer?" Leo asked, using his first name. Up until now, it had been Mr. Blackwood, but Leo had a hard time showing respect to someone who didn't return the favor. It was difficult for him to even use the man's first name. Leo wanted to refer to him as Asshole, or Dickhead, but knew that there was a level of professionalism that he needed to maintain.

"No one, but my wife," Elmer said.

"Where does she keep her keys?" Leo asked.

"Oh hell...I don't know...in her purse...on the kitchen counter... wherever she gets the notion to set the damn things down, I guess. You know how a woman is...her head's halfway up her ass most of the time and the rest of it, she ain't paying any attention. She probably left the damn things in the ignition." Elmer turned to Lashauna, like he was waiting on a comment from her, but she didn't acknowledge him. It seemed to Elmer like she was studying him, and he didn't like it. They locked eyes.

Leo looked over at the two of them and to him it reminded him of two kids having a staring contest. He could only guess, but Elmer, the male chauvinist, wasn't used to having a woman around that didn't bow down and cower in his presence. '*Oh boy Elmer*,' Leo thought, '*you're in for a rough go, if that's the case. This one don't budge!*' "So tell me," Leo said, to break the tension, "when did you first notice the car was missing?"

"That next morning," Elmer said, "it was Thursday, I think." He broke his stare with the black lady cop. She didn't move. He felt like reaching across the table and slapping the moisture from her mouth for being disrespectful. She obviously didn't know her place! He wanted to, but the bitch would only take him to jail. That's probably what she was after. She was trying to bait him into doing something by being a bitch. She was just itching to arrest a wealthy white man, for nothing at all. Elmer didn't like anything about her.

Leo asked, "Is there any chance that somebody from inside the house took the car?"

"Like who?" Elmer asked, "Everybody there's got a car. Hell, the garage is full of cars. If somebody wanted to steal something nice, they damn sure wouldn't have stolen the Lincoln." Elmer looked at Lashauna again, "tell you what I think. I think some vagrant, nigger came wandering by…just like that one did the other day, when you two showed up. He found the keys that my dipshit wife left in the ignition switch, and made off with her car. The son-of-a-bitch is probably still driving it…probably half way to California by now."

Lashauna finally spoke, "Do you know anyone with the last name of Taylor?"

Elmer said, "Can't say that I do."

Lashauna studied Elmer. Nothing in the way that he answered the questions led her to believe that he was not telling the truth. As much as she wanted to run this piece of shit down, she knew that she didn't have anything. If the tires did in fact match Elmer's car it could just be a coincidence. Until they located the Lincoln, there wasn't even any way of proving that the tires actually were a match. Right now. She and Leo were just a couple of barking dogs, trying to scare Elmer into saying something that they could use, but it wasn't working. "Is there anything else that you can tell us, that might help us to locate your car, Mr. Blackwood?" She was still showing a level of professional respect. It didn't go unnoticed by Leo, who was very impressed, since all of Elmer's digs had been aimed at women and blacks.

"No!" Elmer said, "I can't think of anything else."

Leo slid a business card across the table, "If you happen to think of anything…give us a call." He and Lashauna both stood and showed themselves out. Elmer leaned back in his chair and rubbed his face with his hands. He pulled his phone from his pocket, brought up Johnny's number and dialed. It rang three times, then Johnny answered, "What's up, Elmer?"

"Where are you?" Elmer was fuming mad.

"I'm down here at the store getting some eggs and bacon," Johnny said.

"Get your ass over to the hill right away," Elmer barked. The Hill was what the family called the boat house at Violent Hill and anytime there was important family business to be discussed, it took place there.

"I can be there in a couple of hours. Me and Jill were getting ready to have some breakfast," Johnny explained.

"Get rid of her and be there in one hour," Elmer said.

Johnny asked, "Do I need to round up everyone else?"

"No!" Elmer said, "Come alone."

5

Lashauna and Leo sat in the car outside of the Blackwood's dealership. She had the keys in the ignition, but she still hadn't started the engine. Leo waited for her to either drive them out of there, or let him know what was on her mind, but he didn't want to interrupt her thoughts if she was working on something. Finally she said, "That guy is one of the biggest assholes that I have met in a long time."

Leo smiled, "Well, this old world is full of assholes, and the fact that you and I encounter a multitude of them on a daily basis, that's saying a lot. What's your impression? Guilty?"

Lashauna rested her elbow on the window sill of the car door and then her chin in her hand. "As much as I would like to believe otherwise; I'm not convinced that he knows anything more than he's telling us."

"A family member maybe?" Leo said.

"Maybe," she agreed, "Lionel did seem pretty interested in confronting the long haired one that day."

"Do we know who long hair is?" Leo asked.

"No, but I think I know how to find out," She said.

Leo asked, "How so?"

Lashauna took out her cell phone and scrolled through the contacts list. Finally, she found the one that she was looking for. She pressed send and then switched the speaker on so that Leo could hear also. The phone was ringing through the speaker and then someone picked up on the other end. He sounded stiff and robotic, "3rd precinct, Officer Hannah speaking."

"Chris," Lashauna said, "It's Trudeau."

"Lashauna," his whole demeanor changed from strictly business to extremely friendly. "To what do I owe this pleasure?"

"I need a favor." She was to the point. She always was.

"Name it," he said.

Chris Hannah owed Lashauna for going to bat for him. Hannah was involved in a particularly rough arrest one night, about a year ago. When the officer arrived, some lowlife was actively kicking his already unconscious wife in the face with his steel toe work boot. Hannah would later learn that the beating was a result of the wife going to the grocery store earlier in the evening, while her husband was out having some drinks with his work buddies. Apparently, this asshole was serious about his snacks, because the wife bought the wrong kind of potato chips and it set him off when he got home. The man liked his Doritos.

The drunk husband ignored Hannah's commands to stop beating on her and resisted when the officer tried to subdue him. Officer Hannah had grown up with an abusive father and on many occasions had been forced to watch helplessly as his father mistreated his mother. This was a scene all too familiar to Hannah, and when the wife beater started to fight with him, Hannah lost his cool, forgot all about the restraint and discipline that is encouraged at the academy and wound up getting a little too rough with the man. A broken forearm, fractured left orbital socket, and one cracked rib later, Officer Hannah found himself as the focal point of a lawsuit. The lowlife, wife beater filed charges against Hannah and the department. He was even backed up by his wife. She testified as a witness against Hannah, even though she was knocked out cold for the whole ordeal. Her head trauma had still not fully healed, even as she sat on the witness stand.

If it hadn't been for Lashauna testifying on Officer Hannah's behalf, after preforming an investigation on behalf of the department, Hannah would have been in some pretty hot water. Lashauna was able to dig up enough dirt and violent history on the wife beater that the jury sided with the department. For his lack of restraint, and putting himself and the department in jeopardy, Hannah had been delegated to desk duty, though he was able to keep his job.

"I need information on all people with the last name Blackwood, currently in the Pascagoula area. Addresses, arrest records, family trees, whatever you can dig up."

"Every Blackwood?"

"Yep, every one."

"You got it. How quick do you need it?" he asked.

"Yesterday."

He sighed, "I'll do what I can."

"Thank you," she said, and hung up.

She started the engine.

"Let's go grab some breakfast," Leo said, "I'm starving."

Lashauna smiled, "Great idea, you buying?"

6

An hour and fifteen minutes after the phone conversation with Elmer, Johnny pulled his truck up to the boat house. Elmer's Mercedes was already parked along the edge of the road, but Elmer was nowhere to be seen. Johnny put his truck in park and climbed out. He looked to see if anyone else was around, but didn't see anything. Elmer must be inside, Johnny surmised. Johnny pulled his pistol from under the seat and tucked it into the waist of his jeans. He didn't know what Elmer wanted - what could be so urgent, but it wasn't like Elmer to call him out here on such short notice. It also bothered him that he was asked to come alone. Johnny wasn't quite ready to reveal what he'd been working on with Stokes, but if Elmer, or anybody else for that matter, got in the way of his plans - he was prepared to do what he needed to do. Elmer, like Otis, was the past when it came to this family. Johnny was the future - they just didn't know it yet.

The boat house was wood clad and from the outside it resembled a building built around the turn of the century, moss stained siding and all. It had sun dried wood to the point that it appeared on the verge of abandonment. Inside on the other hand, it was a different story. Exposed, freshly stained wooden beams, antique hanging lights and expensive decor maintaining the rustic look. The place was the ultimate man cave, complete with a fully stocked bar and pool table. Aside from just a great place to hang out, the boat house had also been the meeting location for the men of the Blackwood family for the past ninety years. While maintaining the appearance of a shanty, the building had been modernized with today's technology. A few years back a high level security system was installed. From the main control computer inside the boat house, one could view the many cameras around the property, inside the house and outside. The rustic charm had always been preserved, but modern power with a full kitchen and posh furniture, right down to a 60 inch television hanging on the wall along with a small office had been added. The side of the building closest to the boat ramp was outfitted with all of the modern gadgets and lifts that were necessary to house the skiffs, large boat, and jet skis that the family had access to any time they wished.

Johnny found Elmer sitting inside at a small desk, scrolling through e-mails and messages on his cell phone. Elmer looked up from his phone. Johnny stood just outside of the door, suspiciously waiting for something to happen that never did. Elmer barked, "Come in already…what in the hell are you waiting for?" Johnny stepped in and pulled the door closed behind him.

Conrad, Johnny's father, had been Elmer's oldest brother. Kirk and Elmer both idolized Conrad when he was alive. When Conrad joined the Army and shipped off for Vietnam – his two brothers were right behind him. When Conrad came back home and settled in Mississippi with Uncle Otis, again the two younger boys were not far behind him. That was of course, after Elmer recovered from the wounds that he suffered in Nam. He was the only one of the three brothers that had gotten wounded, taking some shrapnel in his neck when the helicopter that he'd been riding in was hit by a rocket. The chopper went down in the jungle and Elmer, who was wounded, was able to pull one of the injured pilots to safety, as he fought off a few enemy soldiers single handed. He'd received a silver star for his actions that day; in his mind it was the greatest day he'd ever lived, and the most horrifying. Elmer came home a hero and even though he'd proven his leadership overseas, at home Conrad was the unequivocal leader for the younger members of the family. Conrad was smart, honest when it was important to be, and solid as a rock. He could also be short tempered and mean spirited. He demanded that everyone around him not only be tough, but self-sufficient. This requirement included his young children, Johnny and Chris, both of whom were left in their dad's care when their mother disappeared one warm June evening back in 1977. In Elmer's opinion, his brother had done the best that he could with his boys while he was alive. Conrad died eight years ago, leaving Johnny and Chris as his only real legacy. Elmer thought that they should both be ashamed of themselves. Johnny and Chris dirty, lying, worthless crack fiend's who had dishonored their father's memory in every way possible. Elmer detested them both. If it weren't for Otis's love for all things family, and the old man's belief that he could trust Johnny with running the very important task of delivering the product to the suppliers, then Kirk and Elmer would have disassociated with the two of them long ago. It was too late now. They both knew too much to ever be excommunicated from the family. The only way for them to go now, would be permanently. Elmer hadn't quite figured out how to do that without Otis and Kirk's approval just yet - but he was working on it.

The man standing in front of Elmer was disappointing. Despite the nearly half a million dollars that Otis had paid Johnny this last year, Johnny looked like a vagrant. He was dressed in dirty jeans and a tattered t-shirt. Although Johnny's clothes were ragged, his complexion and hygiene were even more miserable. His face was covered by the sores that were a telltale sign of a habitual druggie and his teeth were discolored - some missing altogether. It didn't look like he'd seen a haircut in years, and now that he was getting older, it was grey, stringy, and long like a hippie. Johnny wore a goatee that matched the color of his hair. Elmer couldn't figure out why Johnny would even bother with shaving any part of his face at all at this point.

Johnny held his arms out and shrugged. "You mind telling me why you made me come all the way out here this morning," saying it with a little more attitude than Elmer liked, but he maintained his composure.

Elmer put his phone back into his pocket and stood up. "I got an unexpected visit this morning, down at the car lot."

Johnny said, "Yeah...so?"

Elmer hated Johnny's smug arrogance. Ever since he was a little boy, he'd had that attitude. It was most likely the reason that Conrad had to beat the boy so often. There were times back then that Elmer thought the whippings to be excessive – a thought that he never would have shared with Conrad, for fear of his older brother turning that anger on him – but Elmer understood now that it was necessary. Johnny was forty-four years old and Elmer thought that the boy could use a good whipping. Elmer asked, "What was the name of that black fellow who showed up at the cookout the other day?"

Johnny looked confused. "Which one?" he asked.

Elmer raised his voice, "How many goddamn blacks did you see at the cookout the other day, Johnny? I'm talking about the one that came up here, screaming into your stupid face right before the law pulled up." He could see Johnny's face turning red. He didn't know if it was from rage or embarrassment. He really didn't care one way or another.

After a couple of seconds Johnny said, "Oh, that was Lionel."

"Lionel what?" Elmer asked.

Johnny said, "What?"

Elmer repeated, "Lionel what…what's his last name?"

"Taylor…why?" Johnny asked, "Did he go up to the car lot?"

"No Johnny, he didn't, but that half-breed lady cop and her asshole sidekick did," Elmer said, "and you know who they were asking about?" Whether Johnny knew the obvious answer or not, he shrugged his shoulders like he'd just joined the conversation. Elmer shook his head in disgust. "The Taylors, Johnny! They were asking if I knew the Taylors." Elmer waited for Johnny to say something, but he didn't. He just stood by the door of the boat house staring off into a corner of the room. Finally, Elmer asked, "Why?"

"Why what?" Johnny asked.

Elmer lost what little control of his temper that he had left. "Why in the fuck are a couple of cops coming to my dealership and asking me questions about some bastard that I am only connected to through you? Why in the fuck did that same son-of-a-bitch come up here the other day and act like he was ready to stick a knife into your fucking throat? What's going on here Johnny? I need to know. We have a lot at stake and a lot of people involved that I care about. If there is some reason that the cops are sniffing around regarding this friend of yours then you need to clear it up before they stumble upon our business. If that happens Johnny, it won't be good for anybody."

Johnny didn't like to be threatened and he felt like that was exactly what Elmer was doing right now. He could feel the weight of the pistol in his waist band and he would have liked nothing more than to pull it out and ask Elmer to say one more threatening thing to him, but that would have to wait. Elmer was going to get what was coming, when the time came. Instead, Johnny said, "I'll take care of it."

"You'd better, Johnny!" Elmer said. "We all can't go down for something that you let get out of hand…whatever it is."

Johnny nodded and turned to leave.

"One more thing," Elmer said, "Have you heard from Robert?"

"No. Why?"

"Because I got a text message from Nancy…he evidently didn't come home last night."

7

A llen entered the address into his GPS and followed the directions back into town for a short time, eventually winding up on the north side of Pascagoula, where the small businesses begin to change back into the small turn of the century bungalows that seemed to dominate the area. After only ten or twelve recalculations by the stupid machine and an unintentional tour of Big Point, Mississippi, he found himself on Goff Farm Road - now searching for the house number that Demri had written on the bar napkin. When Allen found the address, he was pleasantly surprised to see a small, but very manicured house, white with black shutters, complete with a white picket fence surrounding a freshly cut lawn. It was the kind of home typically found in older areas. Neighborhoods maintained by an aging group of original owners – retired, with time to keep their yards in tip-top shape. The yard that Allen was looking at was spacious - numerous flower beds added a pleasant amount of color to the little white house. He pulled onto the short drive and parked beside the car that Demri had been driving that day at the restaurant. There was a detached garage at the head of the driveway - painted to match the house. Along the side of the garage was a wooden staircase that obviously led up to the apartment, which Allen had come to see.

Demri and her two children met Allen in the driveway as he was getting out of his truck. She looked wonderful, as usual, dressed in a pair of casual shorts and a green tank top. Before he could get the car door closed, Allen was approached by a little girl, who could only be Lindsay. She looked exactly like her mother, only twenty-five years younger. The little girl was dressed in short overalls, a white t-shirt and reminded Allen of a character straight out of a Huckleberry Finn adventure. "How do you do mister?" the little girl asked.

Allen smiled and bent down to shake her hand. "I'm doing fine miss, how are you today?"

Apparently, the little girl hadn't prepared for conversation beyond the introduction, since after shaking Allen's hand she turned and walked back to the porch, taking a seat on the steps. Demri walked over with a small boy in her arms. The child had a Dennis the Menace charm – grinning big from ear to ear, as he surveyed the new arrival and imagined all of the creative ways that he could maintain Allen's attention. His hair was stock blonde and he had a sparkle in his eyes that Allen found to be happy and clever. Demri put the boy down and said, "Landon, can you say hello to Mister Allen?" The little boy contemplated the request and instead of doing like he was asked, he smiled, spun on his heels, and ran to take a seat beside his sister on the porch. Demri smiled and put her hands on her hips. She looked like she'd had been working in the yard and was getting tired. "What do you do?" She said, "Kids."

"I appreciate you taking the time to show me the apartment," Allen said.

"Don't mention it," Demri waved him off, "let me go and grab the keys." She went inside her house while Allen stood in the driveway beside his truck. The kids sat on the steps, watching Allen like they were expecting him to pull out a wand and start doing magic tricks while he waited. Landon smirked at Allen and leaned close to his sister to whisper something into her ear. She smiled at whatever it was that he'd said, but pushed his leg as if to say go away. Landon laughed from the stomach the way that children do when they are truly tickled and the sound of it made Allen happy.

Allen was still smiling when Demri returned with the keys and also with a heavy set woman, who'd evidently been in the house. As they approached, they must have thought that he was smiling at them. "What's so funny?" Demri asked Allen.

Allen motioned to the kids on the steps, "Landon is quite a character, isn't he?"

"You have no idea," Demri agreed, with the exasperation in her voice that only a mother could have for her children. She stepped to the side and introduced the middle aged, heavy set lady. "This is my neighbor, Rachel. She lives right across the street."

"Nice to meet you, Rachel," Allen shook the woman's hand, "Nice neighborhood you guys have here."

Rachel nodded in agreement, "It is! Most of the people around here are retired and keep to themselves. It's a nice, quiet street."

Allen could feel Rachel's eyes searching him. She was direct and looking for any sign that he was going to be a problem. He was sure that Demri had told her that he was related to the Blackwoods. He could only imagine what kind of local reputation his cousins had created over the years. He considered clarifying to the woman that she had nothing to be concerned about, since he wasn't in any way like his cousins, but he decided that he didn't owe Rachel any explanations.

"Well…" Rachel said, "I've gotta' go get some supper started. The women's group up at the church is having a dinner for the deacons tonight and I'm responsible for the cornbread."

"Nice to meet you," Allen repeated, as Rachel said goodbye to Demri and the children. Allen could tell that she and Demri were close - they hugged before she left. After walking Rachel to the edge of the yard, Demri came back and said, "Let me show you the place." He followed her up the staircase. The shorts that she was wearing weren't exactly Daisy Dukes, but they were short and Allen was having a hard time keeping his eyes on the steps as they went up. He wasn't even aware that the two kids' were behind him until Landon giggled, "Quit lookin' at momma's backside."

Demri turned around and Allen who nearly dove headfirst over the staircase railing – plunging himself all the way to the ground with embarrassment. "You kids go and play," Demri said, and the two kids reversed back down the steps. In a few short strides they were running through the yard.

The apartment landing was a small area, only big enough for two chairs and maybe an ashtray if it was positioned just right. Demri opened the apartment door. When Allen stepped in he could smell that the place had been closed up for some time. The place was twice the size of the one that he'd rented in Buckroe and much nicer. The light fixtures were new and the kitchen, although unfinished, was a considerable size given that it was inside a garage apartment.

"It's not one hundred percent finished, but the things that are missing are minor. I can have them finished soon, if you want to rent it," she said.

Allen poked his head into the closet, and opened the refrigerator door. He already knew that he wanted to rent it, but he didn't want to seem too eager, "How much?"

Demri had an expression on her face that told Allen she hadn't thought it through completely. "I don't know...how about six hundred a month?"

Allen thought about it for a second, "That seems kind of light for this place. How about I give you seven hundred and I'll fix the unfinished items."

Demri seemed shocked, "Ok," she said, "but, you really don't need to..."

"Look," Allen said, "In good faith, I can't let you short yourself. I've seen places that were a complete dump compared to this and they were going for no less than eight hundred a month. I insist."

Demri peaked out of the door to make sure that the kids were safe and then she said, "Alright, but there are some rules."

Allen smiled, "Lay them on me."

"First, no crazy stuff, this is a nice quiet neighborhood and we don't do a lot of partying around here."

Allen said, "No problem. I'm pretty mellow."

"Second," she continued, "I've heard all of the rumors about your family and I know a few of them firsthand. I don't want any of the trouble that usually comes with the Blackwood's here at my house. I have my kids to think about and I just don't want that kind of stuff around here!"

Allen wondered what kind of *stuff* she was referring to. What could she possibly know about what his family did? He just assumed that she was being general and he agreed by nodding his head. "I am not part of anything that anyone in my family has going on. I assure you."

She went on, "the rent will be due on the first of every month...no exceptions." She waited for him to say something, but he didn't. "Any questions?"

"No," Allen said, "sounds reasonable." He pulled a wad of cash from his pocket and counted some out. It was the money that Otis had paid him for the swamp run. "Here is the first three months' rent. I want to give that to you now, so that I have time to find a good job before it is due again."

Demri looked at the twenty-one hundred dollar bills that Allen was holding out to her. It was more cash than she'd seen in a while and would go a long way to helping her struggling bank account. She took the money and put it into her pocket. "Good doing business with you, Mister Blackwood."

"Same to you…Miss?"

"Harvell," she said.

"Mrs. Harvell," Allen repeated, "When can I move in?"

"Right now, if you want," she said, and handed him the key.

"How about tomorrow?"

"Suit yourself," she said.

8

O tis was sitting on the plush leather couch in his living room. He was watching as Maury Povich read the results of a lie detector test on the television. Apparently, some ignorant fellow had taken the test to determine if he cheated on his girlfriend with her fat cousin, or not. Otis was disinterested to say the least, but was compelled by the level of self-loathing that it must require to air out your dirty laundry in front of a national audience the way that these people were doing right now.

Juanita, the Hispanic, in-home nurse that came twice a month to take Otis's vitals and refill her medication, was packing her belongings into her bag.

"This here fella, likes the fat women." Otis said, gesturing to the TV. "He said he can't give um' up."

Juanita said, "To each his own," and smiled. "What is it that you can't give up, Mr. Blackwood?"

Otis looked at her with a serious face and said, "I like porkin' Hispanic women." Juanita looked momentarily taken aback. "Now, I can give up pork…but damn those Hispanic women get me."

Juanita laughed out loud. She never grew tired of Otis joking with her. She'd been coming by on a regular basis for the past two years and Otis was never short on things to say.

Suddenly, Elmer burst through the front door of the house and immediately started calling for Otis and Kirk from the foyer. Otis didn't answer at first, but he overheard Kirk reply from the kitchen. "I'm in here Elmer. What in tarnation is the matter?"

Otis knew that Elmer was in a panic, or maybe a little pissed – it was hard to tell the difference sometimes. "We need to talk…" Elmer said, "… there may be trouble."

Otis switched the TV to off and smiled at Juanita. She was an attractive middle-aged woman who had a pretty smile and nice eyes. He'd gotten to know her very well over the years and genuinely enjoyed her visits. She and Otis had talked many times about her husband and son and he felt like, in some strange way, she'd become an extended member of the family. Otis made it a point to give her generous tips here and there, to help her and her family out. Otis also liked to flirt with her on occasion, because it made her uncomfortable and he thought that was funny. He was just getting ready to start in on her when Elmer burst into the house, so instead of flirting – he handed her fifty dollars and said, "Thank you Juanita…I'll see you a week from Tuesday."

"You sure will Mr. Blackwood," She said. She was obviously a little shaken by the way that Elmer came into the house. She kept watching the door to the living room while she zipped up her bag, like she couldn't get out of the house fast enough. "Remember," She told him, "Don't let your heart rate get up. You need to not let things bother you and raise your blood pressure."

"Yes mam," Otis said. He smiled at her again, as she walked to the exit. She and Elmer passed along the way.

"We need to talk," Elmer repeated, when he saw Otis on the couch. Kirk was slowly making his way into the room, breathing heavily as he did so. Elmer looked at the two of them, Otis with his oxygen mask looked like he had one foot and both hands into the grave already, and Kirk, who was only seven years older than Elmer, looked almost as unhealthy as Otis. Kirk wheezed as he sat on the couch beside Otis. Elmer paced the floor in front of the TV. "Something's going on and I can't put my finger on it."

Otis, who was never one for small talk when it came to a business discussion said, "Well spit it out, Elmer."

Elmer stopped pacing and said, "Them two cops that were here the other day showed up at the car lot this morning. I thought that they were there about Patsy's car, but they started asking about somebody named Taylor." Elmer looked at Otis and Kirk to see if there was any indication on their expressions that would lead him to believe that they knew the name. He didn't see anything but question marks on both of them. "I called Johnny out to the boat house and asked him what the confrontation with that fella was about the other day, but he wouldn't tell me. He did say that the guy's last name was Taylor though."

"What could the cops want with you regarding this Taylor fella?" Otis pulled himself up a little straighter on the couch.

"What does Johnny have to do with any of it?" Kirk asked, "Why was this Taylor fella fussing with Johnny the other day in the first place?"

"I asked Johnny those same questions and all he would say was that he would take care of it," Elmer said.

Kirk looked concerned, "That makes me nervous! Especially with us moving the large shipment out of here next week."

"When did Boone say he would be ready to meet?" Otis asked. Boone was the regular buyer that took the Blackwood drugs and moved them throughout the Gulf Coast. Over the years, Otis, Kirk and Elmer had managed to distance themselves from the street level of distribution and only deal in bulk to one customer. Dealing with too many buyers was too risky. They strictly forbid anyone in the family from selling drugs on the street to avoid being caught and bringing attention back to the family. It was a perfect set up for the family - sell in bulk and move the whole shipment to the buyer collecting a healthy sum of money in the process.

"We drop on Friday," Elmer said.

"Did these police officers give an indication that they knew anything regarding what we're doing?" Kirk asked.

"No," Elmer said, "But whatever Johnny's got going on with this Taylor guy could cause problems if the cops are already looking at him."

"I agree," Kirk said, "That damn Johnny's been nothing but problems."

Otis thought for a moment and then said, "We need for this drop to go smoothly. Let's get all of the boys here for a sit down and talk things over. Maybe we can find out what this Taylor mess is all about. On another note, have either of you heard from Robert? Nancy called a while ago and said that he went out last night and didn't come home."

"Yeah, I got a text from her too," Elmer said. "I haven't heard from him since he left here last night."

Kirk asked, "Did he mention where he was going?" Robert had a habit of disappearing from his wife in the past. His absences usually involved him and some greasy hag from the watering hole and shacking up for a day or so."

"Out with some buddies, I reckon," Elmer said. "Sounded like he was going out drinking."

The front door of the house opened and closed and the three men waited in silence to see who'd come in. After a couple of seconds, Tommy and Dewayne walked into the living room. "Hey there boys," Otis said, more cheerily than one would have expected given the circumstances.

"Hey there," Dewayne replied. He was the quiet one - soft spoken and shy - one of Otis's favorites.

"Have you boy's seen Robert?" Elmer asked.

They looked at each other. "That's actually why we're here," Tommy said, "We just left his house and Nancy said that he called her from jail."

Kirk sat up a little straighter, "Jail...what in the hell for?"

"It sounds like breaking and entering," Tommy explained.

"What in the hell is going on?" Elmer asked.

Nobody in the room had an answer.

9

The phone on Lashauna's desk had been ringing off of the hook all morning. Leo considered answering it a couple of times, but decided that whoever was calling would either leave a voicemail, or call his phone if it were important enough. Lashauna was uncharacteristically late getting to work this morning and Leo was using his free time to get caught up on a couple of tasks that he'd been putting off. The two of them had been very busy with the Taylor case lately and he hadn't had time to do some of the non-casework things that needed doing. He sat quietly at his desk directly across from hers, filling out a request for leave that he'd been meaning to put in for weeks now. His wife, Paige, had planned a trip to the Outer Banks of North Carolina in two weeks and he was pushing the deadline on getting his paperwork turned in with enough time to get it approved before their departure date. He was looking forward to the break – he needed a break. He was burning out. This case couldn't have come at a worse time for either of them. Whether Lashauna would admit it or not, the Taylor case was taking its toll on her too. Leo noticed her coming in late more often and he didn't have to ask to know that it was due to lack of sleep. He was sure that she stayed awake at all hours of the night going over the details - searching the furthest reaches of her brain to recall any piece of evidence that they may have overlooked. Leo found himself doing the same things most evenings. It had been three weeks since he and Paige had gone to bed at the same time. He often didn't even think about getting rest until nearly two in the morning. He suffered, just like Lashauna did. His saving grace was that he had the distraction of being married and Paige's need to socialize every now and then about things not involving police work which kept him sane. He imagined that Lashauna, being alone in her apartment, was consumed one hundred percent of the time with the case and without anything to distract her, it was probably driving her nuts. They were both burning out quickly and as he signed the bottom of the request form, he knew that it was what he really needed - time away.

The phone on Lashauna's desk began to ring again. Leo put the form in the outbound box, and stood with the intention of answering it. The constant ringing was starting to drive him up the wall. He reached for the receiver, as the door to the office opened and Lashauna came walking in. By the looks of her, she was still waking up. Her hair was a mess and she didn't carry a purse, opting instead for a military style backpack to hold all of her womanly things – and in her hand, she held a paper coffee cup. "I got it," she said, as she tossed her backpack into the chair. Leo went back to his side of the room and Lashauna yanked the receiver off of the cradle, "Trudeau."

Leo watched her facial expression change from the, *I'm tired and pissed at the world - to a broad beaming smile.* She nodded and said, "Hannah, I owe you big time!" Then she hung up the phone and grabbed her backpack from the chair. "I'm gonna' get cleaned up a little and then we can ride over to the local station. It appears that Robert Blackwood was just arrested on a B and E charge last night. They're holding him with a risk of flight warrant, but Hannah doesn't know how long that that will hold, once his lawyers get involved. We need to hurry if we are going to interview him without the counselor there. He may be able to shine a little light on the Taylor - Blackwood connection."

"What about the rest of the information that we requested?" Leo asked.

"He said that he has some files pulled. We can review them while we're there."

Leo stood and grabbed his jacket, "I'll meet you at the car."

10

The ride to the station took twenty minutes and the lawyer was still a no-show by the time that Lashauna and Leo got there. Ironically, Robert was waiting for them in the same interview room where they'd talked to Lionel, just days before. Hannah handed Lashauna two files when she walked in. One was the report that was taken in the breaking and entering case that was pending against Robert right now, and the second was a small amount of information on the Blackwoods. Lashauna thumbed through the list of arrest records, addresses, and police reports that comprised the folder. After a few minutes - standing in the hallway reading, she was led in to see Robert.

When the three cops entered the room, Robert picked his head up off of the table and wiped the drool from his mouth with the sleeve of his black sweat shirt. Lashauna tried to keep from laughing. Robert Blackwood looked like a stereotypical burglar. His black sweatshirt was matched with black jeans and dark boots. His hair was a little bit messy, but it still had the slick sheen of pomade, and was still mostly combed back in a messy pompadour that seemed to be a Blackwood family staple. Robert started to stand up, but was asked to stay seated by Leo.

"Mister Blackwood, I am Detective Trudeau, and this is my partner, Detective Menard," Lashauna took the lead, "We would like to ask you a few questions about an investigation that we are conducting. We feel like you may be able to shed some light on a few things."

Robert licked his lips and asked, "Can I have a cup of water?"

"Sure," Leo said, and motioned for an officer that was standing outside the room to bring in a cup of water.

Lashauna sat down and opened the file in front of her. Leo and Hannah sat on either side of her at the small table. Robert watched like a dog that was unsure whether or not to trust a human, and before the officers could say anything else, Robert said, "I believe y'all have the wrong fella'. See here…I can account for my whereabouts last night."

Lashauna shrugged her shoulders and said, "I don't know about that Robert. This report doesn't leave a whole lot to speculation. It's pretty specific."

Robert shifted in his chair, as if he couldn't get comfortable, but was trying real hard to appear confident. "What's it say?"

Lashauna continued to read the report silently until she was done - flipping the page over to finish up with the report on the back. "It says here, Robert, that you unlawfully entered the residence of a Mister Evans and his wife, through a bedroom window while they were not at home and proceeded to help yourself to their belongings, including, but not limited to, multiple pairs of earrings, a diamond tennis bracelet, a leather coat, and two hand guns."

"That's a damn lie," Robert said. "I don't even know a person named Mister Evans and I damn sure didn't take any of his shit."

"That part may be true, Robert. You may not actually know the Evans family," Lashauna said, "It doesn't look like any of the stolen property has been recovered, so it will be very hard to prove that you took anything at all…"

Robert confidently said, "Damn right."

Lashauna continued, "…but, the homeowner did notice that the house phone…" she picked up the report again to make sure that she was getting the facts straight as she spoke. "…the portable phone in the kitchen, was left on the couch in the living room."

Robert sat back and crossed his arms, "So, they left their phone off of the cradle, what the fuck does that have to do with me?"

Lashauna smiled, "That's the funny part. Get this partner," she elbowed Leo, "…since the home owners never use the house phone, they thought it was odd that the phone had been moved. Once they realized that their house had been burglarized, they called the phone company to see what calls were made during the time that they were gone."

"That's good police work," Leo said.

"Sure is," Lashauna agreed, "and do you know what they found?"

Robert shook his head.

Leo said, "I can't wait."

Lashauna continued, "The burglar evidently called Mrs. Sophia's Psychic Hotline and ran up charges to Mr. Evans home phone, to the tune of four hundred seventy five dollars and thirteen cents."

"What," Leo said. "Who would break into somebody's house and call a psychic hotline?"

"Well…" Lashauna laughed, "Robert here, either had a moment of severe stupidity, or he was so blitzed out of his mind on something, that he didn't know right from wrong, but lucky for us he used his real name on the call."

Leo and Hannah both laughed.

"What was the matter, Robert," Lashauna asked, "Were you afraid that if you gave them a false name, they might have given you someone else's horoscope?"

Leo was laughing also, "Damn son…they are supposed to be psychics. They should have already known your name."

"I want my lawyer," Robert said.

"He's been called," Hannah said.

"Great," Lashauna said, "Just to let you know, these charges, coupled with your past criminal record, are not going to look very good, even with your lawyer present. My guess is that you will be in jail for quite some time to come." She looked at her partner, "What would you guess Leo? Ten years, or so?"

Leo nodded his head in agreement. "Give or take."

"While we wait for your lawyer, I'd like to ask you a few questions about a different matter. One that I need a little help with," Lashauna said. "If you don't mind of course."

"Why should I help you?" Robert asked.

"Because," Lashauna said, "I might be able to help you out by reducing your charges, if you are willing to cooperate with me." She leaned forward resting her elbows on the table. "Instead of ten years, I may be able to get you five…maybe a little less"

Robert thought about it for a minute, "What do you want to know?"

"Let's start with your cousin, Johnny!"

Allen laid the new toaster and can opener down on the counter and wiped the sweat from his brow. The humidity of the Mississippi summer was brutal and he was unaccustomed to it. Virginia summers had been hot and humid, but nothing like this. The air was so thick here that it made him feel heavy. He closed the exterior door and walked over to the window AC unit that was so new the protective plastic stickers were still over all of the labels. It was one of the few appliances that Demri had up here in the apartment and it evidently didn't get used very much. Allen cranked it full blast and stood in front of the vent. The arctic air hitting his wet skin brought a smile to his face. Once he was satisfied that he was no longer melting, he walked into the kitchen and pulled though the couple of boxes until he found his bottle of Elijah Craig whiskey. He searched around in the cupboards for a cup or a glass, but he couldn't find one anywhere. He considered drinking straight from the bottle, but decided against it. To him, that seemed like a regression in the little civility that he still possessed. Besides, Demri was just downstairs in the yard with her children. He could go ask, if he could borrow a cup until he could buy some dishes.

The afternoon sun was hot on his shoulders; he could feel his skin cooking in the direct sunlight. Allen wasn't used to this kind of heat and humidity. Demri and her children didn't seem even slightly bothered by it. Landon was in a plastic children's swimming pool and at the moment trying to sink a toy boat with waves he created with his hands. Lindsay was chasing a butterfly through the bushes with a net and a mason jar. Demri sat on a lawn chair close enough to Landon to pull him from the water if he needed help. She was wearing cut off blue jean shorts and a bikini top that showed off her amazing figure. Allen was trying very hard to not get caught looking. It was difficult, but the last thing that he wanted was to make things weird with the landlord his first couple of days in the new place. It was a difficult lesson in self-control. One that he was not sure if he could maintan, so he focused on Landon playing in the pool.

"Hey Allen," Landon said, as he pushed the boat under the water.

"Hey there little guy, how's the water?"

Landon was clearly confused by the question and simply smiled as he said, "Wet."

Demri laughed and shook her head. "Sorry, he's very literal."

Allen laughed also, "Yeah, he's funny though. He has a lot of character for such a young kid."

"Tell me about it! What'cha up to?" She asked.

"I just finished moving the last of my things and was getting ready to have a drink when I realized that I don't have any cups. Do you mind if I borrow one?"

"I don't mind at all…on one condition."

"Name it."

"Make me a drink too," she smiled.

Allen went inside Demri's kitchen and after opening four wrong cabinet doors he found the cups - filled them with whiskey and ice and returned to the back yard. Lindsay was now in the pool with her brother. To his surprise, there was a second lawn chair beside Demri's. Allen handed her the drink and thanked her for the chair as he sat down.

"Don't mention it," she said. "Lindsay got it for you."

Allen turned to Lindsay, "Thank you, Little Miss."

The little girl didn't look up. She had a doll in the water with her and was dunking it under. "Mom made me do it."

Allen looked at Demri who shrugged her shoulders. Landon was again trying to sink his boat for the second, or perhaps the one hundredth time. "What are you playing, Landon?"

The little boy perked up and smiled. "This is a bad guy boat and I'm trying to sink it with waves."

"Cool," Allen said.

"Want to play?" Landon asked.

Allen looked at Demri, to ask if it was ok. She smiled and nodded her head. "Sure, enter at your own risk."

Allen put his drink beside the chair and stepped into the small pool with the children. When he sat down, the water level rose to the point that it spilled over the edges and onto the ground. Landon laughed hysterically, excited by the adult getting into the pool with him. Lindsay looked mortified and quickly got out. Allen, feeling guilty about ruining her fun said, "Don't get out, Lindsay. We can attack the bad guy boat with your doll. That is assuming that she is a good guy." Lindsay stood on the edge of the pool and considered the proposition. She looked at the soaking wet doll in her hand like she was asking it for an opinion and then she settled back into the pool.

The water was refreshing, even though it only covered the lower half of his body. Demri scooted her chair all the way up to the edge and put her feet in while the three of them played. Allen spent nearly an hour with the children, and when it was time to get out - the kids needed to eat some lunch - Allen having thoroughly enjoyed himself, was sure that he was the most disappointed of the group, even though Landon protested that he wanted to play a little longer.

As Demri was drying Landon off and Allen was collecting his now watered down drink from beside the lawn chair, she asked him, "What are you doing for dinner?"

"I don't have any plans."

She finished drying Landon and he ran inside the house. Demri started to dump the water from the pool. Allen said, "Here, let me get that," taking over and draining the water into the yard.

"I'm going to make a big dish of Lasagna tonight," she said, "There will be plenty, if you would like to join us."

Allen didn't hesitate, "Sure, I'd love to. Thank you."

She gathered up the toys around the pool. "Say, around six?" She grabbed one of the chairs and began to pull it towards her patio.

"Sound's great," Allen said, and rushed over to help her with the chair, "Don't worry about these things out here. You have the kids to tend to. I'll clean up."

"Thank you," she said.

"It's no problem…I need to earn that dinner," Allen joked.

"No," she said, "not for the chairs…for taking up some time with my children."

"Are you kidding me," Allen said, "they're great kids. I enjoyed it."

She smiled and said, "See you at six?"

"You bet."

12

Allen knocked on Demri's front door at exactly six o'clock. He'd wanted to show up a few minutes late - he didn't want to appear too anxious, but it didn't work out. Save for showing up empty handed, he'd driven up to the local Piggly Wiggly for a pecan pie and some ice cream. Not thinking things through and realizing that if he waited in this heat, he'd show up with a gallon of melted ice cream, he went straight to her door. Demri answered wearing a summer dress that looked like it was specifically made for her. The kids were dressed in nice clothes also and both appeared to have recently taken a bath. Though Allen had showered, he felt a little under dressed wearing jeans and white t-shirt. He wished that he'd put on a polo or a button up – something with a little more class. Demri didn't seem to mind either way. It turned out that Demri was a fantastic cook. The Lasagna was amazing.

After dinner, Demri and Allen served the kid's the pie and ice cream and watched the second half of a cartoon movie on TV. The one with the talking cowboy toy. Allen wasn't sure what he enjoyed more – watching the movie, or watching the kids as they enjoyed the movie. He was aware that this was a special family. There was a lot of love in the room. Allen could almost feel the happiness. Before any of them knew it, the evening had gone and it was getting late. As the credits of the cartoon rolled across the TV screen, Demri announced that it was time for the kids to go to bed. Allen looked at his watch and saw that it was almost nine o'clock. After saying good night to the children, which included a hug from Landon, he waited for her to tuck them into bed, so that he could say goodnight and give her some peace and quiet. When she returned and before he could excuse himself, she asked if he would like to join her on the back patio for a night cap. Without hesitation – he agreed.

As Demri was making the drinks – a couple of delicious concoctions that she called Georgia Peaches – her cell phone began ringing off of the hook. Whoever the caller was appeared to call right back after getting the voicemail each time. Allen watched her from the back patio, through the kitchen window, as she picked up the phone to see who the caller was, and then she placed the phone in silent mode and tossed it back onto the countertop. The air outside was still warm, but there was a cool breeze blowing, making the evening pleasant. Allen thought that tonight would be a good night to sleep with the windows open.

Demri was finished making the drinks and getting ready to come outside when the house phone began to ring. She hurried to the phone cradle to keep the ringing from waking the kids and snatched up the receiver. Allen couldn't hear the conversation, but he could tell by her body language that she wasn't happy. Allen waited patiently for her to finish and when she came outside he said, "If tonight isn't a good night to hang out, we can do it some other time."

Demri rolled her eyes, "No way, I've already made the drinks. Let's enjoy them." She turned on a radio that was sitting on a small table next to the back door. A tune came though the speakers that Allen really liked. It was one that he had on his I-Pod. Noel Gallagher's, The Dying of the Light –– great song.

Amazed at how the right song, at the right time, could completely set the frame of mind, he took the glass that she was offering to him, "You're twisting my arm," Allen said.

"Sorry about that," She said.

"Was that the kid's father?" Allen asked.

Demri looked caught off guard by the direct question and then she shook it off. "No, the children's father moved to Colorado about two years ago, after our divorce was final. He doesn't call much." She sipped her drink and watched as a thousand lightning bugs put on a light show in the darkness of the yard.

"Sorry to hear that. He's missing out," Allen said. "What took him so far away from his kids?"

"A job," she said. "You'd think a father would want to be around his children while they were young. He's missing out on so much."

Allen reflected back when he was a kid and could relate. He'd never known his father and his mother went through quite a few other husbands, but all of them had left for one reason or another and never looked back once they were gone. Allen had never been close to any of them. "It looks like he is at least taking care of his financial responsibilities." Allen motioned to the house and the yard.

Demri rolled her eyes again. It was the second time that she'd done it tonight and Allen found it to be very sassy, but at the same time - very sexy. "Yeah right! Don't be mistaken. My mother and my stepdad bought me this house when I graduated college." She noticed Allen's eyebrows raise and said, "I know, I know..." she said, "why am I a waitress in a shit-kicking country and western bar if I've got a degree, Right? I hear it all of the time. The truth is, I can't make what I make at the bar anywhere else...the hours allow me to be a mother too. I don't usually have to go in to work until near the kid's bed time and I'm off all day.

"So the money's good?" Allen asked, "It's got to be, I'd figure a beautiful woman like you would rake in the cash at a place like that."

"Don't get me wrong," she said, as she displayed a smile that would make any dentist proud, "I think you're a nice guy and all, but I am not desperate for company and wouldn't have ever been looking to rent out the garage if I didn't need the money. That bundle of cash that you handed me the other day is already almost gone to past due bills and they are still piling up. I'm definitely not getting ahead at the bar, but like I said...for a single mother, getting by ain't easy and raising my kids comes first."

"Is your ex not good about helping to support the kids financially?" Allen knew that he was prying into her affairs, but he was trying to understand why she would be struggling if the father was meeting his responsibilities, like he should.

"Richard is a self-centered person. He has a good job, but he only does the minimum of what is required by the court. He could do a lot more, but he chooses not to. He's extremely selfish." She said, "That's pretty much why the marriage didn't work out. He could never love me and the kids as much as he loved himself. He wasn't happy being tied down in a family. He felt like he was dragging an anchor and we were the anchor, so he found a way to separate himself. I should have known, but when you're a kid yourself you tend to see things the way you want to see them."

"Where'd you meet him?"

"High school of course…isn't that always the way the story goes when the result is a woman left to raise two young children all by herself?"

Allen sipped his drink, "Oh come on!" he said, "I don't believe that you are forced to raise these kids all alone. It's a choice…I've seen the way that every man in the Kingfish Lounge falls at your feet. You could have your choice of men."

"Lucky me," she said, "The Queen of the Kingfish Lounge," she laughed.

"Here's to the queen?" Allen raised his glass in a toast.

She smiled and raised her own. "What's your story Allen, why are you single and in a strange place with nothing to show for?"

"Damn," he winced, "it sounds really bad when you say it like that." She smiled and shrugged her shoulders, but didn't offer any apologies. She was looking directly at him apparently waiting for an answer. Allen tried to find the best way to explain his situation. He could say that he was a failure and much like her ex-husband, he ran from any commitment that ever presented itself to him. Or he could tell her that he had lost his job due to the fact that he was a borderline alcoholic and that he was here in Mississippi because he was out of options. None of it seemed like the right thing for him to say to her right now. What he said was "Freedom," that made the most sense.

"Freedom?" She repeated.

"Yeah…" Allen said, "Breaking the chains. I just needed to start over and get away from who I'd become back in Virginia."

She asked, "That doesn't include a wife and children, does it?"

Allen laughed, "No, Not at all. I did have a dog once, but he ran away."

"That bad huh?"

"Must have been," Allen laughed. He watched the lightning bugs and sipped his drink. He thought that she was doing the same, but realized that she was studying him with the same awe that he was studying to bugs. "What's on your mind?" he asked.

"Just wondering how in the world you wound up a Blackwood!" she said. "Which one is your dad?"

"Actually, I was given my mother's last name…never knew my father!"

She shook her head, "Any idea who he is?"

"Some…his name's Stephen Gilmour…from down here somewhere.

He disappeared from my mother's life before I was born. Vanished and never paid a dime of support."

"Tragic!" She held up her glass in toast, "His loss, huh?"

"Yeah…I guess so!"

"You ever thought of looking for him?"

"I've thought about it, but don't really know where to start. My mother has never really been forthcoming about him. She's like that…she is very protective of her secrets. Likes to control her relationships…none more so than the one she has with her son."

"Surprised he's never looked you up. It's not like he would have to deal with your mother, or her family, if that were the problem back then. You're a grown man now, he has to know that."

"Yeah…if he's even still alive." Allen chugged his drink. "Who knows?"

They were sharing some pretty personal things, and although he liked the fact that she was opening up to him – he liked it better when they kept the conversation light. "Hey," He said, "all I know is that the guy Richard must be an idiot. Those kids in there are awesome, and their mother ain't half bad either."

She smiled and it made Allen happy to see it on her face. She still hadn't answered Allen's question from earlier. Who'd called so late in the evening that she didn't want to talk to, if it wasn't the kid's father, but he let it go. It was really none of his business.

"So," she said, "Have you found a job yet?"

Allen shook his head, "No, not yet. I really haven't had a chance to hit the street, but I plan on going out tomorrow to look."

She sipped her drink and then asked, "Do you think you're going to be in Mississippi for a while?"

Allen shrugged his shoulders. "I'll be here at least three months." That was how far in advance he'd paid Demri for the rent. "We'll see how the job hunting goes between now and then."

"What about your family? Don't they own a car lot?" she asked.

"What about it?"

She asked, "Surely, they have something that you can do for work?"

That was a good question. Allen hadn't really thought about working for the dealership. He could probably get his Uncle Elmer to hire him on as a mechanic, or something. He really didn't want to be involved with any of the family businesses, but it was at least legitimate work - above board. "You know what…that is exactly where I am going to start my job applications tomorrow morning."

She held up a second toast, "Here's to successful job hunting." They toasted and then she added, "Let's hope that you're around longer than three months."

He looked at her, the house and yard. It was all of the things that he never knew just how much he'd wanted, until now. As he finished his first ever Georgia Peach, he couldn't help but completely agree with her.

13

ohnny and Chris rode slowly past the Palm Grove Condominium sign for the second time tonight. Chris was behind the wheel, as Johnny peered out of the passenger side window. He searched the parking lot for Lionel's car, or lights in the apartment, or any sign of Lionel at all. Johnny didn't know exactly who the apartment they were watching belonged to, but he'd met Lionel here on more than one occasion. Lionel had always been with that other guy. The one who always wore the Saints jersey - it could be his place. Johnny didn't really care either way. Burying two pieces of shit was no different than burying just one. Johnny didn't care if when he found Lionel the bastard was marching in a fucking parade - Lionel was going to be put down on the spot, along with anyone else who may happen to be around.

Three black guys stood on the corner, under a sign at the condo entrance. Johnny eyed them as he passed. Young thugs with oversized pants pulled halfway down their asses - Johnny hated that. He took offense to it. The three men stopped what they were doing to concentrate on the car that had driven past them twice already. Johnny had the window down and his hand on a pistol, waiting for just one smart remark, or some other challenge that would give him the excuse to hang his arm out of the window, fire a few rounds in their direction and send those wannabes into a panic. Lucky for them, they didn't give him the reason. Johnny decided that if they were still there on the next pass and looked at him that way again, he was going to be sure and let them know who they were fucking with. He hated them, and their fucking culture.

Chris accelerated his Nova up to the posted speed limit and away from the black kids. The engine sounded like shit as he revved it up. It rattled with a distinct knock under the hood, which could only mean something was getting ready to break down. The Nova was a complete junker, inside and out. All of the fenders had rust, dents, and scratches. The interior looked like it'd once been home to a grizzly bear. The seats were shredded down to the foam and wire frame. Chris didn't do much to try and improve the already destroyed interior - constantly throwing his trash into the passenger floorboard and back seat. Johnny couldn't figure out why his little brother had bought this car in the first place. He'd certainly made enough money to buy a new car, if he wanted to. Johnny figured that Chris liked to save his money - probably for his drugs. Johnny couldn't be sure, but Chris's habit had to cost him five thousand dollars a week at least. Johnny couldn't deny that he himself liked to get high every chance that he could, but you also had to use your money to buy the things that you needed, every now and again.

Johnny regretted not driving his car. Riding around in this piece of shit car was like some form of unusual punishment. He watched his brother in the darkness. The only light in the car was the dim dash lights and the occasional street light, as they passed under one every fifty yards or so. Chris was driving along with an ignorant grin on his face and it made Johnny sick. He felt like punching the idiot in the side of his face for being such a fucking loser. Johnny felt like he was playing a complex game of chess with his life and Chris was stuck playing checkers. Johnny felt like god had intended for him to be a king, but saddled him with looking out for Chris, the peasant, as some sick joke, to keep him from achieving his destiny. The thought of it made Johnny hate his dead father even more than he already did, for leaving him with this burden. Chris noticed Johnny looking at him, turned and flashed the tell-tale smile of the ignorant and said, "He ain't there."

"No shit, motherfucker," Johnny spat, "Just hurry up and get us the hell out of this part of town, before I have to kill someone other than Lionel." Chris did as he was told and pressed the engine again. The terrible knocking sound returned. "Quit fucking mashing the gas pedal, you're going to blow the goddamn thing up," Johnny said.

"This thing's stronger'n you think," Chris argued.

"Sure it is!" Johnny said, "When are you gonna get something else to drive?"

Chris shrugged his shoulders, "Whenever I get some money, I guess."

He merged the car onto the highway ramp. "I might get something next week after the run." As soon as he said it, he looked at his brother to see if he'd accidentally managed to light Johnny's short fuse. Luckily, Johnny didn't seem to get agitated over the business run into the swamp, set for next week. Chris thought it would be a sore subject, since Elmer and Otis told Johnny that with all of the heat from the cops, he shouldn't go. It would be the first time since Chris could remember that Johnny wouldn't be on the boat.

"Fuck them," Johnny said to his reflection in the car mirror, "...and fuck that piece-of-shit Lionel. He's the one that caused all of this. I'm gonna lose my damn job over that cocksucker stealing my money."

"You ain't gonna lose your job," Chris said, "They just want you to lay low for a little bit. It's just one run."

"It's the big motherfucking run," Johnny said. "The one that I needed to get my money right, set up the deal with LaRue and Stokes."

Chris looked at Johnny and said, "I been meaning to ask you, what kind of deal is it that you're working with them."

Johnny pulled a cigarette from his pocket and lit it, "You don't need the details little brother. You just need to know that you and me ain't gonna' be taking no more orders from those uncles of ours. We're gonna be running the whole fucking show."

Chris would never claim to be the smartest of men, but he knew enough to see that the only way that his uncles, especially Elmer and Kirk, were going to let him and Johnny run anything was for them uncles to not be around anymore. "What about Tommy, Dewayne and Robert?" he asked.

"What about them?"

Chris searched for the proper way to ask the question, so that it wouldn't aggravate his brother. "Are they going to...be around?" It wasn't an unreasonable question in Chris's opinion, seeing as what happened to those two old people the last time Johnny was in one of his moods.

Johnny thought about the question for a second and then answered. "That depends on them," and then he said, with a smirk on his face, "I'm not too sure about our cousin from Virginia though. I don't think that he's gonna cut it."

That smirk scared Chris because every time he'd seen it before, bad things happened. He didn't ask any more questions. He just drove on through the Mississippi nighttime. It kind of sucked though – he kind of liked Allen.

Johnny was running possible scenarios through his mind of what he would do when he finally caught up with Lionel, when his cell phone buzzed. He checked his instant messages and laughed aloud, as he began typing.

"Who's that?" Chris asked, and Johnny held the phone for him to see.

"She's primed and ready," Johnny said, as Chris read the text and steered at the same time.

Sup?

Blow for Blow!

Meet me at the spot

Your # 1 White Girl

"She's a hooker, she's always ready!" Chris snickered.

Johnny laughed and said, "Drop me off at my truck. This Lionel shit can wait until tomorrow."

V

A HISTORY OF BAD MEN

1

The Mississippi Bureau of Investigations main offices were located on the second floor of the State Police Department building, just a couple of miles outside of Biloxi. The aging structure lacked some of the amenities that more modern law enforcement facilities around the state had to offer, but it had the aura of old time policing that couldn't be found in a modern building.

Lashauna liked working in the old building. The walls were dull in color and the desks were all made of aged wood and had been used by investigators dating back to the civil rights era. There were pictures of wanted criminals posted to the wall, mixed with inspirational posters and the more modern OSHA and Labor Department required information. The building reminded her of the police departments that she'd seen on TV when she was a child - watching reruns of Adam 12 and Starsky and Hutch with her grandmother. Looking back, it was about that same time she'd first become interested in police work. She was no more than eight or nine years old when she'd started reading Sherlock Holmes, Nancy Drew, and the Hardy Boys. She couldn't get enough of the mysteries and crime stories.

A year later, her interest became her obsession the first time that she saw the characters of Sonny Crocket and Rico Tubbs on the show Miami Vice. Police work had gone from tweed suits and stiff characters to white cotton and people that she dreamed of hanging out with. Detective work had become sexy and cool. She knew from the very first moment that she watched the two Miami detectives, in their black Ferrari convertible, chasing bad guys around a 1980's cocaine laden paradise that she was going to become a police detective.

Little did she know that being a real police detective meant years of unglamorous, uniformed patrol work to climb up the ladder to the rank of detective, and the reality of it was that when she reached the goal, there were no black Ferraris. There were no dreamboat partners, no offense to Leo, but he was certainly not Rico Tubbs, and there were not any evil drug kingpins for her to outsmart, arrest, or shoot in a dynamic finale to an investigation. Things were rarely so cut and dry. In the real world, criminals were rarely bad guys all of the time, and good guys could flip back and forth too. There was very little glamour in the real world of police work – especially in South Mississippi. Very few of the people that she encountered during her homicide investigations were anything more than junkies, or some other form of lowlife that never really had a criminal plan. The diabolical plan of the criminal was usually nothing other than trying to score some blow or meth. In homicide, it usually amounted to a momentary fit of crack-filled rage leading to someone else getting dead.

Nevertheless, her job was something that she found pleasure in. She found satisfaction in helping others and took pride in bringing criminals to justice. It didn't hurt that she was good at it. She had the ability to focus on the details of a case and within a very short amount of time, have a good idea where to find the truth.

Lately though, this Taylor case had been the exception. She was no closer to finding the murderers than she'd been a day after the crime. She was willing to bet dollars against doughnuts that someone in the Blackwood family had something to do with the murder, but Robert Blackwood hadn't been willing to help her out with anything more than the names of his relatives and how the branches of the family tree ran. Lashauna pulled through a stack of photos that were spread out across her desk, along with the paperwork from the case file. She held the photo of Johnny Blackwood, just looking at his photo made the hair on the back of her neck stand up. He had the eyes of a wild animal. They were the cold and hollow – frightening. The way that he stared into the police camera reminded her of the photos that she'd seen of Charles Manson. There wasn't anything behind his ice blue peepers but darkness - emptiness. Lashauna thought that the only thing missing on Johnny Blackwood was the swastika inked into his forehead. She didn't like the feel of him at all, and if there were any doubt in her mind of his ability to commit a crime like the Taylor murder, his past arrest record helped her erase it.

His rap sheet read like a novel. Possession of a controlled and dangerous substance, malicious destruction of property, second degree assault, fourth degree burglary and trespassing, possession of a controlled substance with intent to distribute, possession of narcotics, illegal gambling, possession of marijuana, second degree assault of a police officer; the list was extensive and spread out over the past twenty years. Lashauna was shocked that Johnny wasn't rotting away in prison for all of the things that he'd been charged with. She guessed that his remaining at large was the result of having access to the best lawyers that money could buy. She thought about Robert being locked up in the Pascagoula Police Department jail and wondered why these two men from a well to do family would still find it necessary to rob people's homes and sell drugs.

She looked over the notes from her conversation with Robert and pulled the photos of the other family members that were in the file. She matched the photos to the names that Robert had given her. Along with Johnny, *he had the most extensive record*, there was Tommy, Dewayne, and Chris, who were all younger than Johnny, all with trivial arrest records. Elmer and Kirk were the older generation, and then Otis, the patriarch of the family.

One name on the list was Allen Blackwood. The only record that she found on him was from an arrest in Hampton, Virginia, after receiving an assault charge in a bar fight. She wasn't sure how he fit in with the Blackwood family, or why he was here in Mississippi, but maybe she could drum up something if she could talk to him. If he were in fact somewhat disconnected from the core group, he might not know what the family secrets were. On the other hand, he wouldn't know what to hide. It couldn't hurt to talk to him, if she could locate him.

She thought of calling Leo, who was out of the office assisting a local department with a prostitution sting operation today, but decided against it. She didn't want to distract him if he was in the middle of something important just because she needed someone to help steer her back on track. Lately she'd begun to realize that Leo was a vital piece to her process and when he wasn't around, she felt a little - lost.

She was getting ready to put the photos back in the file when one caught her eye. It was a photo that she'd taken herself at the crime scene and at the time, it seemed to her to be nothing more than an inconsequential object. She pulled the photo from the pile and held it in front of her. No matter which angle that she held the photo, it never seemed to say anything different to her conscious. It was always just an object. One that millions of people had used and discarded throughout the last half century, with nothing more than a passing glance. Now however, Lashauna felt like this one had a story to tell. She laid the photo of the discarded 7-11 hotdog box down on her desk with the other articles of the case file and opened up the map software on her computer. She typed in the address of the Blackwood estate into the *From:* tab and in the *Destination:* tab, the address of the Taylor residence. When she hit enter, a blue line was overlaid on the map of Pascagoula filling her computer screen. She hit the gas station tab at the top of the screen and all along the blue route, small icons started popping up onto the screen. She hovered the mouse over each icon until she had the information that she was looking for. There were three 7-11 stores along that route. She jotted down the addresses of each, grabbed her coat off of the rack behind her chair and headed out of the office. It wasn't solid, but it was a little bit more than she had a few minutes ago. She just hoped that the convenience stores saved their video from the surveillance cameras long enough to review images from a little more than a week past.

It took better than two hours for Lashauna to visit all three convenience stores along the route – the same path, she guessed, the murderer would have taken if he'd been coming from the Blackwood estate, on his way to the Taylor's residence. In that short amount of time, she'd learned more about electronic surveillance systems than she had ever wanted to – including the inconsistencies of the systems from store to store. She now understood that all three stores were owned by three different people, even though they all shared the franchise logo. Apparently, the store owner was responsible for the installation and maintenance of their own security systems – including the closed circuit TV monitoring system. This amounted to a series of random camera types, scattered around the premises, with the location of each determined by the owner. The employees at the first store had no problem pulling up the video of the evening that the murders took place and the manager of the store was more than happy to assist Lashauna with reviewing the tapes. In this instance, it was a more modern surveillance system that used a digital recorder, proving much more efficient and organized than some of the tapes that she'd had to review with cases in the past. In fact it was so easy to pull up the video, she should have known it was too good to be true and after watching all of the data of the parking lot from that night - in fast motion to cut down the review time to about thirty minutes – she was convinced that there was nothing on the video from this store that could help with the case. She thanked the manager and was then off to the next location, with high hopes that they all would be that easy to review. She was wrong.

The second stop was nothing of the sort. The video system was not working at all and had not been functional for quite some time. Exactly how long, the absurdly overweight lady behind the counter couldn't tell Lashauna. The clerk had eyebrow piercings and her hair dyed flame red to match her work smock. "That seems a little dangerous, doesn't it?" Lashauna asked.

The clerk just shrugged her shoulders, as if she'd never considered the dangers of working in a convenience store.

Lashauna then showed her a picture of Johnny Blackwood, and asked if she'd ever seen him before. Big Red shook her head no, while taking a deep swig from the straw of a Super Gulp soda.

Lashauna's disappointment must have been evident, because the clerk, feeling sorry for the detective offered, "We give all cops free coffee and sodas."

"I'll pass," Lashauna said, as she walked to the exit door. "Thank you for your time and keep your eyes open."

"For what?"

"Whatever," Lashauna said, "Apparently you're on your own here! You need to make sure that you're paying attention to faces and licenses plates, if anything should ever happen."

The clerk had a dumb look on her face as Lashauna left the store. Strike two, Lashauna thought as she got into her car and drove the ten minutes to the last location. She felt good about this one as she pulled into the parking lot. It was the first store that had been on the same side of the road that the murderer would have been traveling and if there was one thing that she'd noticed about criminals in her nearly twenty years of law enforcement – it was that they liked convenience.

When she entered the store, however, she was once again disappointed to find that this owner didn't even have a surveillance system. Though he had installed dummy cameras to save some money. The fake cameras even had a flashing red light on each to appear real in an attempt to thwart petty thieves, instead of installing an actual system. Lashauna was amazed at the risk these merchants were taking by not having video cameras in their stores. She previously assumed that every place of business would have them to protect the employees and property, but she was wrong and her disappointment was written all over her as she left the store and walked back to her car, feeling like she was right back where she'd started, the only difference was that now, she'd wasted another day.

She stood at the door of her car, trying to decide what she was going to do next. She hated this lost feeling. It was one that she hadn't had to deal with on too many occasions in the past. Lashauna Trudeau had a one hundred percent success rate at closing her cases and she felt like she was in uncharted territory now, by not having a direction to go - no lead to chase down. Her last option would be to find the visiting cousin, if he was still in town, but she was sure that wouldn't pay off either. Even if someone in the Blackwood family was responsible for the murder – she was sure that they wouldn't have told an out-of-town cousin what they'd done. Murder wasn't usually something that people bragged about while trying to get to know a distant relative. She was at a dead end in the case and she knew it.

As she was getting back in her car, she happened to look across the street and a smile instantly crept across her face. What she saw was nothing more than a slim chance. A trail to follow and that's all that she needed. Directly across the street was a two story self-storage building – nothing spectacular to look at. Those types of buildings were designed for function - not aesthetics. This one looked clean and well kept - a bonus, in Lashauna's opinion. Hanging from the roof on both ends of the building were two very large, and very modern looking cameras – and they were both pointing in the direction of the 7-11 parking lot.

2

I t was 8:30am when Allen finally woke to the alarm. He hit the snooze button twice before he forced himself out of the bed. He'd become a bit lazy in the two weeks he'd been in Mississippi. This morning, he wanted to continue sleeping in, but he needed to get started with his job hunting. He and Demri had shared some drinks the evening before. They'd only had a couple on the back patio before Demri excused herself and retired to her house for bed, claiming that she had an early appointment to take her mother grocery shopping.

Allen was more determined than ever to find a job and settle in Mississippi – at least for a while. He was really connecting with Demri and the children. In just the short amount of time that he'd been here, he was beginning to feel like a part of something. Even if vicariously, he was enjoying the beauty of raising kids and being part of a close knit family. He was falling for Demri, but wasn't sure that she felt the same way. There was obviously somebody else in the picture - the telephone call late at night was his only evidence, but he just felt like these was. There had been far too many times in his life that he'd set himself up to be disappointed – and this felt like one of those times.

He lay in his bed, watching the ceiling fan, recalling the details of the previous night. He rubbed his hands across his face and swung his leg over the side of his bed. Jesus, he needed to get his shit together. This girl had his mind all cloudy. He looked around the empty apartment. The only items in the whole place were a couple of half packed boxes, a cheap single bed that he bought yesterday, and a folding chair that was left behind by god knows who. Thrown in the corner – a pile of his clothes. He didn't even have hangers to hang them in the closet yet.

"Who am I kidding?" He asked aloud, to the empty room. He was right. What could he possibly offer Demri and her children? At the moment, he couldn't even offer them a place to sit when they visited his apartment other than the folding chair. He needed to get himself into a better position in life. He promised himself that today was the day that he was going to change. He was going to find a real job and start a new chapter in his life. Hopefully, Demri and her children would have a role in it, but even if they didn't, he knew that he needed to do it for himself. He couldn't remember a time that a drink of whiskey wasn't the main agenda for the day. For the first time in a long time - he wanted to be something more. Someone with a purpose again.

He showered – without soap, because he didn't have any in his shower yet – and got dressed. He checked the cash in his wallet and saw that he still had about two thousand dollars left over from the Uncle Otis job. He put all of it into his pocket. He intended to use some of that money to furnish the apartment this afternoon, after he did a little job hunting. The rest of it may need to go to food and supplies that would get him through the next couple of weeks. He grabbed his keys off of the kitchen counter and left the room telling himself that the first stop that he was going to make was going to be a pharmacy, so that he could get himself some soap, deodorant and cologne. All of this sweating in the Mississippi heat was giving him a complex.

When he got to the driveway, he found Demri there with the hood of her car raised and grease all over her hands. She was wearing clothes that didn't look like she'd *planned* the car maintenance. She was dressed in a nice grey skirt and a white blouse that gave her the sexy receptionist look. "Hell of an outfit to be working on the car," Allen said, as he came around the corner.

She looked at Allen over her shoulder without coming from under the hood. "Very funny! I think the battery is dead." She showed him her grease stained hands, as a sign that she had given it all that she could and was giving up.

He looked under the hood and said, "Turn over the engine."

She got in and turned the key. The only thing that happened under the hood was a bunch of clicking sounds. Allen walked up to the driver side window and said, "You are absolutely right…it's the battery!" He noticed Lindsay and Landon in the back seat of the car.

"What do I need to do?" Demri asked.

"We need to jump it," Allen said.

"That sounds like it could take a while," Demri said.

Allen shrugged, "It depends...do you have any jumper cables?"

"No."

"Then yeah...It could take a while, because I don't have any either."

"Damn it," She said, "I'm already late getting to my mother's." She started to walk back to the house, "I need to give her a call and let her know that she needs to get someone else to take her to town."

Allen stopped her, "Don't do that. You can drop me off at the dealership, and use my truck. I'll get your car running later this evening."

Demri smiled and said, "Allen, I couldn't..."

"Bull," He said, "Come on and load your kids up in my chariot." He opened the door for her and the kids.

"Are you sure?" She asked, "I hate to be a burden."

"Don't be silly...It would be my pleasure."

The drive to the dealership didn't take as long as Allen had hoped. He was enjoying the conversation with Demri as they drove. She pointed out different areas of the town that she remembered from her childhood. She talked about her mother and how she felt a responsibility to take care of her now that she was getting older. Apparently, the old woman had a nervous breakdown a couple of years ago and felt like she couldn't drive her own car any more. Demri made a weekly trip to take her mother grocery shopping and then help her with house work. To Allen, it seemed like a lot of extra burden to assume for a single mother who already had her hands full, but Demri didn't seem to mind. She said that it gave the children a chance to get to know their grandmother. Allen liked the way that Demri saw the good in every situation. He wasn't use to being around positive people like her. The family circles that he was familiar with always seemed to focus on the negative side of things and make problems where they otherwise didn't exist. There was something very real about her – something refreshing to the soul.

He pulled the truck into the expansive parking lot of the Blackwood Ford Dealership and parked next to a line of pickup trucks. "Now that's what I need right there," Demri said.

"Mom, I like the black one," Landon said from the back seat.

"Can we get one?" Lindsay asked, like it was no big deal and the only thing keeping the group from pulling out of here with a new truck was simply picking one out. *Kids*, Allen thought, *how wonderful it must be to live in fantasy land.*

"Can we?" Landon piped in, as if he'd never considered the possibility until his sister mentioned it.

"I wish we could," Demri said, giving Allen a wink, "but we still haven't used up the Nissan all the way yet. Maybe someday soon."

Allen thought that it was good to let them live in the fantasy world for as long as they can. The real world was depressing and full of things that you couldn't have.

"Oh man," Landon said, dejected.

"Don't worry," Lindsay said innocently, remembering the broken down car in the driveway, "It won't be too much longer before the Nissan is completely used up."

Allen and Demri laughed. "Thanks for letting us use your truck," She said.

Allen waived her off and opened the door, "Like I said, don't mention it. I'll catch a ride back to your house a little later."

Demri got out and came around to the driver's seat, "You know…it's kind of your house now too."

Allen liked the sound of that. "Drive safe," he said, "and keep an eye on the dash for red lights. This thing has a tendency to breakdown also." He could see the concern on her face when he said it, and then he added, "Don't worry…you guys will be fine. Call me if you have any problems."

"Ok, See you later," she said, as she put the truck into reverse and backed out.

Allen approached the reception desk, just beyond the top-of-the-line cars, artfully positioned around the showroom. The room was painted traditional Ford white and blue. Neon lights and art deco pictures were hanging from the walls, giving the shoppers the feeling that they were visiting a fancy car museum, instead of a local car dealership. Allen dug the vibe of the place. If he were in the market for a new vehicle, he could see himself giving this place a serious chance to earn his business. In the waiting room, under a large TV screen that currently had the local news team reporting a traffic accident, a few customers were sitting on deep blue leather chairs and a white leather couch. The reception desk was a large wooden piece, shaped like the oval adorning the grills of the vehicles. It was large enough to seat three receptionists, yet all three chairs were currently empty. He waited for a few seconds, listening to a bald man that was much too young in appearance to not have any hair, read the news to the audience. The newscaster said that there would be scattered, severe thunderstorms moving across the viewing area later this evening.

Suddenly, the bald man on the TV was interrupted by a familiar voice. "Hey Allen," Jennifer Blackwood had approached from behind.

"Hey Cuz," Allen said. "Is your dad in?"

She set a file down on the desk, "He is…I think he's in his office. Do you know where it's located?"

"Nope, do you have a map of this amusement park?"

Jennifer laughed, "Follow me." She took him through hall after hall and Allen was glad that she'd led him through because the building was so big, he would have most certainly gotten lost trying to find his own way.

Finally, they came to a corridor lined with wood paneling, just like the hallways in Otis's house and Allen knew that they were getting close. They came to a large wooden door with the name Blackwood intricately carved into it, Jennifer knocked lightly. She opened it slowly to make sure that there wasn't important business being conducted on the other side and when she saw that the coast was clear, she fully opened the door, and said, "Dad…Allen is here to see you.

Elmer Blackwood was seated behind a large desk and wearing a suit that was probably worth more than all of the clothes that Allen had ever owned - put together. He looked more like the president of a Fortune 500 company, than the part-owner of a family owned, local car dealership.

"Allen," he sang, as his nephew walked in. It was different than any greeting that Allen had ever received from Elmer. His uncle genuinely seemed happy to see him. "Come on in and have a seat. You're just the man I've been wanting to see." He motioned for Allen to take a seat in one of the plush leather chairs opposite the desk. As Allen sat, Elmer jumped up, shooed Jennifer away and closed the office door behind them. "Where have you been? I didn't see you around the house the last couple of nights." Elmer sat back down in his chair behind the desk.

"I thought that I told you I found an apartment."

Elmer shook his head, "No, I don't recall hearing you say that. What's the matter with the room at Otis's?"

"Nothing's wrong with the room, at all. In fact, it was probably the nicest room that I've ever stayed a night in, but I felt like a mooch. I needed to get out on my own."

"A mooch?" Elmer repeated. "Hell, you ain't no mooch. You can stay there anytime that you need to...you're family!"

"I know," Allen said, "and I appreciate it, but I just feel like I need to make my own way. Especially, if I'm going to stick around Mississippi for a while."

"Have you decided to stay?"

Allen nodded, "For a little while at least. That's actually why I came to see you."

"Is that so?" Elmer steepled his fingers.

"I was hoping that you could use my help around here...as a mechanic, or something," Allen said.

Elmer opened his desk drawer and produced a cigar box. He put one of the cigars into his mouth and held the box open for Allen to take one - Allen declined. Elmer lit his cigar and puffed away. The tobacco smoke filling the space above his head with a white cloud. "Do you know something about mechanical work?" Somehow, suddenly the aura in the room had changed. Allen could see Elmer's disposition change. His uncle's pretentiousness returned just as soon as he felt like Allen needed something from him. It made Allen wonder what exactly had been on Elmer's mind that had caused the friendly greeting a moment ago.

"Yeah, I do," Allen said. "I can do almost anything to a car..."

"What kind of cars have you worked on before?" Elmer cut him off.

"All kinds, really."

"What do you know about modern cars?" Elmer asked, "The technology has changed so much over the last couple of years that if you haven't been working on them the whole time, you've been left behind."

Allen was getting the impression that his uncle didn't like the idea of giving him a job working on cars. "I'm pretty confident that I could learn anything that the mechanics are doing here. I just need a chance."

"Is that a fact?" Elmer asked, from behind his fat cigar. He glared across the desk with what Allen could have mistaken for contempt. Allen was sure that the attitude had something to do with Allen refusing Uncle Otis's offer to work for the family in other ways. Allen could feel his blood begin to boil. He hated feeling like he was being bullied or taken advantage of. The way that Elmer was looking at him right now, made Allen want to get up and smash the fucking cigar down Elmer's throat.

"Yeah, that's a fact," Allen said frustrated, "...but look, forget it, I shouldn't have just popped in on you like this. I just thought that I'd see if you needed any help around here, before I went looking somewhere else." Allen stood up and offered a handshake to his uncle. Elmer didn't take it. He continued leaning back in his chair, puffing on his cigar.

"Sit down and don't get yourself so worked up," Elmer said. "I'm just trying to figure out why you would want to work here, punching the time clock like these other monkeys, when you could be making money hand over fist with your cousins."

Allen searched for the right words to explain why he didn't want to be involved in his family's criminal activities without sounding holier than thou. "I just don't think that I'm cut out for that type of work," he explained. "I'd rather make my money...honestly."

Elmer leaned forward in his chair and dabbed the cigar into a crystal ashtray. "Let me tell you about honest money. You could work here six days a week, fifty two weeks out of the year, for fifty thousand dollars, give or take a few...or you could work for the family and make fifty thousand dollars in a couple of months, only working for a night, or two total to earn it. I don't see where your hesitation is coming from."

"Fifty thousand dollars in two months doesn't do anybody any good if they are in jail and can't spend it."

Elmer spread his hands, "Nobody's going to jail over here. We have it down to a science. Besides, Robert's not locked up for anything related to the family. He's locked up for being a dumbass."

"Wait, what?" Allen didn't know that Robert was in jail. "What happened?"

"You haven't heard? Oh that's right you ain't been around the house for a few days." Elmer leaned back in his chair again and took a long drag off of his cigar. He smiled a little, even as the smoke burned at his eyes causing him to squint. Allen got the impression that Elmer liked being the boss - sitting behind his desk, in his fine suit, in his fine office, smoking his expensive tobacco, counting all of his money. Allen realized that what Elmer liked the most out of all of this was being in charge. He was the boss and he wanted everyone to know it, even as they were coming down the hallway, admiring the wood, before they even got to his office. Allen guessed that Elmer would give all of this away. Walk away from all of the flair and authority of being the automotive businessman extraordinaire, to be the boss of Otis's little family empire. Elmer explained, "Robert went and got high…broke into the county treasurer's house and did a little vandalizing." Allen must have had a perplexed look on his face, because Elmer said, "I don't know…the boy's a moron! Allegedly, he called his favorite psychic hotline and ran up a few hundred dollars worth of charges. He's going to be locked up for a while, since the district attorney convinced the judge that no bail should be set, based on Robert's propensity for doing stupid shit."

"They call that vandalism?" Allen asked.

"That ain't all," Elmer explained, "He tore up some books and a few of the lady's belongings. Somehow, he managed to tear down some curtains in the living room and get feces on them."

"Feces?"

"Shit," Elmer explained.

"Yeah, I got it." Allen said, "How in the hell did he manage that?"

"Tommy and Dewayne went to see him in jail and they asked him that very question." Elmer toyed with the cigar in the ashtray. "They said that he laughed and said that he'd given the family an upper decker." Elmer raised his eyebrows, "Any idea what *that* is?"

Allen laughed. He'd been in the construction industry long enough to know that an upper decker was when a person took a crap in the top tank of the toilet. "Yeah, I know what it is. The question is, how do *you* know what that is?"

"I know a lot of things, kiddo. Don't make the mistake by thinking that your generation blazed the path that you walked. All you were doing was following the trail left by us old guys."

"I hear you," Allen laughed. Somehow, Elmer could calm someone down, just as quickly as he could irritate them. He was a strange personality indeed. Allen couldn't decide if he liked his mom's twin brother or not.

"So, back to business," Elmer leaned in his chair again. "I need you to

do me a favor and I'm willing to pay you very well to do it. If you want…
after this favor, I will give you a job managing this whole goddamn place,
but I…we…need you to do this for the family."

"What is it and how much are you willing to pay?"

"We need you to make a delivery, just like last time," Elmer said.

"Alone?"

"No. Tommy, Dewayne and Chris will go with you."

"Where's Johnny," Allen couldn't figure out why Johnny wasn't
involved in whatever was planned. He thought Johnny was the uncle's
number one man.

Elmer smiled and said. "He isn't able to go on this trip. He has some
other business to attend to." Elmer didn't want to tell Allen about the cops
sniffing around Johnny. He knew that it would be a deal breaker and they
all needed this transaction to take place.

"When?"

"The night after tomorrow," Elmer said.

Allen was sitting across from his uncle sorting through his moral
dilemma. What kept popping into his mind was Demri, under the hood
of her worn out car this morning and how she'd complained about being
broke the other night on the patio. His mind then flashed to his empty
apartment and how he needed furniture and a normal life, with normal
things. Sure, he could work for it over time, but one evening with the
family, and he would have a pretty good head start. "How much?" He
asked.

Elmer shrugged his shoulders and toyed with a pen that was laying on
his desk. "Oh, I don't know…how does ten thousand sound, to get you
started?"

"Make it fifteen," Allen negotiated.

Elmer stopped playing with the pen and looked Allen in the eye. There
was an eerie silence in the room for several seconds, before Elmer said,
"You got it, fifteen!"

3

I t was a little past five o'clock when Demri returned to her house. She'd taken her mother to the grocery store, drove mom back home, put her grocery's away, and made lunch for the two of them and the kids. Turning Allen's Land Rover into the driveway, she noticed that the hood of her Toyota was raised. She parked, as Allen came out of her garage with a couple of tools in his hand. Demri watched as he resumed working on the car and seemed to not notice them sitting in the truck. When he did notice, he smiled and waved and for a fleeting second Demri wanted him. She watched as he leaned under the hood of her car.

"Mom...are we gonna' get out," Landon asked, still strapped into his car seat.

"Oh, Yeah...sorry," Demri pulled the seat belt off and opened the door for the kids. "I was just thinking about some things."

Lindsay pointed out of the front windshield and said with a disgusted tone, "Mr. Allen isn't wearing a shirt."

"Ewww..." Landon piped in.

"Y'all hush. It's hot and he's working on Mommy's car," Demri helped the kids get out of the truck. Once they were on the ground she said, "Lindsay go inside and get some cartoons going on the TV for your brother. Mommy will be inside in a minute to get dinner started. They took off running for the door. "Hi Allen," Lindsay said, as she ran past.

"Hey Allen, you forgot to put on your shirt," Landon giggled, as he followed behind his sister.

"Hey kids," Allen smiled. Once they were inside – the screen door slapping against the door frame behind them – Allen turned to Demri. She was getting a couple of bags of groceries out of the back of the truck. "Do you need any help?"

"Nah, I got it," She closed the rear door of the truck with her hip, "Let me get these put away and I'll make us a refreshment."

"That sounds great," Allen said.

When she was finished inside, she returned to the driveway carrying two glasses of ice tea. Allen was just finishing up with tightening the last bolt when she got there. "Is it gonna' live?" she asked.

Allen spun around, sat against the grill of the car, and took one of the glasses. "Yeah, I think you will get a few more miles out of it before it goes terminal. I replaced the battery, the alternator, the plugs, and the plug wires. It runs like a charm now." He motioned to the driver side door, "Go ahead start it up."

"My, my, you're pretty resourceful for somebody that has been without transportation all day," She joked. "How did you get to the auto parts store?"

"It helps that you have a very nosey neighbor. I was just going to get the old parts pulled off and wait for you to get home, but Rachel from across the street saw me working out here and came over to see what was going on," Allen explained.

"She's sweet, ain't she?" Demri said, with sincerity.

Allen gave her a funny look, "She's a little bit scary. I got the feeling that she was coming to intervene if somebody was out here screwing with your stuff. I don't think that she knew it was me until she got up close… and she came over to handle the problem empty handed. She didn't even have a cell phone to call the police if I turned out to be a bad guy." Allen laughed, "I'm pretty sure that she was coming over here to fight like a man."

Demri laughed, "Yep that sounds like Rachel. I take it y'all didn't fight though…due to your lack of bruises!"

"No, after a couple of minutes of explaining that your car broke down and you were using my truck, I convinced her to take me to the auto parts store, so that I could have this ready for you by the time you came home."

"Wow, that's so sweet of both of you!" She climbed in and turned the key. The engine sprung to life quicker than she could ever remember since she'd had the car. "It sounds great!"

"It should get a little better gas mileage now too," he explained.

"Allen, how can I ever thank you? I don't know what to say." She got out of the car and hugged him. "What do I owe you?"

Allen shook his head, "Nothing, I did it because I wanted to." Not to mention that he had a pocket full of money again, since Elmer had given him another five thousand dollar advancement on his earnings to come.

"Bull," she said, "those parts weren't free. At least let me pay you for the price of them."

Again, Allen shook his head, "No, it was a favor to you and the kids, for being so nice to me. It was the least that I could do."

"Well, let me cook you some dinner," she offered.

To that, Allen agreed, "Now you're talking."

She smiled and nodded her head. "Give me an hour and I'll have some of the best hamburger steaks that you've ever tasted."

"I can't wait."

"Hey, by the way," She said, "how did your job hunting go?"

Allen wiped the grease from his hands with a shop rag and his eyes fell to the gravel in the driveway. He found that he couldn't look her in the face for fear that she would sense what he was getting himself into, "It went well...I should be back to work in a couple of days."

4

Allen shut off the engine and got out. The rain was coming down in buckets and had been for the last two days. It showed no signs of letting up - the weather man reporting that it could go on for a couple more. As he walked up the driveway, he could see Dewayne and Chris standing just inside of Otis's garage smoking cigarettes. Each of them held a half finished bottle of beer in their free hand. Dewayne reached into the cooler and offered one to Allen as he hurried in out of the rain. Allen declined, he didn't want to drink before the trip into the swamp. He wanted to be on the highest alert and to tell the truth he was a little concerned that the two of them were drinking. He vowed to not let it ruin his good mood, but he could feel his anxiety kick up a notch. He tried to control the nervousness he was feeling with thoughts of Demri and the kids. Things had been going good with his new living accommodations over the last two days. He was starting to feel like there was something brewing between them. He'd been on edge over the last couple of days and he tried to stay away from her as much as possible. The distance seemed to make her even more interested in him. He's used the bad weather as an excuse to fix up his apartment a little, and hadn't gone over to see her once in the interim. He wanted to see her – he couldn't get her off of his mind, but didn't want be around her for her to catch on that there was something worrying him. He kept telling himself that if he could just get through tonight that things would get much better between the two of them, and even though she'd warned him of the no dating the roommate rule - he'd vowed to ask her out on an official date sometime before the next weekend. He was going to offer to pay Rachel to babysit the kids for the evening. All that he needed was for things to go smoothly tonight, but two of the four people that he was relying on to help make things go right, were standing in the garage tying on a buzz - not a good start in his opinion. "Where's Tommy?" he asked them.

Dewayne shrugged his shoulders like Tommy's whereabouts were the last thing on his mind at the moment, "He's around here somewhere."

Chris said, "I think he went in the house, with Elmer."

"Where's the van?" Allen asked. He knew that he was running a little late and would have assumed that the van would be packed and ready to go by now.

"Still in the barn, I guess," Chris said.

Allen checked his watch. Even though it seemed later, due to the early darkness brought on by the grey rain clouds, it was only 5:24 pm. Elmer had gone over the plan with Allen two days ago at the dealership. In order for them to be out in Whiskey Bayou and at the fishing shack by 7:00 sharp, they would have to load the boat and be on their way by quarter past six at the latest. "Is it loaded?"

"Not yet," Dewayne said, "We were waiting for Tommy to come back."

Allen said, "For what?"

"To help," Dewayne explained, in a manner that suggested, why else?

Allen wanted to scream. These ignorant hillbillies were so worried about one of them having to do an ounce of work more than the other that they were going to stand around all night waiting. "You two go down to the barn and start loading the van. Me and Tommy will meet you there in a few minutes."

Chris and Dewayne both stood where they were, looking at Allen like they hadn't heard a word that he'd said. It reminded Allen of being the foreman on the construction site and having to deal with the brick brained workers. Luckily, he was used to motivating people that had more testosterone than brains. Those guys were just looking for someone to take the lead and Allen decided that if he were going to be a part of this thing tonight – he wasn't going to do it their way. Allen was going to do everything that he could do to make sure that things went according to plan. "What in the fuck are you two just standing there for?" He raised his voice and pointed into the rain soaked driveway, "Go get the van... start loading it!"

Dewayne chugged the remainder of his beer and threw the bottle into the trash can. Chris just tossed his in the trash without finishing it and said, "Who made you the boss?"

Allen ignored the remark, since they were both on their way out of the garage.

Once they were firmly on their way, Allen went inside. As he was walking through the foyer, Kirk was coming out of the living room with an older man – one that Allen had never seen before. The stranger had white hair - thinning on the top, yet he still had it long around the edges in the Clark Griswold fashion. He wore a grey double breasted suit - buttoned to cover his oversized belly and he carried a black leather briefcase. Kirk introduced him as Mr. Hackman, the Blackwood family attorney.

"Like the actor?" Allen asked.

"Yes, Yes," the stuffy old man agreed with a fake smile that Allen knew was forced. "Pleasure to meet you," he said, as Kirk opened the door for him.

The two men stepped out onto the front porch and closed the door, just as Tommy came out of the hallway restroom with the sound of a flushing toilet echoing behind him. He noticed Allen standing in the foyer. "Hey Allen…what's up?"

"You tell me," Allen whispered, "What in the hell is the lawyer doing here tonight of all nights?"

Tommy shrugged his shoulders like it was no big deal, "Probably has something to do with Robert. You know they ain't gonna set a bail for him. He could be in there for a whole month before his trial."

Allen realized that some of his own anxiety was due to Robert being locked up. It just increased the potential that his idiot cousin had worked a deal with the cops in exchange for a lighter sentence. Allen had a fleeting image of the cops waiting for him and his cousins out in the swamp, ready to bust them as soon as they headed out with the goods. He pushed the thought from his mind and tried to focus on the money and how having it would benefit him and Demri, "Is that right?" He replied.

"That's what I heard," Tommy said. "You ready to head to the hill? I think Dewayne and Chris are waiting for us in the garage."

Allen shook his head, "I sent them to load the van. Told them that we would be along shortly."

"No kidding…" Tommy seemed surprised, "…and they went?"

"They weren't happy."

Kirk came back inside from the porch. "Whew, it's really coming down out there." His shirt was wet on the shoulders from the rain. "I hope it stops before the cook out tomorrow. You boys are coming aren't you?"

"Sure," Allen said. It was the first that he heard of it, but he was always up for a barbeque.

"It's gonna be a fun trip out in the swamp with all of the rain," Tommy said, sarcastically. "We were just getting ready to leave."

"You boys have your rain gear with you, don't you?" Kirk asked.

Tommy nodded his head affirmative. Allen shook his, "I don't own any."

Kirk smiled at Allen, "Boy, oh boy, are you gonna be miserable. I think I have something upstairs that might fit you."

Tommy said, "You two go on upstairs and see. I need to make a phone call. I'll meet you in the garage."

"Roger that," Allen said, and then he followed Kirk slowly up the stairs, stopping every few steps as the old man paused to catch his breath. Once they made it up the full flight of stairs, Kirk led Allen into his bedroom. It was tidy – a result of Aunt Patsy's efforts, Allen presumed, since Otis and Kirk didn't like to employ housekeepers. They'd told Allen once that they tried it before, but couldn't find anyone honest enough to not steal them blind. Allen guessed that it had more to do with protecting the family business than anything else, but he didn't really care. After tonight, he had no intentions of ever being a part of this again. He just hadn't told his uncles yet. He was waiting for the right time.

Kirk rummaged through the closet, while Allen looked at an ensemble of old photos of Kirk's late wife, Elizabeth. Allen remembered her well and seeing the old photographs brought back fond memories for him - she was a good woman. Allen wondered just how much she knew about the family business herself. The people that he loved and looked up to in his life all seemed to be in on the secret. He was sure that she'd known too, but it didn't define who she was. It didn't define Kirk either. They had always been good to Allen, and their involvement with the illegal family operation didn't change that. He knew first hand, it was easy to get sucked into. He missed her.

"Ah, ha," Kirk said, from inside the closet and emerged with an entire rain suit, complete with pants and a hat, "This should fit." He handed it over and Allen agreed that it looked like his size. "There's one more thing that I've been wanting to give to you and I haven't had the opportunity to do it yet." Kirk was holding a hand towel wrapped around something. He carefully opened the towel to reveal a nickel plated revolver. Kirk handed it to Allen and said, "That there's a .357 magnum. Kicks like a mule, but it should put down just about anything on this side of reality."

Allen held the handgun and felt the weight of it in his hand. He opened the cylinder and found that it was fully loaded. "Seven rounds... not six, huh?"

"A little surprise for the bad guy who can count shots," Kirk said, with a grin. "That's what makes that gun special. I've had it a long time. I want you to have it now."

Allen tried to hand it back, "Uncle Kirk, I couldn't," but Kirk pushed Allen's hand aside.

"Keep it. You may find a time when you need it."

"I don't know what to say...thank you," Allen shook his uncle's hand.

"That will do. Now hurry up. You boys are running late."

5

At the same time that Kirk was giving the gun to Allen, miles away Johnny pulled his truck along the curb at the Pascagoula boardwalk. The beach area was mostly empty due to the nasty weather, so Johnny felt better about the meeting place than he did when Stokes suggested it earlier this morning. Johnny approached the small beachside pub. The logo on the sign was a stupid looking pirate face, smiling and happy with the words, First Mates, under the pirate in big white letters. Johnny wondered if there'd actually ever been any pirates in this part of the world. Probably not, but anywhere there was water, people liked to imaging that they were somehow living like a pirate. *Yeah right,* he thought as he opened the pub door and walked in. He was more of a pirate than anyone he'd ever met in these parts.' He saw Stokes in the back corner of the small shack, sitting alone at a table. A couple of well-dressed business men and a young sailor were at the bar. All appeared to be drinking alone tonight, 'Definitely not the smiling pirates that the sign depicted. Butt-pirates maybe, but not real pirates.' Johnny was getting the impression that Stokes had them meeting in a gay bar, until the bartender appeared from the kitchen. She was young, blonde and had a very curvy body accentuated nicely by a pirate costume. Johnny could see why the single men flocked to a dive like this, in the middle of a rain storm. Stokes held up his hand and waved, as if he thought that Johnny couldn't see him on the other side of the small room.

Johnny walked up to the table, "Put your hand down, for Christ sakes. When I walked in, I thought everyone in here was fags, but now, thanks to you...they think *we* are." Johnny laughed. Stokes evidently didn't think that it was very funny, because he didn't even smile.

"So what's the purpose of this little meeting?" Stokes never stopped eating the ham sandwich that was sitting on the table in front of him. The uneaten half was buried under a mountain of french fries. He got right to the point. "Do you have good news for me?"

"I'm close," Johnny said.

"Close, huh? Well, close ain't doing me any good, Johnny. My boss is getting a little bit impatient and he's not the kind of guy to piss off. I've been telling him that you were close for a month now. So, can you come up with the product, or not?"

Johnny leaned over the table, getting closer to Stokes, so that the other people in the small establishment couldn't hear him. "I said I could and I will. There's just been a couple of setbacks with my finances."

Stokes took a bite of his sandwich, "Setbacks...what kind of setbacks? You haven't lost our money, have you?" As he spoke, pieces of bread fell from the corners of his mouth.

"Just some minor things," Johnny waived his hand dismissively. In reality, the setbacks were huge. Johnny had tried to make a quick profit, not only his money, but Stokes' money also. His plan was to buy drugs at a rock bottom price and sell it full tilt. He turned to his friend Lionel to sell the drugs, since Lionel had connections with some of the street distributors in the black community, but Lionel had never paid him the money back. His assumption now was that Lionel had used up all, or most of his product. He was going to deal with Lionel later and figured on making enough tonight to cover most of the losses, but getting cut out of the trip to the Whiskey Bayou due to the black cop lady snooping around was another major setback. This was one of the two big runs that they made every year. The rest paid chump change compared to what Otis paid them for this one. All in all, he was short about fifty thousand dollars. "Can you spot me some cash?"

"How short are you?"

"About fifty g's."

Stokes let his arms fall to the table, "Now where in the hell do you suppose I'm going to get another fifty grand from? If I had that kind of cash available, then I wouldn't need to be talking to you right now, would I?"

"Well then you're going to have to wait until I get my cash straight. I need to buy the supplies before I can cook the goods," Johnny said. It irked him that right now, at this very moment, his cousins were about to head out to the drop to make some good money and he wasn't going.

"Are you not listening to what I'm saying, Johnny? We don't have a week. If we don't have the…" Stokes was getting loud and caught himself, "If we don't have the stock by Saturday, the deal's off. If the deal is off and we don't have the money to return to Mr. LaRue, things get worse, for both of us."

"What do you mean the fucking deal is off? I've got a lot riding on this, man." Johnny was getting loud now.

"We all do, Johnny and everyone has done their part in this but you. I have done what I said I was going to do. You're the only wild card here. By the way, that was some fucked up shit, you pulling a gun on my brother-in-law!"

Johnny smiled, remembering the look on the fat brother-in-law's face. "I told you to come alone."

Stokes looked at Johnny, "Don't forget who is funding this venture. You piss me off, there's no deal."

"I don't do business with people that don't listen to instructions," Johnny said. "Besides, you're just a middleman. Tell the big boss that next time, I want him there."

"What don't you understand, Johnny?" Stokes said, "You don't get to give any instructions. You get your supplies together and make the meth… that's it." He pushed his plate away from him, like he'd lost his appetite talking to Johnny. "Get the shit cooked by Saturday, so that we can collect our money…ok?"

"Alright, I'll figure out how to make it happen," Johnny said.

"Good," Stokes popped a french fry into his mouth, "Do you still want the other thing?"

"Sure do," Johnny said. That of course was the real reason that he'd called the meeting in the first place.

Stokes slid the bottle of rohypnol tablets across the table under the cover of his palm. "That will be two hundred…but you can owe me," Stokes said. "I'm not even going to ask you what you need date rape pills for."

"Good, don't!" Johnny took the bottle of pills and put them into his pocket, "And I won't ask you why you like to hang out in gay bars," he said, as he stood to leave. He made no attempt to keep his voice down. "You can take the two hundred from my cut."

"This isn't a gay bar," Stokes explained, as the other patrons were now looking at them.

"Tell that to these two," Johnny said loudly, pointing at the two business men sitting at the bar. They both turned and glared at him, but neither of them were about to start anything with the maniacal man who was already on his way out the door.

"Don't let me down on this, Johnny. I've got a lot invested here," Stokes yelled right before the door closed.

Yeah, yeah," Johnny said, as he walked through the rain to his truck, "I'll see you Saturday."

6

The rain was finally lifting by the time that Allen got back to his neighborhood. The wet weather had been relentless all evening. The streets were flooded in areas and getting to Demri's from Violent Hill was a slow, nerve-racking experience – especially for someone not entirely familiar with the area. More than once, Allen had to hold his breath as he entered high water, hoping that he wasn't driving off the road and into the gator infested swamp. The clock on the dashboard of his truck read 2:46 am, as he pulled it into Demri's driveway and his eyes were heavy. He was waterlogged and his back ached. All that he could think about was getting a shower and some warm clothes - because despite the rain gear that Kirk had given him, he was soaked. When he pulled into the driveway, he noticed a strange car parked behind Demri's. He turned off the ignition and grabbed an envelope from the passenger seat. In it was the payment for his work tonight. Elmer had given it to him right before he left Violent Hill. He closed the door to his truck and stood in the driveway for a few seconds, looking at the other car. It was a Jaguar XJS and to be honest, he was a little bothered at the sight of it. He looked through the darkness at the main house and he could see through the kitchen window that there was a lamp still lit inside. At that moment, he felt that if he wasn't so tired, he could sure use a drink or ten down at the pub. Anything to get out of there right then. He wasn't sure if he wanted to get away from whoever owned the car, or Demri, or both. He only knew that he was insanely jealous that it wasn't him inside the house with her.

A breeze blew across the yard, causing him to shiver in his wet clothes. He needed to go upstairs and get dried off. *Oh well*, he thought, *getting a woman like that to pay attention to him was a long shot to begin with*. At least he had a good place to live and he felt like they were at least friends – that was something. He decided that he would take a shot of his own whiskey that he had stashed and as he climbed the stairs of his apartment he thought – maybe two or three shots tonight.

It had been a taxing evening to say the least. He'd been on edge all night and the swamp run was made extremely difficult by the torrential rainfall during the entire trip. It was coming down so hard at times that he and Dewayne had to bail water out of the boat, to avoid swamping while Chris drove and Tommy stood on the bow, looking out for debris in the water. Finally, they arrived at the shack, only this time there were no fires burning as before and the drop off was nothing more than a quick exchange – three bags this time from the Blackwoods, for two bags from the other guys. Within a matter of a few minutes, they were on their way back to Violent Hill. The rain let up a little on the way back and the situation didn't seem so dire, since the boat wasn't filling up with water faster than they could bail it out.

Once they returned, it was much the same process as that first time - Allen and Tommy were left to put the boat and the van back in their proper places while Dewayne and Chris took the bags to the main house. By the time that Allen and Tommy made it to the house, their dinner was ready and waiting. When Allen was called into Otis's office, he was disturbed to find that Otis was not in good health. The old man - who had been dressed like he was headed to church every other time that Allen had seen him – was now dressed in pajama bottoms and a white sweater with his oxygen mask fixed firmly to his face. His color didn't look good to Allen.

"Are you alright?" Allen asked him.

The old man nodded and pulled his mask aside long enough to thank Allen for helping them out tonight and to tell him that he'd included a little bit extra in his envelope. "We're having a cookout tomorrow. Will you make it?" Otis asked.

Allen took Otis's old hand in his own and said, "I wouldn't miss it."

Allen, not wanting to appear rude, hadn't looked at the envelope in the office. He'd come straight home when he left Otis's office, without even telling the others goodbye. He could hardly wait to get inside of his house to open up the envelope to see what, *a little bit extra*, actually meant. Allen took one more look at the Jaguar in the driveway, before closing his apartment door and tossing his keys on the counter. He tore the envelope open and removed the wad of cash. He counted the hundred dollar bills quickly, until he got to fifteen thousand and he still had a large amount of money uncounted in his hand. He counted out another ten thousand before the bills ran out. He took a deep breath and backed away from the pile of money, now haphazardly stacked on his kitchen counter. His legs were tingling and he wasn't sure if it was due to the long night's work, or from the sight of all of that money. He leaned against the stove. A little bit extra in Otis's opinion was apparently an extra ten thousand dollars. Allen let the envelope fall to the kitchen floor and it landed with a small metallic thud. He reached down and retrieved the envelope from the floor - turned it over and a familiar key fell into his hand. With the key, a small note was attached. Allen held the key in front of his face like a mad scientist looking into a vial of his greatest creation and let the envelope slip through his fingers again. He didn't know what it meant exactly, but it looked like his Great Uncle Otis had just given him a key to Violent Hill. He opened the note attached to the key with a small string and in Otis's hand writing it said,

"You will always have a home...right here!"

Allen laid the key on the counter with the pile of money and pulled his bottle of Whiskey from the cabinet. He didn't even look for a glass. He just pulled the top off of the bottle and drank four swigs straight. Feeling like that would hold him over until he got out of the shower, he pulled his wet clothes off and stumbled into the bathroom.

After spending a good twenty minutes under the cool water, Allen got out and put on his shorts and t-shirt. It was his attire of choice when he planned on lounging around for the next day or so. He went to the kitchen with every intention to stack his money and find a good hiding place, when he heard the screams coming from the main house. They were followed by breaking glass. He immediately ran out of the door and back into the rain - sure that the screaming had come from Demri.

7

L ionel slowly drove his car past the entrance to the Blackwood home driveway and parked just off of the road, behind a grove of thick bushes. He thought that no one would be driving on this road so late at night, but just in case he wanted to stay out of sight. He had a perfect view of the Blackwood driveway from where he was - able to see anyone coming or going from the house. He pulled his pistol from the glove box and held it in his hand. He flipped open the cylinder, removed one of the bullets from the chamber and set it on his dash board. Lionel stared at the round for several seconds - a hollow point - the new brass of the casing glimmering in the moonlight. That one was for Johnny. The rest of the bullets in the gun were for anyone who got in the way. He put the round back in the gun, rotating the cylinder so that it would be the first to fire.

He got out of his car and leaned against the fender. Covering the flame of a lighter with his hand to shield it from the rain, he lit a cigarette. He knew that Johnny didn't live here. Violent Hill was his family's home, but the truth was that he didn't know where Johnny lived. He'd considered finding out, but to do that would mean that he would have to go around asking questions. Asking questions may get back to Johnny and Lionel didn't want that white trash, piece of shit to see him coming. He wanted the shock and horror on that cracker's face when Lionel pulled the trigger. Just like he imagined it was on his parents face when Johnny murdered them.

A little over a week since putting his parents into the ground, the grief and rage still boiled inside of Lionel. He considered going through the woods and up to the house right now. He was sure that he could find a way inside. Maybe just put a bullet into the head of one of Johnny's family members for that prick to mourn. No sooner had the thought entered

Lionel's mind, he knew that it was something that he could never do. He couldn't hurt innocent people. His vendetta was against Johnny - that was who he would deal with. Standing in the dark, wet night - tears streaming down his face – Lionel already felt like a killer. He'd envisioned killing Johnny a thousand times. He tossed his cigarette on the ground and got back in his car. It was too late for Johnny to be visiting his family tonight, but tomorrow, or perhaps the next day, he would come – and Lionel would be waiting.

llen lost his footing at the base of the stairs and slid all the way down. He slid in the mud, across the soggy earth like a baseball player, a good five yards before scrambling back up to his feet and sprinting to Demri's back door. He pulled on the handle, but the screen was locked. He could still hear her screaming and now he could hear Lindsay crying in the background as well. He thought of the gun that Kirk had given him - still upstairs in his apartment. He decided against going back to get it when Demri screamed again. This time she was yelling *"get off of me goddamnit... just leave!"* Allen could hear the panic in her voice as she pleaded with whoever was inside of the house with her. He jerked the screen door as hard as he could and the flimsy lock broke. The door swung open. He turned the handle to the main door and of course it was locked too, but now at least he could see inside. Demri was standing in the living room wearing her bed clothes and crying. The kids were visible behind her in their bed clothes also and Demri was pointing her finger into the face of a man that looked vaguely familiar. He couldn't clearly see the man, since the stranger was standing in the kitchen doorway with his back facing Allen.

Though Allen was sure that he'd seen the man before and was actively trying to place him when the man grabbed Demri by the arm and jerked her forward. Lindsay let out a scream and rushed forward to defend her mother. The little girl was pushed aside by the stranger. Demri struggled in vain against her attacker, yelling at the top of her lungs for help and pleading with the man to let her go. Allen had seen all that he needed to see. Later, he wouldn't be able to tell anyone how he'd gotten through the locked door so quickly, but in an instant he was in the kitchen with them. From the other man's perspective it must have looked like the Kool-Aid man had just entered the room by the way that he shattered the door frame.

The surprise of the back door exploding shocked the man into letting go of Demri. Just as he did, Allen was connecting a right cross, flush to the stranger's chin.

As the punch found its mark, Allen could feel the man's jaw dislocate. The attacker dropped to the floor, banging his head off of the refrigerator on his way down to the linoleum. Allen's momentum, aided by the fresh mud caked to his feet, caused him to slip down on top of the man. Allen got his legs under him and grabbed the stranger by his shirt. The attacker had a terrified look in his eyes – shocked by suddenly going from aggressor to victim. Allen didn't waste any time by asking questions. He quickly began dragging the stranger out of the house, and away from Demri and the kids. The three of them were watching with shock and horror at the sudden violent events. Right about the time that Allen and the man reached the busted rear door of the house, the stranger, regaining his senses, began to fight back by clawing at Allen with nails – which were surprisingly long. Allen easily swatted the man's flailing hands aside and got in another couple of good punches before the bones in his knuckles began to ache. The stranger's face was turning into a swollen, bloody mess and his breath reeked of alcohol. It was then that Allen remembered where he'd seen the man before. This was the blue shirt man from the Kingfish Lounge. The one that had watched Demri like a hawk the night that they'd met. Allen stopped punching Blue Shirt when he went limp for the second time and dragged him the rest of the way out into the yard. It proved to be a relatively easy task, once Blue Shirt blacked out and was no longer trying to gouge Allen with his nails. In the yard the man started to wake up and was moaning a deep guttural sound. Allen stood him up by yanking his bloody collar and told him to get his ass moving, pushing him toward the Jaguar and kicking him in the backside for good measure. The kick caused the man to fall to the ground for a third time.

"Allen stop!" Demri was standing at the back door, "He's had enough."

Allen looked at Demri. His rage subsiding, he realized that he'd been close to killing this man. He was breathing heavily and he was covered with mud and blood. Some of it was his own, due to the scratches to his neck and face. He looked down at blue shirt who was pulling himself up off of the ground. Allen said, "It's your lucky day, pal. You get to go home tonight, but if I ever see you over here again, I can't make any promises."

Blue shirt tried to speak, but with his jaw broken he just grunted, as blood drained from the side of his mouth.

"Whatever," Allen said, "I hope you like milkshakes motherfucker, because you ain't going to be eating anything solid for a while. Happy trails!" Allen didn't hit the man anymore, but he also didn't move from between Blue Shirt and Demri. The man stumbled back to his car and except for a few short moments of searching for his keys, he was driving down the road and away from the house rather quickly. Once he was gone, Allen turned around to find that Demri was not in the doorway anymore. She'd gone back into the house. Allen went to the broken door and for some reason, courtesy he guessed, he knocked, "Demri?"

"I'll be right out." She said, from the back of the house. Allen assumed that she was in the bedroom comforting the children. While he waited, he checked the door frame to see what kind of damage he'd caused by breaking it open. It didn't look too bad. He would call someone out to fix it first thing in the morning. He grabbed some paper towels from the roll near the sink and started wiping up blood that was splattered on the floor. After a few minutes in the back, she came into the kitchen, got her broom and started helping him clean up the mess, by sweeping up shattered glass lying near the doorway to the kitchen. The two of them cleaned until the kitchen was tidy again, save the busted door. Neither spoke a word about what had just happened. Once they were finished, Allen stood up and got ready to leave. "Are the kids alright?" he asked.

She nodded, "They were shook up, but they're not hurt." She began to cry, "Landon asked if you were alright when I put him in bed."

"Hey, hey," Allen walked over and put his hand on her shoulder, "I'm fine…are you ok?"

"I'm just a little shook up, but I'll be fine," she said. Her eyes searched his face and she noticed the scratches on his cheek and neck. "Oh god, we need to get those cleaned up."

"What…" Allen touched his neck and saw that his fingers were covered with blood. "Yeah, I'll clean it up when I get back to the apartment." Allen looked down at the rest of him and realized that one side of him was still covered in mud from his fall. "Looks like I need another shower anyway."

"No," she said, "Let me get the first aid kit from the bathroom. I'll clean the open wounds for you."

"You really don't need to..." he began, but she was already hallway down the hall on her way to get the kit.

They sat at her dining room table as she dabbed rubbing alcohol on his face and neck. Along with the alcohol, she had antibiotic ointment, gauze and medical tape. Allen figured that if he didn't call her off after she finished applying the alcohol, he was going to leave here looking like a mummy.

"Who was that guy?" Allen asked.

Demri poured more alcohol on a rag, "That was Bruce."

"And Bruce is?" Allen pried. He figured that she owed him at least that much, after what had gone down tonight.

"An ex," she said. She looked at Allen and saw that he was waiting for more information. "He and I have been over for a month or so and only dated a few times to begin with."

"I'm assuming by the way that he was acting, it was your call to end it?"

"Yes," She said, "he showed up tonight and said that he wanted to talk. It was late, but we were all still awake watching a movie, so I didn't see where it would hurt to let him say what he had to say and be done with it. We really never had the talk, you know? I didn't really feel like we needed one, since we were never really that close to begin with. He was just someone that I went out with and had a couple of drinks with." She must have seen the look on Allen's face, because she said, "It wasn't an intimate relationship...ok?"

"Ok," Allen agreed, wincing as she dabbed one of the particularly deep scratches on his neck.

"Anyway, I didn't know that he'd been drinking when I let him in, but when we started talking I could smell it. He was saying weird things like he couldn't live without me, crazy stuff like that. Like I said, I don't think that we even kissed more than once or twice and never with any passion, so the way that he was talking was kind of creeping me out. I told him to go home and sober up and we could discuss this at a later time, but he started getting angry..." She started crying again.

Allen turned to her and pulled her head into his chest. "It's alright. You don't have to go into any more detail. Let's just start trying to forget it altogether."

She cried hard for a few minutes and then she said, "He'd never been

physical before. He seemed like a good guy. It just didn't spark you know?"
Allen nodded. "I honestly thought that he was going to hurt me and the
kids until you showed up…thank you."

"You don't need to thank me. You are good people, there's no reason
for someone to treat any of you guys like that."

She smiled and was beautiful, even behind her swollen eyes and
smeared mascara. "You really got him good. Where'd you learn to fight
like that?"

Allen shrugged, "Grew up in a rough neighborhood, I guess." He stood
and flexed his aching hand. "I better get back to my apartment and get my
hand on ice. This thing's going to be sore in a little while."

Demri held his hand in her own and inspected it. "Do you think it's
broken?" she asked.

"I don't know…maybe. It's hard to tell right now." Allen moved his
fingers around and said, "I'll check on you guys in the morning."

Demri's voice softened, "Don't go…I'll make you a pallet on the
couch." Allen could tell by her tone that she was still shook up and she
didn't want to be left alone. "I can't even lock the back door. I need you
to stay."

Allen nodded his head, "Ok, but I need to go get cleaned up first. I
can't sleep on your couch covered in mud."

She smiled again, "I'll make you a pallet while you're getting your
shower."

Allen went back to his apartment and cleaned up for the second time
this long, drawn-out night. As he was brushing his teeth he was able to get
a good look at the scratch marks on his neck and face. Bruce must have had
nails like a woman, because a couple of them were pretty deep and were
going to leave scars. He threw on some jeans and a t-shirt along with his
sneakers. To top off the outfit, he tucked Kirk's gun into his waistband.
He doubted that he'd need it, but if Bruce had any ideas of redemption,
he knew that the guy wouldn't show without some back up. In reality,
Allen doubted that Bruce was thinking about anything other than medical
attention tonight, but it was better to be safe than sorry.

When Allen returned, Demri was watching a re-run of That 70's Show.
There was a blanket and a pillow situated neatly on the couch, the way that
his grandma used to prepare it when he was a kid. The blanket was folded

at an angle and pressed neatly into a perfect rectangle across the couch. She also had a glass of wine sitting on the end table waiting for him and one for herself in her hand. "I figured that we could ease our nerves a little before bed," she said.

"How can I argue with that?" Allen picked up the glass and offered Demri a toast, "Here's to broken doors, broken noses, and broken relationships."

"Very funny! Why do you look like you are ready to go to work?" She motioned to his jeans and shoes.

Allen lounged on the couch while Demri sat in her recliner. "I have to get up and go to a family cook out tomorrow and I figured since it is already nearly five in the morning – I could save some time by being ready to go." He looked over at the beautiful woman sitting on the recliner across the small living room and an idea struck him. "Do you and the kids want to go with me? There should be some other kids, food, and a big swimming pool."

Demri sipped her wine. Her gut instinct was to say, no thank you, but the idea of seeing the infamous Violent Hill Estate from the inside sparked her curiosity. "What time?"

"Noon-ish, or whenever we get there."

She finished her wine and set the glass down on the table as she stood. "I'll have to see how I feel in the morning and I need to get my door fixed, but thank you for inviting us." She stretched her arms high over her head, arching her back, "I need to get some sleep."

"I'll take care of the door tomorrow, before I go," Allen assured her. "Goodnight." He watched her walk down the hallway turning the lights out as she went. When she was gone, he kicked off his shoes and pulled the covers back. It was too hot to cover up, so he just laid on top while the ceiling fan buzzed overhead. Within a matter of minutes - he was asleep.

He wasn't sure just how long he'd been asleep, but sometime before dawn, he woke up to a hand on his chest. When he opened his eyes Demri was sitting on the edge of the couch. She was crying and said, "Allen, I can't sleep."

Allen gently put his hand around her shoulder and pulled her close to him. She wrapped her arms around him and held him as close as she could. She laid beside him on the couch - her body half on his and half on the cushions – nothing else was said between the two of them. They held onto each other as they both drifted off to sleep.

9

This particular area of Pascagoula was very familiar to Lashauna. She'd been raised in a small fishing community not far down the road. As a matter of fact, a childhood friend used to live on this very street, many years ago. It seemed like yesterday when her mother would bring her here for slumber parties when she was in grade school, and later for teenage high school parties. She thought back to her first kiss, right here in this neighborhood, after one of those same high school parties – Timmy Shires was his name. She'd been crazy about Timmy back then. He was the running back for the high school football team and everyone – including himself – referred to Timmy as "TD" Shires, or Touchdown Shires.

His parents were the despicable kind. The kind who lived their unrealized high school dreams through their child. They made friends with Timmy's friends and it was a common occurrence for weekend parties to be held at the Shires home. If she remembered correctly, the house was just a few blocks away from where she was right now. The Shires' were friendly and welcoming when they first met her, but as soon as they found out that she and Timmy were dating, they pulled a one-eighty - apparently, mortified by the fact that Timmy was dating a black girl. From then on, she was no longer welcome at the Shires' home. Timmy and her vowed to each other that they would make a stand and defy his parents' wishes, but it wasn't two weeks into that stand that Timmy broke up with her and started dating Trish Johnson, a blond haired, blue eyed cheerleader that was more along the lines of what his parents were looking for. Lashauna had been devastated at the time. It was her first crush and her first break-up. Looking back now, she was a little bit embarrassed to have been so head over heels for Timmy. Unfortunately, the glory of being the high school football star faded as quickly as the stadium lights, and a few years after graduation, TD more commonly stood for "Town Drunk" when someone was referring to Timmy Shires. Years later, when Lashauna had only been on the force a short time and still in uniform, she ran into Timmy Shires at the station, while he was being booked on a drunk and disorderly charge. He'd put on about twenty pounds of beer gut and was already losing his hair. She wanted to go over to the finger printing booth and thank him for doing her a favor all those years back, but decided against it. Timmy breaking up with her, when she was too young and stupid to realize what a shallow piece of poo that he was destined to become, had been the best thing that could have happened to her back then. She smiled at the memories of her youthful ignorance. It was an easier life - a much different life, for sure. It was hard to imagine who she was then, and who she was now, were connected in any way at all.

She drove slowly, looking for the house number. Leo wasn't helping her out very much with finding the address. His attention was focused on a file folder that was laying in his lap. It contained all of the information that they'd been able to obtain on Allen Blackwood – which didn't amount to very much. Leo was pretty sure that they wouldn't even have known where to begin their search at all, if Robert Blackwood hadn't given them a name and the state where he formerly resided. Demri Harvell was a little easier. She was a local Mississippi resident whom Robert was pretty sure his cousin had befriended. Lashauna and Leo pulled Mrs. Harvell's police file also. Aside from a restraining order, placed on her estranged husband after an incident a couple of years back, it was equally devoid of any useful information. "What gives?" Leo shook his head with disappointment. "Don't these people ever commit crimes?"

Lashauna looked at her partner and then went right back to checking the address of the houses.

Leo continued, "If it wasn't for a bar fight in Virginia, back in o-seven, there wouldn't be anything on this guy at all. Not even minor stuff, like a single traffic ticket in the last ten years." He thumbed through a couple of pages. "How does this guy fit in to this Blackwood group?"

"He's family," Lashauna said, "Other than that, I can't see where there's much in common."

Leo closed the folder, "Then why are we wasting our time coming all the way out here to talk to him?"

"I just want to get my eyes on him," Lashauna said, as she pulled the unmarked police car into the driveway of the address that matched the one they had for Demri. There was a grey Land Rover parked along with a Toyota sedan. The Land Rover matched the description of the car that they had for Allen.

"He may be completely oblivious to anything involving the Taylor's murder," Lashauna said, "but someone in that family knows something and I'm pretty sure that we aren't going to get any of the regulars to talk. I'm just kind of hoping that we can learn something from this guy that we don't already know." She parked her car and looked over at her partner who was staring back at her, as if to say, *go ahead…tell me the real reason why we're here.* "Ok," She said, "I also hope that I can rattle a cage. Try to stir up a little activity…you know. I'm getting a little desperate with this case. I don't like not having a trail to follow."

"I feel you partner," Leo said, using his best street slang. "What about the camera lead? Have you heard anything back from the storage building owner?"

"Not yet, his secretary said that he was out of town and should be back sometime this week. I'm hoping to hear back soon. He's the only one who has the access to pull the video off of the cameras. If that doesn't pan out then we're just about out of options with this case, unless Allen Blackwood can help us. I'm pretty sure that's his Land Rover."

Leo looked in the notes and then smiled and tossed the folder onto the dashboard of the car. "Let's go lean on him a little bit then. See if he has it in his heart to help us out in our time of need." As they got out of the car, a beautiful woman met them at the edge of the driveway. Leo looked between her and Lashauna and tried to decide which one of the two might be the prettiest woman that he'd ever seen, but for the life of him he couldn't choose. Either one would be a candidate for 'pin-up of the year' in any of the girly magazines that he'd ever had the pleasure of reading.

Miss July said, "Good morning," as they approached her.

"Good morning," Lashauna said, revealing her badge. "I'm Detective Trudeau and this is my partner, Detective Menard. We're looking for Demri Harvell."

"Well…you found her! A testament to good police work." Demri smiled, but there was something behind the smile that Lashauna noticed.

She'd seen it on the faces of countless women over the years, it looked a lot like fear. But why? Lashauna wondered. "What can I do for you?" Demri asked.

"We are looking for a man that we believe you may have been in contact with recently." Lashauna looked at Leo and he held up the mug shot of Allen from the bar fight years ago. "His name is Allen Blackwood."

Demri looked at the photo and her dread of facing the repercussions from what happened to Bruce last night, quickly turned to confusion. She looked closely at the mug shot, hoping that it wasn't Allen, but if you added a couple of pounds and a few years to the handsome guy in the photo, there was no mistaking, it was him. "Yeah, I know him. He's renting the apartment above the garage." She motioned to the stairs leading up.

Leo and Lashauna were both about to thank her and go knock on the apartment door, when Demri added, "...but he's asleep on my couch right now."

Demri didn't like the way that the Detectives exchanged a glance with each other. "May we talk to him?" Lashauna asked.

Demri said, "Is he in some kind of trouble?"

"No," Lashauna said, flatly, "Just a few questions about a case that we are working on."

"Ok," Demri still appeared a little reluctant, obstinate even, "wait here and I'll go get him."

Lashauna and Leo watched as Demri went through the mangled frame of the back door. When Leo pointed it out to Lashauna, she shrugged her shoulders. "Maybe, she forgot her keys."

Inside, Demri woke Allen by punching him in the shoulder and whispering with obvious panic in her voice, "Allen, get up. There are two detectives outside, looking for you."

Allen sprang from a sound sleep, directly to his feet, "What? Are they here about last night?"

"No," Demri continued to whisper, since the back door was standing wide open. "They said something about a case they were working on. Do you have any idea what they might be looking for?" She was clearly agitated and Allen couldn't blame her, the past couple of hours had been stressful on her, to say the least.

Allen immediately thought about the pile of money laying on his kitchen counter and how he'd acquired it. "No," he lied. He wasn't sure if that's why they were here, or not. He couldn't think of any other reason that the cops would be looking for him in Mississippi.

Demri watched as he peered around the corner trying to peek outside, where the detectives were waiting. "Well…what are you waiting for?" she asked. "Get out there and see what they want."

Allen nodded and pulled the pistol that Kirk had given him from his waistband. He set it on top of her TV stand, so that it was out of the children's reach.

"What the fuck is that?" There was panic in her voice again when she saw the gun, but she was still trying to whisper.

"I didn't know if your boyfriend would be back to cause more trouble, so I brought it just in case," Allen whispered.

"You brought that into my house without letting me know?" she was furious and now, somehow whisper yelling. Under different circumstances Allen would have found humor in the exchange.

"Look," Allen explained, "I was trying to protect you and your kids and I apologize if having it in here offends you, but right now is not the time for you and I to hash this out."

"What the fuck are the cops doing here, Allen?" She was so upset that she was talking in circles.

"I don't know, alright," Allen said, "Let me go find out." He straightened his shirt and out onto the porch with the detectives. It was the same cops that he'd seen at Otis's during the cookout, the day the black guy showed up. The lady cop was a stunner and the man looked strong. Both appeared to be all business. The lady stepped forward and introduced herself and then her partner. Demri stood behind Allen, thinking that it was a good thing that her kids were still asleep. They'd witnessed enough excitement last night and didn't need to wake up to the police standing in their back yard.

Lashauna noted the scratch marks all over Allen's face and neck. Then she motioned to the broken kitchen door, as she turned to Demri, "Who huffed and puffed?"

Demri smiled and said, "Yeah, my kids were locked inside and I panicked." Allen was surprised at how quickly Demri came up with the lie.

"You did that?" Leo asked, and then commented, "…strong woman."

Allen nodded in agreement and said, "What can I do for you two detectives?"

Lashauna didn't believe for a second that the petite lady in the sun dress had kicked the back door in, and done that much damage to the frame, but she let it go, since as far as she could tell, it had nothing at all to do with the reason she was here. "We talked to your cousin Robert, and he indicated that when you arrived a couple of weeks ago, you spent some time at your family's property at Violent Hill when you arrived."

"Yeah," Allen said, "...that's right. How's Robert doing by the way?"

"Good, he's doing real well," Lashauna said. "He looks real good in county orange. I imagine that's the color that he'll be wearing for quite a while."

"That sucks," Allen said. "...but hey, you can't just let people go around running up other folks phone bills, now can you?"

Lashauna laughed, "Yeah, I wish that was all it was."

"I don't know anything about Robert's adventures, other than what I heard after the fact, which I'm sure you already have in a police file somewhere."

Lashauna nodded, "Actually, I'm not here because of Robert's most recent caper. I'm conducting the murder investigation of an old married couple by the name of Taylor. Have you ever heard the name?"

Allen shook his head, "No, I'm sorry, I haven't." He thought about the question for a second and then said, "I'm not sure what this kind of an investigation would have to do with me."

"We were hoping that if you've overheard anything or, if you were to happen to hear anything in the future, you would reach out to us." She handed him a business card with her name and phone number on it.

"I'm not sure that I'm following," Allen said, as he inspected the card. "I don't know who you think that I might overhear talking about something like this. I typically don't associate with people that would be involved in a murder...but I'll keep my ears open."

"That's all we ask." Lashauna said. Her cell phone started to ring. She pulled it from her pocket and excused herself from the conversation. Leo wrapped up the meeting by thanking both Demri and Allen for their time. He joined Lashauna at the car, just as she was finishing her phone call. Leo could tell that whomever she'd been talking with had given her news that made her happy, because she had a smile on her face and Leo hadn't seen that in weeks. "Good news!" She said, returning her phone to her pocket, "That was the self-storage manager. The owner will be there around six o'clock this evening to review the tapes from the night of the murder."

"That's good...but it's not a definite," Leo said.

"It's all that we have right now..." Lashauna said, as she climbed into the car, "...I'm like an ugly nymphomaniac right now, I'll take whatever I can get."

Allen stopped her just as Lashauna was climbing into her car. "Excuse me, Detective."

She stepped back out of her car, "What can I do for you?"

"I'm sorry to hold you up, but a thought just occurred to me and I thought that maybe if I were to do you a favor and keep me ears open for info on the Taylors, then maybe you could do me a favor as well," Allen said.

Lashauna looked at Leo as if to say, *can you believe this guy*? And then she asked, "What kind of favor can I do for you, Mister Blackwood?"

"Steven Gilmour," Allen said, "That was my father's name. He was around here in the early seventies and then took off. I've never met him. Don't know where he is."

"Sorry to hear about your family problems," Lashauna said, "What is it that you want me to do?"

"I didn't know what kind of resources that you had access to. Didn't know if you could find him."

"I'm not a private eye, Mister Blackwood. But I would be happy to refer you to a good one."

"Eh," Allen shrugged, "no worries. Just thought I'd ask."

"Have a good day, Sir." She returned to her car.

Allen and Demri watched the detectives pull away. When they were gone, Allen turned to Demri. She had a confused look that he was sure matched his own.

"Murder?" she gasped.

Allen raised his hands in confusion, "I don't have any idea what that was all about." Allen rubbed his temples with his free hand as he looked over the business card that Detective Trudeau had given to him.

"Was she implying that someone in your family might have been involved in a murder?" Demri asked.

"I think so. That's what it sounded like to me, but I don't have any idea who it could be, or what they expect me to know about it."

Demri stepped close to Allen and grabbed both of his hands. "Look, I know that what happened last night with Bruce was no way for us to start a relationship and I don't want you to get the wrong impression of me based on that. That being said, we would both be fooling ourselves to think that there isn't something sparking here. I have a lot riding on the decisions that I make in my life and I can't jeopardize my children." She let go of his hands and held his face, so that she could look directly into his eyes. "Apparently, I am a terrible judge of character and I have a history of bad men. I can't afford to have you in my life, or even at my home, if there are things going on in your life that could cause trouble for me. So tell me now…is there anything at all that you are involved with, that I need to be aware of before it puts me and my children in harm's way?"

Allen stared into her eyes. He knew what was at stake here – for her, her kids and him. He considered lying saying that he was completely above board with everything, but she was right, she deserved the truth, and Allen couldn't put her and the kid's in harm's way. For some reason, he trusted her, so he started talking, "I honestly don't have any idea what the cops were asking about…" Allen explained, "…but, I have twenty five thousand dollars in cash upstairs on my kitchen counter. I made it last night doing some work for my family."

She dropped her hands from his face. Her mouth hung open from the shock. "What?"

Allen stepped forward and put his hands on her shoulders. "Let me explain before you freak out. I know that sounds really bad, but it was a simple boat ride into the swamp to drop off some black duffel bags and pick some other ones up. I only helped out this last time because family really needed me, since Robert and Johnny couldn't do it. Besides, he promised me a job at the dealership if I helped."

"Boat ride into the swamp…at night? Black duffel bags?" Demri pulled away from him again, "What…was this a fucking movie that you watched? What are you involved with?" The questions were flowing and she didn't give him a chance to answer any of them before asking a new one. "What was in the bags?"

"I honestly don't know. I didn't look," Allen said, "I can only assume."

Demri shook her head in disbelief. "Assume what...Drugs?"

Allen nodded.

"Your fucking family is running drugs into the swamp?" Demri said, a little louder than Allen would have liked for her to, since they were still outside. "...and you're helping them do it?"

"Like I said...I helped them out last night and I have no intention of ever doing it again."

"This last time?" Demri said.

"What?"

"You said, *'this last time'* a minute ago, were there other times?" she asked.

Allen put his hands into the pockets of his jeans like a child that was being reprimanded by a parent. "Yes, once before. Right after I got to town...and before I met you."

Demri stormed back to the house. "I can't believe this. I have rented a room to a fucking drug dealer. I want you to get your shit and get it off of my property, right now."

Allen chased after her, "Wait Demri. Just hear me out."

"Hear you out? You're lucky that I don't call those two detectives that just left here and report you and the rest of your fucking criminal family," She screamed.

"Look at me," he yelled back. It was the first time that he'd raised his voice to her and she stopped and turned around. "You have every right to hate me and want me out of here, and I will leave just as soon as you give me a chance to explain."

Demri had tears in her eyes and sarcasm in her voice, but at least she wasn't yelling anymore, "What would you like to explain to me, Allen?"

The sudden change in tempo threw Allen off for a second, as he searched for the right words to say. He felt like everything he'd been hoping for was right at his fingertips and he'd screwed it up. Looking at her right now, he felt something that he had never felt before, for any woman. The fact that she was crying and he was the reason was almost too much for him to bare. He choked back his own tears and said, "Demri, I haven't ever amounted to much and most of my life, I've been fine with that. I've spent my years hating myself…hating everything and everyone. I have known women before, but it never amounted to anything and there were never any feelings…none at all."

"Allen, why are you telling me this? I don't care one bit."

"Just hear me Demri," he pleaded. "The point is, I have not always been a very good guy, but I have never really been a bad one either. I have always been content just scraping by and minding my business. All too often, I found solace in a bottle - maybe too much at times, but ever since I first laid my eyes on you…I knew that I wanted something more. I've never met anybody that has made me want to be a better person, made me want to have more to offer in life. I knew that I had nothing that I could offer to you, or your children, but I knew that I wanted to give the three of you everything that you ever wanted and I had to take a chance and do it quickly." He looked up at her standing on the porch. She sat down on the steps and Allen thought that was a good sign. "I went into the swamp the first time, before I met you, at the request of my uncle without really knowing what I was getting into. I sort of figured out that we were doing something illegal somewhere in the middle of that first trip. After that one, I told him that I couldn't do it anymore and I had every intention of owning up to that decision. That's when I moved out here with you. My intent was to get a regular job, just like you and I discussed, maybe doing mechanical work…or electrical work…I don't know…something legitimate. Then, I saw that your car was broken down and you were struggling financially and all of a sudden…an opportunity presented itself."

"Don't blame me for your stupid decisions, Allen."

He shook his head, "I'm not blaming you, Demri. What I'm saying is that I saw that you needed money just like I did, and I found a way to make enough to ease the burden for the both of us, while I got my feet under me with something real…so I took the chance. I thought that I could make a few extra dollars on one trip and never do it again."

She looked up at him with her deep blue eyes. The whites were red and bloodshot from the tears, "You're done? Never again?"

"I swear Demri. I planned to tell my uncles today, at the cookout, that I never intended to go again. I want you and the kids to come with me and see for yourself."

"You want me to take my kids to a drug dealing, murderer's cookout?" She spat.

"Demri…it's not like that. It's a family cookout. I can't guarantee that everybody there will be fine upstanding citizens, but there will not be anything that you need to worry about having your children around. I wouldn't even have offered if I thought otherwise." He stared directly back into her eyes waiting for her to say something. "I'll say my piece to my uncles and we can be on our way."

He waited, as she sat looking out over her yard. A bird flew past the two of them and landed in a tree just off of the steps. It was a blue jay and in the lull of their conversation, it called for its mate with a high pitch chirp. Finally, she spoke, "Show it to me."

"What?"

"Show me the money."

He did.

10

Landon splashed the water with his hands, aggravating his sister as only a little brother could do. Demri watched the children from a lawn chair situated on the edge of the pool - close enough to get in quickly if Landon were to go over his head. The boy had a history of losing himself in the enjoyment of his surroundings and was notorious for not paying attention to safety. Even though the Blackwood's had a rope, with blue and white buoys separating the deep end from the shallow end, Demri found that she couldn't relax. She knew that you could have the Berlin Wall between her child and the deep end and he would still find a way over there. She was uneasy about that, but she realized that she was just plain uneasy in general. She also imagined that her uneasiness had a lot to do with the events of last night and this morning. Her nerves were wrecked, and all that she could think was that she would be happy when they were gone from here and back to her house, where she could get some rest.

While still keeping an eye on the kids, she scanned the back yard, looking at all of the people eating their cookout food from paper plates and dressed in their jeans and t-shirts – the girls in summer dresses. By the appearances of everyone, Demri found it hard to believe that this was a family of criminals. She'd always known, as everyone else who'd grown up in the area, that at least the younger version of the Blackwoods were known to break minor laws here and there, but she'd always assumed that petty stuff was as far as it had ever gone. Just some spoiled rich rednecks lashing out - on everybody's town dumbass list, but could afford to be. She wondered just how many of them were in the drug business. How many of them right there around her and her kids at the pool? Who were the dealers? Who was the murderer?

Allen tried to rationalize that maybe the police were just barking up the wrong tree. He told Demri that he didn't think that any of the family that he'd known since he'd been in Mississippi were anything more than a bunch of back wood hicks. Full of hot air most of the time, but they were not killers.

Demri watched a heavy set woman, sitting under an umbrella on the other side of the pool, eating a hotdog. She wondered if the lady knew anything about what the men of this family did for a living. She couldn't help but to stare. Allen told her that the lady's name was Nancy, Robert's wife. Demri had known Robert most of her life, off and on, but had never met Nancy. She didn't think that Nancy had grown up here. To Demri, the other woman looked sad, as she watched her daughters toss a ball with Lindsay in the pool. Demri assumed that her sadness had to do with the fact that Robert was in jail with not much hope of getting out anytime soon. Nancy noticed Demri watching her, forced a smiled and waved. Demri waved back.

Someone to her left started talking to her, "Can I get you a refill on your drink?" Patsy had snuck in close.

Demri rattled the ice around in the empty glass. "Oh, no thank you," Demri said, "Allen went to get me a soda out of the cooler." They both looked and saw that Allen was talking with Dwayne, Tommy, and one of his uncles that Demri hadn't met. Allen had a beer in one hand and Demri's soda in the other. It looked like he'd gotten sidetracked on his way back to her.

"He's a cutie, ain't he," Patsy remarked. "He reminds me of his Uncle Elmer, back when we were first dating. How long have you two been together?"

Demri blushed, "Oh, we're not dating. We're just friends."

Patsy gave her a funny look, "You can call it what you want darling, but I didn't fall off of the turnip truck yesterday. I've seen the way that he looks at you...and I've seen the way that you look at him too."

Demri smiled, "It's obvious, huh?"

"Sure is sweetheart. You two might be telling lies to each other, but it's pretty obvious to everyone else."

Demri bit her tongue to keep from saying that she and Allen weren't the only people telling lies around here. "Well, we'll just have to see how things go. I'm sure that he would agree that if there is anything at all…we intend to take it slow."

"I get it darling, y'all are young, got all the time in the world…why hurry, right?"

Demri smiled and nodded, as Allen came over with his uncle. The man looked like a throwback to the movie cowboys of the fifties. He was wearing a tan cowboy shirt with white piping around the pockets and a Johnny Bravo pompadour. Demri had served what had to be a thousand drinks to the younger members of this family during her employment at the Kingfish Lounge, and had never understood their fashion sense, until now. This guy must have been their inspiration.

"Hey, Demri," Allen said, handing her the soda, "I want to introduce you to my Uncle Kirk."

Kirk offered his hand, as Demri stood and took it, "Oh no, please don't stand up," Kirk said. "Allen has told me all about you."

Demri smiled and looked at Allen, "All good, I hope."

"Of course," Kirk answered for him. "Allen, why don't you go and get a couple chairs from over there?" He motioned to the other side of the pool. Allen did as he was asked. While he was gone, Johnny and Chris came over to where Kirk and Demri were sitting. Johnny was one that she knew all too well from the bar and didn't like him – never had. She tried to ignore him - he was filthy, he was an asshole, and he repulsed her.

"Hey there, Uncle." Johnny said, and then he regarded Demri, "My, my, look at you." He stood in front of Demri, as she tried to take no notice, checking to see if Landon was in over his head the same way that she was feeling right now. "You look even finer in that dress than you do in those tight jeans you wear at the bar. What do I have to do to get you into a bikini?" Johnny continued.

Demri looked Johnny and said, "Oh, I don't know…You leaving the party would be a good start." Everyone laughed, except Johnny. Johnny never laughed. He was without expression and it made her feel uncomfortable.

"I'll be damned," Kirk was still laughing, "She sure did put you in your place, didn't she boy?"

"I need to talk to you," Johnny said to Kirk, as Allen returned with the chairs.

Kirk nodded and said, "In just a little bit, we can go inside and talk, but right now I am enjoying the fresh air." He took a chair from Allen and sat. "Why don't you and Chris go inside and see about Otis. Ask him if he's going to join us out here." On Kirk's direction, Johnny went inside. Allen sat down beside Demri and asked, "What did I miss?"

A half hour later, as all of the guest sat in the humid Mississippi heat and chatted in small groups, like they were in a high school cafeteria, Jennifer wheeled Otis's wheelchair out on to the patio and even though it had only been about twenty four hours since he'd seen his uncle, Allen barely recognized the old man. Otis was slumped forward and to the left like he couldn't support the weight of his upper body. Jennifer had a blanket covering his legs, despite the near ninety degree heat. His oxygen tank bottle was fixed to the back of the chair, with a bracket and the hose was thrown over Otis's shoulder, so that the mask strapped to his face wouldn't hang on something and pull free.

Elmer came out to the patio behind Otis and Jennifer. He was dressed in business slacks and a tie. Allen assumed that he'd just gotten home from the dealership. Kirk stood up and labored himself over to the area of the patio that his brother and Otis were getting settled – taking a seat beside Otis's wheel chair. To Allen, it reminded him of a scene out of the movie the Godfather. The three criminal relics gathered to conduct business under the cover of a family get together. Allen looked on, as Johnny and Chris wasted no time in engaging the men and in some presumably important discussion, based on the way that Johnny kept looking over his shoulder to see who may be in ear-shot. Allen couldn't hear anything that was being said, but he was pretty sure that there was disapproval on Kirk's face at whatever the two brothers were saying. Elmer said something to Kirk, causing the old man to turn in his chair, so he was not facing the conversation any longer, while Elmer and Johnny continued. Poor Otis showed no sign that he was even coherent during the whole conversation.

"Are you going to talk to them today?" Demri asked, as she watched the meeting that was taking place across the patio.

Allen looked at her and gave her a weak smile "Yeah, It needs to happen today, before any more business plans are made that involve me." Allen sounded like he was trying to convince himself. Whatever was going on over there looked like it had made Johnny unhappy now also. Allen guessed that the discussion wasn't going his way. His brow was furrowed, and he was pointing his finger at Elmer. Chris was just standing there looking confused - as usual. Otis hadn't moved from the position that he'd been wheeled out in.

Allen said, "I just wish Otis was feeling better. I'd like to explain to him why I can't be a part of the business. I hate for him to think that I'm being ungrateful. He and Kirk have been nothing but good to me."

"Maybe you can explain to Elmer and Kirk now, and come back when Otis is feeling better," Demri suggested. Allen could tell by the way that she was urging him forward that she wanted it taken care of. He couldn't blame her. He wanted it done too. He nodded and stood, as the meeting on the other side of the pool was breaking up. Johnny, obviously unhappy with the conversation, slid his chair back in a childish fit and stormed inside the house. Chris joined Tommy and Dewayne near the grill.

"Be right back," Allen said, as he walked over to his uncle's table. When he got closer – he could see that both Kirk and Elmer were agitated, thanks to Johnny. Elmer leaned on the table with his elbows, as Kirk absently stirred a spoon around his glass of tea. Otis still hadn't moved. Allen touched Otis's shoulder as he sat down. He could hear the oxygen flowing through the mask attached to Otis and assumed that was a good thing – at least he was still breathing.

"What's on your mind, Allen?" Elmer asked.

Allen found himself searching for the right way to say it…realizing that he really didn't have a plan before he came over. "Well I…" He searched for the right way to present his case, "…about that job at the dealership."

Elmer gave an anxious nod, as if to say hurry up and get on with it. "What about it?"

"Is that still on the table?"

Elmer looked at his brother, Kirk. "We've talked it over and we don't see where you working at the dealership, in between our other business ventures, would be a problem."

Allen shook his head, "No…Not in between…I'm not going on any more trips into the swamp." He looked between his uncles. "I am looking for a legitimate job…that's it…that's all."

Elmer leaned back in his chair and crossed his arms. "Just who in the hell do you think you are, Allen?" He asked in a calm, even tone that Allen found more disturbing than if he'd screamed it across the table. "What makes you think that you're better than your cousins? Or us, for that matter? You look down on what this family has done to survive for generations with contempt. What you don't understand is that it was all done in order to pull ourselves up out of this swamp. Turning your back on what this family does for a living, is just like turning your back on this family altogether. You can't be a part of one – without being a part of the other."

"Allen…" Kirk finally spoke, "Elmer's right. There has never really been a choice for any of us. It comes with being a part of this family…and right now, at this time, we need you more than ever."

Allen heard what they were saying and he understood, but nothing that they could say was going to change his mind – his future with Demri was more important to him right now than his future with a family that he barely trusted. "So it's all in, or nothing?"

Kirk and Elmer exchanged glances again. "We can't help you…if you're not willing to help us," Elmer said, flatly.

"Alright then," Allen stood up from the table, "Thank you for everything that you've done since I've been here." He touched Otis on his frail shoulder. The old man never flinched and Allen wondered if he'd already said his last words to his Great Uncle. He walked back over to where Demri was sitting and motioned for Landon and Lindsay to get out of the pool. Demri met the children with towels, as they climbed the stairs and protested the early departure. While Demri got the kids ready to leave, Allen took a few minutes to say goodbye to his cousins.

Five minutes earlier and inside the house, Johnny sat behind a picture window in a large leather chair overlooking the patio. He wore the scowl of a troubled man, as he sat in silence and watched. Allen, Kirk, and Elmer were talking on the other side of the glass at the patio table. He wondered just what kind of offer his uncles were making to Allen. No doubt, to be Johnny's replacement. The thought of being replaced infuriated Johnny even though he knew that it didn't mean a thing based on his own plans - already in motion. The joke was on them, and before too much longer, he would be running the whole show, although he doubted if any of them would be around to see it happen. He considered going back outside with his family, but found that he really didn't want to be around them anymore. They were left behind. He'd mentally progressed beyond them all. He'd been enlightened somehow, and was now operating on a higher level. He couldn't be burdened with them and their ignorant ways any longer. A smile crept across Johnny's face. Just then, Jennifer came into the room holding Ronnie in her arms. She and the toddler were wet with pool water and still wearing their bathing suits. She didn't notice Johnny sitting by the window at first and when she saw him, she was startled, letting out a little noise.

"Hey Johnny," she laughed, "you snuck up on us." He didn't say anything to her. She sat Ronnie down on the floor and pulled a couple of baby toys from the closet behind were Johnny was sitting. Ronnie immediately picked one of the toys up and started to shake it in front of his face while he stared at Johnny. The baby smiled, showing the two teeth that were just starting to break the surface of the gums. Ronnie let out a sound from deep down in his belly and tossed his toy at Johnny's feet. "He wants to play with you," Jennifer smiled. "Hey, do you mind keeping an eye on him for a second, while I go and get changed?"

"Suit yourself," Johnny said, without turning his gaze from the scene outside. It looked like Allen and his whore were getting ready to leave. Johnny touched his pocket and felt the Rohipnol bottle that he'd gotten from Stokes. Maybe later he would pay a visit to Allen and that stuck up bitch. How dare she insult him while they were on his own family's property. He told himself that he'd be interested to see how smart her mouth was later on, when it was just her and him.

Once Jennifer was upstairs, Ronnie crawled over to the chair and pulled himself up to a standing position using Johnny's pants leg. Johnny looked at the baby boy who was the toddler version of Elmer. The kid had the same shaped head and the same mouth. He also looked at Johnny with the same accusing eyes that Elmer had and it made Johnny hate the child. Ronnie smiled a gummy smile - drool trailing down both sides of his mouth. The child giggled and tossed a toy elephant into Johnny's lap. Johnny picked the toy up and tossed it into the floor beside the toddler. The child didn't go back to the floor with his toy. His smile faded, as his toy hit the floor and he stood looking at his uncle with a confused look - while wobbling a bit from side to side. Johnny stared into the dark eyes of the child and hated what he saw. It was the same contempt for him that he'd seen in the eyes of everyone else and from what little that he could remember - the eyes of his own father.

Johnny grabbed the tiny hand that was holding on to his jeans for stability and pulled it free. He detested the way that Ronnie's little hand wrapped around his pointer finger, as he held the child steady. Ronnie continued to stare into Johnny's eyes with an inquisitive gaze. After a few seconds a smile returned to the child and a fresh string of drool fell from his mouth and on to Johnny's pants leg. Johnny ignored the drool spot on his knee and instead focused on squeezing the child's tiny finger between his own. He was surprised to find just how fragile the kid's fingers actually were. As Johnny squeezed harder and harder Ronnie's smile quickly turned from a smile to a mask of terror. He began to wail loudly, as Johnny felt the tiny bone in Ronnie's hand pop. Johnny pushed the child to the floor, as he heard Jennifer franticly running down the stairs to the crying child. Ronnie lay wailing at Johnny's feet, as Jennifer entered the room. "What happened?" She asked frantically. She scooped Ronnie up off of the floor and held him to her chest.

Johnny shrugged his shoulders and said, "I don't know, I must have stepped on his hand or something. All of this space in this room and he wants to play right up under my damn feet."

Jennifer shot Johnny a glare and walked out of the room, rubbing Ronnie's head and trying to sooth the child, as he continued to scream in pain. Johnny smiled once they were gone. 'Go ahead and coddle him,' He thought. 'Make him a pussy, just like everyone else in this family. They should all enjoy it while they could, because when he took over this operation - they were all going to have to toughen up and he was going to do it the hard way - just like his father had done to him.

263

11

Lashauna put the disc beside her computer and followed Leo into the briefing room. She had every intention of coming into the station first thing and reviewing the video footage from the self-storage building. While she was there, she'd told the manager exactly what time frame that she was looking for, and with a couple of mouse clicks on his computer, the manager was able to capture the segment of video and burn it onto a disk. It had been so easy that she hadn't bothered to review the footage while she was there, thinking that she could come back to the station and review it at her own pace and in the comfort of her own office. Sometimes, it took a considerable amount of time – not to mention a few cups of coffee - to go over video footage thoroughly. And thoroughly was exactly how she wanted to go over this film. This was her last lead and she didn't want to miss a frame. Especially, when she wasn't even sure what she was looking for to begin with. Lashauna had asked that the storage manager provide her with the footage for a twenty four hour period, starting at 8:00 am, the morning of the murders. She felt like if there was anything to be found on the tapes - that footage should cover it.

She was anxious to get started and see what she could find, but was side-railed as soon as she and Leo walked into the station. They were ordered by Captain Harrelson, to attend a briefing that was already underway. The meeting had been called regarding an investigation that was being led by a couple of other detectives, Orsak and Deel. As she stood in the back of the drab, windowless briefing room, she learned that Orsak and Deel were investigating a gang related homicide and through an informant, the two detectives had obtained an address of the possible whereabouts of their prime suspect. The two old-school detectives had been working this case all of two days now, and although Lashauna was very proud for her colleagues for the quick police work, she was a little bit agitated that she was still stumped on her own case, nearly four weeks in. She was also pissed about being pulled off of her own work. Leo joked that at least someone in this office was solving a murder and his sense of humor only irritated her more.

Captain Harrelson stood at the head of the briefing room. It was filled with about fifteen uniformed patrolmen, along with a half dozen undercover detectives. As Harrelson talked, he pointed at a crude map, drawn on a white board with black marker. The map was of a road intersection with a few squares drawn around it representing houses. One of the squares had a red X through the middle representing the perp's house. Harrelson used the same red marker and put dots on the board, as he laid out where he wanted each team to position themselves during the operation. The suspect was to be considered armed and dangerous and they wanted all hands on deck if things got out of control. Lashauna and Leo were going to be positioned in their car one block away from the "X" house and be ready in case the suspect was able to slip through the other officers. Lashauna figured that the rest of her evening was blown and probably most of the coming morning too.

The video review would have to wait until she was finished assisting in the operation. *Oh well,* she thought, *what's one more day?* She'd waited this long to see the video. She'd half convinced herself that watching it would just be another waste of time anyhow.

The briefing was dismissed and most the attendees in the meeting went straight for their cars. Lashauna and Leo did the same, only after a brief trip back to their desks to retrieve their coats. As she headed for the exit door, Lashauna gave one last look at the silver disk sitting beside her computer and wondered exactly what she was going to discover when she found the time to watch it.

12

The coffee pot indicated that it was ready for Allen to brew a mug. It was one of the new models that made individual cups of coffee, as opposed to a full pot. The machine made sense if a person was having a single cup of coffee, but in this case he was brewing two - one for Demri and one for himself and the contraption didn't seem very economical since he had to stand there and wait for it to warm and then brew two different cups. A handyman, ironically named Bob, was finishing up the repairs to Demri's back door, as Allen waited for the coffee. They'd decided to sit outside on the patio, while Bob the Builder worked on the door. The evening had grown cool and Demri wanted to let the kids run off some steam, since it was so nice outside. Allen impatiently waited for the coffee to finish dispensing into the second cup, so that he could get back outside with Demri. She seemed ready to talk about the last few hours, which had been trying on them both, but in Allen's opinion it had given them some hope that they could make things work out. He knew that her going to Otis's with him was a good sign. It looked like she was willing to look past his poor judgement and move forward. He was prepared to accept that he needed to get himself a legitimate job and settle in, which shouldn't be too hard. He could always go back to electrical work. He heard on the TV a week or so back that the local shipyard was looking for electricians.

He at least had the twenty-five thousand to get him and Demri started though he wasn't very proud of the way that he'd acquired it. With it, he intended to help her get caught up on her bills, and maybe have enough to buy a cheap, but reliable car for her to use. The options were rattling around in his mind, as he waited on the coffee machine. Bob was turning the last couple of screws on the new door knob and noticed Allen staring off into space.

"You alright, buddy?" The man asked, as he pulled himself from his knees to his feet.

"What? Oh, yeah...never better..." Allen said, "...never better!" He meant it too. He couldn't ever remember feeling better. The coffee pot finished its process with a spitting sound, followed by a second or two of air leaking out of the hose. Allen carried the two cups out to the patio where Demri waited.

"Thank you," she said, as she took her cup. Allen sat beside her at the iron table under the umbrella. Landon and Lindsay were playing in the yard. Allen listened to the children and treasured the giggles and laughter that the two of them were sharing. It appeared that the excitement of the previous night with Bruce was a distant memory. If the kids had any scary memories of the event hanging around in their heads, they weren't showing any signs of it right now. They were happy and carefree, chasing a butterfly with a net and a sand bucket.

"So," Allen finally said, sipping his coffee. "What's next?"

If she heard him, she didn't let on that she had. Allen assumed that she was putting her thoughts together, so he leaned back in his chair and continued to watch the kids play in the yard. Lindsay was now chasing her brother with a foam sword, as Landon zigged and zagged across the yard, so fast that Lindsay never even came close to hitting him. "She's lucky that she's going to be so pretty," Allen said, "I don't think that she will ever be mistaken for an athlete and heaven forbid she will ever have to run for her life."

Demri smiled, "Oh, shut up. She doesn't have to be fast. She's going to have a knight in shining armor to protect her."

"I hope so," Allen said. "Every girl deserves a Knight." He watched Demri observing her children in the yard. "Demri...I'm sorry for putting you in the middle of all of this."

She nodded, but still didn't look at him. "No one is perfect," she said. "If you remember, I was the single mother of two that had to be rescued last night from one of my own bad decisions."

"Hey, that's not your fault," Allen tried to console her.

Demri waved him off, "I knew that Bruce was weird. I should have never agreed to go out with him."

"Hey, you live and learn." Allen sipped his coffee, "I don't think that he'll be back for a while, if it's any consolation."

She laughed, "Probably not, but I'll need to find a new job. I can't possibly show my face in his bar again."

"Hey, maybe we can go job hunting together for our first date," Allen joked.

Demri looked at him this time, "Let's do that."

Allen stopped laughing, "Do what...job hunt together?"

"No," she said, "Let's start from scratch and go out on a date. A new beginning."

"Alright," Allen said, "A new beginning." He looked over at the kids, as Lindsay screamed playfully. Her brother took the sword out of her hand and began to chase her now. "It just so happens that I have a little extra cash," he smiled.

Just then headlights cut through the early dusk and shined like spotlights on Demri and Allen. When the driver cut the lights off, Allen recognized the car. It was Chris's beat up Nova. Allen sat his cup of coffee down and walked out to the driveway, as Chris got out of the car. He was alone.

"Hey Demri," Chris yelled across the yard, with an awkward wave of his hand.

She waived back and called the children in, telling them that it was getting late and time to get cleaned up. Allen knew that it was Chris that gave her the creeps.

"What's up, Chris?" Allen asked.

"Kirk sent me over to grab you. He wants to meet at the Hill and have a talk...with all of us."

"Who's all of us?"

"Everyone," Chris explained, "I think that the uncles are throwing in the towel on the family business."

"No shit?" Allen couldn't help but feel somewhat responsible if that were the case. Either way, he felt a little relief hearing it.

"Yeah, no shit," Chris said, "Kirk said we'll meet at ten o'clock." Chris looked at Allen and saw the apprehension in his body language. "Look, you can call him and talk to him if you want. I really don't give a shit if you come, or not. I was sent to tell you and my job is done." He got back into his car and started the engine.

"Let me go inside and grab my keys. I'll meet you there," Allen said. Chris nodded and backed out of the driveway. With the grinding of some gears and a puff of white smoke from the tail pipe, he was headed down the street. Allen didn't know what to think about Chris coming all this way just to tell him that Kirk wanted to have a meeting. Something didn't feel right. Allen pulled his cell phone from his pocket and dialed the number for Kirk. It rang twice and then, "Hello," Kirk rasped, from the other end.

"Hey, Uncle Kirk, It's Allen. Sorry to bother you."

"No bother Allen, what's going on with you?"

"Chris just came over to the apartment and said that you guys wanted to have a meeting tonight."

"Yeah, sorry about that. I should have called, but I was a little preoccupied with Otis. He isn't doing very well. Patsy's up there with him right now. Chris said that he was in your neck of the woods when I talked to him, he said that he would get in touch with you. I guess he didn't have your phone number, so he stopped by."

Allen wondered what Chris would be doing in this part of town. As far as he knew, Chris lived out near Violent Hill. Something didn't add up with Chris. Allen figured that once the meeting with the uncles was over, he could ask Chris what he was doing out this way. "Alright," Allen said. "I'll be over there in an hour."

"See you then," Kirk said, and just as he was about to hang up; Allen stopped him.

"Kirk…how bad is Otis?"

"Not good," Kirk sounded sad. "I'll see you in a bit," and then Allen heard the line go dead.

13

As Allen pulled his truck onto the drive of Violent Hill, he had the thought to stop by the main house and see Otis. It was nearing 10:00 pm and Allen was sure that Otis would be in bed resting by now. He decided not to bother the old man and kept driving, promising himself that first thing in the morning, he was going to go over for a visit.

His headlights cut through the thick, wet air and as he neared the swamp – the fog that had settled over the land thickened the closer that he got to the water. Once he reached the boat house the fog was so dense that he could barely see the front end of his truck. He slowed as he approached the building. When he stopped, he noticed Johnny's truck through the fog. It was parked closer to the building. It was pitch dark and coupled with the fog, hard to see, but he was pretty sure there were no other vehicles out here. Maybe they car pooled, or maybe the others just had not arrived yet. Allen checked his watch and noticed that he was a little early. He put his truck into park and stepped out into the evening air. It was so muggy that he could almost taste the swamp. He stood beside his truck watching the driveway through the trees to see if he could spot anyone else approaching. He heard a strange noise come from beside the boat house. It was close to him, but the fog was too thick to see what had caused it. Whatever was out there would have to be right on top of him before he could see it in this fog. He wished that he'd brought Kirk's gun, but he'd left it for Demri, just in case Bruce came back for a second round.

He quickly went inside the Boat House, figuring that he'd probably be better off inside, rather than waiting outside to be eaten by an alligator.

Inside, Chris was in the small kitchen area, putting ice into a glass and getting ready to pour a drink. He gave Allen the universal *what's up*, nod of the head, as Allen entered from the darkness - Allen waved. Johnny was sitting on the couch, watching a CNN report about the removal of the Confederate Monuments from the public buildings in South Carolina. He never looked away from the TV screen when he said, "Can you believe this shit? It's just another attack on the white man. How can they say that the monuments are racist?" He was clearly agitated. Allen didn't respond, he stood behind the couch and watched as the news coverage switched to a group of white supremacists, protesting on the capitol steps. "All of this..." "Johnny continued, "...because some white dude went and shot up that black church. How can they blame that shit on the flag? I bet they don't outlaw Muslim flags...and those bastards shoot us up every day."

"That's a little different, Johnny," Allen said.

"How...how is it any different?"

"I don't know...but it is," Allen said, "Maybe for the very reason that the Muslims are attacking Americans, we should be drawing closer together and trying to get past our own differences to look out for one another...and if the start of that unity is taking down a flag or a monument that represents hatred to a large portion of the country's population...then take it down. What does it change?"

Johnny finally turned around on the couch to face Allen, "Well, well... aren't you a fucking philanthropist. Since when did *you* become a nigger lover?"

Allen felt his blood pressure rise to the point that his ears started ringing. He thought of Randall Jefferson and all of the other decent African Americans that he'd known in his life - who on their worst days, were miles above Johnny and his ignorant, drug obsessed, racist ass. Allen wanted to be politically correct, maybe make a strong argument as to why Johnny was looking at things wrong, but his emotions got in the way and instead he said, "You know what...fuck you, Johnny! I'm sick and tired of listening to your racist shit all of the time. The problem isn't that monument, or those people trying to take it down...the problem is people like you."

Johnny stood up, "What do you mean...people like me?"

Allen and Johnny were chest to chest now, "I've got a little secret for you, Johnny."

Johnny was clearly mad now. His own face was red and he was

breathing heavy. "Go ahead…say something that will give me reason to knock you the fuck out."

Allen looked into Johnny's eyes and although he had never been frightened by the idea of getting into an altercation with anyone before – he felt a shiver when confronted by the hollowness that Johnny's eyes possessed. Allen felt like he was looking into the depths of hell – the blackness staring back at him. "A nigger…ain't necessarily a black person."

"*What did you call me?*" Even though they were virtually touching chests, Johnny took a step closer. Allen didn't back down and was expecting Johnny to lash out at any moment, when Chris stepped between them and said "Alright you two…knock it off. Kirk and the others will be here any minute." In his hands, he held two whisky on the rocks and handed one to Johnny and the other to Allen.

Surprisingly, Johnny took his drink and went back to the couch, not saying another word. To Allen, the drink was exactly what he needed right now. He drank the entire glass all in one long sip. Allen could taste that it was the family recipe, but right off the bat, he noticed something else. The liquor had a bitter after taste.

Allen looked at the bottom of his glass, to see if there was any residue of something left over, but there wasn't anything in the glass but ice. He felt a wave of dizziness overcome him and leaned against the back of the couch to steady himself. He could hear Johnny and Chris laughing in the background, but found it difficult to focus on them - his vision was starting to blur. He heard Johnny talking. His voice was a distant echo, like he was down in a tunnel. Johnny sounded hollow and far away. He was saying, "Wow…that must have been a hell of a shot. How much did you give him?"

Chris chuckled, "Not much…just a cap full, like you told me." Chris laughed again, as Allen felt himself hit the floor, banging his head off of the wooden planks. He was fighting to stay conscious. "I thought you were going to blow it by getting into a fight with him," Chris said to Johnny.

"I wasn't going to fight him," Johnny said, "That would have ruined all of the fun. Get the rope and duct tape out of my truck, let's get him tied up."

Allen lay on the floor and continued fighting to stay conscious. He heard Chris go outside to get the supplies, as Johnny directed him to do. Allen pulled himself up to a sitting position against one of the wooden beams. He rubbed his eyes - they were useless to him. The only images that they produced were blurry shapes. The room was spinning and Allen felt like he was going to vomit. A hazy image appeared in front of him and he felt Johnny grab his chin and lift his head so that they faced each other. "Man, you have a high tolerance. I was told that a few drops of this shit would knock a horse on his ass. If I know Chris, he used more than a couple drops in your glass."

"Fuck you," Allen managed to say, right before he began to vomit.

Johnny laughed. "My, my, you really need to learn some manners," he said and then back handed Allen, causing him to loose what little balance he was maintaining. He fell all the way to the floor again. Johnny stood over him, "I hope that your little whore has that kind of sassy mouth, when I visit her later. I like it when they talk dirty. It makes things more exciting when it gets...rough."

Allen heaved on the floor, "You...you stay away from her."

Johnny laughed again, "I'm going to have some fun with her and then I'm going bury her ass in the swamp. I may even put you both in the same spot, if she's good."

Allen felt like if he could keep Johnny talking – the effects of the drug may wear off some. "You wouldn't. You don't have it in you."

"Who do you think you're talking to?" Johnny asked, "You ain't the first...and you won't be the last."

"The Taylor's..." Allen mumbled.

"What?"

Allen mustered his strength, "The Taylor's...you killed them."

"How do you know about the Taylor's?"

"The...the cop's...I already told the... told them that it was you."

"You didn't tell them shit!" Allen could hear a small amount of panic creep into Johnny's voice.

"They're coming for you..."

"Shut the fuck up..." Johnny used his foot to turn Allen over onto his back and started rummaging through his pockets. He removed Allen's car keys and dropped them on the floor beside Allen's head. He then removed Allen's cell phone and tossed it aside on the ground. The light fixture hanging above Johnny looked like a flashlight pointed directly into Allen's eyes. He couldn't see anything except the white light as it flooded down from the ceiling. Dark spots started to close in around the light and Allen knew that he was losing consciousness. If that happened, he was going to be dead, along with Demri...or worse for her. Allen fought what he knew was a losing battle to stay awake. Whatever the drug Johnny and Chris had put into his drink was working fast. Allen's head felt like it weighed fifty pounds, so he laid it back against the floor. It was then, just as his world was becoming a black hole – he heard a new voice say, "Put your gun on the floor, or I'm gonna kill this motherfucker right here." Then things went black. Allen felt like he as falling - and falling - and falling - into the darkness.

14

Five minutes prior, right before Allen lost consciousness, Lionel crouched in the shadows outside the boat house, trying to get a look inside one of the windows. He wanted to see just how many of the Blackwoods he was going to have to deal with once he went inside. He'd hid at the main entrance until he saw Johnny's truck and then followed it in. The fog had made it easier for him to follow Johnny through property without being seen. Lionel went in on foot, leaving his car in the hiding spot so he could sneak in and out without anyone ever seeing him. Hell, he doubted that anybody would even hear the gunshot this far out. Oh, yes – the stars were aligning and things were falling into place – tonight, there would be retribution. Lionel had watched Johnny and his brother inside the boathouse for some time, planning how he was going to handle them both together. He'd had a plan in mind of killing the brother quick and making Johnny pay slowly for what he'd done, when the third man arrived in the Land Rover. Lionel didn't have any idea who this newcomer was, other than some unlucky fool that had showen up at the wrong place, at the wrong time. Lionel watched from his hiding spot behind some crab pots, waiting for the new arrival to go inside. The man had taken his time going inside until Lionel bumped up against one of the crates, causing it to shift, making some noise. The man, who was still standing beside his truck at the time, looked directly at Lionel, as he was frozen in the darkness and fog. Evidently the man couldn't see him hidden in the darkness and proceeded into the boathouse.

Lionel pulled his pipe from his pocket and quietly moved away from the window, so that no one would see him. Once he decided that he was clear, he pulled a lighter from his pocket and took a hit. *A little something to calm his nerves,* he thought. Tonight, he would make things right for his parents. His muscles changed from tense, tightly bound fibers, into elements of tranquility, in a matter of seconds as the drug took effect.

He was ready. He was making his way back to the front of the building when he heard an argument coming from inside - he pulled the pistol from his pocket. He was just outside the front door, trying to decide on how he should go in – guns blazing, or more collected – when the front door opened. Chris stepped out and headed over to Johnny's truck.

Lionel waited for the door to close and then he hit Chris over the head as hard as he could with the butt of his gun. The blow sent the smaller man straight to the ground in a heap. Chris was unconscious and moaning, as Lionel searched his pockets and found a small gun in the man's waist band. Lionel tossed it as far as he could into the darkness, hearing a splash, as it landed in the swamp. He slapped Chris in the face a couple of times, until Chris regained consciousness. Once he could walk, Lionel marched Chris to the front door, warning him that if he tried anything funny – he would be the first one to die tonight. Lionel didn't tell Chris that no matter what – he didn't have any intention of anyone other than himself walking out of here alive. Lionel held his gun to Chris's back, as they entered the building.

15

Allen was conscious, but was still in a dreamlike state of mind. He forced his eyes open and a blurry, white light burned into his retinas with such a painful sensation, it sent tears streaming down his face. He wasn't sure whether he was back in reality or not, but he was aware that there was a struggle nearby. There were grunts and screams coming from at least three different people and he was mostly sure that he wasn't one of them. He struggled to shake the cobwebs, knowing that he needed to get away from this place and quickly. Memories that were foggy and almost nonexistent just a few seconds ago were flooding back into his mind in torrents. Though it felt like a dream, he remembered that Johnny and Chris were trying to kill him, and Demri was in trouble. He didn't fully understand what was happening with the struggle on the other side of the room, but he knew that he couldn't wait around to see what it was. He also didn't know how much longer he would be able to stay awake.

He felt a new surge of the drug overcome him, forcing him back into the dark oblivion, from where he'd just emerged. He knew that if he were to pass out again, in this room with Johnny and Chris – he was finished. As one of the unidentified men on the other side of the room screamed in pain – Allen rolled to his hands and knees. The room was spinning like a carnival ride and he wasn't even to his feet yet. He felt a new round of vomit blasting its was up his throat, as he struggled to get to his feet. He wasn't sure what side of the room that the exit was on, and since all that he could see were blurry shapes – he picked a dark square and hoped for the best. He only had one shot at escaping - this was it.

He stumbled to the dark spot on the far wall, as he vomited down the front of his shirt. At least his body was fighting the drug, maybe he could lessen the effects if he could continue to throw it up. Allen fell as he reached the dark spot on the wall and luckily a door opened. He landed half inside the building, and half out. Although he still couldn't see, he was aware that he was in a patch of dirt. He quickly pulled himself to his feet again and started to run – if stumbling from side to side was actually considered running. He was in total darkness and fighting for his life. Suddenly, he remembered how foggy the night had been when he arrived and felt like it may give him a chance to survive if he could get far enough away and hide before they came after him. He was stumbling and running just as fast as he was able to will himself to do – nearly falling again as his foot struck something hard on the ground – maybe a rock. The drug was making his muscles fatigue faster than he anticipated and his burst of adrenalin was wearing off. He felt his consciousness slipping again and forced himself to keep running. Behind him, he heard multiple gunshots from the direction of the boat house. He couldn't tell if they had been directed at him or not, but he never turned around to see, one way or the other.

Suddenly, the ground fell from beneath his feet, and he was abruptly aware that he was in water. His drugged mind took a few seconds to process what had happened as he splashed desperately in the darkness. Realizing that he must have fallen into the swamp river - he composed himself and tried to relax. Flailing around wouldn't do him any good. It would only attract attention his way – from Johnny and Chris, or maybe worse – the gators! The drug had exhausted him and he wanted to close his eyes – just go to sleep, but he knew that he had to swim. With muscles that felt like they were literally on fire – he managed to pull his upper body out of the water on the far side and into a thicket of weeds along the bank. He could go no further. He lost consciousness and fell into the darkness once again.

16

Lashauna hung her coat on the wooden rack behind her chair and sat at her desk. She was exhausted and buried her face in her hands. It had been a long night already and she still had work to do. The stakeout in Deel and Orsak's case had been uneventful, since all of the action took place inside the suspect's house and out of sight from where she and Leo were positioned in their car. Fortunately, there had been no violence as the team of police officers surprised the occupants of the house - rushing through the door and catching three small children – one of them an infant - in the living room watching TV. They'd quickly secured the children and searched the rest of the house, finding the children's mother, the suspect, and a third adult male, presumably the mother's boyfriend, all in the back room, hiding in the closet. All three of the adults were high as hot air balloons, and the police team found enough heroin in the bedroom to keep these role models, *along with the rest of the neighborhood*, jacked up for a couple more days. Orsak and Collins were on cloud nine - not only getting their murder suspect, but two additional drug dealers as well.

Once the group was in custody, Lashauna's night should have ended, but seeing as she was the only female involved in the operation, an always borderline male chauvinist, Captain Harrelson, asked her to stick around to comfort the children until social services arrived. She agreed and Leo, late for a planned dinner with his wife already, caught a ride home with another officer. Lashauna was one of the last to leave the scene and wound up transporting the children to the police station with her, where she met social services and made the transfer. It was heartbreaking to witness kids being treated so carelessly by the ones that were supposed to love and protect them. These children didn't have a chance to live a normal life. It was either going to be an orphanage, or worse if left to their worthless mother. Lashauna couldn't help but wonder if someday, down the road, she was going to see these kids again, either arresting them for a crime, or investigating their own murder. It was a vicious cycle. So sad.

A couple of other officers had come back to the station to pick up their cars, but no one other than Lashauna stayed. She looked at the clock - it read 10:31 pm. She'd considered going home and getting some much needed rest, but she knew that she wouldn't be able to sleep until she watched the surveillance video. She picked up the disk and inserted it into her computer. Even though she was sure that it would be another dead end – she couldn't give up on the hope that there would be a trail to follow by watching it.

The video was black and white - but surprisingly clear. One of the cameras had a focal point that didn't give her a view of the 7-11 parking lot, but in a reversal of her recent bad fortune, the top portion of the second camera had a perfect view of the gas pumps and parking area of the convenience store.

Evidently, whoever set up the camera system, wanted to get a shot of the street in front of the storage building. She focused her attention on that one and hit the button for 6x video speed. The images sped across the screen in fast motion, as Lashauna constantly watched the monitor for anything to catch her eye. She had her head propped in her hand with her elbow on her desk and felt herself dozing off once or twice. On one such occasion she reopened her eyes just in time to see a car pulling out of the parking lot of 7-11. She quickly clicked the button that slowed the video down to real time, then made a few frantic clicks to reverse the video. Slowly, the video reversed and she watched a Lincoln Town Car move backwards from the main road, back to the gas pumps. Lashauna almost asleep a few seconds ago – was fully alert now. She reversed the video all the way to right before the car pulled into the parking lot, and then she hit play.

The video flickered and then started forward at real speed. What she was watching brought a smile to her face. At first, she only had an idea that the car was the same as the one reported stolen by Elmer Blackwood a couple of weeks ago, but now she was sure that the car in the video was in fact Elmer's car. She verified that the date and time on the video matched the Taylor's murder - it did! The video that she was watching was recorded

45 minutes before the Taylors were murdered. She paused the video when the driver got out to pump gas and after several attempts, she was able to figure out how to zoom the image, so that she could get a close up of the driver. The man finished filling the tank and went inside to pay. After a few minutes he emerged from the store carrying something in his hand. She zoomed in on the object and felt her heart skip a beat - it was a hotdog box. The same type of box that she'd recovered from the Taylor's driveway the day of the murder. When she saw who it was and what he had - she leaned back in her chair and stared blankly at the screen. Suddenly, everything began to make sense. The day that Lionel made his impromptu visit to Violent Hill, he was focused on one individual in particular and she should have picked up on it, but at the time she hadn't.

Lionel must have known who'd killed his parents all along. Lashauna was willing to bet that the old folks weren't the targets, but had just gotten in the way. She double clicked her mouse and hit the print button. A crisp picture of Johnny Blackwood and the Lincoln emerged from the printer. Examining the photo, Lashauna could tell that there was another individual in the car's passenger seat, but with the angle of the camera and the distance – she couldn't tell who it might be. She went back to the computer screen and tried to zoom in closer to the passenger window, but she still couldn't get an image of the face behind the window – it was just the shape of a person in the car. But it confirmed that there was a second suspect involved in the murder.

She knew that it wasn't exactly the smoking gun that she would prefer, but it was a step in the right direction and it was enough to bring Johnny in. For starters, why he was driving a car that was reported stolen just hours after the video was recorded and in the vicinity of a double homicide. Not to mention, it looked like he was very likely holding a piece of evidence that was found at the crime scene. She sent an e-mail to the evidence department, asking them to pull any prints that they could from the hotdog box and to cross reference them to the ones that they had on file for Johnny Blackwood. Then, she pulled the last known address for Johnny. It was a house near the Biloxi boardwalk, ten minutes from the station where she was. She opened her phone and dialed Leo. He was probably at home asleep by now, but she needed him to go out to Violent Hill to detain Elmer until she could get there to question him. She couldn't tell who the second person in the car was, but given that it was Elmer's car, she was going to start with him.

Leo answered on the third ring, "Lashauna, what's up?" He was whispering, apparently trying to avoid waking Paige.

"Hey, are you still up?"

"I am now." He sounded agitated, "What's going on?"

"I think I found something on the video," She said.

"Are you still working?"

"Listen," she said, "I'm pretty sure that it was Johnny and an accomplice." She explained to him what she found and told him that she needed for him to go over to the Blackwood estate and to not let anyone leave until she got there. She was headed out to see if Johnny was at home.

Allen gradually started to regain consciousness. His eyes were still blacked out, but he could hear a frog croaking, seemingly right next to his ear. The bullfrog carried on incessantly, as if to say *Hey there, dumbass…I know you aren't dead…get up…you're in my spot.* Allen wasn't sure if he agreed with the frog, or not – he actually felt like he may be dead in fact. Then again he hoped that when he died – his head wouldn't continue to hurt quite as much as it did right now.

After a few minutes of lying motionless in the tall weeds, listening to his new friend argue over the spot – he began to hear what must have been a thousand frogs croaking in the distance. Soon, his eyes cleared and although his vision was still blurry, he could see the moon hanging overhead, like a bulb attached to a pitch black ceiling. Every muscle in his body shrieked in agony as he forced himself upright. He was soaking wet and shivered violently in the cool evening air. He wasn't sure how long he'd been out, but the fog that had been hovering over the land was completely gone and the moon illuminated the area all the way back to the boat house a little ways across the river.

He willed his aching muscles to move, getting back in the dark murky water and waded across – though this time fully aware of the dangers that lurked all around him. He considered himself extremely lucky that he'd been laid out unconscious on the river bank and had not been eaten by an alligator or bitten by a snake. As he reached the far bank, the fog in his mind began to clear as it had on the swamp. Confusion and panic from what Chris and Johnny had done replaced the fear of being eaten by a swamp critter. It felt like some horrible dream in his cloudy mind, but he knew that it wasn't, and Johnny and Chris had actually tried to kill him.

He needed to get to Demri as soon as possible. He prayed that he wasn't too late.

Out of nowhere, he remembered the detectives at Demri's house yesterday morning and their talk of a killer. He didn't actually believe that there were killers in the family. He assumed that the cops were just following some weak trail or protocol. Deep down he knew that if any of them were capable, it would have to be Johnny or Chris, but he was genuinely shocked at what had happened just a little while ago. How long had it been? For the life of him, he had no idea. He'd done some pretty good drugs back in his youth, but whatever his cousins had slipped into his drink was some of the heaviest stuff he'd ever experienced. He reached solid land and took off in a sprint. As he approached the boat house, there was an eerie silence and he wondered whose body he was going to find inside. As his memory returned, he recalled overhearing the struggle – the one that ultimately allowed him to escape, and the gun shots – ringing out as he was running away. Had they been directed at him? He doubted it! There was definitely someone else there. Someone had interrupted what Johnny and Chris had in store for him. He owed someone a big thank you – he only hoped that they were still around to receive it. He knew that it was a long shot, but he was wishing that he would find Johnny and Chris lying dead - he couldn't be so fortunate, but he couldn't help but hope. Whoever had come in was more than likely on the victim end of those gunshots. As he neared the building, he noticed that the vehicles – including his own - were gone from the road. Allen felt like he was cracking up a little at this point, because given the entirety of the situation, all that he found himself repeating in his head were the words, *Those motherfuckers stole my truck! Those motherfuckers stole my truck!* Then he realized, *I'm fucking stranded! I need to get to Demri!* A helpless, panicked feeling engulfed him. He stood there in the driveway a full minute, before it occurred to him that there was a phone on the boathouse wall and if he were lucky, his own phone may still be in there too.

He tiptoed to the boathouse door, stopping and listening for any signs that someone might still be inside - silence. There was absolutely no sound, other than frogs off in the distance. He pushed open the door and stepped in. The darkness of the room hid any evidence of the violence that had transpired the last time that he was in here. He wondered just how long he'd been passed out along the river bank.

There was a disturbing stillness inside the wooden walls. Alone in the darkness, the place felt hollow, like it had been empty forever. Allen searched for a light switch and found one behind the door. Once the lights were on, he found the room relatively tidy, except for a missing chair at the card table - one that he knew had been four before and guessed that it must have been broken in the scuffle. Other than that – nothing else indicated foul play. He searched for his phone unsuccessfully, it was nowhere to be found. He knew that he needed to call Demri and the police and in that order, so he rushed over to the desk, in the corner of the room and picked up the phone from the cradle. It was a relic, but his only hope of connecting to the rest of civilization, way out here. His hopes of hearing a dial-tone on the line were quickly dispelled, when all that he heard was the dull absence of sound in the ear piece, so he tossed the receiver aside. He was walking back to the exit, gearing himself for the long trek back to the main house on foot, when he noticed a small amount of blood seeping from under the throw rug, beside the door. Using his fingertips, he carefully grabbed the corner and pulled it back. Underneath the expensive Isfahan area rug was a very large pool of blood that was beginning to soak into the wood floor. Allen dropped the rug and stepped back away from it. The sight of the blood took his breath. He wondered who it belonged to but then decided that it didn't matter. Unless it was both Johnny and Chris, he still had major problems. Johnny had told Allen of his plans with the intention that Allen would never again leave that boathouse. The words echoed through Allen's mind again as he reached the doorknob to the outside. Johnny had said, *I hope that your little whore has that kind of sassy mouth when I visit her later.* Allen lost his breath as the thought that he was already too late crossed his mind. He sprinted from the boat house and across the field toward Uncle Otis's house. As he raced past the mound of dirt and grass – the one that had become the namesake of the property - the all too fitting namesake. All that he could think was that Demri was in danger – real danger.

18

Winded by the long run, Allen finally arrived at the main house. His level of concern rose when he found that it was just as dark as the boat house had been. Praying that the reason for the darkness was that everyone inside had retired for the evening, he tried the front door - it was locked. He then went around to the side entrance – it was the way that most of the family entered the house. This one opened and Allen stepped into the kitchen. All of the lights were turned off except for a table light that Patsy liked to keep lit during the night, just in case someone needed to come down to the kitchen for a midnight snack - safety first in this household. Patsy didn't want anyone to break their neck tripping in the dark. Any neck breaking done here would be at the hands of Johnny and Chris. Allen almost laughed and caught himself, wondering how in the hell he could find any humor in his present situation. He must still be a little loopy from the drugs that he was slipped. He went to the kitchen phone hung on the wall near the sink. Allen crossed his fingers and prayed that it still had service – hot damn, it did! He quickly punched Demri's number, hoping that he had it right. In the age of cell phones remembering numbers was a thing of the past. Luckily, she had written it on the napkin not long ago, and Allen remembered the order. He had butterflies in his stomach as the line made a couple of clicks and then began to ring. "Come on… pick up, come on…pick up," he kept repeating underneath his breath. It rang six, or seven times and he was losing hope – just then, the other end was answered, "Hello." It was female, but it wasn't Demri.

"Hello," Allen tried to control his anxiety, "Who is this?"

"This is Rachel…who in the hell is this?" She sounded a little anxious herself.

"Rachel, its Allen, where's Demri?"

"I was hoping that you could tell us the answer to that question," she said.

"Us…who's us?" Allen asked.

"Me and the kids," Rachel said, "We've been looking for her for an hour." Allen's stomach dropped down to his knees and he felt weak. Rachel continued, "Lindsay came over to my house a little while ago upset, saying that she was scared and couldn't find her mother. She said something about someone trying to hurt them the other night and the back door getting broken in."

"I don't think that the two are related," Allen explained.

"Related to what?" Rachel was getting loud. "Ever since you moved in to the apartment out back, it sounds like some weird shit has been happening, Allen. You had better hope that Demri is ok. I will personally kick…"

"Rachel," Allen cut her off. She was worked up, and rightly so. "I didn't even know that she was missing until right now, at this very moment, but I am going to do whatever I need to do to find out where she is."

"We've tried your number a dozen times and it keeps going straight to voicemail," Rachel continued, like she wasn't listening to anything that he was saying.

"I lost my phone," Allen said, and it wasn't entirely a lie. He didn't see where it would do any good explaining what happened with Johnny to Rachel and the kids. It would just upset them more. "What time is it?"

"Eleven twenty seven. Where are you?" Rachel asked, and then she said, "I called the police a few minutes ago and I think that they might want to talk to you."

"I'm at my uncle's house at Violent Hill. Call them back and tell them to be on the lookout for Johnny Blackwood…and tell them that he is dangerous. I'll be here when they arrive."

Allen could hear Rachel's voice drop, so that the kids couldn't hear what she was saying. "Allen, is Demri alright?"

Allen truly didn't know how to answer. He wanted to say that she was, but there was really no telling at this point. "I hope so. I'm going to find out. I'll call you back in a little while. Stay with the kids." Allen hung up.

He stood with his hands on the counter top trying to keep from falling to the floor. As he stood there he thought that he heard a moan from the dining room area. He held his breath and listened closely, to see if it was just his imagination playing tricks on him. He stared into the pitch dark dining room and couldn't see much farther than the door frame. On his way to investigate, he removed a kitchen knife from the butchers block by the stove.

Slowly, he crept into the dining room. He was holding the knife like he was expecting something to jump out from the darkness at any moment and impale itself upon the blade. He heard the sound again and this time there was no mistaking that it was a moan. He reached in and flipped the switch, lighting up the large room and the family dining table. The table was set with a single plate of dinner on the far side of the table. The dinner was half eaten and a spilled red wine soaked the tablecloth around the plate. Allen slowly walked around the table and found Elmer on his back, lying on the floor. There was a dinner napkin still tucked into his shirt, like a baby's bib, and what looked like mashed potatoes caked around the corners of his mouth.

Allen would have liked to believe that Elmer was just knocked out, or drugged like Allen had been not long ago. Unfortunately, there was an open gash along the front side of Elmer's neck revealing a much sinister fate had befallen his uncle. As a parting gift, the killer had left the knife imbedded in Elmer's chest, the handle protruding from his now stained, white designer shirt. Allen took another look at the spilled wine glass and wondered if Elmer's drink had been spiked, leading to letting his guard down. Perhaps due to their failure in finishing Allen off at the boathouse, Johnny or Chris had been a little more thorough on Elmer, once he'd passed out.

Allen was shocked and enraged at the sight of his uncle lying in the dining room floor. Elmer moaned again and Allen went to his side and cradled his head. He considered removing the knife from Elmer's chest, but had read somewhere that he could cause more damage to the victim by removing it. Elmer was trying to say something, but whatever it was, the words were getting garbled in the massive amount of blood collected in his throat. Allen grabbed the tablecloth and pulled it off of the dining room table, causing all of the dishes to crash to the floor. He used the cloth to apply pressure to Elmer's neck and then put Elmer's hand on it to hold it into place. He ran back to the phone and dialed 911. He put the receiver to his head and waited for it to ring - it never did. He hung up and dialed the numbers again, but it still would not ring. Was it still connected to Rachel? He tried again and listened for a dial tone, but now there wasn't one. Somehow, the phones had been disabled in the short time since he'd talked to Rachel.

"Goddamnit." He slammed the phone back down onto the cradle and ran back over to Elmer. He searched for Elmer's cell phone. Allen had an overwhelming rush of dread surge through his body, as he thought that Otis, Kirk and the rest of the family could be upstairs in a similar state. He needed to go and check on them. The problem was that the last he'd seen - Johnny and Chris had guns - and he didn't. Not finding a phone in Elmer's pockets, he told the wounded man that he'd be right back. Maybe, he could find a phone upstairs. He tiptoed to the foyer and looked up at the second floor landing. It was dark, like the rest of the house. He could barely see the outline of the banister. He moved slowly – ready to dive for cover, as soon as someone emerged from the darkness and started shooting. He was finding it difficult to keep his composure. He wanted to turn and run out of the front door, and straight out of Mississippi.

He got choked up when he thought of Demri, and what she must be going through right now. It motivated him to continue up the stairs. He put his hand on the banister and his foot on the first step – just as there was a knock at the front door. Allen waited for a moment, to see if anyone else was coming to answer the door. There was no sound at all, not from anywhere in the house, just complete silence. Either everyone else was already dead, or they were drugged and laid out somewhere. Not even Jennifer's baby, Ronnie, made any sound. Maybe nobody else was here. Allen crept to the front door and opened it, hiding the knife behind his back. He was taking no chances if it were Johnny or Chris - he planned on plunging the blade as deep as he could into whichever neck he could get to first. When he opened the door, it was quite the relief to find the stocky detective standing on the porch. Allen opened the door wide. Detective Menard must have seen the panic, because when he saw Allen's face, he said, "Are you ok, Mr. Blackwood?"

"No...not at all," Allen said, in a panic, "Call the medics."

"What?" The Detective was confused. "Why do you need a medic?"

Allen led Leo to the dining room and to Elmer. He began explaining what happened at the boathouse, all the way down to the stranger coming in and interrupting Johnny and Chris's plans to kill him. He told Leo about Demri's disappearance and what Johnny threatened to do to her before Allen had passed out. He told of waking up along the bank of the river, coming here to use the phone and finding Elmer in the dining room.

Allen found himself short of breath as was finishing the story. He'd always considered himself a tough guy, able to deal with trying situations, but he was really shook up at the moment – more so since the detective had shown up. Having someone there, on his side, allowed the adrenalin to wear off a little and the reality of the situation was setting in. Just as he finished, as if on cue, the lights went out. Allen tried the switch, flipping it up and down several times - nothing happened. He looked into the other room, at the table light that Patsy kept burning; it was off also. Someone had cut the power in the house, just like they'd cut the phone line. Leo pulled a flashlight from inside his suit jacket, and scanned the dark room. Satisfied that there wasn't any immediate danger, he knelt down beside Elmer, checked for vital signs and then pulled out his cell phone. He dialed Lashauna, and as it was ringing he looked at Allen. "Mr. Blackwood, for your safety and mine, please put that down." Allen realized that he was still holding the knife from the kitchen. He tossed it onto the dining room table. Allen listened, as Leo carried on with his phone conversation.

"Hey, are you still in the car?" Leo asked, speaking to Lashauna. "Good, listen…call in medical. Tell them to hurry to Violent Hill. We have a critically injured person here and I haven't cleared the house, yet…" Leo listened, "…I don't know what going on exactly, but from talking with Mr. Blackwood…it sounds like we've got some big problems out here." He listened again as his partner said something and then to punctuate the situation at hand he said, "Hurry up," and closed the phone.

Allen could tell that the detective was nervous. Despite the anxiety - the detective had a business as usual way about him that Allen admired. Detective Menard looked Elmer over in the dark and rubbed his chin, as if he was trying to decide what would be the best course of action here. Elmer was now moaning and gurgling so loudly that it was drowning out all other noise in the house. Leo knew that there could still be someone in the house. There was definitely someone on the property, due to the cut phone lines and power. He didn't like being in such a confined space as the dark house. If someone were stalking them, he would rather have open room to see them coming. Leo turned to Allen and said, "Let's get him outside, where it's safer."

Allen didn't protest. He was content to follow the detectives lead and wait for back up if that's what the detective had in mind. They worked together to pick Elmer up and had just about gotten him to the front door, when a scream echoed from upstairs. It was an ear-piercing roar, one that someone made when the knife of a madman made contact with their skin. They laid Elmer on the foyer floor near the door and Detective Menard drew his weapon. He gave Allen a terrified look. "What the fuck was that?"

Allen shrugged and tried to speak, but the lump in his throat prevented him from producing any sound. Leo ran toward the staircase. Allen instinctively followed, since the scream had come from a woman and along with Demri, he knew that Patsy and Jennifer were probably in danger as well.

From the top of the landing, the upstairs hall branched both to the left and to the right. Leo stopped unsure of which way to go. For good measure he tried a light switch, but again - nothing. The power was cut throughout the entire house. He shined his flashlight down both ends of the hall and didn't see anything either way.

"Mississippi State Police," Leo yelled into the darkness, "Whoever is up here, step out where I can see you with your hands shown." They waited – still nothing, just eerie silence. Leo handed Allen a small flash light - the kind that you would attach to a key chain - and motioned him down the hall. "Open the first door...and keep out of the way," Leo instructed. "I'll cover this end," he gestured to the hall to the left. "I can watch your back. I don't want anyone sneaking up on us and I have a good vantage of the whole upstairs from right here." Allen nodded in agreement and slowly walked to the first bedroom door - the small beam from the pocket light barely illuminating the area in front of his feet. "Any sign of trouble...you hit the floor," Leo added.

Allen pushed open the first door and shined the light in - an empty bedroom. He looked back at Leo who was still on the landing with his pistol ready. The cop motioned for him to keep going. Allen crept to the second door, which was Otis's bedroom. The door was slightly ajar, Allen pushed it open. Across the expansive bedroom, Uncle Otis was lying in his bed with covers drawn up to his chin. "Otis?" Allen called out to his Great Uncle. There was no response - nor any movement. He stepped further into Otis's room, scanning the corners with the tiny flashlight. As he got to Otis, his fear was confirmed. The old man's eyes were wide open and staring blankly at the wall beside the window. Allen felt Otis's lifeless hand - it was as cold as ice.

"Is he dead?" Allen was startled, he hadn't heard Leo come in behind him. The detective was standing in the doorway, still guarding the hall.

Allen nodded, "Yeah." He wondered if Otis's death was the direct result of Johnny and Chris, or if Otis was lucky enough to go on his own, before he had to witness the self-destruction of his family. Either way, it was heartbreaking. Allen never really had a chance to know Otis. Now, he never would. All that the old man had worked his entire life for – keeping his family together – was now disintegrating away before their eyes.

Otis must have known that this was the likely end for them – he had to have. Not long ago, Otis had spoken of the business as if it were a living beast. Something dangerous, something that would devour everything that came into contact with it, if left unchecked. He was right! It was loose and they were all paying the price. Allen bet that Otis never figured that the real danger would come from inside his own family. He protected them all from the world outside, but Johnny was already inside the gates. Poor Otis, Allen hoped that he died peacefully, and didn't know what was really happening here. But, just like Otis had warned him, it was the nature of the beast and the beast always wins. "Ain't that right Otis?" Allen whispered.

He gently closed Otis's eyes and pulled the covers up over his face. On the bedside table there was a photograph. It was of Otis and his family from sometime back in the depression era. In it, Otis and Artie were in the foreground. Clyde, Ellie and Bessie were on the porch of the old family home - the very one rotting away on the other side of the property. All of the people in the photo had smiles on their faces. Allen realized that with Otis's passing, everyone in the photo was now dead. He looked at the family in the photo - his grandfather, Otis, their mother, father and sister. Where had it all gone so wrong? He set the picture back on the table, gently rubbed Otis's bald head, and joined Leo at the bedroom door.

"What in the hell is going on here?" Leo asked.

"You mean other than the fact that we keep finding my family members fucked up?" Allen remarked.

"Keep your eyes peeled and stay close to me."

Allen nodded and followed the detective out into the hallway again.

Together they slowly approached the next bedroom. Allen knew it as Elmer and Patsy's room, and this time the door was closed tight. Leo posted up and took aim at the door. He motioned that he was ready and Allen pushed it opened with a creak. When the beam from the flashlight hit the room, Allen's heart skipped a beat. The light was faint, but there was no mistaking that there were two people tied up, back to back, in the middle of the room.

For a brief second, Allen thought that one of them was Demri and he recklessly rushed into the room. When he got closer he found that it wasn't Demri, but instead Patsy and Jennifer - their hands and legs bound with rope, and duct tape across their mouths. After quickly examining them, he was relieved to find that neither were injured beyond some rope burns and being completely terrified. They looked like they had been through quite an ordeal and just as Allen and Leo were about to free their hands – another scream echoed from down the hallway. Allen recognized the voice as Uncle Kirk. His heart dropped from his chest and he prayed that Kirk wasn't hurt badly, but the cry indicated otherwise. Leo hurried back through the doorway in the direction of Kirk. Allen gestured to the girls that he would be right back. As Patsy and Jennifer protested being left tied up, Allen ran into the darkness of the hallway following the detective down the hall and towards Kirk's scream. They reached Kirk's bedroom at the very same moment that a baby started to wail from behind the closed door.

Leo took a deep breath and pushed the door open, pointing his gun inside the room as it swung wide. The room was a little better lit than the rest of the house, since a lantern was burning on the bedside table. Allen couldn't see into the room very well, mostly because the detective was standing in the doorway. Suddenly, Leo began to yell, *"Get on the ground! Put the child down, and get on the ground!"*

Leo moved inside the room and Allen followed. Chris Blackwood was standing on the far side of the room, near the window and he was holding baby Ronnie up in front of him like a shield. In his free hand, he held a knife and it was pressed against the baby's bare belly. Chris ignored the demands of the detective and stood there facing Allen and Leo with a blank expression on his face. In Allen's opinion, Chris looked like a deranged lunatic, or a person so drugged out of his mind that he wasn't able to comprehend what was going on. Historically being personally incapable of making an intelligent decision, Allen had a bad feeling that Chris, or Ronnie, or both were not going to make it out of this scenario.

"Chris," Allen tried to reason. "Put Ronnie down. You don't want to hurt him." It didn't look like Chris could even hear him, and he made no indication to suggest that he had. "Chris" Allen tried a second time with more force, "Whatever is going on here...I'm sure that we can work it out. Come on...put the knife down. Put Ronnie down!"

Chris was a statue, on the far side of the room. His expression hadn't changed. Not even with the detective's pistol pointed right at his head. Ronnie, sensing that things were very wrong, was crying loudly and with his limited vocabulary kept saying, "Momma...Momma..." over and over again.

Allen tried to coax the child, "Don't worry Ronnie...Momma's in the other room...she's fine. She will be here in just a few minutes."

"Put the baby down," Leo instructed again. He had Chris dead to rights, but still didn't want to jeopardize the baby. "There's no way you walk out of here with the child. Put him down and I'll let you go...for now." This proposal seemed to spark some deliberation from Chris. He at least appeared to be considering the option.

Just as Allen was sure that Chris was about to make the deal, Kirk walked into the room from the dark hallway, surprising Leo and Allen. "What in tarnation is going on in here?" He asked.

Allen was startled, yet relieved, to see his uncle. He'd assumed that Kirk was somewhere in the house hurt - or like Otis, dead. The fact that he was walking freely around the house and not suffering the effects of the drugs that Johnny and Chris had given Elmer and himself was a little bit surprising. "Uncle Kirk," Allen said, "stay back."

"Chris," Kirk said, "what in the hell are you doing?" Kirk was reprimanding his nephew the same way that one would expect if the offender had drunk straight from the community milk carton, and was not high on drugs and threatening a baby with a knife. Allen looked at Leo. The detective still hadn't taken his gun off of Chris - waiting for him to drop the baby. "Goddamnit Chris," Kirk said again, more forceful this time. "I thought that I told you to kill these sons a bitches."

Leo quickly swung his gun from Chris to Kirk, only getting it about halfway before the room erupted with a blast from a pistol. It came from Kirk, who was standing in the doorway with a smoking gun. Leo fell to his knees, clutching his stomach. The blood was already starting to saturate his shirt, turning it from crisp white, to a dark red around the wound. Kirk turned his gun on Allen, and said, "Sorry kiddo," calm and even keeled, as if he were apologizing for not allowing Allen to borrow the car.

Allen stood in shock, waiting on the inevitable flash to come, as he stared down the barrel of Kirk's gun. He could see the muscles in the old man's finger twitch just as Kirk began to apply pressure to the trigger. Suddenly, a shot rang out - but not from Kirk's gun. The wood above Kirk's head splintered, as a bullet made impact with the door frame, missing its mark by inches.

Leo was up to his knees and had gotten off a shot. Allen was amazed that the cop missed at such close range, but given the fact that he was wounded - it was understood. Kirk turned his gun back onto Leo. The two of them fired several shots at each other, at close range - the room erupted into a deafening racket. The wall and door frame behind Kirk was filled with holes from the detective's bullets and the table and lamp behind Leo exploded into pieces, as most of the rounds from both guns missed their mark. Allen didn't see how they both didn't have at least one new hole each somewhere in their bodies. Surprisingly though, Kirk didn't fall from the exchange, but instead quickly fleeing from the room and back into the darkness of the house.

Leo blindly fired a couple more shots out into the dark hallway and then he fell all the way to his butt, slumping over against the nightstand, knocking over the lantern in the process.

During the gunfight, Allen had taken cover on the ground, at the foot of the bed. Once Kirk was gone, Allen got to his knees and noticed that in the melee, Chris had tossed the baby onto the bed. By some sort of miracle, the child had not been hit by a stray bullet. Allen quickly grabbed Ronnie and shielded him, just in case the shooting was to continue. From where Allen was kneeling, he could see Detective Menard slumped against the night stand on the other side of the room. Leo didn't look good. In fact, he'd received a couple more bullet wounds to his shoulder and chest during the exchange with Kirk. Allen was in shock. He was still trying to come to grips with the fact that Uncle Kirk had shot the detective. Confused and shaken, but feeling like the gunfire might be over, Allen pulled himself to his feet. He knew that the detective needed some immediate first aid – until proper medical attention could arrive. Just as he got one leg under himself – a foot hit him in the side, flipping him over onto his back. Ronnie fell from his arms and into the floor. The baby was back to screaming at the top of his lungs – terrified by all of the noise and violence. Allen fought back the pain of what felt like a broken rib. He looked up into the blank hollow eyes of Chris – now standing over him with the knife clutched in his hand. In Allen's opinion, it looked like all negotiating was over and Chris no longer had the slack jawed look of an idiot, but the clenched expression of a madman - his intent, to kill - here and now.

Chris lunged with the knife at the same time that Allen kicked, catching Chris in the chest and lifting him completely off of his feet. Chris sprawled against the far wall, as Allen scrambled up to defend himself from the next attack. Little Ronnie let out a new barrage of howling, at the resurgence of violence and it distracted Allen momentarily from Chris. Allen knew that he couldn't defend them both if Kirk were to return, not to mention keep Patsy and Jennifer safe. With a fleeting thought, he wished that he'd taken the time to untie them. Chris shook off the blow and the impact with the wall and struggled to get back to his feet. Allen grabbed Ronnie and ran to the doorway, deciding that his best option was to get the baby to safety.

He almost made it into the hallway before he felt the blade of the knife slice through his t-shirt and into the flesh along his shoulder. Luckily, the blow wasn't a stab, but a slash, which didn't go very deep, but the pain knocked Allen to his knees again. He held Ronnie tight and fought to keep from falling on the child, as he went to the floor. Allen looked over his shoulder and saw Chris coming in for another strike. This time Allen didn't have a chance to raise a defense. Chris was too close and in such a position that, with the child in Allen's arms, he couldn't shield what was coming. Allen closed his eyes and waited for the blade to make contact with his skin again. The room detonated with gunfire again, startling Allen, causing him to collapse to the floor once again. He turned and watched as the bullets from Leo's gun tore into Chris's lower body hitting him in the legs, stomach, and at least one round directly in the crotch. Chris shrieked, letting the knife fall from his hand, as he collapsed to the floor beside Allen and Ronnie.

Allen didn't waste any more time cowering on the floor. He quickly jumped up onto his feet and scurried over to Leo, who was breathing laboriously. The detective was thankfully still alive and for the second time in the last couple of minutes, saved Allen's life. Allen held Ronnie in one arm and helped Leo to his feet with the other. Allen had to get the five of them, counting Patsy and Jennifer, out of there right now. Though Chris was down, Johnny was still nowhere to be found and now they had Kirk on the loose. Allen was sure that Kirk hadn't gotten too far with his breathing problems, so he was cautious helping Leo out into the hallway and to where the women were restrained. Allen cut Patsy and Jennifer loose, using Chris's knife and handed Ronnie to his mother. Jennifer held the baby close to her chest and cried along with the child. Patsy was crying also, as she coddled Jennifer and Ronnie. She put her hand over her mouth as she realized that the detective was bleeding badly. Innocently, she asked, "Allen, what's going on? Why did Chris and Kirk tie us up?"

Allen answered honestly, "Patsy, I honestly don't know what is going on, but they are trying to kill us and we need to get out of here." He motioned for her to take his place holding the detective, who was now on the verge of passing out, "Here, take the detective outside to his car. You guys get out of here. His phone is in his pocket...use it to call the last number that he dialed. It's his partner...tell her what happened and tell her to hurry up."

Patsy was confused, "Where are you going?"

"I'm gonna get Elmer and meet y'all outside. Then I have to find Demri."

"She was here," Jennifer said, "After we were tied up, I heard her downstairs, yelling for help. Johnny was with her...then they left. It sounded like she was fighting him the whole time."

Allen's heart sank again, "Do you have any idea where they went?" he asked.

"No," Jennifer said, "but when he was here, I heard him talking to Chris. I'm pretty sure that he knows where Johnny was headed."

Allen could hear Chris moaning from the bedroom down the hall - his balls, hopefully blown into small pieces by the detective's bullet. Allen, feeling no remorse for his recently castrated cousin, prayed that the asshole could still talk. He took the gun from the detective's hand. Somehow, Leo was still holding on to it, even though he was in and out of consciousness.

"You guys head outside...I'll be right behind you," Allen instructed.

He waited for them to get down the stairs, just to make sure that they didn't need any help with Leo. Patsy and Jennifer were stronger than Allen gave them credit for. They navigated their way down the stairs with no problems at all. Once they were outside, Allen returned to Chris.

19

From the distance, Allen could hear the sirens of the first responders on their way. He wasn't sure if it was the police, or medical personnel, or both, but he knew that someone was going to be here soon – which meant that he needed to hurry. He went back into the room with Chris and pushed the bedroom door closed. His cousin was still laying in the floor and despite the other bullet wounds in his body, he was holding his groin, which was a dark red bloody mess. Turning the lock with his left hand, he felt the surge of pain in his shoulder, a result of where Chris had stabbed him. The locked door was not to trap Chris; Allen was pretty sure that the wounds were too severe for Chris to move anywhere on his own. It was to prevent being surprised by Kirk, or anybody else who may be hiding in the darkness of the house. Allen would let the police deal with the problem of securing the house when they got here – right now, he was only interested in getting some specific information.

Chris was laying on the floor beside the overturned lantern, moaning in pain. Allen picked up the battery powered lantern and set it down beside Chris's head. His cousin's eyes were rolled back, showing only the whites, and for a brief second, Allen felt a twinge of pity for Chris. The pain of being shot in the groin must be excruciating. Allen pulled a wooden chair from the writing desk over to his cousin and sat down. The severely injured man opened his eyes, looked up at Allen sitting over him and said in a quick short breath, "Help…get help…help me."

"Where's Demri?" Allen asked.

"I dunno," Chris licked his dry lips. "I need some…water."

Chris's hands were holding the spot on his bloody jeans that used to be his penis. Allen took his foot and placed it over Chris's hands. He began to

299

put pressure – slowly at first, and then more and more, before Chris started to moan in agony. Allen let off and then asked again, "Where's Demri?"

"Joh…Johnny has her," Chris withered in pain on the floor.

"Where?" Allen asked.

Chris shook his head. Allen kicked the chair out from under himself, so that he could get down on the ground beside Chris. He pressed Leo's gun to Chris's crotch and leaned down into the wounded man's face. "I will blow off what little balls that you have left, if I have to ask you again. I can't guarantee if you will live, or not, but if you do, you will live the rest of your life pissing through a plastic tube and wishing like hell you had a small piece of that little fella left to rub from time to time." Allen could hear the sirens getting closer and knew that his time was running short. He hoped that Chris wasn't also paying attention to the sounds outside.

Chris swallowed hard and said, "The lab…at…the old house."

"What? What old house?" Then as soon as he asked the question, he thought of the picture on Otis's bedside table. Things started to make a little more sense as to why the dilapidated old house was still standing and hadn't been bulldozed. They were making drugs on the property and somewhere in the old house was the lab. The basement - that was why Otis had discouraged Allen from looking around the day that they were over there. Otis was about to let him in on the secret, but Allen backed out of the deal right before the details of the operation were revealed to him. Johnny and Kirk would go there to hide. That's where they feel safe that nobody would look for them, and that's most likely where Johnny had taken Demri.

Allen stood up and leveled the gun on Chris's head. He thumbed the hammer back, as Chris held out a shaky hand between the gun barrel and himself. "No, please…" he cried.

Allen wanted nothing more than to pull the trigger - as payback for what Chris had done, but he couldn't bring himself to do it. Allen lowered the gun and said, "I hope you enjoy prison. Keep your jaw loose, it'll be your only way to get cigarettes without your giggle stick. Have fun." Allen unlocked the door and left the room. He rushed down the stairs and out the front door.

In the driveway, he found an ambulance and several squad cars pulling into the driveway. Jennifer and Patsy had dragged Elmer outside once they got Detective Menard safe and they were all gathered at the front of a police sedan. Patsy was crying, cradling Elmer's head in her lap and running her fingers through his hair. In Allen's opinion, Elmer didn't look good. His skin was chalk white, as the medics moved in to administer first aid. Surprisingly, Detective Menard was alert and sitting up against his car fender. One thing was for sure, the man was tough. Kneeling beside him and wiping his forehead with a handkerchief was a familiar woman.

Lashauna stood up as Allen came out of the house. She held her gun in her hand and leveled it on Allen when he reached the bottom of the steps. The other officers who were still assessing the scene, did the same. "Down on the ground...now," she said, forcefully. Allen put his hands up into the air. More screeching tires could be heard coming up the long driveway, flashing blue lights reflected through the trees. "I'm not going to say it again...on the ground!" The tone of her voice removed any doubt whether she was serious or not.

Allen complied, knowing that every second wasted lessened the chances of saving Demri from whatever horrible ordeal she was going through – if it wasn't too late already. As he got down on his knees, he explained, "You're making a mistake. We need to hurry before someone else gets hurt."

The officers circled him with their guns drawn. Allen could see the medics tending to Elmer and Detective Menard. Elmer was being loaded onto a gurney. Leo was pushing the medics out of his way, trying to get Lashauna's attention. She was focused on Allen like a pit bull and didn't hear him at first. After several attempts, one of the officers standing next to Lashauna got her attention. She lowered her gun and went to Leo. "Somebody pat him down," she said, pointing at Allen.

Allen watched Detective Menard, as he laboriously said something to Lashauna. His breathing had shortened and there was obvious pain in his facial expressions. Allen hoped that the responders would do something for him soon to save him. Without Detective Menard as a witness to what happened inside the house, Allen was sure that he would have a tough time clearing himself with the police from this madness. Two uniformed officers came from behind and pushed him down to his stomach. They patted him down and removed the pistol from his waistband. Lashauna saw the gun and stood up from where she was talking with Leo. She touched her partners head, as the medics began carting him towards a waiting ambulance. Lashauna returned to Allen, just as the cops were synching the cuffs around his wrists. "You can take those off officer," she said. The uniforms looked at her with confusion, but did what she instructed them to do. Neither of them were ignorant of the reputation that Lashauna had in the department. What she said was always backed up by the Captain.

"Did you want us to give him back his gun too?" One of the cops asked, holding up the pistol retrieved from his belt.

"Actually," Allen explained, "that belongs to Detective Menard."

Lashauna took the pistol from the officer. She faced Allen and said, "You had better start explaining what went down here."

"No problem," Allen said, "but first, a couple of things. There is one of the bad guys upstairs, he's pretty banged up thanks to your partner." The uniformed were headed toward the front door. "Be careful," Allen cautioned, "there's an old guy running around somewhere with a gun." If they heard him they didn't respond, but they did draw their weapons as they went inside the front door. He spoke directly to Lashauna, "I think that Johnny is on the property at another house and we need to hurry. I'm pretty sure that he's responsible for the murder of those old folks. He, along with his brother and our Uncle Kirk, are most definitely responsible for this mess here, and he kidnapped Demri."

"Where on the property?"

"I'll show you. Can we take your car?" Allen asked.

Followed by a couple of uniformed officers, they jumped into Lashauna's car. As they were pulling away – Chris was being brought out of the house on a stretcher. Allen couldn't help but to feel sorry for Chris. He was a dimwit and a druggie, and most likely had just been led down this dark road by his older brother. The poor guy was going to have a long road ahead in the slammer, if he survived his wounds. Allen turned his attention to the situation at hand and directed Lashauna onto the dirt road that led to the old house.

"It sounds like we're on the same page with Johnny," Lashauna finally spoke. She'd been quiet for a few minutes, probably trying to digest all that had gone down in the past hour. "Do you suppose that his brother was his accomplice to the Taylor murders?"

"I'm not sure," Allen said, "were more than just two people involved?"

"No, the evidence suggests just two."

"Then it could have been him...or Kirk."

"Kirk?" She asked, as they bumped along the dirt road in the dark.

Allen said, "Turn here..." and pointed to the right. "He's our Uncle and unfortunately...the one who shot your partner."

Lashauna shook her head, "What would make these well to do old timers get involved in shooting cops and killing innocent people? It doesn't make any sense."

Allen shrugged, "I'm pretty sure that there are drugs being manufactured here on the property, and I am one hundred percent sure that they are running them out into the swamp."

Lashauna gave him a dubious glare, "How are you so sure?"

Allen met her gaze, "How much can I say...without having a lawyer present?"

Lashauna stared out of the window - the trees blew past her headlights at a high rate of speed for such a small road – especially in the dark. After a few seconds she said, "Look, I am here to apprehend a murder suspect... or suspects. If I was to witness anything else illegal...I would have to act as an officer of the law...otherwise, if I don't see it happen...it's just hearsay."

"Alright," Allen said, "I think I know what you're saying." He contemplated leaving out specific details, but in the end, he decided that he needed her help. Demri needed her help too, and coming clean was the only option, if she was going to be able to help them both. He just hoped that she was a woman of her word, "I helped them a couple of times with the deliveries, without actually knowing what was in the bags. I could only assume."

She gave him the look that said, *give me a break*.

"I swear to you, I have no reason to lie," He said, "The money was good and I really didn't care to know what was in the bags." He pointed out of the front windshield, "Slow down, its right through these trees."

Lashauna killed the headlights and the officer in the car behind her did the same. They crept slowly down the tight path and through the brush – the same brush that had scratched the Charger – and pulled slowly up to the front of the abandoned house. Johnny's truck was parked on the side of the house as they pulled up. Otis's golf cart was parked out front near

303

the front porch. "I think both Johnny and Kirk are here," Allen said, "I just hope that we're not too late to help Demri."

"What's Demri got to do with all of this," Lashauna asked, as she shut off the car's engine, "Why would Johnny want to hurt her?"

Allen thought about it, "Other than the fact that he's a complete lunatic, maybe he thinks that I know more than I do, and maybe he thinks that I told her. That's the only thing that makes any sense to me."

"Do you?" She asked.

"What? Know more?" Allen asked, "No…I've told you everything."

Lashauna paused a minute with her hand on the door handle. She was looking in his eyes to see if she saw anything that would make her not trust him. Evidently, she didn't find anything since she pulled the handle and opened the door. As she got out, she said, "Stay close to me."

20

The uniform officers were standing ready, with shotguns and vests, with State Police written across the chest. Lashauna directed one of them to the back of the house to cover the rear exit and the other she wanted out front. "Nobody comes out of this house without me," she instructed the nervous looking officers. They went to their positions and Lashauna joined Allen, already on the porch, looking through the large plate glass window. "What's in there?" Lashauna asked.

"I can't see anything." Allen said, "It's too dark." A bead of sweat rolled down his face – Mississippi humidity, or elevated blood pressure, or both. He wiped it with his shirt sleeve, the cut on his back sending shockwaves of pain up his neck.

Lashauna noticed him wince, "Are you alright?"

"Yeah," Allen answered. A missing arm wouldn't keep him from continuing the search, until he found Demri. "We need to hurry," he said, "If she's in there, she's in big time trouble. Especially, now that Kirk is here too." Allen nodded at the golf cart. "He's bound to have filled Johnny in on what's happening at the main house."

"Have you been inside this shithole before?" Lashauna asked, trying to devise a plan on the fly.

"Yes, I was here a couple of weeks ago."

"Do you have any idea where they would have her, if she's in there?" Lashauna asked.

Allen nodded his head, "I think I know where they are." He remembered the basement door and how Otis had steered him away from going down there. "There's a basement."

"A basement…in Mississippi?" Lashauna asked, "Can't say I've ever been in a house with one around here!"

"I haven't been in it either, but when I was here with Otis, he acted weird when I got near the door. He didn't want me to go down there. It's just a hunch."

"Did you say a hunch? Who are you now, Inspector Clouseau?"

Despite the situation, Allen couldn't help but smile. He found it humorous that she – a strictly business police detective, in the middle of a life and death situation - would reference the Pink Panther. "We need to hurry," he said.

Lashauna looked around the property. It was too dark to see beyond the beam of the patrol car headlights. But there was nothing but wilderness for miles and it was unlikely that even the heartiest outdoorsman would brave the swamp on foot in the dark. She was sure that in the daytime, the Blackwoods, who had grown up on the swamp, could disappear quickly and never be found. She had to make sure that if they hadn't already fled, they didn't squirt out when she went in. With only the two patrol officers and her on scene, her options for backup were limited. She couldn't risk taking either officer inside, just in case Johnny and the uncle were able to slip out. She knew that she should wait for backup, but Allen was right. If Demri wasn't hurt already, she didn't have long before Johnny cut the dead weight, and the last thing that Lashauna wanted was another innocent person getting killed. The porch decking felt soft under Lashauna's feet. She wondered just how decayed the inside of the house was. There were no lights on and it would be dangerous going inside, especially if the floor was rotted out. She couldn't go in alone. She needed someone with her, just in case. Against her better judgement, she made her decision and pulled Leo's pistol from the waist band. She handed it to Allen, who took it with a curious expression on his face.

"It's better to have it and not need it…and all that shit," she said. "Are you ready to go?"

"What about the backup," there was more concern in Allen's voice than he'd like to admit. "Don't we need to wait for them?"

"They could be a while," Lashauna said, "These two guys need to stay outside to cover the escape. You're the only backup I have right now."

Allen nodded, like he was trying to convince himself, "Ok," he said, "Do you have an extra flashlight?"

Lashauna motioned for one of the uniformed officers to come

over. He'd been positioned behind his vehicle, following her first set of instructions. She asked for his flashlight and said, "We're going in. Watch the exits and when the other units get here, make sure that they don't come in with their guns blazing. I don't want to be shot by some rookie with a nervous twitch."

"Yes, Mam," The officer replied and returned to his position.

She handed the flashlight to Allen and said, "You lead...no way am I having you covering my back."

"You've got it," Allen said, as he turned the door knob. The door was unlocked and opened easily.

Inside, the place smelled stale – maybe more so than when Allen was here with Otis. It had been daytime then and the rainstorm of the previous evening had dampened the old wood. It was also missing the homey feeling that Allen felt the other day. Now, it was just dark, damp, cold, and musty - like a tomb.

The flashlight sent a crisp beam into the living room, cutting through the darkness and revealing the eerie interior – complete with vintage wallpaper peeling in the corners. Water marks stained the plaster, adding dark shapes to the sinister atmosphere. The furniture still covered by the sheets, was making more shadows on the walls, making Allen feel uneasy. There was a coat rack standing in the corner with a dust sheet thrown over it. When Lashauna's light skirted past it, the shadow it created looked like a human to Allen's over active imagination, nearly causing him to empty his gun in its direction. Luckily, he caught himself before actually pulling the trigger – not wanting to waste his ammunition. The moment sparked a thought, Allen wondered just how many bullets were left in the clip after Leo and Kirk's shootout. Now was not the time to check - that opportunity had come and gone, but it was cause for concern. He hoped that there was at least one left – he may need it.

He carefully began working his way over to the door. The one that led to the basement. The one that Otis had kept him from entering. The old wood floor was creaking below his feet with every step. The detective - right on his heels - was causing him some concern. The weight of the two of them on the same spot on the floor couldn't be a good thing. Allen was anticipating the soft spot that was going to send them both crashing all the way down. They would get to the basement the hard way. With any luck, they would land on top of Johnny and Kirk and end it all in one shot. The way that Allen's luck ran - he would be the one to break his neck. He would rather not take the chance, so he turned and motioned for Lashauna to stay back several feet, to lighten the load on the floor. She backed away a few steps. Just as he was turning around to resume his tiptoe routine to the basement door, Allen heard the distinct popping sound of the brittle wood giving way under his feet and before he knew it, Lashauna and the living room were floating away, as he fell through the hole. He banged his shoulder and head off of a beam on the way down. Hitting it so hard that he saw stars. The fall wasn't as far down as he imagined, so his body was still stiff from falling through the floor when he landed amongst dirt and broken wood. He felt his knee give out with the impact – the pain shooting all the way up to his hip, as he settled on the floor.

Allen hurt all over! Now, along with the cut on his back, his knee throbbed and his lower back ached from the hard landing. He didn't have any idea where he was. He lay on his back, in total darkness, until Lashauna appeared at the edge of the hole above and shined her flashlight down. He pulled himself up to a sitting position and looked around the room, only it wasn't really a room at all, it looked more like a tall crawlspace under the house.

"Allen…" there was real concern in Lashauna's voice, "…are you alright?"

"No," Allen replied, "I think I'm dead." He looked around trying to adjust his eyes to the total darkness. He wasn't sure, but he thought he could see a door on the far wall. "Can you pass me my flashlight? I think I dropped it when I did my gainer through the floor." Ironically, he'd held on to his pistol throughout the fall. He heard her scramble around upstairs, as he pulled himself to his feet and then she was back at the hole.

"You ready?" she asked.

"Yeah, drop it."

She did, and he was able to catch it before it hit the floor. He shined the light around the damp room. Dark water streaks ran down the block walls from the ceiling and formed a slimy greenish black substance along the edges of the floor. It was an empty space – maybe it had been a storage area at one time or another, but was long ago deserted. The good thing was that it was nothing like Otis had described, as being full of swamp water and snakes. Allen was pretty sure that he could hear the sound of a small engine running – maybe a generator - somewhere in the distance. There was a door on the far wall which was covered top to bottom with cobwebs, leading Allen to believe that it hadn't been opened in quite some time. He shuffled over to the door – his knee aching with every step. "I found a door." Allen said, "Head down the stairs and I'll meet you at the bottom."

"Be careful," she said.

"You too! I'll see you in a minute." He heard her footsteps on the flimsy floor above, as she tiptoed the rest of the way to the basement door. Dust and dirt drifted down through the cracks and floated past his flashlight beam with every step that she took. Allen reached the door and cleared the cobwebs with his hand. He turned the old knob and felt the parts and pieces of the ancient contraption moving and clicking inside, as the door freed from its frame for the first time in many years.

He pushed the door open and stood back to avoid being surprised by whatever may be on the other side. The large room that he was looking into was lit by a single electric light bulb, positioned in the center of the room that illuminated the middle, leaving the outer edges of the room dark. It was a clean, modern looking area. There were stainless steel tables and machinery everywhere that the light shined. There were mixers and ovens off to one side. There were also plastic oil drum size containers in the far corner. Allen was no chemist, but they were most likely full of whatever substances were used to manufacture the drugs. Beside the blue plastic drums, there were several five gallon gasoline cans. The hum of the generator was louder now and Allen figured that it was the source of the power for the light bulb.

He pushed the door open further. When he did, he could see that there was someone sitting in the center of the room, under the light bulb. Their hands were bound behind their back, with rope tied around their waist, securing them to the chair. Allen was looking at the person's back, but he knew right away that it was Demri. His heart jumped from his chest as he rushed into the room. As he cleared the frame, in the corner of his eye, he caught a glimpse of something moving from the darkness behind the door. He barely got his head turned to see, before he was struck in the side of the head with something solid. He crashed to the floor at Demri's feet – his gun and flashlight going in different directions across the floor. The blow didn't knocked him out, but now his head hurt like hell - just like his knee and his shoulder. Demri was staring down at him through teary, terrified eyes. Thankfully, she didn't look hurt, other than being tied to the chair and a piece of duct tape across her mouth.

Through blurry eyes, Allen tried to see what had hit him and saw Kirk standing behind the door with a baseball bat. He held a lit gas lantern in his other hand. Why he hadn't shot Allen was a mystery. He could only guess that Kirk had shot all of his bullets at Detective Menard, during their exchange. Kirk was bleeding from his stomach – another result of the encounter.

Evidently, the good ole detective hadn't missed all of his shots as Allen thought. Standing there in the corner, Kirk didn't look good. He was pale and sweating badly. It appeared to Allen that by swinging the bat Kirk had used up what little strength remained in his body. Now, he was leaning against the wall, holding his gunshot wound - his head cocked weakly to the side. Allen was grateful for Kirk's weakened state, since he was sure that the blow from the baseball bat would have done more damage if it hadn't come from an old man with one foot in the grave.

Demri started to buck and pull at her ties, Allen rolled over to see what she was excited about. When he did, he was staring down the barrel of a gun. Johnny must have been covering the staircase, while Kirk covered the back room after hearing the crash through the floor. Johnny had an empty look in his eyes and his face was tight with rage. "You know what," Johnny said, "I am kinda glad you didn't die back at the boathouse with your black friend." Johnny smiled a rotten grin. "I'm gonna enjoy killing you in front of this whore," he motioned at Demri.

"What *friend* are you talking about, Johnny?" Allen asked. He thought that if he could buy a few minutes, he could think of a way to get from under Johnny's barrel. He already knew that Johnny was referring to whomever had interrupted them earlier while Allen was drugged at the Boathouse. That explained the blood that Allen found under the rug.

"I hope you know that you're responsible for all of this." Johnny continued, "You're the reason things wound up this way."

"Johnny, what in the fuck are you talking about?" Allen pulled himself up to his feet. "You're the one holding the gun. You're the one who killed his own family."

Johnny shook his head, "No, not me." He motioned at Kirk, "The only family that I was willing to kill, was you. He did the rest. Elmer, Otis, and the girls…it was all him."

Allen didn't mention that Jennifer and Patsy were alive and well – Elmer too, as far as he knew. He and Leo must have showed up just in time to prevent the rest from being killed. "Why?" Allen asked, "I don't understand. Why would you kill the person that has taken care of you your whole life? Uncle Otis was nothing but good to all of us."

"No," Johnny shook his head, "Otis made us what we are. We were his prisoners - Slaves to his machine. Sure, he made it sound like a family business, but it was Otis's business and we were tired of being in chains. We wanted to be the one holding the whip for a change. We knew that Otis was dying, and only Elmer was in our way…" Johnny shrugged his shoulders, "…then you showed up. For some reason, Otis took a liking to you…you know the rest."

"Johnny, shut the fuck up and shoot him, so we can get out of here." Kirk wheezed from the corner of the room.

Allen smiled at Johnny, "Looks like you're still not holding the whip, Johnny. Just a new master is all."

Johnny leveled the gun at Allen's head and Allen knew that talking was over. He looked at Demri. She was crying and Allen hated seeing her like she was – hated what he'd gotten her into. Suddenly, from the stairwell behind Johnny, Lashauna's voice called out over the sound of the generator. "Drop the gun and get on the ground."

"What the hell, Allen? How many friends do you have with you?" Johnny smiled and lowered his arm. He turned to face Lashauna. She was pointing her gun at Johnny and slowly walking down the last few steps. "Alright…alright," Johnny coaxed her, as if he were talking to a child, "I'm not going to hurt you. Look, I lowered my gun," He nodded toward his gun now pointed at the floor, "Now, you put yours down, so that we can talk about this."

Lashauna stopped at the base of the stairs. Aim never wavering, "I said put the gun down and get on the floor…last warning."

"Look," excitement started to build in Johnny's voice, "I don't take commands from no bitch. Now, you can lower your gun and we can talk about this or we can…" Two shots rang out in quick succession and Johnny toppled over backwards, like a tree that had been cut at the base. When he landed, Allen could see two bullet holes in Johnny's chest that were quickly turning deep red from the blood - one of them, directly over his heart. Allen knew immediately that Johnny was dead.

Lashauna quickly turned her gun on Kirk, who had emerged from the corner during the showdown and was now standing near the chemical containers. He was still holding his lantern, but he no longer had the baseball bat. Instead, he held the gun that Allen had dropped.

"Drop it and get on the ground," Lashauna commanded, in the same even tone in which she'd just spoken to Johnny, only this time her barrel was still smoking from the rounds that had ended his life.

Kirk didn't acknowledge her. He talked directly to Allen, "This is the only way that it could end, you know?"

"It doesn't have to be like this, Kirk," Allen pleaded. "Put the gun down."

"I'm an old man." Kirk said. "I was just trying to be free."

"Free of what?" Allen asked.

Kirk took a deep breath of the stale air, like he was savoring the aroma of the decrepit old building. While doing so, he tossed the lantern onto the gasoline cans and they quickly caught on fire. He spread his arms out wide as the flames picked up behind him – they began to climb the wall, "All of this," he said. He then turned the gun on himself and Allen's question as to if there was any ammo left in the magazine, was answered with another crack of gunfire, as Kirk's head blew apart and his body crumpled to the floor.

Demri screamed from behind the duct tape and Allen suddenly realized that they had a major problem. If the chemicals in the barrels were to ignite, this place was going to blow. The old house was like dry kindling and would probably burn down in a matter of minutes. Allen grabbed the ropes holding Demri to the chair and hoped that there was still enough time to free her. He pulled at the knots and they began to loosen. The fire was climbing up the wall as he freed her hands and began to work on her waist. Demri pulled the tape from her own mouth and began to cry, as she helped Allen pull at the ropes. Lashauna checked both Johnny and Kirk to see if either of them had any life left in them. They were both dead, so she rushed over to help Allen free Demri.

The plastic containers were beginning to bubble under the immense heat of the fire. It was just a matter of seconds before the chemicals inside the drums reached the temperature that made them volatile. Finally, Demri was freed and the three of them were running for the stairs. Allen brought up the rear, limping on his injured knee.

By the time that Allen had made it all the way up the stairs – Demri and Lashauna were already outside of the house. Allen sidestepped the hole that he'd fallen through. Smoke was billowing through it, like a smoke stack from the inferno below. For some reason, Allen felt compelled to stop at the doorway and look back into the old house. Smoke covered the top half of the living room, quickly engulfing all of the Blackwood family history. Flames were coming up through the floor boards now, catching the sheets that covered the furniture.

Lashauna yelled at him from behind her car, "ALLEN RUN!" She and Demri were following the two uniform cops down the old dirt drive and away from the house. Allen hurried behind them and as he reached the tree line, the house exploded like a bomb, sending pieces hundreds of yards in every direction. The force of the blow knocked Allen down, and when he looked back, all that was left of the house were two of the first floor walls that were burning so brightly they lit up the night sky.

VI

MONEY AND GEOGRAPHY

1

Lashauna steered her police cruiser off of South Beach Road, and into the nearly empty parking lot of the Gulf Coast Inn. The patrol car was a new model Crown Victoria – a replacement for the one that was destroyed in the explosion at the Blackwood estate, three weeks earlier. It still had the new car smell and the shiny paint that Lashauna was certain wouldn't last very long, given the abuse she tended to inflict on her work vehicles.

The new car felt empty without Leo sitting next to her. At least he was at home and on the mend. Lashauna had stopped by Menard's house to check on him just this morning. He was more than ready to get back to work. Paige was driving him nuts with all of the pampering and rules. Worst of all, according to Leo, was that the doctor had been very specific about what he could eat, since one of the four bullets that hit him had damaged his intestines. Leo loved eating junk food, but Paige wouldn't even allow it to be in the house at this point, and Leo was craving some potato chips and dip. During the visit, when Paige left the room, Lashauna agreed to smuggle some Ruffles in on her next visit. She didn't actually have any intention of doing so - she wanted him back on his feet just as quickly as Paige did, but she hated to tell him no in his present state. Lashauna smiled as she thought of the hopeless look in his eyes, as she was saying goodbye. He hated not being able to go with her. Maybe not as much as she hated not taking him along though.

The Gulf Coast Inn was nothing more than an efficiency, built sometime during the eighties, and other than being on prime beach front real estate, it left a lot to be desired. There was a weird, *forgotten in time* vibe that the place had. She remembered seeing places like this all over the coast when she was a kid, but most of the old buildings had been renovated, or torn down over the years. Not this one.

Somehow, the GCI had been overlooked. Its paint was faded and peeling, revealing grey, sun-bleached wood that looked brittle to the touch. There were broken chairs on weathered porches and at least one Confederate Flag being used as a curtain in a window near the main office. A drunkard with a long beard and torn clothes stumbled past her car, doing the stiff legged shuffle, as he made his way out toward the beach. She thought that he would make an excellent extra in one of the Pirate movies that she'd recently seen. The man was so drunk that he'd be lucky to make it through the day at the beach without drowning. She considered intervening, but she wasn't here to hassle drunks.

She pulled her cruiser into a parking space next to a Mercedes that looked about as out of place in the GCI parking lot as she did. She gave a second glance at the Confederate Flag in the window. The redneck ambiance didn't bother her - she wasn't here to rent a room. She got out of her car and ran her hand along the fender. She walked to the building with certainty that who she'd come to see was still here.

The door to the small hotel room was open and Allen was inside packing a suitcase that was laid on the unmade bed.

She stepped inside and said, "Nice atmosphere, I really like the white supremacist flavor of the place."

Allen looked up from what he was doing and smiled, "Hey, Detective. What brings you out here?" Allen noticed that she was holding a legal envelope in her hand.

"Where're you headed?" She asked.

Allen shrugged, "Not sure exactly. I was thinking Florida, maybe."

Lashauna leaned against the dresser. "What's in Florida?"

"I don't know...fishing...a job...hopefully, a new start."

"Have you talked to Demri?"

Allen tossed the t-shirt that he was holding onto the suitcase. "Yeah, we talked."

"Maybe you should give her some time," Lashauna said, "Being kidnapped and nearly murdered is not something that is easily gotten over. She'll come around."

Allen didn't have to sit in on all of the police interviews that Demri had gone through to know that she blamed him for putting her and her children in the position that they'd been in. He had been through more than a dozen interviews himself. As a matter of fact, it seemed that other than attending Otis's and Elmer's funerals that was all that he'd done over the last couple of weeks. Both of his uncles were laid to rest in the family grave yard at Violent Hill, near the charred ruin of the old house. Ironically, the place was still smoldering behind the yellow police tape in the distance as the bodies were placed into their graves. Just days before, Kirk and Johnny's charred remains were removed from the basement of the house and taken to the county morgue where, after autopsies, they were cremated. Patsy and Jennifer refused to claim the remains of either, so there were no actual graves created for those two.

Allen felt like they were laid to rest beneath the rubble of the old house. Chris, who was recovering from his wounds in a guarded hospital room, was helpful in piecing together most of the events from that night. He was more than willing to cooperate for a reduction of his own charges, which to Allen didn't make a lot of sense, based on the amount of felonies that he was facing. When you were facing multiple life sentences, what good was it to knock off twenty years? Either way, Chris wasn't ever going to be mistaken for an intellect, and it was good to hear how the story had actually played out.

It turned out that Chris wasn't with Johnny the afternoon that the Taylors were killed. Chris claimed that Kirk was the second person in the car. It was an allegation that couldn't be confirmed, but Lashauna bought it, based on the evidence. It also turned out that Kirk and Johnny were apparently trying to raise money to start their own criminal empire, once Otis and Elmer were out of the way. For a short time they had used Lionel Taylor to sell their drugs. Chris claimed that Lionel had sold a couple thousand dollars worth of heroin and meth, but had not paid them the money. Chris also told the police where they could find Elmer's stolen Lincoln. He also confirmed that Johnny took it and used it during the murder.

The Lincoln was fished from the river behind Violent Hill, along with Allen's Land Rover. Inside the Land Rover the police discovered the body of Lionel Taylor. He had been shot multiple times and driven into the swamp while buckled into the passenger seat of Allen's truck. It turned

319

out that inadvertently, he had been the one to actually save Allen's life that night by coming in and distracting Johnny and Chris long enough for Allen to get away. Allen wished that he could thank him.

With all of that testimony, Lashauna had everything that she needed to close her case, except a murder weapon. None of the guns used in the spree at Violent Hill the evening that Kirk and Johnny were killed matched the gun used in the Taylor murder. It was a critical piece of evidence that she assumed she would never be able to locate. She supposed that, like the vehicles, it had been thrown into the swamp, but she'd never know for sure.

Lionel was laid to rest beside the fresh graves of his mother and father and at the expense of the Blackwood estate. The estate was currently controlled by Otis's lawyers and the lawyers had been fighting the State of Mississippi over the property. The state wanted to seize all assets due to the illegal activities conducted on the property. The lawyers argued that the illegal activities were only conducted in the abandoned house, and that was now destroyed. Furthermore, there was no proof, other than the confessions of a known druggie, that Otis Blackwood had any knowledge of the illegal activities being conducted on his property. It was also presented to the court that it was a probability that Otis was killed – suffocated in his bed by Kirk Blackwood – because he'd found out about the operation and was going to reveal the activities to the police.

Allen knew this to be totally inaccurate, since he knew for certain that Otis was in on the illegal activities just like everyone else, but Allen never said anything to the contrary. It looked like all of Otis's assets were clean. Allen's role in the operation was never revealed by Lashauna and he was free and clear of any charges related to the ordeal. When he and Lashauna were alone outside of the police station one afternoon, Allen asked her why she didn't spill the beans on his involvement. She simply said that everybody makes stupid decisions sometimes, but his actions didn't have any bearing on the murder investigation that she was conducting and therefore were of little interest to her. He was a free man, and was being given another chance to get himself straight. Though she did mention that if he were to break any more laws in the state of Mississippi, she was going to be there to bust his ass as soon as it happened. Allen believed her.

She tossed the envelope that she was holding onto the bed beside his suitcase. "I thought that you'd like to see that."

Allen looked at her funny and picked it up. When he opened it, he saw that the heading was Norris, Brinks and Hackman, Attorneys at Law. He recognized the name Hackman as the family attorney that was leaving Otis's house the rainy evening that Kirk had given him the gun. He still couldn't figure out why Kirk would have given him a gun – especially if Kirk was planning to kill him. Then it hit him, *Kirk had given him the gun*. Allen let the paperwork fall to his side and he looked at Lashauna. "I think I know where to find the Taylor murder weapon."

She raised her eyebrows and said, "Read that, and then tell me more."

Allen breezed through the paperwork that was more lawyer talk than he cared to read. All of the jargon made his head hurt, as he flipped the pages not really understanding what it all meant. "Ok," he finally said. "You care to translate?"

She stood, took the papers from his hand and flipped to the second page where he'd seen his name on multiple lines. She pointed to it and then to a bunch of numbers beside the line. "That's two point five million in cash and property, and possession of the Violent Hill estate, along with all of the assets that are on the property…furniture, cars, all of it."

"What?" Allen felt the air leave his lungs.

Lashauna said, "You're rich, courtesy of your Great Uncle Otis. He left all of the others a little something, but you got the bulk of it. Patsy and Jennifer got enough to live comfortably along with the car dealership and Elmer's share. Robert got a few hundred thousand which is being held in a reserve fund, until he gets released from prison next year. Tommy and Dewayne both received a few hundred thousand. Chris even got a nice chunk of change that he will probably never be able to spend, since he'll likely never see the outside of a prison again. Kirk and Johnny's inheritance were returned to the estate and added to your total, since you got everything else." Lashauna patted Allen on the back. "It looks like Otis amended his will just a few days before he was killed."

Allen thought about the night that he had seen Mr. Hackman leaving the house and shook his head in disbelief. "Jesus, I don't know what to say."

"How about telling me where I can find that murder weapon."

"You hungry?" Allen asked.

She smiled, "I could go for some eggs and bacon. There's some other paperwork that we need to go over while we eat. You buying?"

SHAWN A. LAWSON

While they were sitting in the beachside diner, Lashauna produced another legal sized envelope and set it on the table between them.

"What is that?" Allen asked.

"That's the entire police file on Stephen Gilmour."

"My father?" Allen scooped it up and opened the folder.

She nodded while she sipped her coffee, but didn't speak while he read. The file was substantial and there was no way that he could read it all in one sitting. The front page had a police mugshot of Stephen, most likely taken around the time that Allen was conceived, based on the fact that he had the same haircut as the photo seen in the picture at Otis's. Behind the front page was a hand written report of his arrest. Strangely, the author of the report kept referring to Stephen as *the informant*. Behind the initial report, there were some files that had Federal Bureau of Investigation written across the top. Allen closed the file. After a few minutes of silently looking out of the window, he asked, "Does this mean that he was a police informant?"

"Yes," Her voice was softer than normal, respecting the sensitivity of the matter. This was probably more information on his father than he'd ever known before – and most certainly, the truth.

"Have you read it?" Allen asked, his eyes focused on her new cruiser in the parking lot.

"Yes."

He set the file back down on the table. "What does it mean?"

"Well," she chose her words carefully before continuing. Allen was learning that it was her way – complete professionalism. "The file is old...and despite the best efforts of the authorities, FBI included, when your father disappeared from you and your mother's life...he literally disappeared. March 27th, 1974 was the last time that he was seen on this earth."

"So what?" Allen laughed, "This guy was running from my mother so hard, that he changed his name and started a whole new life? Meanwhile, the FBI and the State Police were wondering where their informant had run off to?" He took a sip of his coffee. "How do you hide from the FBI?" Allen asked, almost innocently.

Lashauna didn't laugh with him. A slight smile to not seem insensitive, but no laugh. "If you read further into the file, you'll see that they don't

322

think that he eluded them." She paused and Allen looked at her with an expression that said that he was beginning to catch on. She continued, "In the file, it states that Stephen was a State Police informant, not FBI. He'd been arrested trafficking a large amount of cocaine. Even back then, the Blackwoods were on the police radar and the arresting officer knew that Stephen worked for the family. As part of his plea agreement with the DA, Stephen agreed to help gather evidence on the family from the inside. About two weeks later, he disappeared."

"So he ran?" Allen asked, "What...to avoid having to snitch on his friends...his future in-laws?"

Lashauna shook her head, "I'm afraid that's not what the evidence shows. See, his mother and father were still living at the time, and by testimony of a couple of his close friends at the time, your dad was a serious mama's boy. Her health was failing at the time and it was highly unlikely that he'd just up and leave her. As a matter of fact, she's the one who filed the missing person report. She was very outspoken in her demands that the FBI locate her boy. They were called in to assist with the investigation."

Allen didn't need her to finish to know where this was heading, but he wanted to hear it anyway. He needed to hear it. "What did they find?"

"Not much. The guy literally disappeared from the face of the earth. Through interviews it was determined that Conrad and Kirk Blackwood were the last people to see him alive, and even admitted as much when they were interviewed, but they both claimed that at the end on the day on March 27th, Steven Gilmour got into his car and drove off into the sunset. Never to be seen again."

Allen took a deep breath, "You think that they found out about him talking to the cops somehow, killed him and buried him in the swamp?"

"I do."

"Jesus," Allen rubbed his temples. "Who in the fuck were these people, and how did they get away with it for so long?"

"Money and geography, my friend. Money and geography. They were able to operate in an area that most people wouldn't have been able to survive. Develop a system, a way of doing their business that had very few holes and they thrived. They learned the trade, passing it along generation after generation. It took you, an honest Blackwood...maybe the only one ever, to bring it down."

"Don't know if I should feel like the redeemer, or the betrayer."

"That's something that you are going to have to work out for yourself." She smiled at him. He couldn't help but to smile back – who could resist? She was perhaps one of the most beautiful women he'd ever met, but he knew that underneath that beauty lay one of the most vicious beasts imaginable, waiting for some unsuspecting criminal to bring it forth – so that it may devour. She was a rare specimen, one of a kind and Allen was glad that she'd been there for him - for him and Demri both. "What now?" she asked.

"Honestly, I don't know. I don't think that I could ever live at Violent Hill, but I don't think that I could bring himself to sell it given the family history – violent or not. Do you believe in a place being cursed?"

"I don't know," Lashauna shrugged her shoulders, "I think that people make the place." She sipped her coffee. "I think that Otis loved his family so much that he over looked the evil that existed within some of them."

Allen set his fork on the table and wiped his face with his napkin. He looked at the beautiful detective sitting in the booth across from him and asked, "Why did you ignore all the details that I told you about my involvement in the business?" Allen had never said a word to anyone about Tommy, Dewayne, or Robert being involved also. He didn't see where bringing the heat down on them would do anybody any good, and as far as Allen knew – they didn't have anything to do with what Kirk, Johnny, and Chris were planning. He admitted his own involvement and he admitted Elmer's involvement, since that was the only explanation for Kirk killing Elmer. "Why not bring me down too?" he asked.

Lashauna looked out of the window, as a family passed the diner carrying their beach gear. Dad was loaded down, struggling along with beach chairs and a small cooler, while mom followed with towels, holding the hands of two small children – a boy and a girl – both of whom were already wearing their water wings. She smiled as they passed and said, "That's why I do it." Allen looked at the family and laughed when the dad dropped a chair just as he was stepping from the pavement onto the hot sand. The man was struggling to pick it up, without dropping something else. "My job is to protect them...the good people." She looked directly at Allen again with her piercing blue eyes, "I hunt down bad people and put them away. I don't worry myself with good people who may make a bad decision once in a while. Especially, if I feel like they might be of some assistance to me at some point down the road."

The two of them finished their breakfast. As the waitress was clearing the table, Lashauna looked at her watch and said, "I really need to be getting back to work. I have a murder weapon to collect."

Allen smiled, and said, "Please express to Demri how sorry I am for what happened to her."

Lashauna stood up and said, "Why don't you go tell her yourself?"

Allen shook his head, "She doesn't want to see me. She made that very clear, as she was demanding that I get my stuff off of her property."

"She was upset," Lashauna reasoned, "In time, she'll get past that. You were the one who mistakenly put her in danger, but you were also the one who saved her."

Allen asked the detective a question that had been burning inside of him ever since that night. "Did she ever say that Johnny put his hands on her?"

"No," Lashauna said, "She was even checked out at the hospital and there was no evidence that she was mistreated in any way, other than being slapped around a little bit." She put her hand on Allen's shoulder, "It's not your fault, Allen."

"Thanks," he said, "For everything."

"You bet," she said, "It's my job." She walked to the exit door and said, "See you around."

He watched her get into her car and leave the parking lot. He wasn't sure if he would ever see her again, but deep down he hoped that he would.

2

Two weeks after having breakfast with Lashauna Trudeau, Allen pulled Otis's 69 Charger off the interstate – trying to find his way through a relatively unfamiliar town in a vehicle without GPS. It had been over two month since he was last here. Summer was gradually turning to fall and the air was cool in Greenville, South Carolina - a welcome change to the humid air of the Gulf Coast. Allen rumbled down a small two lane street as onlookers gawked at the Charger from the curb. One man, wearing a trucker hat and a Lynyrd Skynyrd t-shirt, gave him a thumbs up as he passed.

All of the vehicles in the garage had meant something to Uncle Otis and therefor they were special to Allen too - but this one was extra special. Several times during the trip from Mississippi to South Carolina, Allen had looked over at the passenger seat and imagined Otis sitting beside him - a big smile on his face as they cruised down the highway. Allen had only known Otis for a short time, but he missed him. He still had a hard time believing all that happened in the past couple of months. It was tough for him to imagine the broke alcoholic that had come through Greenville back then. He didn't feel like he even knew who that person was. Now, he was in possession of an estate that the lawyers estimated to be worth a total of about six million – not to mention the nearly three million in cash that was now spread out over four bank accounts. He hadn't touched a drink since he was living at Demri's, not since Johnny and Chris had poisoned his drink at the boathouse that night.

He turned the Charger onto a familiar road and up ahead he could see the white block building that he'd driven the nearly thousand miles to see. Somehow, this felt like home - as if it had always been so. It was a feeling that he never got from anywhere else. He guessed that was why he didn't bat an eye when Tommy volunteered to watch Violent Hill for him while he was away. Allen had the lawyer, Mr. Hackman, draw up a lease for Tommy to live on the property with only one condition. Allen wanted to make sure that Patsy, Jennifer and Ronnie were taken care of for as long as they wanted to stay there. Allen was happy to have family in the house – it was how Otis would have wanted it.

Allen pulled up to the front of the garage bearing the MacAulay's sign over the doors and got out. The rumble of the Charger's 426 engine was too much for any self-respecting mechanic to ignore, so it was no surprise that Allen was met in the parking lot by MJ, Tony, and a customer who was evidently waiting on service for his own vehicle inside the shop.

It took MJ a second to recognize Allen, since his focus initially was on the car. When he finally recognized who it was, a shocked look sprang upon his face. "Allen?" MJ hurried over and shook Allen's hand with a smile. "How have you been, son?" MJ removed his greasy trucker's hat and scratched the bald spot on top of his head. "Where in the hell did you get that thing?"

"My uncle left it to me." Allen would explain more some other time.

"Lookee there," MJ gawked, inspecting every detail of the car. "All original huh? What's it got under the hood?"

"426."

MJ smiled and popped the hood. As he regarded the showroom condition of the engine compartment he said, "This thing must be worth a mint."

"That's what I understand," Allen agreed, "It's a gem." He looked around the lot and realized that not much had changed. The amount of cars lined up, waiting on service, had the lot bursting at the seams. "You looking for any help around here?"

MJ came from under the Charger's hood and looked at Allen, gauging to see if he was serious. "Planning on sticking around a while, are ya?"

Allen thought of Demri back in Mississippi. Other than with her, this was the only place that he wanted to be. He nodded, "Yeah, I think I'm going to hang out a bit."

MJ smiled, "Sure, sure thing kiddo. I'd love to have your help. I can't say that I'll be able to pay you much. Things are real tight," then he added, "as usual!"

Allen waived his hands, "We can work all of that out later."

"Alright," He patted Allen on the back, "I'll have Tony clean out the room in the back of the shop for you."

"Don't bother," Allen said, "I'm thinking of buying a house."

3

As fall turned to winter, or as much as it did in the south, Allen fell in working full time at the Auto Repair Shop. In that short time, he'd also become one of the regulars around the small town. He frequented some of MJ's favorite spots like Sal's Diner, and Edward's Tavern. Still not finding his taste for alcohol, he usually drank coffee, even on Friday and Saturday nights, while everyone else was letting loose. He felt that even without the alcohol, getting out and being around other people was easier than sitting alone in his house – there, all that he could think about was Demri.

He'd bought a nice brick rancher, just a few blocks from the MacAulay's home – the selling point was the large detached garage. In it he parked the Charger to avoid wear and tear and bought himself a Dodge pick-up truck to get around town in. It took some time to get used to having the kind of money that he now possessed. Feeling guilty for having so much while others had so little around him, he rarely even passed a lemonade stand without making a donation. In a state of perpetual disbelief, he checked his accounts periodically, expecting to find that the money was all gone and, to his amazement, they all seemed to be growing instead of getting smaller. Being well to do was certainly something that he could get used to, but he was also learning the hard lesson that poor people had told themselves for as long he could remember, *money don't buy happiness*. He would have to agree. Sure, he was grateful for MJ and all that the folks here in Greenville had done for him. He did everything that he could to help MJ out also, like working for half of the wages that MJ would have had to pay someone else and buying new equipment for the shop out of his own pocket when things broke. But as much as Allen cared for MJ and his family, they didn't make him feel complete. They just eased the affliction of loneliness to some degree.

Once he was settled into his new place, Allen reached out to Lashauna by phone with the excuse of calling to see how Leo was doing, though they both knew that his real question was how was Demri doing? Lashauna was busy, and didn't have very long to talk, but she said that Leo had made a full recovery and was back to work. Before they hung up she asked if he'd talked to Demri. He told her no and inquired why she'd asked, but all that the detective would say was that he should call her. Allen wanted to, but he couldn't bring himself to do it. He was afraid that calling her would dredge up painful memories of what had happened to her, and he didn't want to do that. If she could move on and have some piece of mind, he wanted that for her – even if that meant without him.

Allen tried to distract himself by staying busy at the shop, working on the endless amount of vehicles that MJ had lined up. He put in countless hours, working late into most evenings, in an effort to keep his own mind off of all that had gone down in Mississippi – to keep his mind off of her.

One cold night, a rare one that he wasn't working late, he sat down with a glass of scotch, *his first in over three months,* and began to write his mother a letter. When he started, he didn't have any intention of actually sending it, but when he was done, he found himself placing a stamp on the letter and dropping it in the mailbox around the corner from his house. He didn't use his own mailbox, or current address, because he wasn't ready to fully open the door just yet. He knew that sooner or later, they were going to have a talk. He wondered just how much she knew about what happened to his father. Was she privy to the family business back then, just like Patsy and Jennifer were now? Of course – she had to be. She had to know that her boyfriend was working for the family – did she also know that Conrad and Kirk had murdered him? Buried him out in the Whiskey Bayou for talking to the police? Is that why she left Mississippi when the rest of her siblings stayed? Did she know that she was pregnant? Did she run to save him? There were still so many unanswered questions. Maybe they could sit down one day, have some coffee and talk – maybe one day.

Many times since Otis's passing, Allen wondered why his Great Uncle had left him with the bulk of the inheritance. Why not Tommy, Dewayne, Jennifer, or Patsy? Those that had been around longer – that he was closer to. Otis had amended the will in Allen's favor at the last minute, even without knowing that Elmer was not going to be around - still he left Elmer only a small amount by comparison. Allen could only assume that Otis was trying to make amends. Unlike Clara, Otis without a doubt had to know what Conrad and Kirk had done to his father. It may have even been Otis's order. Maybe it was the guilt from that. The guilt of knowing that he had killed Allen's father, robbing Allen of something that he could never repay. No amount of money would make that up, but he did what he could to atone for it. That could be the reason, or it could be because Otis knew that Allen would do what he himself had always tried to do – Allen would take care of the family.

So before Allen sealed the envelope to his mother, he slipped in a check for fifty thousand dollars and a note that if she ever needed anything more, she could contact Patsy at Violent Hill, and leave word for him.

One night in early December, as the cold wind bit so bitterly that Allen and Tony were struggling to keep the shop warm, MJ poked his head into the garage from the door that led to the front of the shop. He didn't spend a great deal of time in the garage these days, since it had gotten so cold. He claimed that his arthritis wouldn't allow it – which may, or may not have been true, but Allen and Tony didn't question him one way or the other. He'd put in his time and the younger guys were happy to give him a break.

"Allen," MJ said, "There's a young lady at the counter to see you."

Before Allen could ask who it was and what they wanted, MJ had closed the door and was gone back to the front. Allen finished tightening the bolt on an engine mount, laid his wrench down and as he walked through the door, wiped his hands on a greasy shop rag.

It was not uncommon for customers to return to the shop after having their car serviced. Occasionally they had questions or complaints, and either way, it was a bother for the mechanics to have to leave their real work to go speak to the customers. They hated it - it had become a sort of competition in the garage between him and Tony to see who could get the least complaints every month. Allen could only guess what was waiting for him at the counter. He passed the main office where MJ and his wife, Trudy were going over the books for the day. Their daughter, Joy, was sitting on a couch, in the corner of the office, feeding her and Tony's newborn baby girl with a blanket thrown tastefully over her shoulder to conceal her breast. Allen went in, "What's up MJ?" Allen asked, not wanting to be blindsided by an angry customer.

"I don't have any idea," MJ said. "I don't think I've seen her here before, but when I asked if I could help, she asked for you." He looked at Trudy and then back to Allen, "You have a girlfriend that we don't know about?" Trudy stopped counting the day's take and looked both shocked and disgusted at her husband's rudeness. "What?" MJ smiled at her, "I can tell the difference between a woman looking for a tire rotation and a woman looking for her man, and this ain't no tire rotation."

Allen felt a lump form in his chest and immediately left the office, as MJ was saying something else - Allen didn't hear him. The hall to the waiting area was a short one, and Allen took it in two steps. When he reached the front, her back was to him, but he knew right away who it was. He felt his eyes well up, as he fought back the urge to cry. She was standing in the middle of the area watching Gilligan do something goofy, causing the Skipper to hit him over the head, skewing his hat to the side and making the fake studio audience erupt in laughter. She was dressed unpretentiously, in dark pants that showed her amazing figure and a long tight fitting sweater – with her coat, folded in her arms. Allen wanted to walk up behind her, wrap his arms around her waist, and hold her like that for the rest of the evening, but resisted the urge. "Demri?"

She turned around and even though she'd lost some of the bronze tan that she had during the summer - her face was even more beautiful than Allen could remember. She smiled and after a few seconds with Gilligan's antics going on in the background, she said, "You sure came a long way to find a job."

Allen couldn't speak. He nodded and smiled as a tear fell from the corner of his eye. She walked towards him, touched his cheek with her hand, and wiped the tear away. Now that she was closer, Allen could see that she was crying also – the mascara running from the corners of her eyes. He put his hands on her waist and pulled her closer. She wrapped her arms around his shoulders. "I'm glad you came," he whispered.

"I couldn't stay away."

"Where are the kids?"

"There at home, with Rachel. I thought that we needed some time to ourselves," She laid her forehead against his.

"What do you have in mind?"

She pulled her head back and looked into his eyes. "How about that dinner date you owe me?"

Paying no attention to the old blue hair lady, sitting in the corner, reading a Cosmopolitan and waiting on her car to be fixed, they kissed – and then kissed some more.

Epilogue

The Mississippi State Penitentiary, also known as Parchman Farm, was founded in 1901 in the northern Mississippi delta. It is, and always has been, a working prison, rotating crops season to season and year by year. Only custody level A and B prisoners have the privilege of working the fields, cotton is the crop in season at the moment, while C and D level prisoners are confined indoors, in the more maximum security sections of the prison. The walls are constructed of thick concrete and block, the bars are a vintage style regularly seen in old black and white movies - still effective nonetheless and the hallways are well lit with modern fixtures that look out of place in such an old building. Near the front entrance is the visitation room, not much more than a line of stools facing a thick sheet of Plexiglas, lorded over by two sheriff deputies, standing at either end of the room. A thick metal door separates the prisoner side of the glass from the rest of the prison and it is through this door that Robert Blackwood is ushered, wearing foot and hand restraints, due either to the close proximity to the front of the building, or for show to discourage the visitors on the good side of the glass from breaking the law. Robert's greasy pompadour is gone, due to the lack of pomade in his current situation. His hair, longer now, hangs straight into his face partially hiding his purpled, swollen eyes – the result of a lunchroom disagreement. His fingers are raw - dirt stuck under his nails from the cotton fields, but otherwise he looks healthy – especially so, since he's been removed from a lifestyle of constant drugs and alcohol.

Robert is directed to a stool, situated on the far end of the room and designated with a large stenciled number 4 above the window. When he is sat down he is alone with no one on the other side of the window, so he turns to the guard who is standing behind him, with his back to the wall. The guard uses his finger and makes a twirling motion, indicating for Robert to turn around and when he does, he finds a stranger sitting on the other side. The stranger takes a few seconds to look at Robert through the glass and then he slowly picks up the phone receiver and holds it to his ear. Robert is trying to place the man, knowing that he'd seen the face somewhere before, but not sure where it might have been. He was older, maybe in his sixties, very well groomed with a head full of white, flowing hair sticking out from underneath a fedora, and a pencil thin mustache that turned up slightly over the corners of his mouth. He was wearing a white suit with blue pinstripes and thin hands were sticking out from the sleeves. Robert focused on the man's long, filed fingernails, as the bony appendages gestured to the phone. Robert reluctantly picked his side up.

"Good afternoon, Robert." The man said, speaking like they were old friends. His voice more of a gravelly whisper.

"Afternoon," Robert answered, "What can I do for you?" and then he added, "Do I know you?"

The man on the other side of the glass rested his elbows on the countertop and took a deep breath. It was then Robert recollected the other times that he'd been down to this room for visitations. Nancy had brought the girls to see him a couple of times, and Patsy had come with Jennifer once, last Christmas. Every other time he'd been in it, the room had been full. There were nearly five thousand prisoners housed in this prison, and if it were visiting hours, there was always a line of family members waiting to see their loved ones. Oddly, at the moment, they were the only people in the room. Robert looked into the man's cold, dark eyes and even with the barrier between them, he shuddered. "Who are you?"

"You don't know me," the man answered, "but you may have met my former associate, Henry Stokes. He did a lot of business with your family over the years."

Robert knew of Henry. Though he never really communicated with the guy, he'd done enough deliveries into the bayou to remember the name. Stokes was the buyer on most of the drug runs and as far as Robert knew, he was also Johnny's buddy. "I know of him," Robert said, "Why did you say, *former associate*?"

"Let's just say, due to some bad deals he made with my money, he and I no longer do business together."

Robert turned to see if the deputy was hearing this saucy talk, only to find that the deputy that used to be behind him, was now on the other end of the room and out of earshot. He grew more nervous. What kind of man has the power to set up a secret meeting in a state prison – and what in the hell did this guy want with him? Robert said, "Ok…what's all that got to do with me?"

The man grew visibly irritated at Roberts apathetic attitude – though it was just Robert's way, the man was clearly annoyed by it. "What it has to do with you, is that I want my money back."

Robert sat up straight on his stool and said, "Look here, sir. I don't have your money and I ain't never made any deals with Henry Stokes. You're barking up the wrong tree."

The man smiled, and his shoulders relaxed again. The mood swing frightened Robert even more than if the man had remained terse – he was not stable. "No, Robert," he said, as he laughed. His breath heavy in the earpiece of the phone. "No, sir…I've got the right tree. You see, Stokes didn't just make a deal with Johnny…he made a deal with the Blackwoods…and one of you has my money."

Robert began to sweat. He had enough worries trying to maintain his anal retentiveness on a daily basis here in prison. The last thing that he needed was pressure from a man like this – one that could no doubt reach him on the inside and make his life a living hell. "What is it that you're here for?" Robert asked. "I'm sure that you're aware of my current financial situation." Robert tugged at the orange jumpsuit he was wearing to punctuate the statement. "There's nothing that I can do to help you."

The man smiled again, "I know that you can be of little help in there, Robert." His heavy breathing was making Robert want to pull the receiver away from his head. "How is Nancy and the girls?" He asked, and without waiting for a reply, he continued, "Those sure are some sweet looking young ladies. Are they…active, yet?"

"You motherfucker…" Robert yelled. One of the guards from the other end hollered for him to hold it down. Robert lowered his voice, "You better stay the hell away from my family."

"Or what, Robert? What is it that you are going to do, if I don't?"

Robert didn't speak. He was breathing heavily himself now.

"I can't promise you that I will stay away from your family, but if you help me, I can promise that I will stay away from your girls."

They sat there looking at each other through the glass for a moment, and then Robert asked, "What is it that you want me to do?"

"I want you to find out where the gate keeper went."

"The...who, what?" Robert was confused.

"The man with the keys to Camelot. Your cousin, Allen." The stranger stopped smiling, "I understand that he controls the business now."

"And?" Robert asked, still fuming mad.

"Tell him that I would like to speak to him...so that we can figure out how I can get my money back." The man stood up, still holding the phone to his ear, "Will you do that for me, Robert? For your girls?"

Robert thought for a moment, but there really was no choice. He was helpless to protect his family in here. He nodded and then asked, "Who should say is looking for him?"

"Oh, how rude of me...my name is Fintan LaRue ...and I'll be in touch."

The End.

Acknowledgment

First and foremost I want to thank my wife of 20 years, Deborah Lawson. You have been my motivation for all that I do. You are the hub of the wheel and make it all work. Thank you for taking care of me and our children, Lindsay, Landon and Leif, unselfishly, all of these years.

Thank you, Trudy Hannah, for reading my gibberish and somehow being able to see the picture that I am trying to paint. Your guidance and editing has been a tremendous help.

Thank you, Steve Hannah, for the cover art. As always, you seem to capture the essence of the story in the art work. Much appreciated!

Thank you, Joy Calloway, for being my sounding board and reading Uncle Otis early on. I appreciate you spending your valuable time reading my stories.

Last but not least, thank you to any who read this, or any of my stories for that matter. I set out a few years ago to create something that I could leave behind when I am gone - some evidence that I was here. I wanted to leave something that future generations could read, and hopefully be entertained with. If nothing else, these books are a moment in time. Although it takes months, and sometimes years, to write (I got a little bit over ambitious with the Black Flag) every word, every situation, I mill over for quite some time before I write it on paper. In some way, I hope that those down the line, who may, or may not ever even know me, can catch a glimpse of who I am through these books.

All of this was really put into perspective this year with the birth of my new grandson, Benjamin Owsley. Congrats to Lindsay and Greg, you guys are fantastic parents and I am very proud of you both. And for Benny – welcome to the party; I can't wait to get to hear your thoughts on some of these stories. Though, I am sure it will be awhile before your mother lets you read anything that I write.

That said, I hope you all enjoyed Uncle Otis.

Until next time,
Shawn